ONCE UPON A DREAM

A TWISTED TALE

LIZ BRASWELL

DISNEY PRESS

Los Angeles • New York

Copyright © 2017 Disney Enterprises, Inc.

All rights reserved. Published by Disney Press, an imprint of Disney Book Group. No part of this book may be reproduced or transmitted in any form or by any means, electronic or mechanical, including photocopying, recording, or by any information storage and retrieval system, without written permission from the publisher. For information address Disney Press, 1101 Flower Street, Glendale, California 91201.

Printed in the United States of America
First Hardcover Edition, April 2016
First Paperback Edition, January 2017
5 7 9 10 8 6
FAC-025438-18264
Library of Congress Control Number: 2015936643
ISBN 978-1-4847-0730-2

Visit disneybooks.com

SUSTAINABLE
FORESTRY
INITIATIVE

Certified Chain of Custody
Promoting Sustainable Forestry
www.sfiprogram.org
SFI-01054
The SFI label applies to the text stock

For my daughter, Ivy. Wake up, grab your sword, defeat the twin dragons of doubt and uncertainty, conquer the world. I will always love you.

Also, stop drinking my coffee.

—L.B.

Once upon a time I was in an endless dark forest. No—
actually endless, I tell you! In another world! I wandered
for ages all by myself in the woods. My wife died years
ago, you see. I don't know where my oldest boy was.
My little girls and lads were safe at home, I think.

Once upon a time, we were all together, in a castle,
you know, but things change. Wives die and eldest
sons grow up and chase after princesses and
peasant girls, riding away from you forever. . . .

—King Hubert

Consider the Dragon

A dragon was dead.

A giant black and purple fire-breathing dragon from the very pits of hell itself was dead somewhere outside the castle. Thorns were falling from the battlements like rain, making curiously pleasant wooden sounds on the grounds of the bailey. Many strange and dire things were happening to an ancient keep that had already endured enough unusual treatment for the past sixteen years.

The handsome prince had killed the dragon with the help of the three strange little fairies he now followed. Without them, he would have done no good whatsoever.

Without them, he would never have been able to hurl the sword magically into the one spot that would easily kill the beast. Without them, he wouldn't have had the enchanted sword in the first place. Without them, he would have still been rotting in the evil fairy's dungeon, waiting impatiently for a hundred years to pass so he could break his true love's spell—as a doddering old man.

Still, the dragon nagged at the back of his mind like a mosquito. A slain dragon should be *something.* There should be a pause, an astounded moment of silence, when he and the fairies and anyone else watching would take a breath and acknowledge the incredible deed that was just accomplished. He had no illusions that it was all due to him; still, he was a prince, it was a dragon, the dragon was dead—shouldn't there be an intermission? *Something?*

And also. There were some unresolved details about the dragon and its death. The fire, for instance—it looked like the dragon had set most of the forest alight. Was it still raging? Would it ignite the woody thorns that surrounded the castle and the village? Was the whole place just one giant bonfire waiting to explode?

Was there, in fact, any dragon body left at all, or had it turned back into Maleficent?

Had he been battling a dragon that had temporarily been in fairy form, or had the fairy transformed herself into the beast?

Was it really from hell? Or was that more hyperbole on the fairy's part?

And yet still he climbed steps in the silent, drowsing castle. The girl who was destined to sleep a hundred years had only been unconscious for a few hours, along with the rest of her kingdom. Already the inside air had that cool, musty smell usually associated with the bedrooms of those who didn't move much: very great-grandmothers, for instance.

The fairies' wings fanned up tiny tornados of encroaching dust.

The dragon faded in his mind as he fought off the strange presence of magical sleep, the good fairies' spell affecting even those it wasn't meant for. Murky, dim halls only added to his feeling of swimming through the castle while kicking his legs toward the sun.

For that is what he attained in defeating the dragon: the girl—sunlight herself.

He first saw her in a ray of sunshine. She was dancing and singing in a forest clearing, her golden hair sparkling as it swirled around her. Her voice was the very essence of a happy, sunny day distilled into song. She was as weightless on her toes as golden motes in a drowsy beam, floating their way up to the ceiling.

Very soon now he would kiss the girl, break the spell, wake the girl—wake *everyone*—and they would marry, and there would be happily-ever-afters for all.

Or something. The fairies weren't exactly explicit when they had come out of nowhere, freed him, helped him kill the dragon, and led him to this set of stairs that they were presently climbing.

Somehow his girl from the clearing was mixed up with fairies and witches and dragons and castles—this familiar castle, where he had been taken as a child to see the drooling baby he would someday marry. It turned out the forest girl *was the princess*—not that it mattered to the prince; he was willing to upend convention and marry a peasant for love.

This was, however, *a lot* more convenient for everybody.

As he entered her bedroom, these thoughts were discarded to the same mental pile of ashes where the dragon lay.

For there was his sleeping beauty—no peasant girl she. Now she wore the proper attire of the princess he must have somehow always known she was. A blue gown as pure as the sky, white wings of cloth above her shoulders like an angel's. Lips closed but not tight, dreamless, without the tension of any emotion.

Phillip paused, overcome by her beauty.

Did a fairy make a noise? Did he feel some external force pushing him to hurry up with it? The dragon was dead, there were a million explanations waiting, there was a sleeping girl before him dying to wake up.

He knelt, pressing his own lips ever so softly to hers.

Immediately, his knees crumpled.

He fell, his head hitting the soft quilts and satin bolsters on her bed.

His last thought, before sleep and someone else's dreams overcame him:

That damn dragon.

Did anyone make sure it was actually dead?

Happily Ever After, Redacted

Once upon a time there lived a king and queen who ruled their kingdom as their forefathers had—but with even less wisdom. They hunted unicorns in the deep forests until there were none left. They banished all of the wise old men and women, witches and hermits, priestesses and shamans, who advised them to follow a more prudent path. They threw parties for neighboring kings and queens that fairly bankrupted the castle—which led them to levy even higher taxes on the poor. Then they looked around at those neighbors' lands with covetous eyes, wishing they had more for themselves. But as it was mostly a peaceable country, they had no military recourse.

After some years the queen gave birth to a girl, which was something of a disappointment since they wanted a prince who would inherit the kingdom and become king one day. At least she was beautiful and sweet-tempered, with a halo of golden hair that made her look like a cherub. Everyone who saw the baby princess fell in love with her.

For the baby Aurora's naming ceremony the king and queen invited everyone they knew, as well as three evil fairies who lived in the darker parts of the land. Every guest dined on rich delicacies kept warm under golden domes and they ate with golden forks and golden knives. Every banqueter was allowed to keep their golden dinnerware as well as the jeweled goblets that held ancient, priceless wine.

And all the guests gave gifts to the beautiful little baby: snow-white ponies, pillows of velvet and silk, toys carved by the cleverest dwarves.

And then it was the three evil fairies' turn.

"Here she is, as promised," said the king.

"Now it's time for your gifts," said the queen.

The first fairy laughed wickedly. "Hmmm. How about beauty? She may as well be pleasant to look upon while she slaves for us eternally."

The second fairy said, "I'll give her the gift of song and dance. Perhaps she can entertain us."

The third fairy said, "I give her parents the power they

wish and supernatural help they need to attain their hearts' desire. And on her sixteenth birthday, we will claim the princess as ours."

The three wicked fairies laughed and tittered in unsettling peals.

"*No!*"

Hidden among the guests was one of the last remaining *good* fairies in the kingdom, who had kept a low profile since the banishments began.

"My lord and lady," Maleficent said, coming forward. She was an impressive figure, young and comely. "You cannot do this. You cannot *sell* your child to the likes of these."

"I thought we had done with the last of you," the king growled. "Do not meddle in the affairs of kings, hag. It is not your place."

Maleficent looked sadly down at the helpless little baby, who was still smiling despite what was going on around her.

"Poor child," she murmured. "My powers are not strong enough to prevent this wicked transaction. Not the way matters stand now. But I swear on my own life I will be back and set everything to rights. On your sixteenth birthday, goodness and nobility will be restored to this wretched kingdom."

And she vanished in a puff of green smoke.

As the days wore on in the wretched kingdom, the little princess Aurora grew in grace and beauty. She sang and danced to the delight of everyone around her.

Her parents, meanwhile, made good use of the powerful demons and fearsome magics given to them by the fairies. They waged strange and terrible wars upon their neighbors that not only decimated their enemies but punished the land itself, rendering it infertile and foul. Only horrible black and twisted things grew where the king and queen's army had passed.

Soon that was most of the known world.

The peaceful valleys, lush orchards, sparkling rivers, and snow-capped mountains that the queen and king had so envied and wanted for themselves were now nothing more than a blasted wasteland blown through by hot and deadly winds, occupied by only the most vile, unnatural creatures born of darkness and magic.

And the monsters, having consumed everything else, began turning their hideous eyes to their masters' castle.

Meanwhile, the good little princess was mostly neglected by her parents and often wore rags—except for the rare occasion when the king and queen noticed her and decided to dress her like a proper member of royalty, so all who remained could see and admire her.

Aurora took her mistreatment surprisingly well, making

friends with the dwindling number of cats, mice, dogs, birds, and squirrels who lived within the castle walls. All the people who still made the castle their home loved her utterly.

But they were frightened of her parents more.

At sixteen years of age, Aurora, now a beautiful young woman, knew full well that her birthday celebrations were less important than the apocalyptic events that were occurring in the world around her. She forgave her parents in advance for most likely forgetting that special day—as they had for the last fifteen.

Still, she dressed in her finest gown and prepared to greet everyone with the grace and good humor for which she was known. *Someone* would remember and wish her congratulations, perhaps whispered so her parents wouldn't hear.

As the clock struck noon in the middle of her birthday, the three evil fairies appeared.

"We have come for what we have been promised," the first one said.

"We can no longer control the magics you gave us!" the king protested.

"Perhaps you shouldn't make deals with the devil," the second fairy said.

"You must save us!" the queen cried.

"No," the third fairy said. "Now hand her over."

Confused, Aurora looked from her parents to the fairies.

"What . . . what is meant by all of this?" she asked, hoping against hope she didn't understand.

"You must go," the queen said wearily, gesturing to the fairies.

"*NO.*"

As had happened sixteen years previously, there was a puff of green smoke. Maleficent appeared. She did not look like she had before; now she leaned hard on a staff, and her beautiful face was drawn and hollow. Black robes wrapped around her like she was an ancient pilgrim at the end of a very long journey.

"It has taken me the full sixteen years to prepare, but now I shall do my best to prevent further evil in this kingdom," she said, her voice still strong. She raised her staff and green light glowed from the crystalline orb at its top.

"You have no power—" the first fairy began.

"*BEGONE!*" Maleficent cried. She threw both her hands into the air and green fire shot from her body.

The three fairies shrieked and dissolved backward, the essence of their being returned to whatever evil place had spawned them.

"Oh, foolish king and queen," Maleficent said. "What evil you have done can*not* be entirely undone. The land will shriek forever from the pain you have caused it. Perhaps, however, I can save what little is left."

She raised her arms again and chanted. Green fog flowed out from her fingertips and through the delicately paned windows of the castle. It ebbed around the black and twisted trees that now grew in the dried-up moat. Vines and thorns began to sprout from the ground. These grew rapidly and reached up over the castle walls, crisscrossing quickly like the warp and weft of a spinster's loom. Soon the whole castle was enveloped in a dark green shadow.

Unholy cries of frustration rang out from the blasted land beyond.

Spent, Maleficent fell back, her white face even paler than before.

"We are safe."

The king, about to give her royal thanks or some such, was not allowed to speak.

She held up her hand and he was silenced.

"*You*, however, will receive a punishment far kinder than you deserve considering the things you have done," she said coldly. "For selling your own daughter to the Dark and destroying the world outside these castle walls, you *should* die. But as the new queen of this castle, I will show leniency and lock you in the dungeon forever, where you may think upon what you have done and repent."

And the guards of the castle, and the people within, did nothing to stop this—and may, in fact, have helped push their old king and queen down the stairs.

"Sold me?" Aurora murmured. "I don't understand. . . ."

Maleficent put her hand on the poor girl's head.

"I am so sorry, child," she said. "This is a terrible thing to have happened to you and the world you knew. But at least now you and those still here may live, and we shall survive and prevail."

And so Queen Maleficent, Aurora, and the survivors in the castle lived happily ever after, while the world lay dead and deadly around them.

Status Quo

The princess Aurora was spinning again.

She couldn't help it.

When the corridors were wide, inviting, and empty . . . When bright bands of actual sunlight slipped through the vines and the windows, golden and slow, puddling on the ground the way she imagined it did in real forests . . . When the soft carpet beckoned, patterned with dark colors and bright spots the way meadows were supposed to be . . . Then she would sing and spin, twirling down the corridor, feeling the warm moments of light on her skin as she flung her arms out. Trying to recapture snippets of dreams that once in a while involved the woods.

Sometimes she took off her golden shoes.

She would sing whatever came to mind and seemed appropriate for the moment—bits from the nicer tunes the minstrel taught her, proper ballads from her music tutor, half-remembered lullabies, snippets of her own invention. Sometimes, right before sleep claimed her, music rang in her sleepy ears, entire orchestras and choruses proclaiming sternly but joyfully some unremembered thing. Sometimes she would try to remember those tunes, and sing them, too.

This was usually a good corridor for twirling. It was on the southern side of the castle, just above the great hall, and if the hot winds outside managed to scrape away the layers of smoke and soot, sunbeams would sometimes form. The far end of the corridor led to a wide set of formal stone stairs that had balustrades good for dragging the tips of her fingers dramatically along while pushing herself back and forth to each side, like a deer happily tumbling down a waterfall.

Or maybe it was fish who did that. She couldn't keep them straight.

At the bottom, she tried to cross and uncross her feet quickly the way she had seen some of the troubadours and girl performers do. Her golden hair fell like a ripple of costly fabric, first down one shoulder and then the other, as she quickly shifted position. She lifted the hem of her dress so she could watch her feet and make sure they were doing what they were supposed to. But it was all so utterly grace-ful that anyone watching would have thought it was part of the performance.

Of course, anyone watching might also have wondered at a young woman—much less a royal princess—prancing about like that.

She pirouetted alongside a table in the lesser banquet hall, did a little leap through a side pantry, shuffled past an only *slightly* surprised serving boy, and briséd through what was once an orangery but whose glass was now covered in thick, protective vines like the rest of the castle.

Aurora only paused her singing and dancing when she came to the wide ironclad door that led to the *special* dungeon.

At the bottom of a long, winding flight of cold stone stairs were several small, rounded chambers that looked like the lairs of mud dauber wasps. Most of them were empty—there was little to no crime in the castle since there was no place else to go, no one you could escape from in a remaining population of less than a thousand. And nothing worth stealing.

When the minstrel got a little too drunk and out of hand, the queen would throw him in the stocks. Only once did she ever send him to the dungeons to dry out.

No, the only people down there now were the architects

of the end of the known world: Princess Aurora's parents, King Stefan and Queen Leah.

Once she had snuck down there, to look upon her progenitors.

Her aunt Maleficent had never forbidden her from doing so—her aunt had never forbidden her anything. Aurora didn't know why she felt she had to do it on the sly.

But she had waited until Maleficent had been down and come back up so she knew there would be torches still lit and the way would not be utterly black. Aurora had slipped off her golden shoes and tiptoed, sticking closely to the rough-hewn walls, flattening herself like a child playing hide-and-seek.

The king and queen had been daze-eyed and silent, sitting on the one hard bench in their tiny cell, staring at nothing at all. There was no emotion on either of their faces. They were like statues waiting for the end of time, for the castle itself to crumble down around them.

Chilled, Aurora had fled back upstairs as quickly as she could and found her aunt Maleficent and wrapped her in exactly the sort of hug the older woman didn't like but put up with on occasion, for the sake of her adopted daughter.

Aurora had no intention of ever going down to the dungeon again.

For now she just shivered and moved quickly past the

dungeon door, all desire to dance withered and gone.

Her parents had danced, it was said, as the world tumbled down around them.

Their sickness, their evilness, their greed and heartlessness that ran so thick through their blood—it was in Aurora's blood, too. Naturally.

Feeling a rise of panic, she began to race to the throne room, stopping just before the door to enter at a more regal rate, smoothing the front of her dress.

Maleficent sat upon the throne with an easy elegance Aurora wished she had. Her long fingers languidly pointed here and gestured there as she spoke. It was almost time for the Midvember ball; a full month had passed since the previous festivities. The room was filled with servants and minor royalty, all with last-minute requests for magical adjustments to their costumes, or additions to the menu, or royal approval of a certain dance.

Some of the servants weren't strictly human.

Some of the servants were black and gray and strangely shaped. They had beaks instead of mouths, or pig snouts, or, worse, no mouths at all. Their feet were cloven hooves or spurred chicken claws or huge, splayed trotters.

But they were needed to keep the fouler monsters at bay, the ones from Outside. Maleficent summoned them out of clay and spirits from another world—a not very nice world, the princess guessed.

Their intelligence was negligible. Their silence was insisted upon by the queen, who saw the effect they had on the uneasy human residents of the fortress. Aurora was torn about this; the good-hearted girl rued the unfairness of the strict orders they were under.

And yet they were so unsettling. . . .

Maleficent's eyes caught Aurora and her face cracked into a pleased smile.

"Come, my girl, over here. You're a welcome break from these weary preparations."

"Auntie," Aurora said with relief, approaching the throne and standing beside the queen. As always, her fears and doubts subsided the moment she was near the Savior of the Kingdom. She felt *safe*. "Really, you shouldn't bother yourself with all this. You do so much else for the kingdom!"

"Ah, but this is important for morale, my sweet," Maleficent said, raising an arched eyebrow as she smiled down upon her ward. "With none of us able to leave the castle until the world heals—well, we *need* these diversions to keep our spirits up." She lifted a long finger and tucked a lock of golden hair behind Aurora's ear. "Besides . . . your parents neglected you for *sixteen years*. Sixteen years without a ball or a birthday for a royal princess! Even peasants do more for their children."

"Thank you, Aunt Maleficent," Aurora murmured, lowering her head. She felt nothing but gratitude toward the woman who cared for her—but she still couldn't look her aunt directly in her yellow eyes. They never seemed to focus on anything. It was impossible to tell precisely what the woman felt except when she made an effort, by moving her mouth.

"I like the theme you chose this time," Maleficent said, a smile twitching at the edge of her lips. " 'Sky and Water Blue.' Very poetic."

"I have to use my imagination," Aurora said. "Since I've never seen the sea or a river."

In her dreams, sometimes tinkling streams flowed past cool and shaded mud banks—but obviously that was a product of her own starved imagination, and often it was all in shades of brown.

"You've done quite well." Maleficent petted Aurora on the head like—well, like a pet. A funny stroking motion that seemed meant for something else. Another curious habit of her aunt's. "Now listen, you know the ball is going to go very late tonight. Why don't you run along and take a little nap, so you'll be refreshed? I know how much you love to dance."

"But I want to help. . . ."

"Another time, dear," Maleficent said, touching her gently on the cheek. "There will be plenty more of these in the years to come."

"Yes, Aunt Maleficent. Thank you, Aunt Maleficent," Aurora said dutifully, then leaned forward and snuck a quick kiss on her aunt's hollowed cheek.

Maleficent's eyes darted nervously.

The powerful fairy had not *asked* to be the savior of the only people left in the world. She had not asked for the world to be destroyed in the first place.

She had not asked to become the parent of a neglected princess.

She probably wanted to just live by herself in her old castle, practicing her spells and communing with powers beyond the ken of mortal men, happily ever after.

So if she wasn't used to the hugs or kisses or other displays of affection Aurora had not received from her own parents, well, they would just both have to learn. Aurora would wear her down eventually.

The princess walked slowly back to her room.

The hall was wide, empty, and inviting, but she didn't feel like twirling this time. She felt useless and desultory.

"YOUR HIGHNESS."

A hand clawed her shoulder from behind.

Aurora spun around—but it was just the old minstrel. His face was pale, and his long, narrow nose was pinched beyond its usual extreme. He seemed more degenerate and wild than ever; his clothes were torn in a dozen different places, and there were scratches near his eyes that made it look like he was crying blood.

"You are unwell, Master Tommins," Aurora said gently. She couldn't *smell* anything about him—not even the home-brewed moonshine some of the peasants had begun to amuse themselves by distilling. But he was so far gone that sometimes *not* having a dram drove him to fits.

"It's out there. It is! There *is* an *Outside!*"

He looked behind himself wildly and then grabbed her hands and pressed his own around them. "Your Highness, *I escaped!*"

"Unhand me, you are sick," Aurora repeated, only a little alarmed at his behavior. She was more concerned about his health—and what would happen if anyone caught him touching her in such a manner.

Familiar and ominously irregular footsteps came toward them. The sound drove the minstrel to hysteria. Aurora reached out and put a hand on his shoulder.

"Perhaps you should have a little lie-down. . . ."

But it was too late. Shuffling around the corner were two of Maleficent's private guards: oily black-and-gray monsters who moved ponderously along, barely upright. They looked like they had been put together wrong.

The minstrel's eyes widened in naked terror when he saw them, but he didn't take his attention off the princess.

"Your Highness . . ."

"Come away from her, singing human," the more pig-like creature snuffled loudly. *"Maleficent commands you sleep it off and leave her heir alone."*

"You are the key!" the minstrel whispered, throwing himself at the princess so his lips touched her ear. She tried not to pull away. *"You!* It's all still *out there!"*

"MINSTREL!" said the other guard, the one with the comb of a cock and the yellow eyes of a demon.

They each put a horrible clawed hand on the poor man's shoulders. They swung him aloft like he was no more than a speck of dust.

"Your Highness!" the minstrel cried.

The monstrous guards laughed.

"Sing for us, and we might not hurt you too much on the way to the dungeon!"

"Please be easy on him," Aurora urged. "He is having a fit of some kind. He needs a doctor, not a beating. . . ."

"SING!" the second one commanded, ignoring her. Neither monster bothered to bow as they walked away. *"SING!"*

The minstrel tried his best, tears running down his bloody face, borne aloft on the shoulders of nightmares.

"Douce—douce dame jolie . . ."

Aurora watched him go with sadness and horror.

And maybe, just maybe, a tiny spark of something too

hideous to admit. *Relief* that the afternoon had become more interesting.

After they were out of sight, all that remained was the quickly fading song, streaming through the hall like smoke.

> *"Pour dieu ne pensés mie*
> *Que nulle ait signorie*
> *Seur moy fors vous seulement. . . ."*

Aurora noticed her hands were still clasped where the minstrel had held them. When she pulled them apart, she found he had pressed something there for her to hold.

She held it up in wonder.

It was a single brilliant blue feather.

"Douce Dame Jolie"

Without thinking about it, Aurora used her thumbnail to crease the spine, to see if it felt like a real feather. It did. She twirled it between her fingers thoughtfully.

There were still pigeons, of course— quite a flock of them in the courtyards now (which peasants occasionally trapped for dinner, not always trusting magical food). They didn't have feathers like this.

There were some chickens and ducks left, but even the prettiest, most iridescent-winged drakes didn't sport a blue of this purity.

There were a few descendants of foreign birds from the jungles kept safe in golden cages, but the blue ones were very light, like the tiny flowers in ancient tapestries. Not like this.

She held the feather before her as she—much more thoughtfully—made her way to her room.

Aurora lived in a prettily decorated suite on the second floor of the castle. All the surviving royalty and lesser nobles lived in the main keep, as well as those foreign dignitaries trapped in the kingdom when the world outside finally collapsed. The . . . *lesser* survivors, the peasants and servants, lived in a hastily erected shantytown in one of the larger courtyards of the bailey.

If Aurora didn't look too hard at the thick vines covering her window and there was a good strong lantern glowing, she could pretend it was a completely normal royal princess's bedroom. There was a frothy and beribboned pink canopy bed on a raised dais, a wardrobe with gilt moldings in which hung a stunning number of beautiful gowns, a vanity with a pitcher and basin of beaten silver, a tiny couch with silk pillows, and a lovely little table by the fireplace with long, elegant legs.

There was also a bookcase full of books that hadn't worked properly since the world had ended.

Most were missing great patches of text and illustrations. Many were simply blank. The words that remained were often in languages that weren't even real. An effect, Maleficent had explained, of the world-destroying evil magics that King Stefan and Queen Leah had unleashed.

They had literally broken the land and the minds and inventions of men. The queen's powers were not great enough to restore everything fully—they were barely enough to keep the remaining population alive.

And so the books remained mostly blank, and cloth had to be woven from thread summoned by magic. Spinning wheels hadn't functioned the way they were supposed to in half a decade.

Right then, Aurora's bed looked especially inviting—the servants had made it up all plump and pretty. And she *did* love dancing, and she *was* going to be up late that night.

There was also the little matter that when she wasn't twirling, her favorite thing was lying down and dreaming the hours away. Her bed was always her favorite place to be; she could spend the entire day in the dark under its covers. Eventually night would come and sometimes things were more interesting at night . . . as much as anything was ever interesting in the castle at the end of the world.

And when the nights weren't particularly interesting, well, at least she had passed another of the endless days away.

She gave in, collapsing on her back onto the fat mattress full of feathers. She twirled the blue feather in her fingers. She had never seen the minstrel in any of the outer courtyards or baileys. He tended to stick to shadows, internal rooms, secluded areas—like a burglar or a cat. Bright light hurt his addict's eyes, and he was more uncomfortable than most looking up at the giant vines that blocked the sky.

Perhaps that's what he meant by being "outside." Not . . . *Outside.*

Poor crazy, drunken fool.

She sighed and reached up over her head to grab one of the broken books, one with an easily memorable design on its cover, and started to place the feather between its heavy, insane pages.

At the last moment, she changed her mind and put it in the little silver pouch attached to her girdle by her chatelaine. A once living thing, wherever it was from, didn't deserve to be pressed like an inanimate object—filed away like an ancient manuscript. The princess would keep it with her until she figured out what to do with it.

She thought of a different feather she owned and let out another sigh.

Instead of going to sleep, she sat down at her pretty little table, took up her white swan quill, and set herself to solving the math problems on the precious scrap of vellum before her.

After fortifying the castle, making living arrangements for all within, and working out whatever magical source of food she managed, Maleficent had turned to Aurora's education. The king and queen had neglected everything for their unwanted daughter—basic reading and writing skills, needlework, the sort of useful hobbies royal ladies were supposed to know, even etiquette and geography. The new queen immediately set out to rectify this with a half-dozen tutors, adding things to the mix that weren't necessarily "princessy."

Like math.

Which Aurora was terrible at.

Some things came to her naturally: singing, playing the recorder, kindness, patience in sewing—even if it would be years before her needle skills were up to that of a twelve-year-old's. Her fingers were often covered in tiny pinpricks from embroidery, and Maleficent had suggested, with a kind laugh, that she put off carding and spinning until she could be trusted with the sharp point of a drop spindle.

But numbers . . . and anything having to do with numbers . . . that was another thing entirely. Aurora privately wondered if there was a reason princesses weren't taught math or alchemy or the workings of the world; maybe they just couldn't grasp it.

Still, she forced herself to pay attention when the old castle treasurer patiently demonstrated the magic of adding and subtracting amounts with tally sticks and abaci, and the castle carpenter showed her the measurement of forms with string and weights.

When she tried to do the exact same problems on her

own, however, they never made sense. The numbers swam in front of her and the little counting lines seemed to multiply of their own volition. Her ability to draw was negligible, and her squares often looked like mush.

But Maleficent was trying so hard with her adopted niece that Aurora forced herself to keep working in secret, in private. She kept herself going by imagining the look on her aunt's face when she finally showed how she could divide an ink flock of sheep into five equal smaller herds.

Aurora drew a tiny ugly scribble of a sheep. Then she drew four more. She counted them. There were five. She drew two more, farther away. Now there were six.

Aurora frowned, looking at the paper.

Maybe seven. Eight?

She tried it on her fingers, pretending each one was a warm white ball of wool.

Did you count the beginning one *and* the last one, too? Or was it like pages of a book, where you didn't count both ends?

She spent ten more minutes trying to make the two groups of sheep add up. She was pretty sure it was around seven, but the lack of precision was giving her a headache.

Finally, she threw herself on her bed in frustration.

She would never be as smart and powerful and elegant as her aunt.

Sometimes she felt that the queen was just humoring her.

Sometimes she felt the slightest stirrings of anger at always being told what to do. *"Go take a nap."* What was she, a child? *"Oh, you couldn't possibly help out with these* unimaginably complex *party preparations."* Aurora was meant to be queen someday! She could handle a party.

Sometimes, in the secret safety of her canopied bed, in the blackest reaches of her mind, she wondered if her aunt really had the best intentions for her.

Why couldn't she be let in on the magical runnings of the castle? Why couldn't she watch and maybe learn how Maleficent summoned the food, drink, and other luxuries they managed to consume despite the destruction of the world Outside?

And how long did they have to stay cooped up in the castle anyway? When would it be safe enough to go Outside—even for a short while?

There was a story a priest had told her once—the poor priest who somehow wound up Outside the castle when everything happened—about the first time the world was destroyed. By water, not monsters. After enduring the flood in a boat for weeks, the surviving humans had sent out a dove or a hedgehog or some other bird to see if there was dry land anywhere yet.

Couldn't *they* do that?

Couldn't they send out one of the inhuman guards? Couldn't *they* leave to explore and come back—using some of Maleficent's magic somehow to protect themselves?

Had the minstrel really made it *all the way* Outside and back?

The Exile, the only one ever forcibly sent out of the castle, had never returned . . . but he probably didn't want to face the queen's wrath. He had challenged her right to rule; *he* was a *real* king, he had said, not "some strumpet of a fairy too big for her britches."

It was, upon reflection, lucky for him she didn't just obliterate him on the spot. Maleficent had a streak of temper, though she tried to shield her niece from it.

Aurora grumpily spun over on her bed and put her pillow over her head. These were the thoughts she was most ashamed of. Ungrateful thoughts about the woman who had saved what was left of the world. Aurora had too much of her parents in her. She seemed to lack basic human gratitude for what she had.

She wished she had magic powers.

No, her mind quickly said, not like what her parents had received. Not even as much as Maleficent had. Just a little. Just to be able to *see*. Either what the world was like out there now, how it was changing or healing . . . or what it had been like before, back when there were animals and people and the books all worked properly. It was getting hard to remember, another effect of the evil, changed land.

She wished . . .

. . . and a book fell on her head.

In the Cards

Princess Aurora sat up, surprised by the sudden cascade of parchment pages that fell to the floor. Not a book . . . a deck of cards. Brightly colored, intricately painted cards whose pictures were all still intact.

She picked them up with just the tips of her very careful fingers, as if at her touch they would disappear back into her imagination.

The first few were familiar. They were the kind used for games that people in the castle often played to pass their long hours of confinement. A three of swords, a nine of cups, a two of hearts, all in the bright and simple heraldic colors of the kingdom. An eight of chairs. A thirteen of dolls. A zero of castles.

The numbers were elegant, elongated, and golden, just like the ones she drew in the air when math was easy.

A strange ache throbbed where she had been hit in the head by the cards. What golden numbers? When was math easy? That never happened, except perhaps in a dream. . . .

She shook herself and flipped to the next card.

A *joker*.

Aurora frowned at this one. The figure sported the usual impish grin of his kind—but his motley seemed ragged. His face was long and narrow, and instead of a scepter or wand he carried a lute. He looked, all things considered, a trifle too much like the minstrel.

And after *him* came even stranger cards of equally bizarre suits.

A one of suns: a shining yellow ball, golden rays streaking out sharply to the edges of the card. Aurora held it close to her face, wondering at the detail. She wished the artist had left some room for a hint of the blue sky she couldn't remember anymore. The sun seemed so joyous at its own energy that its eyes were simple curves, squinted shut, its mouth almost nonexistent.

Did the real sun actually have a face?

Aurora wasn't sure. She couldn't remember.

In the picture below it, a naked child happily rode a pony over hills so green she was tempted to pick at the paint with her fingernail. His mount was dappled white and black and had a horn and a beard. None of the remaining horses in the castle looked anything like it.

The next card was of a girl who looked, at first glance, like Aurora herself, arms wrapped lovingly around the neck of a lion. The lion was tawny and orange and red, and the girl's golden hair was so thick and manelike she could have been a version of the sun itself. Aurora knew lions because they were carved into decorations around the castle and inscribed upon heraldic shields.

On the card after that, a girl—who also looked like her—was touching a different beast on the nose. Aurora had no idea what animal it was. Tiny like a squirrel, but with overlong, soft ears that were as ridiculous as the horn on the pony. Its pink nose sprouted long whiskers that were so carefully painted Aurora felt her heart break. She wished she could touch such a creature, like the girl in the picture.

And finally, there was an animal by itself in an open green patch surrounded by trees. It looked a bit like a horse but for its shorter body and more slender legs. It had no mane, and its tail was short and fat. Its head was turned backward, cocked, as if listening for danger.

Aurora looked around quickly, suddenly nervous. No book in the castle had *all* of its pictures, and even the tapestries were blurry. It seemed like this strange deck was complete. Why these? Why now?

"Princess? Your Highness?" a voice called from outside her door.

Aurora quickly swept the cards into an ungainly pile and, looking around for someplace to stash them, shoved them into the pretty little velvet bag set out to go with her gown that night.

Without waiting for an answer, the owner of the voice swept in: tiny, round-faced, and as delicate as a dragonfly.

Aurora felt a burn of guilt heat up her face and breast. Lady Lianna was her handmaiden and closest friend. And the princess was *her* only friend; she had been part of a visiting envoy when the end of the world had come, destroying her homeland, her parents, and everyone she had ever loved.

Despite her completely appropriate dress and the very stylish, intricately braided buns of ebon that covered her ears, there was something unmistakably foreign about her large black eyes and grayish skin. Other members of royalty in the castle tended to shun her.

"You're not even *partially* dressed yet," Lianna scolded, but she didn't click her tongue the way another might have. She flowed from one side of the room to the other, gathering things for a ballroom transformation: brush, ribbons, underskirts, golden tippet, golden shoes.

"Um," Aurora said. Up until a moment ago, the ball had been arguably the most important—or at least interesting—thing in her life. The one and only event there was to look forward to every month.

But now all Aurora wanted was for Lianna to go away so she could go back to lying on her bed, looking through all the cards.

The handmaiden planted herself behind the princess and began to unlace the back of her day dress.

"Your second cousin, Mistress Laura, refuses to wear the gown you so generously gave her that bolt of cloth for."

"Really?" Aurora asked, momentarily distracted. "I thought she would look nice in that dark aqua. It matches her eyes."

"I think it was less the *color* than who chose it," Lianna said crisply. Having finished with the laces, she firmly but politely turned Aurora around and started helping her out of the long, buttoned sleeves.

"Oh, bother. Well, she's just a girl," Aurora said, shaking her head—and her arms, to get the long sleeves off.

"She's fifteen, Your Highness," her friend said with a barely audible hiss. "I would keep an eye on her insolences. You have many years of close confinement with her—and her admirers—ahead."

Aurora shook her head with a smile. "Lianna, this is not like the court where you're from. There are no conspiracies. There are no plots. She is a girl who doesn't want the future queen choosing a dress for her. I understand—I don't like it when people tell *me* what to do, either."

There was a moment of silence. Aurora realized that last bit had come out far more vehemently than she had meant.

Lianna's large eyes were unreadable, as always.

"Oh, absolutely. And the Exile was just a friendly neighboring king."

"That was different," Aurora said, uncomfortable at the memory. "He *wanted* to take over the castle. He actually tried to organize a coup."

"It started with *talk*, Your Highness. He told Queen Maleficent she had no place ruling. That he was better suited. It started with talk and ended with him being thrown Outside for all of our safety. If you truly like Mistress Laura, you will caution her to curb her tongue and to obey those above her without question."

The princess was silent. All she remembered from that confusing time was a white-bearded, fat little blustery man, shouting and arguing like a storm against the cool, sharp figure of her aunt. The fury of his words had been split and dissipated by the calmness of her demeanor.

And then his cursing when the inhuman servants threw him Outside.

Lianna relented, seeing the troubled look on her mistress's face.

"Come," she said. "Get out of that, and we'll put you in *your* dress."

She turned to the wardrobe with the precision of an insect. Aurora shivered out of her dress, letting it fall to the floor. It was a fun, dramatic moment, but Aurora was a good girl and could not resist immediately stepping out of it, picking it up, and smoothing it out. The way she had been taught to take care of clothes.

No, wait . . . no one had taught her. She had been ignored and left to run wild with the servants and dogs for years.

She put a hand to her head.

"Here, now, look at this," Lianna said quickly, bringing the new dress over. "*This* is a dress for a royal princess."

It was indeed, and Aurora couldn't help smiling. The skirt and bodice were as dark blue as she imagined the sea had been, dotted with golden shots of thread, the way she imagined the ocean had sparkled under a golden sun. The girdle matched her tippets, both made from the same golden cloth taken from one of the old queen's dresses.

Palace seamstresses and ladies of the court had worked day and night on it—on *all* of the outfits for the ball.

"It is so nice for everyone to make this for me," she murmured.

"It's generous of you and the queen to give the ladies something to do," Lianna almost snorted.

"What do you mean? This took *weeks* of work," Aurora said, showing her the fine seams.

"Seamstresses must sew. Ladies must dance. Everyone does what they must do or we will all go mad here," the handmaiden said, holding the skirts so Aurora could step into them properly. "I have seen them work, their needles flashing in and out, like they are driven by the devil. Even the peasants brush their donkeys and slop the pigs and try to grow little vegetable gardens despite the food our loving queen provides with her magic. They cannot stop themselves. Everyone must be what they must be."

"And ladies in waiting?" Aurora said with a gentle, teasing smile.

"We wait," Lianna said with no hint of humor.

"But you don't *have* to," the princess said gently. "It's nice that you're serving me, and I love you as a friend, but . . . do *you* want to do anything different?"

Lianna stared at her, wide black eyes unblinking.

"I am only here at all because of the grace of our loving queen," she said flatly. "I am grateful for my continued existence."

Aurora bit her lip. What she had mistaken for insensate following of orders was actually overwhelming gratitude. Lianna felt blessed that she was simply still alive; *anything* she did now was a joyful celebration of that.

"I'm sorry," Aurora said softly, taking her hand. "I didn't mean to insult what you do. I just wanted to say . . . if you *wanted* to do anything different . . . marry someone, maybe . . . I don't know . . . I'd miss your constant presence, but I completely encourage it."

Lianna finally blinked.

"Th-thank you, Princess," she said.

Then the moment was over and the quick, knowing smile returned. "For *now*, the princess must have her hair brushed and arranged by an expert. Sit."

Aurora let herself be gently pushed onto her pink-cushioned chair. She looked into the hazy silver mirror as Lianna took her locks and brushed down, down, long strokes, over and over again until they shone.

"Your hair is so beautiful," the handmaiden sighed. "Like spun gold."

Even though she always said this, she said it with feeling every time. Aurora looked into the mirror and smiled. She *was* pretty. She *was* a royal princess. There was about to be a ball. These were things she could, once in a while, allow herself to be happy about.

The Ball

Everyone in the Thorn Castle attended the monthly balls. Well, the peasants were in the secondary hall, and the servants were, of course, serving, but no one was left out. Everyone got wine, cider, food, salt, and a chance to hear the musicians play.

Long silk swags in every shade of blue hung from the walls and billowed out over the ceiling to suggest what the sky used to look like. Magical bronze fountains bubbled water that was tinted slightly blue for effect. Artificial streams ran down troughs in the middle of the great tables like—like actual streams once did, perhaps. Although they didn't quite tinkle properly, as they did in Aurora's dreams. The tables had been draped with old blue and green tapestries. Their pictures were blurred and gone; blue dishes and golden plates were arranged to cover them up so no one would see and grow uneasy. There were *always* golden plates at the feasts. It was the only thing Maleficent ever insisted on. Golden plates and golden domes over the food to keep it warm. Seeing them always made the queen smile, though she never said why.

Chandeliers and great pillar candles and torches in the walls all flickered with dancing blue flames thanks to Queen Maleficent's magic.

The musicians played in the space in front of the three great tables, long blue streamers tied to their horns and mandolins. They sat in what looked very much like a broad wooden washtub, but which people who remembered insisted was a boat.

Even the minstrel was there—albeit with discreet golden chains holding him to the closest pillar and a guard standing nearby. He had apparently been allowed a furlough from his forced recuperation just for tonight. And though his eyes were red, bloodshot, and watery, he was picking his lute with the speed and skill he was renowned for. And acting otherwise completely like his normal self.

Aurora found herself heaving a sigh of relief—and disappointment. *Guilty* disappointment. She genuinely liked the minstrel and didn't really want anything bad to happen to him . . . but with him playing and everything back to normal, it really did seem like what he had said about the Outside was nothing but the raving of a drunk. Everything would go on as it had before. . . .

She forced her attention away from him and back to the revelers.

The nobles of the castle were dressed in brilliant blues: Prussian velvet doublets, cerulean linen skirts, periwinkle bodices, sapphire roundlets, cobalt capes, all swirling and undulating as people talked or danced or made their way around the room.

Aurora watched the scene from her vantage point next to the throne with a satisfied smile. On the royal dais, looking down at the entire room, she imagined she was also on a boat, watching waves crash against each other in dance after dance.

Maybe it really was like a sea.

Maleficent wore all black as usual, but with a nod to the theme of the festivities, she had changed her horned headpiece to a slightly iridescent blue and wore matching iridescent wristlets.

Aurora shifted her legs in a slightly unprincessy manner; her decorative bag hung heavier than usual. It was only when she looked down that she saw the uneven corners of the cards sticking out the top of her velvet pouch.

"Something the matter, my dear?" the queen drawled.

"No. It's just . . ." Aurora fumbled with the bag and loosened its drawstrings. "I found these earlier. I was . . . I was going to ask you about them."

As she handed the deck over, she wondered if that was strictly true. She had no hesitation in showing them now, but if she hadn't been caught, would she have?

"Ahhhh." Maleficent's eyes widened for a moment, but the sound came out of her mouth long and quiet. Aurora had no idea how to interpret it. "This is how the world was before. Before your parents destroyed it. Behold: the sun. A unicorn. A lion. A rabbit. A deer . . ."

As the queen named each card, Aurora found herself mouthing the words she didn't know after her, trying to remember.

"And so on. You shouldn't look at these, dear. They will only make you sad. They are all gone from this world, never to return."

Maleficent let the cards tumble from her fingers to the ground.

Aurora watched, tears springing to her eyes.

"Couldn't you," she whispered, "couldn't you with your magic . . . ?"

"There is no magic in the world powerful enough to bring back that which is truly dead and extinct. I'm so sorry, my dear. You should, sadly, put it completely out of your head. It can only cause you sorrow."

Aurora nodded mutely, trying not to sniff.

Maleficent put a finger to her niece's chin and gently forced her head up. "See? It is already ruining your fantastic party. It's unfortunate you ever saw these."

The princess took a deep breath and tried to compose herself. Through the blur of her unshed tears, the golden numbers on the cards gleamed and twinkled from the floor, refusing to be trash.

The queen also regarded the cards on the ground and began to tap on the edge of her throne with her long black fingernails.

"Where *did* you find these, anyway?" she asked casually.

Aurora shrugged. "They fell off my bookshelf. I never noticed them before. All of the other books are, you know, senseless or blank."

"Of course they are," the queen said, nodding, seeming relieved. "You must be careful, my Aurora. The Outside has ways of getting *in*side. My powers can stave off the physical attacks, the bigger monsters and obvious threats of invasion . . . but evil has a way of slipping in—through the cracks in your mind. Wishes are powerful and dangerous things. Do not wish for things that can never be."

"Yes, Aunt Maleficent." The woman's words had been

said as gently as possible, and there had only been the mildest tone of chastisement. Yet the princess was once again filled with shame at her ingratitude, her silly little-girlishness in wishing to see something that would never be again. Things that were long ago destroyed—by her own parents. And *their* evil wishes.

"Oh, darling, don't be grumpy," Maleficent said with a smile. "Enjoy your party, dear! Look how much fun every-one is having, thanks to you!"

The queen indicated the crowd with an elegant and dramatic wave of her fingers. While she was looking away, Aurora quickly used an agile foot to sweep a few of the cards out of sight, under the train of her gown. Only then did she follow her aunt's example and look around.

Lianna was clapping along on the far side of the room; she never danced. When she saw the princess looking at her, she nodded her head slightly. Aurora turned to follow the direction of her nod and saw, dressed in a worn velvet doublet that was certainly not his own, the stable boy, Cael. He had his head thrown back in laughter at something one of the serving girls said, his thick brown hair tossed behind him like . . . like . . . like a mane. But his eyes were directed at Aurora, and he grinned.

She didn't particularly fancy him, but grinned back anyway. A young man who wanted to dance was a young man who wanted to dance, and in the castle at the end of the world, there weren't a whole lot to choose from.

On the other hand . . . there was also Count Brodeur, who never looked away from her eyes when they talked, who flattered her and spoke sweetly. An older and wiser man than a silly stable boy. Someone she could *discuss* things with.

She picked up her skirts—and, secretly, the cards—and hurried down to join him.

"Your Highness," the count said, turning and executing a low, sweeping bow the moment he saw her. His blue cape flew out behind him like the tail of a magnificent bird: a peacock or a badger or something similar. His peppered-gray mustache tickled the back of her hand as he kissed it.

"A word, if you would?" she asked, trying not to simper and giggle, though she couldn't stop the smile forming in the corners of her lips. It was also hard not to look at her hands as they stuffed the cards back into her bag.

"You may have *all* my words, forever, Your Highness," he promised, only the twinkle in his eye betraying any admission of hyperbole. "Also, all my dances."

He put his arms out, and Aurora gracefully scooped up the train of her gown and let him lead her delicately out onto the floor. Their fingertips just touched in this most proper of dances. When she spun, she saw Cael miming an arrow striking his heart and feigning big tears. But he had another drink of cider and didn't seem overly concerned as he chatted up the maid who had brought it over.

"May I ask you a question, Count Brodeur—discreetly?" she asked, turning so she avoided looking at the stable boy.

"Always, Your Highness," the count said, his interest definitely piqued. "Intrigue? Schemes? *Anything* to relieve the boredom around here?"

Aurora chose not to think about the rumors concerning how Brodeur relieved his own boredom. She also chose to ignore Lianna, who was watching them closely with what looked like a frown on her otherwise placid face.

"Nothing, perhaps, so interesting," she slipped a hand into her pouch and pulled out the feather. "What do you think of *this* . . . ?"

The count squinted at it, disappointed. "It's just a feather. So what?"

The princess bit her lip, a little taken aback by his reaction.

"But . . . it's not a *pigeon* feather," she pointed out. "Or a sparrow's, or . . ."

"Is this for a scavenger hunt?" he asked, getting excited again. "Is someone organizing another scavenger hunt?"

Aurora frowned. *Scavenger hunt?* Were there all sorts

of games going on that the royal princess wasn't invited to?

"No," she said impatiently. "The minstrel said he got it from the Outside. . . ."

"OUTSIDE?"

The count stopped dancing and grabbed her by the shoulders in an entirely indecent and improper manner.

"Good sir," Aurora said as politely as she could, looking around nervously.

"When did he go? He's back in? *How did he get out?* What did he see?" the count demanded, almost hissing like her aunt.

"I don't know. He was drunk. He's always drunk. He may have been lying," she stammered.

"DID HE REALLY GO OUTSIDE? Is the air out there good and sweet? He survived? *You must tell me!"* he said, practically shaking her.

"Please—you're hurting me," Aurora said, fighting tears. People were watching. Despite the occasional breach of etiquette in the endless confinement of the castle, attacks on the royal princess—in public, no less—just didn't happen.

Two of Maleficent's servants were instantly on either side of her, bronze spears held at the ready.

The count paled and immediately let her go.

"My apologies, Your Highness," he said, making an

extremely low bow and touching his heart. "I was . . . overwhelmed."

His face was red and his eyes were darting, unsettled.

Aurora noticed that, despite this, he had carefully phrased his apology such that it could be misinterpreted as to mean he was overwhelmed by *her*—her beauty.

Everyone was staring.

Including Queen Maleficent, whose yellow eyes watched unblinkingly to see what she would do.

The princess wanted nothing more than to run away. To pick up her skirts and run out of the room, away from the faces—to run to bed and her solitude and her silence.

But she was a royal princess in the Thorn Castle at the end of the world.

And the wrong word from her would send this *stupid* man to his death.

She drew up her shoulders, trying to channel her aunt.

"There is no trouble here," she said, voice quavering. "As the count said, he was merely overwrought. You may return to your posts."

The creatures slumped but obeyed, looking disappointed they didn't get to rough someone up. The crowd turned away—also disappointed that the excitement was over.

The count gave a subdued, if sullen, bow. She hurried

away from him, anywhere—toward Mistress Laura, who was sporting an extremely bright orange dress instead of the aquamarine she was supposed to.

And Aurora kept the feather and the minstrel's secret to herself from then on, as safely locked in her heart as they all were in the castle.

We're All Mad Here

A month passed.

Soon it was time for another ball.

This time the theme was "Gold."

People assumed it was the bright metal kind, in coins and necklaces. But that wasn't the sort of gold Aurora was imagining.

She was imagining the sun.

She *tried* not to think about it. She tried not to wish for it. She tried to be like Lianna—thankful and grateful just for being and there being a sun somewhere up in the sky at all. She spent a lot of time lying down these days, trying very hard to be grateful—when she wasn't just staring into space. Trying not to feel restless and caged. Once in a while, the sun would push one ray through the protective vines on her bedroom window and its thick, heavy light would make its way to her bed. She would lie in its warmth for hours, like a cat in front of the fire, wishing it would cover her entire body.

Sometimes she would spend a whole afternoon watching little motes of dust doing their slow dances in the golden light like lazy, otherworldly fairies. Sometimes it seemed that if she just concentrated hard enough, she could make them dance the way she wanted them to. They performed whole ballets and routines just for her, each one unique, each little dancer jagged and golden. Sometimes she drifted off during the performances, which might have been rude but was also unavoidable.

Sometimes she would waste the hours observing a single spot of sunlight slowly moving across the room and up the wall before disappearing.

She slept a *lot*.

Lady Astrid, a second cousin from somewhere on her father's side, was one of the few nobles who noticed her complete dropping out of even the tiny and desperate life those in the castle led.

The short, plump woman showed up at her door in the middle of one of the many endless afternoons with a needle and a frame and a look of steely determination.

"Your Royal Highness, I think maybe some useful work would help you cheer up and pass the time constructively."

"Mmmfh mmmng mmmmbr," Aurora said into her pillow. She didn't *have* to get up for a lady.

"I beg your pardon, Your Highness?"

"Thank you, but not today, Lady Astrid. I'm not feeling up to it."

"Your Highness," Astrid said through clenched teeth. "I do believe this is for your own good. Prithee get up off that bed and start acting like a princess and not a lazy, spoiled brat."

Aurora sat up at that, shocked.

"If the queen's servants heard you speaking to me that way, they would throw you into the dungeon."

"Fat lot of difference that would make around here," the older lady said pleasantly. "And there aren't any around. Thank heaven for small miracles. Now, are you coming? There's no seat in here comfortable enough for my robust, aging backside."

And Aurora, whose basic mode of being was to not do *anything*—or to do whatever she was told for want of any good reason to do otherwise, followed Lady Astrid meekly to the closest study.

It was a slightly more interesting way to spend time than staring into space—despite the little pricks of blood on the cloth, the countless times she had to squint and rethread the needle, and the general mess she made of the piece. Fortunately it was just a sampler, nothing fancy.

Eventually, she got into a groove and made little rows of knots that weren't too terrible.

"You do this every day?" Aurora asked, frowning at where the needle was stuck on the backside of her cloth.

"Every afternoon," Lady Astrid said briskly. She sat in a larger, more comfortable chair, closer to the fire. Her brows furrowed as she did a tricky bit, beautiful arched brows above her plump and sagging face. "After lunch, before the *nones*—my midafternoon prayers."

"You have a *schedule?*"

"Of course. You have to keep a mind and body busy. Idle hands are the devil's playthings. Rise, dress, stretch, *matins*, breakfast, a brisk walk around the castle for digestion, *lauds*, midmorning snack if it's available, a visit with some of the older residents—or laundry inspection, mending, et cetera—*terces*, perhaps a little liturgical discussion with Lady Carlisle or the Marquis Belloq, lunch, say a quick prayer for those precious souls we have lost since our confinement here, review of the stores or, alternately, review of the servants, a tour of the lamentable remaining greenery in the courtyard, see if there's anything for arranging or decorating . . ."

"Goodness," the princess said. "You have every minute of the day planned."

"I would go mad if I didn't," the lady said, half under her breath. "And more people would do better if they did," she added pointedly.

The princess paused in her work and bit her lip, regarding the funny little woman. Some of the nobles—like Brodeur—had fallen into strange excesses during the confinement—which everyone tried to keep Aurora from hearing about. Here was a plain Jane sensible old lady who, despite being a little boring and plenty judgmental, had adapted to life in the Thorn Castle as best she could and made herself useful wherever she could. Levelheaded.

Aurora fingered the little pouch on her chatelaine. She had decided not to tell anyone about the feather since the incident with Brodeur. But this prudent—and low-profile—woman didn't seem like the type of person who would make a fuss. Like Brodeur.

After a moment, she came to a decision and pulled out the feather.

"What . . . Lady Astrid . . . what do you think of *this*?"

And for once, the lady looked astonished.

Her face softened when she saw it, crumpling into something like wonder.

"It looks . . . *fresh*," she said softly. "Not years and years old. And it's too . . . *imperfect* to be magic. It looks like it's from Outs—"

She started to reach out her hand for it and then curled up her fingers at the last moment.

"Where did you get it?"

"I'm not sure I can say," Aurora admitted, thinking about Brodeur's reaction. "Do you know what kind of feather it is? What bird it's from?"

"Do I *seem* like some sort of expert on animals—on birds and other winged things?" Astrid asked sharply, regaining her composure. "Since it . . . cannot be . . . from the *Outside* . . . I'm going to assume it's from a pigeon or one of those other flying rats that haunt the bailey."

She went back to her work.

Aurora looked at the feather glumly.

"I wouldn't talk to anyone else . . . *inside* the castle about the feather, Your Highness," the lady added quietly after a moment. "If you ask me, people are a little tense and stir-crazy . . . and the walls have ears. Your—blessèd—aunt has saved us all, but she gets very touchy about anything having to do with the Outside. For good reason, I suppose. I'll keep your secret. . . . There are others who wouldn't."

The princess nodded—again, glumly. She wished she had spoken to Astrid *before* the last ball. Was Count Brodeur already telling everyone her secret? Or worse, would he tell her aunt? Aurora wouldn't get in trouble, most likely, but the poor minstrel . . . Right now he was enduring her wrath for his public drunkenness. How much worse could it be for him if her aunt found out he went Outside?

Aurora put the feather away and went back to sewing.

It was better, she supposed, than doing nothing at all.

The days leading up to the ball were particularly grim.

Though sometimes *days* were hard to count, with little sun and no moon and clocks that didn't keep hours in any way that made sense.

But even with the world changed, seasons run amok, the moon gone, and the protective vines keeping the castle dwellers safe from the unnatural world that raged Outside . . . there were still some markers of the course of time.

At the beginning of each year of their confinement, for instance, a strange bell would toll across the land. Once or twice a day for several days it would strike, its reverberations lasting for hours at a time, gradually increasing and echoing in the corridors until everyone was fairly shaken and crazed. Everyone from the lowest peasant to Aurora herself stuffed their ears with wool and cowered under their pillows trying to escape the sound. Even Maleficent seemed to be gritting her teeth and on edge.

The passing of weeks could be observed by keeping careful track—or observing how the queen herself waxed and waned. By the end of each ball she was healthy, energetic, and her magic was at its most powerful: for many days after, meals were interesting and fantastic, new diversions were summoned, clothing was refreshed, and the stores all restocked. Everyone rejoiced, and life in the Thorn Castle was bearable for a time.

But . . . after a while . . . the queen began looking more tired, with deeper shadows under her eyes and a languor that surpassed her usual show of ennui in the days furthest from a feast.

Meals were still served, but the food was gray and bland and hard to remember. The fires and candles and lanterns, all burning with magical fuel, dimmed. People clustered closer to them and went to bed earlier, terrified of the thought they might go out entirely. Between the constant grayness of the keep and the strangely forgettable meals, time lost all meaning entirely, and people began to lose any remaining hope they had.

They flitted through the halls like ghosts, silent and gloomy.

Often this was when they finally noticed that someone had disappeared from their dwindling ranks, and found the body of someone who just couldn't take it anymore.

At these times, when morale in the castle was at its lowest, when even the peasants seemed to give up on their little gardens and things grew dusty for lack of the servants' care and no one reprimanded them—no one had the energy—at these times, Maleficent would ask Aurora to sing.

For everyone.

All would gather in the great hall: nobility and royalty in front, of course, on chairs and cushions arranged for them. Behind them were lesser nobility and the remaining artisans, merchants, and freemen, on stools and rugs. Then the villeins and peasants and servants, wherever they could fit themselves. They all forgot their hunger, their confinement, their growing insanity the moment her voice rang out its very first note.

The princess sang for hours, for everyone—at a time when she least wanted to see *anyone*, much less sing.

"I can't do it this time, Lianna."

Aurora sat, slumped, on her pink-cushioned chair, her hair around her in very slight tangles—which was as messy as her handmaiden ever let it get.

Lianna regarded her princess with impassive eyes. She was the only one who seemed unaffected by these doldrums and had little patience for those who were.

"You must," she said simply. "It is a much-needed, pleasant distraction for the people."

"Distraction?" Aurora asked, momentarily roused by the odd word choice.

Lianna shrugged impatiently. She picked up her brush and began brushing. "From their depression or sadness or whatever. Whatever it is that has you people so low. And besides being just a nice thing to do, your queen asked you. You should obey—happily."

"I know," the princess sighed, slumping again. "I just . . . hate it. I *hate* standing in front of everyone . . . singing. . . . Singing is just something I do. For *me*. I feel like I'm on display up there."

"You *are* on display," Lianna said with her usual bluntness. "You are their beautiful princess. A shining beacon of hope. You were given beauty and song and a royal title and . . . absolutely *gorgeous* hair. Being on display is one of your duties. And speaking of hair . . ."

She picked up a single long, golden lock and began to systematically brush it.

"I didn't ask for any of these things," Aurora mumbled. She pulled the feather out of her chatelaine and began to roll it desultorily through her fingers.

"*Nobody* asks for the things they are given, most of the time. I didn't ask for . . . black hair . . . or . . . my clumsy feet . . . or . . . what I am now. *Where* I am now. Would you rather you were a servant, forced to scrub all day? Or one of those peasants out there, pretending you're still farming the land? It's rather ridiculous, you know. I actually heard several of them discussing the prospect of breeding those sad, silly sheep they keep in that . . . *petting zoo*, trying to save the line. And the horses."

Aurora smiled knowingly.

"You don't like animals much, do you?"

Her handmaiden shrugged.

"They have their uses I suppose."

"I love them. I wish there were more of them. I wish . . ." She stopped herself, thinking about what Maleficent had said about wishes. Lianna cocked her head at the princess curiously. Aurora quickly changed the subject. "Did you . . . did you ever have a pet or anything at all? Where you grew up?"

The girl stopped brushing. Her eyes grew unfocused, like Aurora had never seen before. Her face softened at an unseen memory.

"I . . . I had a bird once. A raven."

Aurora blinked in surprise.

She stayed as quiet as possible, not wanting to disturb Lianna out of her story.

"He had fallen out of his nest. A fledgling. His flight feathers hadn't come in yet. I picked him up and brought him home. Raised him from a baby."

Without realizing it, Lianna was miming the motions of what she had done, making her hands tuck the invisible bird into some soft cloth, carrying it delicately.

"He lived. He grew into a strong, healthy man-bird with ebon feathers and a bright yellow beak. Such bright eyes, too! He went with me everywhere. He sat on my shoulder. He sat on the back of my chair, behind me, at meals. He never left my side. . . ."

Lianna trailed off, lost in the memory.

Aurora didn't want to break the spell, but couldn't help asking.

"What . . . happened to him?"

And the spell was broken.

Her handmaiden shook herself. "He was turned into stone. By a fairy. A stupid, stupid fairy. The only thing I ever loved, and she killed him."

"I'm so sorry," Aurora said, reaching out to clasp Lianna's hand. "It seems like fairies do nothing but evil. To all of us."

The other girl looked down at her princess's hand clasping hers, then up into Aurora's face. A rare confused stream of emotions ran across her own.

"I know a song about ravens," Aurora said brightly. "I'll sing it tonight, just for you. In memory of your friend."

"Thank you, Your Highness," Lianna murmured. She

smiled, too—a genuine, rare smile from her heart.

Unused to the expression, her face only allowed half of her mouth to tilt.

But if the royal princess could bring even a *little* happiness to people tonight, as she had her handmaiden, she would absolutely do it. And do it gratefully and happily every time Maleficent asked, Aurora decided.

No matter how much she hated it.

The Bluebird of Happiness

The concert was a rousing success. Aurora sang beautiful songs that made people sigh with wonder, sad songs that made people weep for things that were never real, and *almost* bawdy, funny songs to bring them back from the brink. When she sang "The Raven of the Evercliffs," she looked at Lianna. Her handmaiden's eyes remained wide and unblinking for the entire song.

As a surprise encore, a little servant boy sang a simple country ballad that had everyone clapping and shouting. Aurora held him high in her arms so the whole crowd could see.

For one evening, at least, everyone was happy again. There was a little bit of hope in the Thorn Castle once more—enough to get them through to the next ball. Even Maleficent seemed cheered.

All this strengthened Aurora's new resolve and crystallized her intentions. She came up with a Plan.

A Plan to improve herself. To keep herself busy (like Lady Astrid). To make what was left of the world better for those around her (like Lianna).

The Plan was this: each month she would work on one quality she felt she was lacking in until she was a better person. First was Gratitude. Next was Patience. After that was Pure Thoughts.

She made lots of wonderful little lists chock-full of ideas for exercising each deficient part of her psyche. It was much easier than math.

One of her first to-dos for Gratitude was to give a thank-you speech at the Gold Ball as a surprise for her aunt.

"And we thank you, gracious queen . . ."

Aurora held the carefully penned speech in her right hand and moved her left hand across her body, indicating an imaginary crowd. It didn't feel right. She should be gesturing at the *queen*, not the audience. Or maybe if she just emphasized the *we*.

"*We* thank *you*, gracious queen, for our safety, our health, our well-being, our very lives! Without your foresight and kindness, we would be as dead as the world around us, as extinct as the rabbits. . . ."

She faltered on that word. She tried not to th
the playing card with the tender brown-furred thing lifting
its nose to the golden-haired girl—who resembled her so
closely. She tried not to think about what the animal would
have looked like in real life, whether it was really that friendly,
if its fur was soft, if its nose twitched or stayed still. . . .

"Extinct as the rabbits." She began again, taking a
breath. "For . . ."

A movement flickered at the edge of her vision. At the
base of her desk, next to one of the long legs that ended,
ironically, in paws.

There, of course, was a rabbit.

Somehow she had known what it was before she even
made herself look at it. And now that she had, she felt her
heart beating out of control, her breath catching in her throat.

It looked both exactly and not at all like the picture.
Its eyes were brown, large, glistening, and mostly empty. It
leaned forward, hesitantly, to sniff the leg of the desk, putting its whiskers and silly long ears back. It turned its head
to look directly at Aurora. It had no tail, only a stupidly
endearing puff of white on its rear end.

"You're not real," Aurora said, hopefully and doubt-
ingly. "You're extinct."

The rabbit cocked its head and turned its ears like
a windmill. If she hadn't known better, she would have
thought its face showed the animal equivalent of a smile.

Oh, she wanted to touch it.

She wanted to bend down and put her hand out, the way she did to the few baby goats and sheep that were born to the castle each year. She wanted to be the girl in the picture and have it breathe its warm, moist breath on the palm of her hand.

She thought of Maleficent's words. About the Outside finding unexpected ways into the castle. About the implication that she was weaker than most in this respect because of her parents, because of her tainted, evil blood.

Aurora closed her eyes.

"You're not real."

When she opened them, the rabbit was gone.

What she felt then had nothing to do with relief or thankfulness. It was as if all of her little stores of energy, of hope, of happiness, were now suddenly being forcibly drained from her and into the floor. She let the speech drop in a sad flutter and lay down on her bed, too empty to do anything else.

Lianna was starting to worry about Aurora.

She even tried to arrange a tryst between the princess and Cael; difficult, because he couldn't read the notes she sent. Aurora just didn't care that much. The stable boy would always be there. He would be there next month, if she cared by then. And so would the ball. And so would the musicians and the food, and then there would be another month. . . .

"Besides, stable boys are no fit match for a royal princess," she said aloud, imitating Maleficent's voice and dramatic speech. She sat alone at her desk, playing with her tiny pile of illicit treasures—the three cards she had managed to keep, the blue feather—instead of working on math or her lists. "They're all dirty and work with animals and live outside and . . ."

She stopped, and it wasn't to wonder—as she occasionally did—who *would* be a fit match, since all the princes in the world were dead. No, it was a murky, intriguing thought, involving stable boys and *animals.*

She picked up the feather, regarding it.

Lady Astrid was right. She *couldn't* talk to anyone about it *inside* the castle.

The old lady had said it very specifically and carefully.

The stable boy was *not* inside the castle. He lived in the stable. In the bailey.

And *he* knew something about animals. Birds, maybe . . .

This was an interesting idea. An idea that actually involved *doing* something. An action of some sort. Which was where things usually fell apart for Aurora. Actions were tiring. She mostly found it better to lie on her bed and *think* about actions. Just the thought of getting up these days seemed exhausting and unreasonable.

Sometimes she had to *surprise* her body into doing something.

So without thinking, she leapt off the bed and fastened her chatelaine to her girdle. She hurried to find Lianna before she could find some reason to change her own mind.

The handmaiden was sitting in front of a woodless magical fire, just staring into it, warming her hands. Which would have been odd if Aurora didn't know that she came from a hot country.

"I think . . . I think I'd like to have a word with the stable boy, after all," Aurora said. It wasn't a lie.

But she still felt guilty when the usually impassive Lianna leapt up immediately, joy and mischief in her big black eyes.

"We will go out through the summer kitchen," she said, clasping the princess's hands in her own. "Come! When we get down to the outer courtyard I will run ahead and prepare the way. We will say you are just visiting the animals, as you love to do."

The two girls hurried through the passageways, hand in hand. When a stolid-looking matron of the lesser nobility rounded a corner, the girls immediately slowed down to a more decorous pace, nodding serenely at the woman. As soon as she was out of sight, they raced ahead again.

"Wait here. I'll wave to you from the dairy window when it's safe," Lianna said at the door before the courtyard. She started to open it then stopped and turned, suddenly seized with conscience. "Whatever you do . . . do not—do not do anything that would shame yourself. He *is* just a stable boy."

Aurora smiled. "I plan on just talking. Thank you for your concern, though," she squeezed Lianna's arm. "You are *such* a good friend."

The girl cocked her head at Aurora with an unreadable expression; the princess could not help being reminded of the imaginary rabbit she had seen. Then Lianna was off through the dark greenish-black murk of the courtyard. It wasn't long before her head popped up across the way, and she waved her hand frantically, like a little child.

Aurora waved back and stepped through the door.

She didn't like leaving the castle; only the prospect of petting animals could draw her out. Despite her longing for sun and sky and freedom, she felt safer under mountains of cool gray rock. Inside, you could almost forget there was an Outside, that anything had happened to that Outside.

In the courtyards and bailey, there was no possibility of forgetting. Giant black-and-green vines, some as wide as a man was tall, arched up overhead from beyond the castle walls. They twined and joined and wove themselves in strangely nauseating patterns. Humungous thorns, some the size of swords, clasped and gouged and held the vines together; the plants' skin puckered where they pierced, almost like it was painful. A few thin, unhealthy-looking leaves decorated the undersides of the largest branches as if they were merely an afterthought on the monstrous plants.

The whole bailey and all of the courtyards were bathed in a perpetual twilight. On good days it was shot through by narrow beams of sun, but even those seemed sickly by the time they reached the ground. The peasants had managed to arrange long, thin, unhappy-looking gardens that traced along the route of the feeble light that made its way through.

Aurora hurried as daintily as she could, trying not to close her eyes. She wrapped her shawl tightly around her.

One peasant had been killed by a falling thorn.

As soon as she was under the overhang of the stable—at one time necessary when clean rain fell freely from the sky— she breathed deeply. Royal princesses were not supposed to show fear. But only when she was under the cover of real shadow from solid dead wood and stone walls, and enveloped with moisture from cool, dark interiors and the breath of animals within, did she feel safe.

Once recovered, she turned to pet the nag Fala, who was old when the world was destroyed; even the stoniest-hearted peasant wouldn't think of putting her down now. Aurora kissed the horse's warm nose and stroked the muzzle below her blind eyes. Then, slowly, as if it was something she was just attending to, she went into the stable itself.

It smelled strongly of strange, magicked hay, of horse and cow dung, of leather and oils and humans who didn't bathe as often as a royal princess. She didn't mind.

"Your Highness!"

Cael came forward out of the gloom, no longer wearing his borrowed finery. In a loose tunic and carefully bound-up, ancient leggings, he still cut just as handsome a figure. In his own territory, he certainly had more swagger and braggadocio.

"Cael," Aurora said, tipping her chin gently. If this was an actual—illegal, unsanctioned—tryst, what would come next? Would it end with him trying to kiss her? Would she pull him into a clean pile of hay, as she had heard some of the serving girls whisper about?

"How may I be of service?" he asked, a twinkle in his eye. "It's not the best weather for a ride around the kingdom today, I'm afraid. What with the monsters and demons and everything being dead and all."

"Yes, I am aware of the present circumstances of the world we live in. I came to ask you a question. What is *this*?"

She took the feather out of the silver pouch on her chatelaine and held it up.

"Why, it's a feather, Your Highness," Cael started to

joke. Then he stopped, suddenly peering at it harder. He took it from her without asking. Aurora saw the intrigued look in his eye. "Well, smack my flanks—it's a *bluebird* feather. Wherever did you get it?"

"How do you know it's from a bluebird?" she asked, ignoring his question.

"I'm a few seasons older than you," he said, touching his forelock in a sort of salute. "My memories are still cloudy, like all of us. But when I was a babe, I remember being left outside on my own with my siblings supposing to care for me, a heel of bread for my lunch. Birds would come peck at my crumbs. Sparrows and others and even a couple of these fellows, as blue as the sky on a winter's day."

Aurora listened to his story with wonder. *Imagine having birds as playmates . . .*

"May I ask where you got this, Your Highness? It doesn't look like it's from a hat or a pin or a cloak . . . it's too small and not crushed at all."

"I don't think I can reveal that," she said slowly, taking it back.

"Oh, aye," the stable boy said slowly. "But . . . if . . . it's from *Outside* . . ."

Aurora looked at him sharply.

"Begging your pardon," the boy mumbled, looking down, suddenly seeming years younger. "It would just be . . . a miracle . . . a godsend . . . to know there was still bluebirds out there."

Aurora felt herself melt. Here *she* was feeling caged and useless, a princess who spent her whole life inside castle walls, and there he was—one of many who had lived most of their lives Outside. Those who *knew* what they were missing, even if they couldn't precisely remember it. Who had, in some ways, lost far more than she had.

She reached out and clasped his hand.

He looked at her, surprised.

"On my honor, as soon as I work out this little . . . mystery, I shall let you in on it," she promised. "As soon as I hear word about . . . the safety of going Outside, I will let you know. Myself."

"Th-thank you, Your Highness," he stammered. He offered her a spontaneous, jerky bow.

"Good day, Cael," she said with a royal nod of her head.

"Good day to you, Your Highness," he said solemnly back. "You're . . . as wise and kind as you are beautiful."

The glow that rose up on her cheeks warmed her on the walk back to the castle.

He might not have been her *favorite* boy in the castle—but he was a boy. And it felt nice.

A strange, quick hissing noise caused her to look up.

Lianna was standing, otherwise motionless, near the

door of the summer kitchen, a basket over one arm as if she had been intending to do something useful. Two bothersome, gossipy girls stood with her: none other than Mistress Laura herself and her chaperone, the only *slightly* older Lady Malder. Neither had seen the princess yet.

Lianna shook her head very slightly. Aurora could not return to the castle that way.

The princess bit her lip and quickly dashed to the stone wall, pressing herself up against it as closely as she dared without ruining her dress. The next entrance was all the way around the side, where the chambermaids went to empty the pots and the cooks tossed the offal. It stank, but no one would see her there. She hurried as carefully as she could, holding the train of her dress high out of the dust.

As she rounded the corner, she saw one of Maleficent's servants nosing around the door.

Off duty?

Did they even *go* off duty?

It was on its knees and hands, snuffling in the midden like an animal.

Aurora had to turn her head when it found a length of entrails and worried it out of the pile, stretching it until the tube of flesh snapped.

Holding her nose and gagging, she slipped past it. The last entrance that was unlikely to be guarded was a once-upon-a-time secret passage for quick escape in case of invasion. Almost everyone knew about it now—there were few secrets left in the remaining population. But it was rarely used because the stairs were slick, the tunnels dark and damp . . . and they led right past the chamber where King Stefan and Queen Leah were imprisoned.

The princess pulled aside what looked like a set of heavy rain barrels and stepped reluctantly into the dripping hole they revealed. She descended slowly, almost slipping twice in the first few feet and jarring her head badly. She cursed, using a word that she had heard Cael use once—and found it *did* make her feel a little better.

The way ahead was pitch-black, but there was no way she could get lost; there was only one way to go.

And she kept telling herself this as she moved slowly along, a hand on each slimy wall to steady herself.

She tried to distract herself with the important thing she had just learned: that the feather was from a bluebird. A bird that only existed on the Outside . . .

. . . an Outside that was supposed to be a wasteland, devoid of all but the most noxious and evil life.

An Outside that the minstrel had apparently escaped to and returned from, not entirely worse for wear.

But was there still a possibility that he was just drunk and mad? That he had simply found a feather somewhere and concocted this crazy story?

Well, then life would go on. As it had.

But if he really *had* been Outside . . . and things *did* live there . . .

The princess picked up the hem of her skirt as she stepped delicately over a pool of muck. There was a little light now that reached her from the flickering torches in the dungeon proper. She slunk against the far wall to the stairs on the other side, unwilling to see or be seen by the prisoners.

And then . . . she heard voices. Her *aunt's* voice. And— her parents?

She slowed down and pressed herself against the cool black wall to listen and watch.

"Oh, enough already," Maleficent said with a tired— though dramatic—wave of her arms. "There *is* no way out. You will eventually die. And I shall live again."

"But our daughter . . ." the old queen said, coming forward and holding the bars. It *almost* sounded like she cared.

"Your *daughter*?" Maleficent asked, her voice rising in dramatic surprise. "*Really?* What kind of loving mother hands her *daughter* off to the fairies for sixteen years?"

Aurora frowned. That was wrong. She was to be given to the fairies on her six*teenth* year, not *for* sixteen years.

"It was to protect her!" King Stefan protested.

"Really?" Maleficent swung around, arching her arms and fingers like an animal, lowering her yellow eyes to their level. "You couldn't think of *any other way* to 'protect' your daughter? Better guards? Higher walls? Runes and spells *inside* the castle? Really? Let me tell *you* something, dearies."

She lowered her voice and spoke with a hiss through lips that barely moved.

"You may think I'm more evil than any demon who ever walked this earth. And you may be right. But if *I* ever had a daughter, you can be sure I would keep her close, and teach her well, and school her in the arts of magic, and make her strong and powerful enough to protect herself, and I would *never let anything come between us.*"

Aurora felt something strange inside her. Maleficent was never this uncontrolled, this furious. Her words rang somehow truer now than in all of her carefully composed, dramatic speech.

"Or." Maleficent recovered herself. She straightened back up to her full height and adjusted her cloak. "Or admit the truth to yourselves. It didn't matter much either way, because in the end, you really would have preferred a *son.*"

And with that, she spun and strode out of the dungeon.

Aurora was so confused she didn't bother trying to hide herself. Her aunt almost tripped over her.

"Aurora," she said in her normal voice, faintly surprised. "What are you doing here?"

"I . . . was playing a game of hide-and-seek with some of the servant children," she stammered.

She had *never* lied to Maleficent before. But overhearing that conversation had unnerved her.

"Oh," her aunt said, accepting her explanation but still confused. "That's rather . . . gracious of you, my dear. I wouldn't encourage them to hide down here, however. Lest they come under the evil spell of your parents."

"Or the minstrel," Aurora added quickly, relieved her lie was taken up so quickly.

"The minstrel? He's not down here."

"But he's not in the stockades, so I assumed . . ."

"Oh," Maleficent's face fell into a mask of sadness. "He's gone, darling. Apparently the poor drunken fool actually did make it Outside somehow. I thought it was just his usual drunken ramblings. . . ."

"What?" She just barely caught herself from adding, *So it's true. . . .*

Maleficent regarded her with intelligent, unreadable eyes. "Outside and back *in*, over a month ago. I just found out the truth of it myself. I have no idea how he did it. There's a hole in the security somewhere. I must recast my spells and protections. Who *knows* what he could have brought in with him. . . ."

"Where is he now?" Aurora breathed, thinking about her feather.

"Back Outside. Where he so desperately wanted to be. For *good*, this time. I . . . didn't stop him."

Aurora felt like throwing up. Her head hurt. She had the feather. Should she tell her aunt? Tears sprang to her eyes.

Maleficent misunderstood, reaching out to pat her on the shoulder.

"Darling. Don't over mourn. His time wasn't long here anyway, the way he was living. But—and this is important—*you must never* talk about this with *anyone*. People get funny, wrong ideas . . . there is nothing Outside. Nothing that will keep you alive for long. We don't want anyone starting rumors."

She pulled her cloak around her and started to go.

"Aunt . . ." Aurora began, not sure what she was going to say. An admission of everything. Something about the minstrel. Something about a feather. Questions about the Outside.

But that's not what came out.

"What if *I* could do it? What if I could learn magic? Would you teach *me* your powers? Would you raise me to be like you? And we could rule the world together, and maybe make it back to like it once was? Before my parents destroyed it? Together?"

Maleficent blinked at her once with her slow yellow eyes. For perhaps the first time ever, an ironic remark, a dramatic observation, a meaningless quip didn't form on her lips.

She seemed *uncomfortable* thinking about the question, and twitched her shoulders.

"But you can't," she finally said. "You're just not capable, dear."

And she swept up the stairs, her cape trailing out majestically behind her.

Aurora sank down on the cold stones. She didn't go down to confront her parents. She didn't go up. She stayed in the comforting darkness and wept over things she couldn't even name.

Dancing While the World Burns

The morning of the Gold Ball, Aurora was in bed, as usual.

With the minstrel gone, there was no way she could find out the truth of the matter. Either he was dead, or he was free of the castle, living with flocks of mutant bluebirds or whatever—and in neither case would he be coming back.

She flipped wearily through the blank pages of one of her books. The back of her mind was playing with the idea of wishing for images to appear. Of wishing for the darkness from the Outside to come in. Could it be any worse than living in the castle with the same people for the rest of her life? Worse than blank books and hateful parents? Worse than being confronted every day by your own stupidity—so stupid even your own aunt patronizes you?

She imagined the one brief glorious moment of false paradise the Outside would bring: birds and trees and bunnies and other animals everywhere, flooding the castle halls, singing and purring and leaping in people's laps—and then it all exploding in one final, rapturous apocalypse as the monsters came in and everyone died.

She sighed, turning over in her bed. She knew exactly how ridiculous she was being. As a princess—a *living* princess—at the end of the world, she was far luckier than those who had died, and her life was far better than the lives of most of those who remained.

With great effort, she pushed herself up until she was at least sitting on the edge of the bed. Her head felt weary with all the terrible thoughts weighing it down. She felt sick— and that idea appealed to her very much. Of crawling back into bed and sleeping and having Lianna wait on her, and then go away . . .

Sparkles appeared at the corners of her vision. She was both relieved and scared; she really *was* sick. About to faint, even . . .

But the sparkles weren't golden or silver as they were normally when she felt light-headed. They were red, green, and blue. They coalesced into three distinct balls of color instead of dissipating when she took a few deep breaths.

The little balls danced around the room in a manner

that suggested intelligence: as if they were investigating the cracks, the crevices, the nooks, the crannies. Like they were looking for someone or something that might be hiding.

As Aurora crawled back onto her bed away from them, she noticed detachedly that when they came close to a solid object, their pale lights illuminated it and cast its shadow. Like real lights. Not hallucinations.

Finally, the three balls must have decided it was safe and grouped together, hovering right in front of Aurora.

She blinked, her eyes taking a moment to get used to their brightness being so close. As soon as she could see properly again, Aurora realized that there were *things* in the centers of the lights.

Little *living* things.

Things that looked suspiciously like tiny women. One in each light.

"Oh, dear," Aurora said aloud, trying to steady herself.

The first thing spoke. Its voice was too high-pitched and tiny to hear.

Aurora shook her head and pointed at her ear.

The balls bobbled a bit.

Then they suddenly puffed up in size.

Now Aurora was faced with three—still smallish—flying ladies engulfed in light.

The princess began to panic. These were fairies. That

was startling enough. There *were* no fairies left, except for Maleficent. And certainly not any good ones . . .

But—far more importantly—there was something terribly *familiar* about them. Something her body immediately recognized but her mind didn't; she was overwhelmed with an urge to put out her hand and have them land on it. To try and hug them.

Why?

"This is not the world in which you are supposed to reside," the green one said. The voice was still very high-pitched, but Aurora could just make it out this time.

The blue one rolled her eyes. "You are running out of time. Years and hours are tangled, it's true, but both go fast. If you want to save yourself and those you love, you need to figure out how to get out of all this."

"Wake up, you don't *belong* here," the third one, the red-lit one, piped up. "Wake *up* already! *Do* something!"

There were footsteps in the hall, Lianna's strange, syncopated gait.

No, wait, just a moment. . . . Aurora was torn between panic and frustration.

"Time for your bath."

Her friend appeared at the door holding a towel and a brush.

The fairies were simply gone. Like they had never been there at all.

The princess succumbed to her bath thoughtfully. She had accidentally wished . . . and *something* had happened.

Aurora was glorious in her golden gown. Without a trace of envy, Lianna declared it was the most beautiful the princess had looked yet; somehow the seamstresses had managed to create a dress several perfect shades lighter than her hair, and it sparkled when she moved. With her tresses up in intricate loops of braids and a golden diadem on top, the royal princess was an image of the sun itself, her tippet and skirts rays that just touched the earth.

Probably. No one could quite remember the sun.

Aurora gave her speech of gratitude and thanks to her aunt with verisimilar emotion. And by the end of it, she actually felt the way she had when she first wrote it.

The queen wore golden horns that night in deference to the theme. She kept her eyes modestly lowered during the speech and then thanked her ward warmly when it was over. The crowds cheered. Everyone seemed a little wilder that night. Dancers danced faster and harder. The musicians played like the devil was after them now that their leader was truly gone. Laughter was far too loud, and the drinking far too copious. Time may finally have taken a toll on the survivors in the castle.

Aurora watched it all distractedly from her usual spot next to Maleficent's throne, but she wasn't really paying attention.

What if the fairies were actually evil demons from the Outside trying to get in? What if they had discovered her mind was weak, like the drunken minstrel's? A perfect, pliable vessel on which to work their evil influence. Wasn't she *just thinking* about how great it would be if everyone died before the fairies arrived?

What sort of person even *thought* those kinds of things? Who imagined opening a door and letting death in?

A new idea interrupted this familiar spiral of thoughts she had been torturing herself with.

What if she wasn't the only person these visions appeared to?

What if there were other minds in the castle, as weak and diseased as her own, prone to self-destructive thoughts— gateways of evil?

Like the minstrel . . .

Aurora looked back and forth over the golden-hued crowd, searching for something. Some sign of a weak or evil mind. Nothing immediately revealed itself.

The laughter may have been borderline hysterical, but that could have been relief that things were back to . . . "normal." If they questioned the source of their magical banquet, the gilded quail eggs and golden soups, they were at least eating it. If the musicians sorely felt the absence of the minstrel, still they played in key for the twirling golden dancers.

There wasn't an off note anywhere, actual or metaphorical.

"Why aren't *you* dancing?" Maleficent asked. She clasped a golden goblet that held some thick black wine. Her eyes were shadowed, and her movements were slow. She would be her old self again, in just a few hours. . . .

Aurora bit her lip. She was almost overwhelmed with a drowning sense of déjà vu. She had done this before. At least once. She would do it again at the next dance probably. And again and again and again . . .

Panic was building in her head, and she wasn't sure what to do with it.

"*Go,*" her aunt said, flicking her wrist imperiously, shooing her away. Aurora nodded and obediently trotted off, glad to have an order to follow and give her body something to do.

But her mind wasn't on the dance. It was on the fairies and traitors and what the Outside really looked like. It was on what had happened to the minstrel and the feather and her aunt. Her feet were merely going through the motions with no joy. No one noticed, however; the princess's innate grace and skill and beauty and poise made her the most beautiful dancer in the room without her even having to try. Golden torches were reflected a thousand times in the soft golden folds of her dress; her golden shoes sparkled like candle flames.

Count Brodeur avoided her like the plague, not even looking at her face when they twirled around each other in the middle of a set.

In the middle of an endless chain dance, Aurora saw Maleficent get up quietly and slip away from the throne, out of the room.

Maybe it was a good time to take a break. Get a mug of cider. Clear her head. Over by the bowls of punch, Lady Astrid had a grim smile on her face and a flagon in her hand and was nodding at something the much older Countess DeShabille was shouting in her ear. Just a week—or whatever—ago, the princess wouldn't have given a second thought to either one of them. She would have danced, flirted politely with the cuter boys and men, and done anything she could to impress her aunt.

But now . . .

Lady Astrid seemed like a breath of fresh air in the tightly locked castle and Aurora's own head. At the very least, the lady deserved to hear the truth about what had happened with the minstrel and where the feather had come from.

And then two of Maleficent's servants came up to the lady. The cockscomb one and the doggish one—very obviously flanking her. They spoke tersely and gestured with their spears; the lady looked confused.

Aurora apologized to her partners, disentangled herself from the other dancers, and made her way over as quickly as she could. But by the time she got there, all three were gone. No one else seemed to have noticed. Countess DeShabille stood still, nodding to herself, humming quietly.

"DID YOU SEE WHERE LADY ASTRID WENT?" Aurora asked carefully and loudly, knowing the woman was mostly deaf.

"VERY COURTEOUS AND NICE WOMAN," the countess shouted back. "SHE CHECKS IN ON ME EVERY DAY, YOU KNOW, TO MAKE SURE THAT I AM ALL RIGHT."

"WHERE DID SHE GO?" Aurora repeated, trying not to be rude.

"ALL OVER, I THINK. SHE AND HER HUSBAND LIKE TO TRAVEL. NOT ME."

The princess couldn't stop one huff of disappointment, but she forced herself to nod courteously before rushing off to the closest stairs.

Where were Maleficent's guards taking Lady Astrid? And *why*?

Maybe there was something wrong with one of the residents of the castle. Lady Astrid was the closest thing the nobles had to a nurse.

But as Aurora looked all over, running through the

castle halls and ducking into every likely place—and finding nothing—she began to suspect that it wasn't for so noble
a cause.

With a sickening twist of her stomach, she thought
about the feather. Of her ill-advised revelation to Brodeur
and then Lady Astrid . . . and the implications of where the
feather had come from. . . .

The minstrel was gone, Count Brodeur was on edge.
Astrid herself had said the whole matter was dangerous.
And now the lady had been whisked away by royal guards.

Praying she was wrong, Aurora hurried up the last
flight of stairs. The one that had originally led to her father's
solarium, which Maleficent had claimed as her own chambers. She chose it out of respect for Aurora—not wanting
to appear to replace her parents entirely, especially in their
own bedroom. Plus, it was a little removed from everyone else and in a tower, just the sort of thing a fairy queen
would like.

Aurora paused just outside the door and took a deep
breath.

She moved to go in . . .

And then stopped.

Whatever she had expected to see—Maleficent talking
with her guards, Maleficent chastising or questioning Lady
Astrid, Maleficent standing in front of her large mirror,

adjusting her outfit—none of it was what was actually happening in the room.

Lady Astrid *was* in there with Maleficent. Gagged and tied up. The rope cut into her flesh and made her gold dress balloon in ridiculous folds between the cords. She was only upright because she was held that way by the two guards. Astrid's face, pale and sweaty, strained her gag and her gold-and-white wimple.

"An excellent choice, my pets," Maleficent was saying with a throaty laugh. She looked like she wanted to stroke one of the horrible guards, but pulled her hand back at the last moment and clasped it into a fist. "The lady is certainly . . . robust. True royalty would be the best—their blood would be the strongest. A pity about the Exile being gone—that was a mistake. But *she* will serve for now."

The queen reached deep into her cloaks. She pulled out a strange ripple-bladed black stone dagger that looked sharp but awkward.

Before Aurora could even guess what it was for, Maleficent plunged it deep into Astrid's chest. The movement was swift and yet unending; the queen had to jiggle it back and forth to get all of its sinuous bends into the woman's flesh.

Astrid screamed, or tried to, the muffled cries sounding wet and useless behind her gag.

The guards holding her whistled and hooted with glee.

With a determined set of her jaw, Maleficent wrenched the dagger out.

A fountain of blood streamed from the poor woman's chest—too purely, too neatly to seem possible considering the jagged imprecision of the wound.

Aurora ground her knuckles into her mouth to keep from screaming.

Maleficent chanted:

> *"Magic of the darkest power,*
> *Grant me this, but one more hour.*
> *I give thee blood for one who sleeps.*
> *My body dead, but my spirit keeps*
> *Alive in her thoughts and dreams—*
> *Though to her this world seems*
> *As real as the waking one.*
> *I will live again, my will be done."*

Almost delicately, like she was watering a fragile flower, Maleficent took her staff and held the crystal orb at its tip in the stream of blood. The world blurred; the orb was a hole in the air itself and the blood bent and gushed into it, pulled into its vortex. Somehow it passed through the wall and filled the glassy vessel, churning and frothing redly.

When it was full, the queen pulled her staff back and gave it a dramatic twirl. The blood inside glowed and bubbled furiously. Then it changed, losing its redness and becoming the familiar bright, glowing green of Maleficent's magic.

The queen sighed, shifting her shoulders and stretching out her arms as if she had just woken from a long, restful sleep or come out of a hot bath. The shadows under her eyes were gone. Her skin looked fresher, plumper.

But she didn't look entirely happy.

"It wasn't enough. It's taking more and more blood from those idiot nobles to sustain me for fewer and fewer minutes. . . ."

Lady Astrid was apparently already forgotten. The two monsters let her fall forward. Blood pumped out of her in ragged spurts directly onto the floor. Blood moistened her gag as well, and began to collect in large, heavy drops on her chin.

Aurora found herself praying that the lady was dead. There was something about the way the guards couldn't keep their eyes on their mistress but let them slip to the pale body they now held. Their tongues hung out of their mouths and they slavered hungrily.

Maleficent moved her staff in a circle.

"Spirits of evil, open the window to that other realm!" she commanded.

The orb traced a silvery outline in the air that shimmered and shivered. The view through it was of the same room, but distorted. Or . . . *less* distorted. The details in the image were somehow more distinct than reality, the colors more complicated. It was both uglier and more fascinating than the real room.

But that wasn't what caused Aurora to gasp.

In that other room, through the shimmering window, the queen's bed wasn't empty; Aurora herself slept in it.

The princess fell against the castle wall. It wasn't like looking at a statue or a painting of herself; *it really was her.* She knew it. She knew there would be a teeny tiny freckle on the inside of the left pinky finger. She could feel the way her belly flattened out when she lay on her back. She knew her own breathing.

Which . . . the other Aurora . . . wasn't really doing. . . .

She who sleeps.

Aurora was the one who slept.

Though to her this world seems
As real as the waking one.

This . . . wasn't real. . . .

The whole *world* wasn't real.

As soon as she thought it, she knew it was true. *Felt* it was true. Over there, in that complicated, ugly world, *that* was reality.

This was all a dream. . . .

Aurora felt like fainting. Just letting go. Letting whatever insanity that made up the world continue on without her.

Maleficent looked at Aurora's bed thoughtfully.

"All I need to do is hold on for a little longer," she murmured. "Until the clock chimes twelve and her sixteenth birthday is over. . . ."

She regarded the blond hair, the petite frame, the delicate feet, the pixie nose of the sleeper.

"I suppose her body will have to do until I can find better," she added with an only slightly disappointed shrug. "But I will have an entire kingdom at my disposal at that point."

Do not faint.

A tiny voice, a tiny glimmer of a voice insisted annoyingly in Aurora's mind. But it was her *own* voice, from inside her head, not a hallucination or a visit from an Outside fairy.

Passing out would not solve anything. This was all very real. It was happening. It would not go away. She would have to deal with *thinking about* it and *processing* it and *weeping* over it—and all of the real ramifications—later.

Right now *she had to run.*

"Your Majesty, Princess Aurora is . . ."

Lianna had been hurrying up the stairs but stopped

when she saw Aurora in the shadows. The two girls regarded each other.

Then Aurora's eyes drifted from the other girl's face to her feet.

Lianna had picked up the skirt of her dress to run quickly up the stairs, just as the princess had. But where Aurora had golden shoes, Lianna had . . .

Trotters.

Splayed, ugly, fleshy trotters.

Which was why she always walked so oddly, Aurora realized. It wasn't a foreign habit.

She was one of Maleficent's creatures.

"Your Highness," Lianna whispered, addressing the princess this time.

Somehow *this* spurred Aurora into action. She swept past the other—*girl?*—quickly down the stairs, slamming her shoulder into her as she went.

"TRAITOR!" she hissed, almost like her aunt.

Where could she go? Her first urge was her bedroom. Safe, lonely, comfortable bed.

That was dumb.

Her second thought was to hide *under* her bed. Like a little child. Which was also dumb.

Her third thought was a broom closet, which—with the *entire castle* of monstrous guards and a powerful fairy queen after her—was also dumb.

She stood for a moment, frozen, terrified. There was no place to go.

There was only one place to go.

Outside.

She moved like she was diving, lunging toward the back entrance, where just days ago she had gone to meet Cael. Aurora didn't have the time or energy to be terrified of the dark green dome of vines overhead; she just made straight across for the outer defenses of the keep. One lone old crone marked the princess's presence with a vaguely curious raised eyebrow as she emptied a water skin over her parched plot of beans. Golden ball or not, things died without help in this world.

The princess dashed into the nearest tower in the outer wall. Even through the heavy stones, she was sure she could start to hear movement, an alarm raised once it was realized she had fled.

Up, up, up, she climbed the staircases she had played on as a child, free to roam the castle at will like a rat.

Her dress kept tangling with her legs despite her nimbleness and grace; she paused just long enough to rip the train off. She felt a twinge of sorrow for the women who sewed the cloth and the old women who wove it. But her legs were now free, and she could take the steps several at a time.

She doubled her speed past the floors with barracks. Not all the human guards had gone to the ball; people still had to patrol, despite the safety of the thorny barrier. They looked up at her from benches where they were sharpening their swords or polishing their helms. Perhaps they were not as surprised as guards might have been in other castles, in other times, with princesses who stayed nicely in their rooms and chapels and gardens.

Aurora paused at the top of her tower and looked around wildly. Her goal was the barbican: the main entrance to the castle with the portcullis and drawbridge. It was the point that stuck out farthest from the keep and leaned farthest into the vines.

But the passage to it from where she had emerged was a terribly exposed length to run. The tall crenellations on the right of the stone walk were meant to protect guards from invading forces. There was nothing on the left but a low wall; who would attack a castle from within?

In the courtyard below, a half-dozen misshapen figures tumbled together out of the castle, armed with bows and slings. They had a perfect view of her.

"There she is!"

One pointed an arm that terminated in a single terrifying hooklike claw.

Aurora ducked and ran.

Maleficent appeared at an arched window in a castle tower, fury informing her every gesture. *"Guards, seize the princess!"* she cried. "She means to do herself harm!"

But at the same time, she raised her staff and began to mutter an incantation.

The princess willed her feet to move faster. She narrowed her vision to the path before her, the ancient rocks that slipped by on either side of her. The barbican was once a place of extreme security, with murder holes for dropping boiling oil on the heads of invaders, but had been more or less abandoned since the world had ended. The giant gate was sealed in place; there was no cause to raise it, ever. The platform on top was now just used as a private escape for castle teens and drunken servants. Aurora hadn't expected to find anyone there.

To her dismay, the shiny helms of guards began to pop out of the narrow entrance to the stairs like moles.

"Your Highness!" one called, immediately leaping to grab her.

Up here the vines were distressingly close. They laced together just a man's height above her head before bending over and shooting straight down a hundred feet, where their thick trunks made a living wall just outside the castle's stone ones. The moat was gone, the water sucked up by their greedy, unlikely growth.

The foul dust of their aging and shifting lay brownly over everything. It smelled unwholesome.

Aurora looked around wildly, unable to believe she was about to do what she was about to do.

A guard lunged for her.

She leapt.

Aurora fell harder than she thought she would—and landed on a thick branch. She coughed and gasped, the breath knocked out of her. Her ribs were bruised and her stomach hurt. But that was all.

Now that she was within the tangled world of the plants, it would be a piece of cake: climbing down from one closely entwined vine to another.

The guards continued to shout from somewhere above her.

"My lady!"

"After her!"

"Queen Maleficent, what do we do?"

With a grin she wasn't sure why she had, Aurora began her descent.

And then the vines began to move.

Not the oldest, thickest trunks; small whippets of young vines, curlicued like a cucumber's tendrils. They shot around her legs and arms and pulled.

"*NO!*" Aurora cried out, frustrated with the world. She shook and pulled and kicked. The greenery snapped away as easily as bean sprouts.

The princess was taken aback by her own ferocity and its accomplishments. She really hadn't expected it to be so easy.

A little less cocky but more resolute, Aurora moved more quickly downward.

Then thorns grew much faster than they were supposed to, erupting wide and thick and unseemly in the way they pushed through the skin of the vines and each other. They pierced Aurora's flesh, sharp as needles. Everywhere she tried to place her hands, they sprung up. Very quickly, she was covered in cuts and punctures and rivulets of blood.

Also, they screamed.

They screamed as they forced their way through their own stalks and into one another; they screamed in delight when they pricked her.

They grew strange faces, long and lined like old men's. But when they managed to speak, they sounded like Maleficent.

"Go back. . . ."

"There is nothing for you out here. . . ."

"Return to the castle. . . ."

Aurora bit her lip and tried not to sob. She couldn't move for the sharp thorns everywhere.

"GO AWAY!" she shouted in rage and bitterness. "I wish you would just *disappear!*"

The thorns receded, melting like lumps of sugar in hot tea.

Aurora blinked. She wanted to think about what had just happened.

But she had to move quickly, before Maleficent attacked again. Throwing herself with almost careless abandon, she plummeted down, bouncing from branch to branch like a pebble tossed down a deep well.

She hit the dark ground with a sickening hardness. Her head was snapped back and jarred so badly that everything went blurry. It didn't help that the air was thick and dusty and in a permanent twilight.

But there, some distance away from the castle, just barely visible through the interlaced vines, she could see a faint flicker of yellow light.

Golden and bloody, Aurora straightened her shoulders and walked toward sunshine.

Interlude

A castle lay asleep. A kingdom lay asleep. The people, horses, mice, and even fountains and gnats lay asleep. A hush lay over everything, and all seemed sweet and peaceful at first. Beautiful, ancient-looking brambles protected the sleepers within and occasionally bloomed pink honey-scented roses.

There were only two groups of things that didn't sleep. One was the dead.

The other was a trio of concerned-looking fairies who flitted around the castle and watched over the sleepers—especially the royal princess.

Aurora lay perfectly, beautifully, hands clasped below her ribs like she was in constant prayer. Her lips were parted. Her eyes rolled. Something was happening in what was supposed to be a dreamless, swift sleep.

Collapsed in an ungainly heap on the floor next to her was Prince Phillip. The one who was supposed to wake her up and end the whole thing.

Instead, the silly boy had *fallen asleep himself* . . . the first hint the fairies had that something was terribly amiss.

And then the people had started dying.

Flora, the fairy watching over Aurora, had a worried, weary hand to her head. Her strange, flowing vestments of red drifted sadly around her like mist rather than cloth. Her face appeared mostly human except up close. There was a strange serenity behind all her normal-seeming emotions.

Her companions, a plump little pixie in blue and a hamadryad in green, floated in from their rounds.

"All's quiet," Merryweather, the one in blue, said. "I mean, they're all still asleep. So of course they're quiet."

"She's doing it again." Flora pointed at Aurora's face. For a split second, the beautiful princess's features twisted up in agony or upset. They recomposed themselves almost immediately.

Fauna, the one in green, moaned in despair. "I cannot *believe* this is happening. We were supposed to *save* the princess and everyone. Not just hand them over to Maleficent. We're *sure* they're all in there?"

"Sadly, yes."

"How did she ever plan all this?" Merryweather demanded.

"I don't think she *planned* it," Flora said, sighing. "I think she just took advantage of the situation. I think she always had sort of a . . . backup plan in case she was ever killed."

"If *I'm* ever killed, I want you two to resurrect me," Merryweather said with a humph. "If she actually had friends, she could have done the same."

"Be kind!" Fauna admonished her, swooshing back and forth in the air. "If she *actually had* friends, maybe she wouldn't have turned out so nasty and evil. And besides," she added reluctantly, "if she actually had friends, we'd be in worse trouble now."

"*Worse?* How could it be worse? We can't wake up *anyone* here. Not with a spell, not with foxglove, not with holy water."

"We have not ruled out everything," Flora snapped. "We haven't *tried* everything."

"True. Have you tried kissing anyone yet?" Merryweather asked archly.

Flora gave her a withering look.

A horrible, piercing cry rang out through the castle.

"*Oh, no.* Not another one!" Fauna cried in alarm.

Immediately, the three fairies shrank into red, blue, and green balls of light and went whisking through the air, will-o'-the-wisps on a mission. They streaked through the bailey, the courtyard, the bedrooms, and the chapel until they found the source of the scream: Lady Astrid, asleep at her needlework, her face a mask of horror and fear.

The three balls quickly resolved into human-sized figures who gathered her up in their arms. Fauna kept the woman's head upright; Merryweather grabbed a cloak and crumpled it up, to try to prevent what would come next. Flora regarded the dreamer with a critical eye.

All seemed fine at first.

And then thick dark blood began to soak the lady's gown, over where her heart was.

Merryweather immediately pushed the cloak onto the wound, pressing it down with her hands as hard as she could. Fauna closed her eyes and invoked the healing power of the woods, an ancient, usually infallible, incantation. Flora drew symbols in the air with her naked ring finger, trailing gold behind it in a strange three-dimensional rune.

It was no use.

Lady Astrid screamed and screamed and screamed. She was somehow aware, despite the strange half-life she lived between dream and sleep, that her death was coming, and it was unavoidable. Her cries were of pain and fear and anger and horror and everything terrible the fairies had never felt themselves—in human quantities.

The blood came faster until it was gushing through the cloth like a fountain, heaving with each pump of the heart.

And then the heart stopped.

The silence of the sleeping castle was complete and utter once more.

Merryweather dropped the bloody rags in sadness that disguised itself as disgust.

Silver tears formed in Fauna's eyes as she stroked the dead woman's hair back up under her wimple.

Flora clenched her fists in frustration.

"Damn that Maleficent," she swore, using the worst human phrase she could think of. "She's worse than we ever could have imagined. She's a murdering, life-draining soul leech."

"And why these two?" Merryweather asked philosophically. "This one seems harmless, and really—that peasant was quite literally a nobody. Nice man, but a strange choice."

"Well," Fauna said softly. "Both are equally dead now, noble or not. And Maleficent has bought herself another hour."

"Only two more before her hold over Rose becomes complete," Merryweather added. "I mean, *Aurora*."

"We have to try again," Flora insisted. "I felt like we

actually *did* something that time. That we reached her, a little."

"It's all we can do," Fauna agreed. "So let's try it again."

The three fairies held hands and closed their eyes, preparing to dream a fairy dream.

The Inevitable
Forest Primeval

She pushed her way through the tunnel of vines with calm deliberateness, beyond the dangers of the castle now. She couldn't even hear shouts from above or the commotion in the courtyard. There would be no lifting of the portcullis anytime soon, and Maleficent couldn't aim her spells at the princess if she couldn't even see her. There might be *new* dangers ahead, but the old familiar ones were receding like shadows.

The plants around her were twisted and enormous, solid and unmoving. They didn't seek to bar her way further. She dragged her hands along them, feeling the leaves crumble away under her fingertips like they were ancient, long dry and dead.

She paused, suddenly remembering. She looked around and called out tentatively:

"Minstrel? Master Tommins?

"Exile?

"Hello?"

No response.

She looked at the dusty ground as she walked—if there were any human footprints in the lifeless soil, they were old and long lost among the strange traceries that time and wind had made. There was no sign that anyone had ever been Outside besides her.

She shivered. The drunken, narrow face of the minstrel would have been a comfort. Even some sign of the Exile would have been reassuring. That he had managed to live—to survive—on the Outside for all these years.

The shadowed world of the enormous plants eventually ended at an archway that revealed nothing but the golden inferno of light she had glimpsed before. There was no hint of what lay beyond.

She shielded her eyes and stepped out.

She didn't breathe for the first moment, afraid of what she would smell. Afraid of what poisons she would suck in. She felt the heat on her skin and admired the redness of the light through the cracks where her fingers met one another.

Slowly she removed her hand.

She thought she was hallucinating again.

The air was mostly still and the light, yes, golden—but soft now that she had grown used to it. The "inferno" was nothing but strong afternoon sunlight. Little motes floated in the air, larger and fluffier than the dust that haunted her bedroom. She held out her finger and one landed on it: a feathery seedpod, its milk-white strands anchored to a beautiful brown teardrop.

She let it go.

The princess stood in what looked like a small grassy meadow . . . on the outskirts of a *forest*. A proper one, not a barrier of magicked plants. Trees with light gray trunks and insanely bright green leaves dotted the edges shyly, a mild invitation to the dark woods beyond. Before the trees, dark green and amber grass grew in large clumps. Tiny light-blue flowers with pale eggy centers burst forth with sprightly enthusiasm.

A breeze made whickery noises in the tree leaves and older grasses.

Aurora knelt down and put her hands on the ground.

She closed her eyes again, feeling the sun-warmed dirt. She took a deep breath, inhaling the scents of grass and brown and mud and . . . *water*? It wafted from somewhere, moist and metallic and *full*. She had no idea you could actually smell water.

She made a silly but heartfelt vow to never, ever live *inside* again.

She opened her eyes, and it was all still there.

It had been, she realized after a moment, *always* still there.

While . . .

The thorns. The eternal dusk of the castle. The always being cooped up with the same people. The eating of pigeons, the hiding of cats and dogs.

None of that was necessary.

Outside was an *entire world* with trees and flowers and rivers and . . . other people? And . . .

What was it all for?!

Why did Maleficent keep them all imprisoned? What had *happened*, if her parents hadn't destroyed everything? How did they all live in the strange dreamworld, not realizing the truth?

A strange *qwork qwork* from above startled her.

Slowly, calmly making its way across the open blue sky was a raven, its large wings pushing aside the air like it was a god. No thought at all to the royal princess below it or the castle of insanity just beyond.

Birds were real. Beyond pigeons and parakeets.

Probably even *bluebirds.*

She stood up and stumbled toward the trees, overcome with a desire to touch the bark.

But as she stepped over a clump of grass, the meadow began to swim in front of her eyes, and her perspective shifted. As her fingers brushed the wood surface, the inside of her head broke open.

It was familiar.

She didn't know *this meadow*, exactly. But she was familiar with the concept. The types of plants. The *raven*, which she knew was too big to be a *crow*. The trees: the way the trees circled meant there was probably a bog or a stream in the middle, where the land dipped. She *knew* that. She knew that beyond these leafy trees would be gnarled, thicker trees with dark green leaves. And beyond them, pines. And under their heavy boughs, there lay a friendly darkness so complete it put the vines over the castle bailey to shame.

She fell.

She felt the soft yet hard ground beneath her, comfortingly supporting her as the sky and world whirled. It kept her from flying off.

There was another meadow. Warm and sweet-smelling, like this one. But much larger—or was she just smaller? Tiny legs thumping the ground. Tiny *naked* legs. She was warmed by the sun tickling her skin and always two steps behind a large, languorous butterfly. It flapped its oversized wings like a joke and the tiny girl giggled, chasing it but not really wanting to catch it, because that would end badly.

The world was safe and wonderful and soft and warm, and at home . . .

At home there was a cake. A bright pink-and-blue cake, lopsided, covered with mounds of frosting. She clapped fat little hands and laughed, then sank her entire face into it.

Three pleased and happy faces above her, smiling and serene. And relieved.

Wait—

She tried to sit up.

They looked like . . .

They were the three ball-of-light fairies who had visited her in the bedroom.

But they *weren't* fairies. They were her aunts, who had adopted her when her parents died. They raised her in the forest and—

No, her aunt was *Maleficent*, who had adopted her when she defeated Aurora's parents, who had destroyed the world.

She doubled over, the conflicting images in her head flickering too quickly. Her stomach began to roil.

An older girl now, pretending to be a princess.

Pretending? But she *was* a princess. . . .

Her three aunts had fashioned a costume for her: a gown of found feathers and flower petals and large green leaves. It was cinched at the waist with a girdle of plaited river reeds and decorated with an incongruous sparkly blue stone that the aunts had found somewhere. A matching reed tiara rested on her shaggy, half-braided hair. When she twirled, feathers and leaves spun out, and she was the queen of the forest.

No, the only queen was Maleficent, and she was the *real* queen. And everyone lived in the *castle*, in a proper bedroom, with a fancy bed—

"STOP!" she moaned, rocking back and forth.

But the memories kept coming.

Lying on the forest floor. For hours.

Watching the light change as it moved along the mossy ground like the snails she often played with. Its slow, miraculous journey over a sprouted nut, the magic of the sun causing its first leaves to unfurl toward the sky. The light moving on. Sleeping some. Not feeling like picking berries. Wanting something *new*, something exciting, beyond seeing what was under the heavy rocks by the creek.

Twirling through shadow and light, across grass and carpets of pine needles, happy but feeling like things hadn't started yet. Wondering when they would.

Her three aunts arguing when they thought she was asleep. Sweet voices, and sometimes sharp. Things she couldn't understand; sentences that began one way and didn't make sense by their end no matter how hard she concentrated.

Utter, utter confusion when she got her moon blood.

The memories slowly wound down. The searing pain behind her eyes dimmed. She rubbed her temples and noticed distractedly that she was curled up in a fetal position so tightly that her legs ached. She cautiously stretched them out, the fear of a muscle cramp momentarily overriding the mess in her head.

She eased herself into a sitting position, the movement grinding dirt and twigs and mushrooms into her beautiful ball gown.

Where were you raised, a barn? Lianna had once asked in disgust, having found the princess in one of her moods, curled up on the ground in the corner of her room, among the dust balls and far too close to the chamber pot.

"No, I was raised in the *forest*," she now said aloud, giggling a little.

And her aunts were . . . *fairies*. Living like feral peasants, dressed in shabby but cheerful shifts and aprons. They had been uncomfortable in human clothes, Aurora could see in hindsight. Presenting her with food and strange habits and love. They tried so hard, and sometimes they failed, but the love was constant and would last well beyond the end of her own short life.

She thought about the funny, badly made costume gown.

Why didn't they just use their magic? The way her aunt Maleficent did?

Her . . . *not* her aunt.

Not a princess. Not a childhood in a castle.

Not Aurora.

Rose. Briar Rose. She was named after a flower that was thorny and green and strong and beautiful, with moments of unbelievable softness in white and pink.

Sixteen years as Briar Rose, living with three crazy aunts in the middle of the forest.

Not a princess. Just a girl.

The girl, grown now—years older now. How had that happened?

The girl at the edge of the meadow sat up.

She couldn't think here. She had to start moving. She would go mad if she stayed still.

She staggered into the forest—but was careful not to touch any of the trees.

Sixteen years of alternate memories of life in a forest. Sixteen years in the dark corners of a castle, running around like a bedraggled mouse while the world crumbled around her. Several years beyond that with Maleficent—*aha, that's where they came from.*

But . . . was this the forest where she grew up? It didn't feel *exactly* right, but she couldn't quite put her finger on it.

The last thing she had seen in the castle came back to her: the image of her own body in that bright other world beyond the orb on Maleficent's staff.

What had the queen said?

> *I give thee blood for one who sleeps.*
> *My body dead, but my spirit keeps*
> *Alive in her thoughts and dreams—*
> *Though to her this world seems*
> *As real as the waking one.*

So . . . this was all a *dream*? Even the forest she was in now?

Unless she was just hallucinating in the last gasps of a fever, and her body was actually somewhere asleep, dying, in the poisoned wastelands of the Outside.

Aurora Rose grabbed the roots of her hair, feeling like she was going mad with indecision and panic.

She spread her hand before her and looked at the tiny freckle on her finger. The one that matched her sleeping form. She felt a breeze on her fingertips.

"This is all I have," she said aloud. She needed to hear it with her own ears, outside the voices in her head. "What I know by touch and smell and sight—is *all* I know. Let's say this is real now. Let's start with that."

She put her hand out to tentatively touch a tree as she passed. No painful opposite memories flooded her this time—just the comforting recollection of *tree* itself. Her skin remembered the pines' rough bark better than her mind and appreciated the sticky sap even when she first recoiled at its touch.

By reflex, her psyche tried to grab at the snippets of dark memories that were starting to shrink now, like the skins of discarded fruit.

But . . . Maleficent.

That great woman who had swept in as a savior, who had kept her parents from handing her over to—wait, that wasn't real, was it? Well, she would work that out in her head in a while. Maleficent had swept in, magnificent and regal and commanding, and put a protective arm around the scared and neglected princess.

And in the years since . . . how Aurora had waited and prayed for and then treasured the moments when her aunt dropped the drama and graced her with a genuine smile of fondness. How she did everything to impress the beautiful, royal, and commanding lady. How Maleficent filled her waking thoughts with awe and gratitude . . . when the princess wasn't mired in restlessness and its twin, languor.

Aurora had *loved* her. With all of her innocent heart and soul.

She saw, with a ripping in the very essence of her being, Maleficent standing at the balcony and ordering her capture. The words the queen had spoken hadn't matched her face: she had talked of clemency for a deranged princess, but her lips had been peeled back in a grimace and her eyes had been filled with hate. There had never been *any* affection there. It had all been a ruse.

Aurora Rose felt the tears spill out soundlessly and endlessly.

The worst part was that she would have forgiven Maleficent everything—even what she had done to Lady Astrid—if only the queen had lied about it. If she had taken Aurora into her arms and said, *Shhh, it's all over, I do love you.* Even if Aurora didn't believe her aunt entirely, she would have forgiven her and forgotten it.

"I . . . am so . . . *pathetic!*" she shrieked, letting the terrible, climbing, hysterical, inhuman cry overwhelm her tears and take over her whole shaking body.

It felt good, but it didn't get her anywhere.

When she opened her eyes, she was surprised to see a little bird before her, sitting on a branch and giving her a skeptical look.

Aurora Rose had the urge to look around to see if anyone else had noticed.

The bird stretched out and gave a single impatient *cheep*. Puffing its chest in the sunlight, it revealed a coat of feathers that were the purest sky blue imaginable.

The princess gasped. She went to find the feather the minstrel had given her, to see if it would match. But her chatelaine was gone, along with the cards and the feather and everything else. It must have been torn from her in the escape.

Muscle memory prompted her, without thinking, to start patting the rest of her ripped dress. Did she have anything in her pockets for the little bird?

It cheeped at her impatiently.

"Sorry," she said with a weak smile and a shrug. "Not myself today."

She knew this bird had a name. It wasn't *bluebird*. When as a child she had asked her aunts what kind of bird it was, Fauna had dismissed her question as irrelevant. Aurora Rose couldn't have pronounced what the birds called themselves to distinguish them from other types of birds, and *little blue bird* was just as meaningful as anything else. But, of course, birds were individuals, and it was rude to address one by the name of its whole race.

The bird seemed to do the bird equivalent of rolling its

eyes and set about preening itself, as if it had never *really* been interested in a handout, anyway. Aurora Rose smiled. Leave it to a bird to make the situation all about him.

She rubbed her face in exhaustion, smearing it with pine pitch in the process and not caring. Everything was insane.

At the base of the closest tree was a clump of wild mint. She broke off a stalk and chewed it, beginning to walk again. The world was beautiful. There was an ancient oak tree heralding a shift in the forest. At its roots underground would be the mushrooms the wild pigs liked.

Hey, if wild pigs are still around, are unicorns, too?

She closed one eye, trying to remember if she had ever seen one as a child. She had seen a magnificent white stag once, with golden antlers, but nothing with one horn.

The world Outside . . . outside . . . was just as amazing as she had always wished in the Thorn Castle. She could live in this forest and meadow happily until the thoughts inside her head sorted themselves out.

Enter the Prince

Of course, as with everything in her complicated, unreal existence, that was not the way things played out.

She was wandering around the twisty bend of a game trail, humming a little half-remembered song to herself, when she came upon a scene out of a tapestry:

A deer. A *doe*, she knew, not just from its lack of antlers but also the shape of its face and the size of its flanks. Beautiful and large and slim and as elegant on its tiny toes as any made-up fairy-tale creature.

Standing some distance away from it was the most breathtakingly handsome man Aurora Rose had ever seen.

Not that she had seen that many, of course. In either of her childhoods.

He was as magnificent as the deer: tall, well-muscled, sleek, and healthy. He tossed his head of thick, shining brown hair like an animal's mane. His face looked like it had been carved by an ancient sculptor whose skill had never been surpassed: strong nose, strong chin, high cheekbones whose apples were still a little soft and pink with youth. Long eyelashes. Sparkling brown eyes.

He was reaching out to the deer with one upturned hand.

Suddenly, she noticed a shining steel sword on his hip, its grip in easy reach, its blade no doubt deadly sharp.

He was going to kill the deer. He was *hunting* it.

"*NO!*"

Aurora Rose ran forward, throwing herself at the handsome, awful man.

She had rediscovered a world of beauty and nature and life and animals, and not ten minutes later, here was someone all too ready to destroy it.

"STOP IT! STOP!" she screamed.

The man looked up, alarmed.

The deer cocked its head and bounded off.

The man blinked, and his face broke into a happy grin.

"It's *you!*" he cried.

Just as she was about to pummel him with her fists, he put his arms out and wrapped her in a gigantic hug.

"What?" She pushed at his arms desperately, with a growing panic. "LET GO OF ME! GO AWAY!"

"I can't believe it's you," the man said again, heedless of her actions. He closed his eyes and squeezed her like a bear. She stopped fighting for a moment, suddenly wondering how she knew what a bear squeeze felt like.

"Who the hell are you?!" she finally demanded, getting ahold of herself. With one hand free, she managed to lean back and slap him across the face.

She wasn't sure who was more surprised, him or her. She had never done anything like that in her entire life. She had never hit *anyone.* In any memory.

The man put her down and looked less hurt than confused, like a boy whose toy had stopped working correctly. The red marks of her fingers angrily stung his face, but he didn't seem to notice.

He stepped back, taking in her tangled hair, her ragged dress, her bloody and pitch-covered face, the mint stalk still hanging out the side of her mouth. "You escaped? From the castle, right? Are you all right?"

"I . . . *did* escape," she allowed.

He waited.

She continued to regard him silently.

"You don't remember me?" He tried very hard not to sound hurt.

"I remember a *lot* of things," she said. "*Too* many things. None of it makes sense. I don't really remember you. Things are kind of confused."

She hated sounding apologetic. The man had basically just assaulted her.

"Oh. Well—that's all right," he said brightly. "Even though *I* remember *you*—and we completely *did* meet, even if you don't remember it—we were never properly introduced. So you can't remember my name, at least, because you never knew it."

"All right," she said slowly. Despite her initial distrust, his glibness, his sunny smile, and—she had to admit it—his general gorgeousness were melting her fairly quickly. His speech seemed genuine and completely free of nuance, unlike if Count Brodeur had been saying the same words.

"I'm Phillip. *Prince* Phillip."

He executed a beautiful bow but finished it with a boyish grin.

She found herself smiling, unable to stop.

"I am Princess Aurora," she said with the slight curtsy of one member of royalty greeting another. "Or . . . possibly . . . Briar Rose, peasant and lady of the forest. It's a little confusing right now."

"No, that's actually beginning to make sense," Phillip said with a thoughtful nod.

"Well, I'm glad it is for *somebody*," she said dryly.

"I like *Rose* better, I think. *Aurora* implies something ethereal and unattainable. Not like a beautiful, sweet-smelling flower. May I call you Rose?"

"If you like. You could also call me Henry for all it really matters," she said, deciding to ignore the implications of "unattainable." Also, there was the whole double meaning of "plucking a rose," the verbal path down which Count Brodeur certainly would have gone.

"I don't like Henry so much. Doesn't roll off the tongue," the prince quipped. "*Aurora* does, though: Aurora, Aurora, Aurora. Oh . . . maybe it doesn't."

Why, when just moments ago she had been having a crisis over her very existence, torn between two lives she seemed to have led, was she suddenly being so ridiculous? This prince was completely distracting her.

This prince whom she had caught *hunting* in her dreamworld.

"Why were you killing that deer?" she demanded, recovering her anger.

"Killing?" he asked, eyes wide with confusion. "I wasn't trying to kill it. I was trying to talk to it."

"You. Um. What?"

"You . . . I was trying to rescue you. In the castle." He pointed. She looked. She felt a moment's stinging disappointment. Here she was thinking she had wandered off into the wilds of the world, away from everyone, never to see another living human again . . . and there loomed the castle, just one ridge of trees away. Covered in thick black vines and floating in a murky haze of dust. A little flock of blackbirds flew by in the foreground, not giving a whit about the strangeness of the scene or the plight of the humans captured within.

"There's some sort of force keeping me out, though," he said, frowning.

"Thorns. They're called thorns," she said helpfully.

"No, besides that," he said with a gentle smile. "I keep hacking at the vines, and they grow back thicker. Then I remembered how close you were to the animals of the forest, and I thought maybe they could help. I was trying to talk to the deer."

"You were . . . trying . . . to talk to the deer? To get it to help rescue me?" she asked slowly, trying to make sure she understood correctly.

"Well," the prince stammered, suddenly flushing. "I mean, it seemed like *you* could almost talk with the animals. They were all around you when I met you, all these wild animals—very close to you. It didn't seem unreasonable. . . . I don't know . . . I ran out of other options."

"Oh, oh, you were, ah . . ."

She was in danger of falling into hysterics. She could

see that. She tried to control her laughter. She only half succeeded.

"Talking to a . . . no, that's sweet."

The prince shrugged helplessly and smiled again. She felt herself warming to him. A person—a boy—who could laugh at himself was instantly likable. Maleficent might have been many things, but self-deprecating wasn't one of them.

"All right, *Prince Phillip*," she said. "You were trying to rescue me. How did you *know* me? Before?"

"I didn't *know* you," the boy said with a sigh. "I *loved* you. We loved each other."

"We did?" She blinked in surprise.

He looked less *hurt* this time than *frustrated*. "What's the last thing you remember?"

She shook her head. "It's not like that. I just told you. I have *too many* memories. Why don't *you* tell *me* about *us*, starting from when we first met?"

"We met once upon a—" He stopped what he was saying suddenly, and shook his head. "I came upon you in a clearing deep in the woods. I was on my way to the castle. I was supposed to meet the princess I was going to marry. For the first time. Meet, I mean. Not marry for the first time. The whole thing was arranged when we were children."

She stared at him hard. There was too much information in what he said; she had to untangle it from the beginning.

"That castle," she finally said, pointing at the vine-covered monstrosity that was now behind them.

"Yes. That castle."

"You were riding to *that* castle. There."

"In the real world, yes," Phillip said.

"To marry the princess of that castle."

"Yes."

"Oh." She twisted a lock of hair around her finger, thinking. "Who was it?"

"It was you!" Phillip said, exasperated. "But I didn't know it at the time. *You* were the princess I was supposed to marry."

"But I wasn't in the castle. I was in the clearing when you met me."

"Yes, well." Phillip pushed his thick hair off his forehead and managed to get in what seemed to be a very satisfying scratch of his scalp in the process. "As I understand it, you were sent to live out in the woods to stay safe until your sixteenth year, at which time you would come back to marry me."

Aurora Rose examined the tendril of hair she had been playing with. Her distant, unthought-of goal had been to chew the end of it, but now she didn't have the urge. Nothing in her life, real or dreamed, made any sense at all.

"Maybe . . . Maybe let's get back to the part where we were in love."

"I met you in a clearing deep in the woods," Phillip said eagerly. "We fell in love. *Instantly*."

"That sounds nice."

It didn't sound like *her*, exactly, but it did sound nice.

To be fair, most of her memories were still of her time in the Thorn Castle, which she had spent with the same people she had known since she was a baby. Falling in love *instantly* with someone you had seen grow up—and use the same privies as you—was not really possible.

"It was. *Is*," he said, taking her hands in his. "*You* are the best thing that ever happened to me."

She looked up into his face. His clear brown eyes moved earnestly back and forth, trying to find some trace of recognition in her face. He was far more handsome than Cael. And to be the subject of this much attention and scrutiny from someone with his physique was more than a little pleasing—even if she didn't know who he was.

"Do you remember that song you were singing when we met?" he whispered, pushing a dirty lock of hair from her face. "The lullaby? 'Once Upon a Dream'?"

Aurora Rose staggered back as if slapped.

She *did* know that song.

The lyrics cut through her memories like a hot knife.

She put a hand to her head as flashing, too-bright scenes sped before her eyes: dappled forest, the *whuff* of a horse, a boy, *this* boy, arriving out of the woods like a spirit. Large hands, but not rough. Clear brown eyes gone soft because of *her*. Her stomach and heart flopping as she waited to be taken into his arms. . . .

Back in the present, the prince also had her in his arms. Which was useful, since she was about to collapse onto the ground again. It was also a little strange. She wasn't used to being held that closely by anyone, much less someone she hardly knew. His hands on her were strong but a little alien. His arms were muscled but unfamiliar. The heat of his skin against her wasn't unpleasant—just unexpected.

She steadied herself, pushing him gently away.

It was another odd thing to see this boy, so handsome, so . . . well-dressed, right there in front of her after all her visions. It really was like she had dreamed him, and like a wish that had been granted, he appeared when she awoke.

"I think I remember something," she finally whispered.

The happiness that flashed from his smile and glinted in his eyes was blinding. She flinched, not wanting to disappoint him by telling him how little she remembered, or how getting to ride on his horse was at least equal to the part where they almost kissed.

"So you knew me when I lived with the . . . uh . . . my aunts. . . ."

"*THE FAIRIES!*" he cried with joy, startling her. He picked her up by her shoulders and swung her around. "Of *course*! They helped me defeat the dragon! They could help us now!"

"Fairies," she said, teetering a little as he set her down. "Right. My aunts were fairies. I understand that now."

She put a hand to her head, just the way Aunt Flora used to when she felt exhausted or defeated by her young ward. "I don't think I knew that then. When I lived with them."

"You didn't know you lived with *fairies*?" Phillip asked, confused. He held her at arm's length to look her in the eye.

"No," she said, a little put out that he didn't believe her—and, yes, that she hadn't known it herself. *How* could she not have known it? "I don't remember them doing much in the way of magic. . . ."

"Well, never mind that. All in the past. What we need to do now is get ourselves out of here and home to put an end to Maleficent once and for all."

The prince gave her shoulders a friendly squeeze before finally letting her go.

The afternoon was soft, and the light was golden. Phillip was a handsome young man who seemed content just to be with her again, to now have a quest and a purpose and direction. His hair glinted in the sun like a topaz.

This was already better than the Thorn Castle or being alone and bored in the Forest Cottage.

"Wait," she said after a moment. "There was a *dragon*?"

Once Upon a Time
as It Really Was
(as Told by the Prince)

In a faraway land, long ago, lived a king and his fair queen. Many years had they longed for a child and, finally, their wish was granted. A daughter was born, and they called her Aurora—for she filled their lives with sunshine. Then a great holiday was proclaimed throughout the kingdom so that all of high or low estate might pay homage to the infant princess.

Good King Stefan and his queen, Leah, especially made welcome a neighboring king and lifelong friend, for on that day would they announce that Phillip, his son and heir, to Stefan's child would be betrothed and thus unite the two kingdoms forever. And so the young prince looked, unknowing, on his infant future bride.

Also invited to this happy occasion were the good

fairies: Flora, who blessed the princess with beauty and grace, and Fauna, who gave her the gift of song.

But before the third good fairy, Merryweather, could bestow her gift, the evil fairy Maleficent appeared, angry she had not been invited to the happy occasion. She, too, gave a "gift"; but it was a terrible curse: before the sun set on Aurora's sixteenth birthday, she would prick her finger on the spindle of a spinning wheel and die.

The king and queen were deeply grieved by this—but all was not lost. For the good fairy Merryweather still had her gift to give. She said:

> *"Sweet princess, if through this wicked witch's trick*
> *A spindle should your finger prick,*
> *A ray of hope there still may be in this, the gift I give*
>   *to thee:*
> *Not in death but just in sleep*
> *The fateful prophecy you'll keep,*
> *And from this slumber you shall wake*
> *When True Love's Kiss the spell shall break."*

King Stefan, still fearful for his daughter's life, did then and there decree that every spinning wheel in the kingdom should on that very day be burnt. So it was done.

To further protect the king's beloved daughter from evil mischief, the good fairies suggested that they raise Aurora in secret and safety, disguised as peasants, in the middle of the woods far away from everyone. So the king and his queen watched with heavy hearts as their most precious possession, their only child, disappeared into the night.

And so for sixteen long years, the whereabouts of the princess remained a mystery, while deep in the forest, in a woodcutter's cottage, the good fairies carried out their well-laid plan. Living like mortals, they reared the child as their own and called her Briar Rose.

One day, many years later, Briar Rose was singing and playing with her animal friends in the woods, when a handsome young man came wandering through the forest, lost. It was Prince Phillip, on his way to marry the princess he had been betrothed to sixteen years earlier—Aurora herself.

But upon seeing the beautiful maiden, all thoughts of marrying royalty disappeared; Phillip fell madly in love with Briar Rose. And although she, too, was instantly smitten, the shy girl scampered away like the very deer she befriended. She did promise, however, to meet him again that night.

Alas for poor Briar Rose, that was also the night of her sixteenth birthday—the night she was to be returned to the castle. Her sorrowful aunts revealed the truth of who they were, and who she was, and how she would marry the prince of the neighboring kingdom on the morrow.

At the castle, weeping and alone in her new gown and tiara, the princess Aurora fell victim to the spell cast by the evil Maleficent. She followed the evil fairy's voice through a secret door and found an enchanted spinning wheel, the last one left in the kingdom. Compelled by Maleficent, Aurora reached out and pricked her finger on its spindle. Immediately, she fell into a deep, deathlike sleep.

The three good fairies then put *everyone* in the kingdom to sleep so that upon awakening, Aurora wouldn't feel strange and alone.

Just before falling under the fairies' spell, Phillip's father revealed to King Stefan how his son had unfortunately fallen in love with a peasant girl and intended to marry her. The three fairies instantly realized what this meant: that Prince Phillip was Aurora's one true love and could break the spell that held her. They raced back to their cottage in the woods, where Phillip was to meet Briar Rose.

Unfortunately, the ever-scheming Maleficent had arrived there first and grabbed the prince, throwing him into her deepest dungeon.

Using stealth and magic, the three fairies good managed to free the prince. With the help of an ensorcelled shield and sword, Phillip defeated the evil Maleficent once and for all, even after she turned herself into a sulfurous, fire-breathing dragon.

The three fairies then led the victorious prince to the chamber where Aurora slept. Upon seeing his beautiful Briar Rose, Prince Phillip knelt at her side and immediately gave her True Love's Kiss.

Princess Aurora woke, saw the prince, and was overjoyed. The two were married the next day, to the rejoicing of all, and lived happily ever after.

The Denouement

"But that last bit didn't happen," Aurora Rose said thoughtfully.

"No." Prince Phillip sighed. "But it *should* have."

"So, somehow, instead of waking *me* up, *you* got sucked into my . . . this . . ." She indicated the world around her with a vague wave of her hand.

"I guess Maleficent was more powerful than anyone thought. Her soul didn't die when I killed her . . . it went into hiding. Into *you*, somehow."

Aurora Rose shivered. The boy next to her had no idea how correct, emotionally and metaphorically, he was.

"I loved her," she said.

"Good God!"

For the first time, his eyes weren't focused on her; they were focused inward and saw something that must not have been a fairy-tale dragon: something monstrous from the pits of hell. Something that he never ever wanted to see again.

And so she told him *her* version of the story. Which didn't involve Phillip at all. Which might have been why she had trouble remembering him clearly.

"Good Lord!" Phillip swore again at the end of it. "That is one of the most terrible things I've ever heard. You were all stuck inside that nightmare castle, believing it was the end of the world and you were the last survivors?"

"It *was* kind of brutal, now that I think about it. But we had food. And parties. Oh . . . that sounds stupid. . . ."

Phillip frowned. "But if she controls the dream, why *not* have the entire world be like that? Like, actually utterly destroyed? Why have a place for you to escape to?"

"I don't know, why would an evil fairy respond to not being invited to a party by *cursing the baby it was for?*" Aurora Rose said wearily. "None of this makes any sense. I don't think I'll ever understand what a normal life is like. With two parents and no magic and one version of reality."

"You know, now that I actually think about it, it *does* seem a bit extreme, cursing a baby and all," Phillip said, nodding.

Then he began to smile goofily.

"What?" Aurora Rose asked, suspicious.

"I'm inside your head. I didn't know your name before and now I'm *inside your head*." He could barely contain his grin.

"Huh."

It was true, and it was a very strange thought . . . that led to a whole passel of other strange thoughts.

"So all the other . . . people . . . in the castle . . . They're all real people . . . *inside my head*."

She put a hand to her head; it suddenly felt much heavier, even though she knew she was imagining it.

"Are you sure?" Phillip asked. He pointed at the castle. "Like, those thorns aren't in the real world. I mean, there are thorns all over the castle, but they're normal and tiny and have flowers. And I can tell you from experience the land around here looks all screwed up. There should be a whole little village right there and a crossroads over there. And the forest should begin much farther away—it's all fields and farms for several miles around.

"So maybe the other people aren't all real—maybe they're characters made up in your dream. I mean, you couldn't possibly have *known* all the real people in the castle because you grew up in the woods. You never met them."

Aurora Rose frowned. The poor Lady Astrid came to mind, and the things Maleficent said about her and her death.

"Well—you've been out and about and . . . 'prince-ing' more than I have. Have you ever heard of a Lady Astrid?"

Phillip frowned. "Maybe. Who's her husband?"

The princess gave him a steely look. "Not that it *matters*, but Duke Walter of the Five Trees."

"Oh . . . yes! Retiring little fellow. About yay high," Phillip said, his hand held below his shoulder. "Sensible man, my father always said. Lady Astrid is also a bit short, yes? And . . . kind of . . . rounded? And a bit of a religious fanatic?"

Aurora Rose had never thought of her that way—in the Thorn Castle, reading the same prayers every couple of hours seemed as useful a way to pass the time as any.

"What about Mistress Laura?"

"Oh, yes, I know her," Phillip said with a rueful smile. "She moons after me all the time. Pretty little child."

"And Count Brodeur?"

"Decadent, useless, scheming gossip," the prince answered promptly. "But mostly harmless."

"Well," the princess said slowly, "then I would say yes—most of the people in the castle *are* real. I didn't know any of them when I lived in the forest, but I've known them all for years here. And . . . I think . . . Maleficent needs to kill people and have them die in real life, too—to maintain herself here."

"Good Lo—all right, I'll stop saying that."

"So maybe the world isn't completely destroyed because she doesn't have *complete* control over it. She needs real people to keep her going. And—it's *not* her dream. It's mine. She's merely using parts of it. And she came up with an easy trick to keep everyone in line. An easily believable lie. 'Don't go out there—it's all dead and poisoned. Stay here. Where I can watch you and use you.' "

"Or maybe," Phillip said thoughtfully, "maybe she *did* try to create that nightmare world. Maybe she couldn't—because you're too strong."

The princess blinked. It hadn't even occurred to her as a possibility.

The cards. The bunny. The visions of the outside world. They weren't monsters from the Outside trying to invade; that was her own self, trying to wake up. The fairies . . .

What had they said?

"Wake up, you don't belong *here. Wake* up *already! Do something!"*

Her brain was weakly, slowly, but finally drawing the threads of connection between things.

"The fairies were there when you . . . uh . . . kissed me, right?"

"Yes—as far as I know they're still there, in the real castle."

"The castle is in the real world, and it's here, too." She thought hard. It hurt. In neither life had she been called on to think things out. But she needed to now. "Maybe they— and you—can't get into the dream castle easily because of Maleficent's spells. The fairies definitely *tried* to reach me and tell me things, but they vanished as soon as one of her minions appeared. So maybe . . . maybe if we found the cottage I think I grew up in—where they *raised* me, we could find them there? Or find some way of contacting them there? Instead of just waiting around for them to find *me* again?"

"That is an *excellent* plan!" Phillip said, picking her up and swinging her around again. She smiled cautiously, pleased that he liked it. He didn't seem like someone who lied for the sake of someone's feelings. She didn't feel . . . humored.

He put her down and looked around them, evaluating the scene and the situation. Confidence seeped from him like the purest sweat. "As I said, this land is strange, but it sort of mimics the real world. That path over there will take us deeper into the forest, in the right direction."

And so they began their adventure.

The way was easy but winding. Phillip would occasionally stop to climb a tree to see where they were in relationship to the castle. Otherwise he was just happy to be there by her side: he kept looking at her secretly, out of the corners of his eyes, picking little nuts and pretty leaves to show her, and generally acting like a boy madly in love with the creature next to him.

It was a little embarrassing, but not unpleasant.

"So we were in love?" she ventured.

"Madly. Still are!" Then he looked at her sideways, anxiously. "At least, I am. . . ."

"But . . ."

"But *what*? What do you need me to do to prove it? I'll do anything, my lady!" He stopped and got down on one knee. "Send me on whatever quest you will! Wouldst thou have me fetch thee the prettiest rose from the farthest reaches of the east? I shall! Bring thee an ancient sparkling treasure from cursèd ruins? Absolutely! Slay a dragon? Oh, wait, did that one already. . . ."

Aurora Rose laughed. It tumbled out of her unguardedly and unstoppably—a thing she had experienced very rarely in the Thorn Castle. The prince smiled, pleased by his effect on her. She gave him a playful shove on his shoulder to force him to get up and start walking again.

She wouldn't have dared try a gesture so familiar with anyone in the castle except for children—or *maybe* Lianna. But it just felt . . . *right* with Phillip.

Still . . .

"No, I mean, but—we only met *once*. Right?"

"Yep!" He reached his hand up and slapped a leaf unconcernedly.

"Isn't that . . . I don't know . . . kind of . . . strange?"

He looked at her, shocked.

"No. It was love at first sight. That's what it means. First. Sight."

The princess scratched the back of her ear uncomfortably. It was an odd thing to find herself happy and free from everyone for the first time ever in her dreamworld life . . . alone . . . and then, suddenly, to just bump into a prince who, while handsome, funny, and *nice*, informed her that they were already life companions, basically betrothed.

"How long have you been out here, trying to get into the castle to rescue me?"

"Oh, I don't know," he shrugged carelessly. "Time is strange here. I swear I saw the moon and the sun in the sky together at night once. Months? Weeks? Weeks, likely. Haven't been that hungry."

"Months?"

This was a problem that involved adding things: units of measurement, time . . . difficult, slippery concepts to contain at once. She thought about the image of herself sleeping, the slowness of her breaths.

"I've been in the castle my entire life. . . . How long were you in Maleficent's dungeon? How much time was there between my falling asleep and you kissing me?"

"I've no idea. A few hours, maybe? The fairies were pretty quick."

"So—time is much slower out there . . . in the real world . . . or much faster here."

"That makes sense," Phillip said, nodding. "I thought you looked older."

"WHAT?"

Phillip shrugged sheepishly at the look she was giving him.

"I mean it in a nice way! More mature. More . . ." He started to move his hands—to indicate what, she could only guess—and then wisely hooked them onto his belt. "Um, mature."

She humphed.

"Mature. Like a matron or some old mother or . . . mother . . ." She stopped, a wide black void opening up in her mind. "Mother . . ."

Five years old, curled up in Merryweather's lap, getting a little big for such pastimes.

"Where is my mother? Where are my real parents again? I mean, *you're* my real parents," the chubby little girl said solicitously, touching her aunt on the chin. "I mean the ones who made me."

The woman in blue looked up anxiously at Flora and Fauna, who were busy with little, quiet evening chores across the room.

"You know—they're . . . dead," Merryweather said.

Perhaps Flora and Fauna frowned at her across the room. She shifted uncomfortably.

"Yes, but *where*? Can't I visit where they are buried? Gather acorns or flowers from the land around so I may bring a piece of them home, to keep?"

Flora dusted off her hands on her apron and hurried over, as did Fauna.

"Little flower, they are all around you, don't worry about that."

"But what did they *look* like?" Rose pressed.

"Like you. But less pretty," Fauna said, touching her on the nose.

"My *father* looked like me?" the girl asked, giggling. "Even though he had a . . ."

"Mustache, yes," Flora finished quickly. "But your eyes are a bit like his. Kind and large."

Rose sighed. "I wish I could have *seen* them, at least."

And the aunts didn't answer, but hugged her tightly.

"Steady," Phillip was saying.

She was swaying, hands to her temples, trying desperately not to pass out because *this* memory brought up a lot of important things. Things she didn't want to forget while she was being sick or unconscious.

"My parents aren't dead," she croaked through her dry mouth. "And they didn't destroy the world. And they're not evil. And my aunts lied to me. For sixteen years. And Maleficent lied to me. And OH MY GOD they were in the dungeon all those years and they weren't under a spell like the rest of us!"

The conversation she had overheard between them and Maleficent when she was sneaking back into the castle . . . it all made much more sense now. Part of the queen's cruelty was keeping them the only sane people left in the kingdom.

"I'm so stupid. . . . All of those years! If I had just *talked* to them! What wasted time!"

"You're not stupid, sweetest," the prince said, running a hand through her hair. "Maleficent is a very clever, very powerful woman. She probably arranged things so that there's no way you could have."

That was true, but in a much more subtle way. The king and queen were set up as destroyers of the world, authors of the apocalypse everyone was hiding from. They were thrown into the deepest dungeon. Everyone *knew* they were insane and evil.

The one time Aurora had snuck down there she was too terrified by them to speak.

"I'm a *coward*," she amended her previous statement. "Why didn't I question anything, ever? Why didn't I—*see* what was happening around me? Why didn't I pay attention to the inconsistencies?"

"Because despite your—um, comely maturity—you're still an innocent young—woman," Phillip said.

She caught the pause and glared.

"I'm not a child! I'm—wait." Her indignity faded with realization and weariness. "How old am I? Really? Oh, never mind. I'll give you the 'innocent' part. I've never been outside my forest cottage or my dream castle. I've never known anyone beyond my aunt, a few villagers, and a limited number of castle refugees who are all asleep."

She thought of Lady Astrid with a quick pain in her heart. She would have liked to have known the lady in real life. Would she have been the same sensible little woman?

"I just wish—I wish I had been a little bit less dense. Or something." There were too many new ideas and old memories to keep track of. She still felt shaky from the last one that hit her. Maybe someday, when this was all over, she would have time to sort them all out.

The sooner the better.

"Are we getting close?"

"I don't think so," Phillip said slowly, reluctant to disappoint her. "When I found you it was closer to the other side of the woods, not so far from the last town before the deep forest began. It was several hours by horseback, so even in this land it will probably take some time."

Time again. Time was confusing and made no sense.

She wasn't sure she could stand *some time.* If she let down her guard, mad streams of memories flowed and swirled around each other and crashed like competing currents in a creek; where they met, foam and chaos erupted.

"So you actually slew a dragon?" Aurora Rose pressed quickly, trying to quell her rising panic.

"Yes, I did, actually," the prince said, cocking his head, enjoying the thought. "It was epic! When was the last time *that* happened? People will be singing about it for *ages.* . . ."

He stopped, grinning ruefully. Aurora Rose found herself mirroring his smile, almost involuntarily. He had that effect on her.

"Well, to be honest, the fairies rescued me, gave me these magic items, and basically guided the sword into her heart," he admitted. "Which did not, let me hasten to add, take away from the extreme fear and panic I felt as I faced the giant fire-breathing monster."

"You were scared?"

"*Terrified.*"

"Really?" She was intrigued. On the one hand, she had this hazy memory of a beautiful boy with a shining steed.

On the other hand . . . it was kind of nice to hear that he was human.

"It's not bravery if you don't feel fear, right? If you're not afraid, then you're not really forcing yourself to do something brave."

It sounded like he was quoting something he had been taught, but it also seemed like he truly believed it.

His face grew dark and clouded. "Her eyes were full of hate. *Full.* And . . . at the same time, empty. Soulless. Like those horrible creatures she keeps around her. The dragon was frightening . . . but *Maleficent*, she was bone-chilling."

"That sounds terrible," Aurora Rose said. It came out more fatuously than she intended.

He looked at her with wide, hurt eyes.

"I'm sorry," she corrected herself. "It really must have been terrible. But . . . you faced a dragon and killed it, and it was over."

"Well, obviously not . . ."

"All right, but *I* have just learned that the world I thought I lived in for the past nineteen years is all unreal. A *dream*. It didn't *feel* like a dream at the time—it still doesn't, exactly. Each one of those years really, fully happened to me. And now I have these *other* memories, sixteen years' worth, of what is supposedly the real world. . . ."

"It is, trust me. I've lived there my whole life."

"It was real for *you*, because you knew who you were, and you were raised by your own parents and lived in your own proper home. I was lied to about who I was, who my parents were, where my real home was, and *what* my aunts were! The real world, as you call it, was all a fake.

"So it's a little hard to deal with right now, thank you. I would rather kill a dragon and get it over with than have to think about all of this!"

She was close to shrieking, despite trying very hard not to.

"Even the fake people in my fake dreamworld were fake. Er. Faker." She paused to wipe her nose and tried not to feel like a child as she did so.

"Tell me about it," Phillip said softly.

Replacing the anger were now tears that spilled down her cheek as she spoke. She wasn't sure which she preferred.

"There was this girl, Lianna. She was my . . . this is so dumb . . . she was my best friend. When we all were confined to the castle, Maleficent found a girl close to my age and made her my handmaiden. Her parents were far away, killed by the demons of the Outside. . . . Not really, though, I guess. Forget that part. The point is, she was odd but we were close. I told her *everything.* All the time. Who I liked and when I had my moon blood and everything."

She stopped still, remembering Lianna being as confused by it as her fairy aunts had been. Of course, it made sense now; like them, she wasn't human. She was a creature, a spirit called up from the depths and forced into the awkward shape of flesh Maleficent had managed to form.

I'm the opposite of Lianna, she realized. Aurora Rose had a body—a natural, real, pretty princess body that different lives and memories and ideas had been forced into. A real mother had given birth to her.

It was her thoughts and memory pictures and everything else that were false.

"As I was escaping, I saw her feet. They were pigs' feet. She was one of Maleficent's creatures. She was working for the queen the whole time, telling her everything. Just pretending to be my friend."

"Oh, Rose," the prince said sadly, running a hand through her hair. It got stuck in some pine pitch.

She began to sob. "I don't remember much from the real world, but I'm pretty sure I didn't have any friends. Except for squirrels and rabbits. No one my own age or human or anything. Lianna betrayed me! I mean, I know it wasn't her fault. She couldn't do anything else . . . she's not even a real person! Not even a real *dream* person. But . . ."

The prince put his arms around her and pulled her in close. She crumpled into his shoulder, feeling so small. Small as a dormouse. She enjoyed the weight of his chest and arms and the darkness when she closed her eyes, and she wept for many things, not just Lianna.

Meanwhile, Back at the Castle . . .

"THAT WRETCHED PRINCE!"

Maleficent's lips stretched taut and thin over her teeth until even her molars were bared in a rictus of frustration. She was not very pretty.

In the air before her was a scene of almost ridiculous pastoral romance: a shabby but beautiful girl in the arms of a prince on a path in the woods. They were quite obviously— and ominously—headed toward the fairies' house.

"That murdering, foul swine," she hissed.

Her hand moved unconsciously to her chest, feeling a place over her heart, which, even in the dreamworld, still bore the ugly scar of a sword.

Her guards, the misshapen horde summoned from the dark places below, remained silent and shuffled uneasily. Even when things went a *little* bit wrong, the punishments were painful, random, and certainly not evenhanded.

This was major.

Alone among them, unmoving, was a single human-seeming girl—though ragged skirts revealed her trotters. Her eyes were large, unblinking, and black, fixed entirely on the vision in the air. A thin film of wet coated them.

Maleficent held her staff aloft. The blood in the orb glowed bright green. She swirled it, slowly, carefully, like a wine connoisseur examining a particularly tricky vintage. From inside the green, a strange, strung-out drop of red began to pulse, caught within but not *part* of the rest of the liquid.

"The battle has just begun," Maleficent said with a knowing leer. "I still have the dreamer's blood from the spindle. It may be time to use it. . . ."

Feeling Ravinous

Three extremely concerned aunts came upon her lying in a hollow at the bottom of what she called Fern Hill. It was after dusk, growing dark, and she should have left hours ago . . . but the hollow was *so* comfy and she didn't feel like moving.

"Briar Rose!" Flora said with a spank in her voice. "We were looking *all over* for you!"

There was real emotion on her face, the thirteen-year-old Rose had noted. On all of their faces. The usual presence of serenity was gone.

The girl knew she should feel bad—or at least concerned—but she didn't really feel much of anything. It was like they were far away.

"You can't be in the woods after dark!" Merryweather scolded. "Wolves could get you! Or bears!"

"They won't hurt me," she had said, slowly getting up. The words came with difficulty. Like she was speaking through a mouth full of honey.

"Bunnies and owls are one thing," Fauna said with a gentler tone of caution. "They are not the same thing as bears."

"Or rapists," Merryweather added.

The two other aunts glared at her.

There was something they weren't telling her, some great fear adults had for children that they never shared. Rose was only vaguely intrigued. She let them lead her back to the house. She apologized, because she was a good girl, and promised she would try not to let it happen again, because she was a good girl.

Then she went straight to bed and slept for thirteen hours and still didn't want to get up.

She came to on the ground, the sickening smell of bile filling her nose and mouth. Phillip was kneeling next to her, holding her hair and shoulders, looking into her face with concern.

The memory had hit her like a sudden falling tree: out of nowhere, splitting her head open. It was so real. . . .

. . . but, of course, it *was* real. *That* really had happened. Her mind was just recovering all of those lost moments.

There was a strangely comforting familiarity in the sadness of the memory. It felt like so many similar days in the castle . . . sleeping the hours away, staring at nothing. Not wanting to do anything. Hoping to disappear.

"I'm fine," she said, before Phillip could ask her. Her head felt like it was sloshing around some but, other than that and a little lingering dizziness, she really was good to go. She put her hand out to the comforting solidity of a tree root to push herself upright. Funny little memories streamed up her arm and into her head. Before she could process them, the prince was helping her. His arm was as sturdy and unrelenting as a rock. She felt no weakness or give when he lifted her.

The path remained steady for a time before dwindling down to dusty silt. The sky opened above as trees fell away on either side. To their right, the land dipped down into a tiny, almost impossibly beautiful valley. A stream ran through its lowest point, its bank lined in pink lupine. Before that, tall, dark green grass sparkled with white flashes in the sunlight. Late season dandelions and breathy, tiny white flowers on slender stems were avoided by bees, while purple thistles and asters thronged with them.

"I could do with a little bit of a break," she said, looking longingly at the soft, moss-covered braes above the tinkling water.

The prince made a big show of cautiously surveying the scene. Aurora Rose hid a smile. Nothing seemed harmful. "All right," he finally said. "My face could definitely do with a wash. Feels all dusty."

They stepped down into the quiet valley that smelled like all of summer crushed into a single flower. She collapsed with thankfulness on a soft sunlit patch of moss. The prince carefully lay down on his stomach and cupped his hands in the stream.

"Wait—should we drink this?" he suddenly asked. "I mean, in fairy tales they always get you with the food or drink."

"We're already trapped in a dream. How much more *trapped* could we get?"

"Hm. Excellent point," Phillip said, and lapped up several mouthfuls.

"So . . . my parents," Aurora Rose mused, chewing on the sweet end of a stalk of grass. "Who are, by the way, *not* evil. They did, however, give me away to a bunch of fairies when I was a baby."

That was the part that was currently confusing her the most. Maleficent was obviously terribly clever in the way she had constructed the false world with its false history;

it sinuously, evilly mirrored the real one—and in each, her parents had given her to fairies. For different reasons and at different times.

"Why, exactly, did they do that? And keep it a secret from me?"

"They thought it was the best way to protect you, I gather," Phillip said. He picked a clump of moss and soaked it in the water, then handed it to her. "Here, maybe you can use this like a sponge."

She smiled and dabbed her face slowly, still thinking. Unconsciously, she began to rub the itchiest bits, where the pine pitch was.

"But if Maleficent's curse was that I should die—or fall asleep—or whatever on my *sixteenth* birthday, then who cares what happened until I turned that age?"

"I think there was some question of how enraged Maleficent was at the way her curse was mitigated," Phillip said with a shrug. His word choice cut through her thoughts; there were moments when the silly, handsome boy almost sounded like a future king. "And that she would just come at you some old-fashioned way, with her army or something. Me, that's not the way I would have handled it. I would have kept my daughter at home where I could keep an eye on her, and surrounded her with armed guards at all times, and had those fairies hang out around the castle."

Those words sounded strangely familiar. . . .

Suddenly, Maleficent's speech to her parents made sense.

Let me tell you something, dearies. If I ever had a daughter, you can be sure I would keep her close, and teach her well, and school her in the arts of magic, and make her strong and powerful enough to protect herself, and I would never let anything come between us.

Or admit the truth to yourselves. It didn't matter much either way, because in the end, you really would have preferred a son.

Aurora Rose rolled onto her stomach, spreading out full-length on the moss like a little girl. She stared at the dirt, part of her marveling at how from this close she could see individual grains and the perfect eyes of ants. How everything tiny was magnified like magic by the globe-shaped teardrop that landed on a patch of moss.

Tiny like a princess. Useless. Unwanted. A girl tossed aside until it was time to marry. A strategic alliance. A useful pawn.

"Hey," Phillip said, noticing her sudden change of mood. He put his hand on her back. Despite the warmth of the sun, his fingers were warmer. "Does it matter now? Didn't you love your aunts—didn't they *really* love you? Surely they must have."

"I guess."

"Believe me, *I* can tell you, as someone who was raised 'properly,' a royal prince in a royal castle, you probably had more love and freedom and fun than any prince or princess I know.

"Before she died, *my* mother was someone I saw once a day at the end of the day for a very proper kiss on the cheek and recitation of the day's lessons. And my dad . . . well, my dad was pretty great. Except when he was punishing me. But all of his lectures, all of his lessons, all of his time with me— it was all only to groom me to take his place. Think about *that*. My one role in life was to prepare for the day the man I loved most would die. Birthdays were marked by the sigh of accomplishment that I had made it that far and the worry of how many years I had left before I turned eighteen—and could rightly rule if something happened to him."

She remained silent, giving him that point.

But she couldn't let it go.

"At least you *knew* what you were in for. I never knew what was happening to me—or what was *going* to happen to me."

"Yes, that was a tactical error, I think we established

that," Phillip said, a little impatiently. "But the *point* of it was to keep you safe. You understand that, right? I'm sure in their own weird way your parents cared about you. Maleficent, despite her . . . *act*, most assuredly did not."

Aurora Rose allowed herself one moment of crazy thought: what if Maleficent *had* loved her? What if her heart had melted just a little and she had really adopted the princess? And brought her into her evil ways, and taught her the great summoning spells, and made her ruthless and strong and magical? Was *that* an unhappy ending? The princess would have become a villain but would truly have had a mother. She would've been ruthless but independent.

Those thoughts drained away as she remembered the uneasy look in Maleficent's eyes whenever the conversation drifted along those lines.

It was never a possibility. The princess wasn't the right kind of daughter for her. She was too weak, too kind, too dumb. . . .

"And bad at math," she said aloud with a bitter smile.

"What?" Phillip asked, confused.

"I was just thinking about my relationship with Maleficent. I just meant . . . on top of everything else, being this stupid princess, I can't even do the math they tried to teach me."

"The fairies taught you math?" he asked, confused. "I didn't even know fairies did that kind of thing."

"No, Maleficent tried," she said with a sigh, picking a fresh stalk of grass and starting on it. "She hired a tutor for me, but I was terrible at it."

"Where?"

"In the castle, silly. In my bedroom or the library."

"Yes, but *that* castle over there? In this dream?"

"*YES*, Phillip. Maleficent didn't melt out of the woods to teach me math while I was being raised by the *fairies*."

Phillip had the indecency to laugh at her.

"Of course you couldn't do math here, silly! You can't do math in dreams."

She sat up.

"What?"

Phillip shrugged, dismissing the whole thing with one boyish expression. "Everyone knows that. For some reason you just can't. Everyone I know—even Sir Gavin, who's like a hundred years old—has these nightmares where you're sitting at the desk with an abacus and the teacher above you, smacking your fingers with a rod for being so stupid. Equations don't make sense. Even simple ones. *I* can't do Latin in dreams, either. I don't know if that's true with everyone else, though. I always start out *hic haec hoc* and then things get weird. In fact, just thinking about it *now*, none of it makes sense. What *is* a declension, anyway?"

Phillip prattled on, but Aurora Rose ignored him.

Even the most *aggravating* parts of her life were a lie.

Math wasn't real in this world. About twenty years of false history and they couldn't even be useful. The time she had spent, the tears of frustration, how *stupid* she thought she was. Stupid pretty princess.

She looked up at the heavens. The amazement at there still actually being a natural world and her being in it hadn't quite worn off yet. The sky was a light blue and large, puffy clouds moved slowly across it. The ground was uncomfortable in a few places under her but not enough to really matter. The breeze was warm when it blew.

Phillip leaned over her and, for a moment, she caught her reflection in his eyes—but then lost herself in them instead.

"Can I kiss you? Would that be all right?" he asked softly.

She graced him with a smile.

"Is this because I look like I'm sleeping?"

"No!" Phillip said, pulling back. "Deuce it all, you just looked beautiful and I love you."

"I was kidding, Prince Serious. You may give me one small kiss. On the cheek. For now."

He leaned over and kissed her, but he lingered a little more than she had imagined he would. She felt his breath, warm and moist but not unpleasant. Their faces stayed close for another moment, sneaking in a second almost-kiss.

He sat up and looked at her face, into her eyes. He pushed a tendril of her hair back over her head.

She was enjoying it immensely.

"I think . . ." he finally said. "I think we should probably get moving. It's kind of amazing that Maleficent hasn't found us yet."

"I don't think she can leave the castle," Aurora Rose said lazily, stretching. She wasn't sure how she knew this. "If she could have she would have. In the last few years. Certainly by now."

"Well, it wouldn't hurt to get a good head start. *She* might not be able to leave the castle, but she could send someone."

Someone *else* outside?

The *Exile*. The *minstrel*.

She had completely forgotten about them.

"Have you seen anyone else out here? Sort of a . . . wasted individual? Might have a lute? Or maybe you know him—our court minstrel, Master Tommins."

Phillip raised an eyebrow. "I haven't seen a soul or sign of anyone since I got here. It felt like I was alone in the world. Once in a while, I could hear faint sounds from the castle courtyard, mere whispers on the wind. That's how I knew there were people inside."

"No one? Not even a . . . sort of fat little older man, white mustache . . . thinks he's a king . . . ?"

Phillip's face went ashen.

"Who is this you speak of?" he asked, trying to control his emotion.

"The Exile. He was thrown into the Outside years ago for high treason. We all assumed he died—but I guess out here he could have lived, after all."

"What was his name?" Phillip demanded, putting his hands on her shoulders. "There is only one other king for leagues in any direction around here."

"We never spoke of his name—it was forbidden," she stammered. "Hugh? Hugley? Humboldt?"

"HUBERT," the prince said with a cry, falling back.

"Hubert, that's right," Aurora said with relief. Then she suddenly got it. "Oh . . ."

"He's my *father*, Rose," Phillip said bleakly. "He's been out here all this time and I didn't even know it. Of course, he would have been in the castle, too—I forgot. He and your parents were in the throne room when it all happened, waiting for the wedding ceremony."

"I'm so sorry. . . . Well, sort of," she added, thinking. "Perhaps it was better for him to be out here than in there all this time. Maleficent could have killed him for his blood in there."

"We've got to find him," the prince said, leaping up. "He's lost out here, somewhere."

"Phillip," Aurora Rose said gently, standing up and putting her fingers on his arm. "I think the best thing we can do now is escape this whole place ourselves and wake up—rescuing everybody in the process. His body, his real self, remember, is still in the other world."

Phillip started to argue, then stopped.

"You're right," he said with a deep breath. He squared his shoulders and set his jaw. "That's the right thing to do. That's what . . . *he* would want me to do. That's what a king would do."

They made their way stoically—if regretfully—back up the side of the pretty valley, Aurora Rose putting a comforting hand on the prince's arm. He smiled and patted it—but that couldn't disguise the worry that floated just below the surface of his eyes.

When they were back on the path, she took a last deep breath of the wildflowers and turned back down the path, toward the woods.

"All right, but both of my, um, potential lives involved being stuck. Stuck in a castle—the real one, I mean, in the real world—until I was sixteen and married off like a real princess," she chatted, trying to distract him. "Or being stuck in the woods with nothing to do and no one to see. So what do normal people do? Like *not* princesses, or those cursed by wicked fairies? Like, a normal girl?"

"Well, I . . ." the prince trailed off, staring at the dust on the path.

"You don't know, do you," she said, nodding. "Because you're not normal, either. I mean you're *normal*, but a prince. Not like a farmer, or—"

"Rose, look," he interrupted, pointing. "What's that?"

Aurora Rose couldn't see anything out of the ordinary. Just a little area where the dust was shifting in the breeze.

And then settling down on itself like an ant lion building its pit trap just below the surface.

And then getting bigger. Spreading out like a sinkhole. Like . . .

"GET BACK!" Phillip cried, spinning around and grabbing her to run.

She stumbled, unable to process what he said and what she saw and what her feet should do at the same time.

She landed hard in the dust, on the same bruises she had made falling from the top of the castle. Her left leg was twisted underneath her.

She rolled over onto her belly as quickly as she could, trying to untangle her stiff appendages—and saw the world open up before her.

Like a devouring mouth, like nothing she had ever seen before or could possibly imagine: the ground itself was falling away into a yawning crack that gaped wider and wider, pulling all the surrounding dirt and rocks and grass with it.

It devoured the path, coming toward her as fast as a horse at full gallop.

"*ROSE!*" Phillip shouted, spinning around when he realized she wasn't behind him.

Without a second thought, he ran back and grabbed her, reaching around her waist and throwing her over his shoulder.

He staggered under her weight for a moment and then began to run.

"Put me down!" she shrieked. "I can walk!"

She watched, upside down, as the earth continued to be eaten away, the edge of the abyss now almost at his feet.

"Didn't seem like it," Phillip huffed.

"*PUT ME DOWN!*" she screamed. "*We'll go faster!*"

Swearing, the prince did, pausing only a moment to set her on her feet.

He did not let go of her hand.

The two took off, and he only had to pull her a little. *Grace*—the fairies' gift, according to his story—seemed to pertain to her running as well as dancing. She might not have been as fast as he, but she was nimble and fleet and didn't need to look at her feet to avoid stumbling.

But it didn't help her with stamina.

She pushed hard, almost crying at the effort. There was a tiny part of her that just wanted to give up and admit there was no escape and no sense wasting energy trying. But she was astonished to see that weak impulse completely over-come by the immediate will to survive. She couldn't have stopped running if she wanted to.

She also chose not to look back; the screams of the ground and the cracking, rocky noises behind them were enough to speed them on.

She suddenly realized they were running back the way they had come, back toward the castle.

But surely, if this was an attack from Maleficent, it wouldn't destroy the *castle*, would it? With her and her min-ions and her victims all still in it?

The princess yanked Phillip's hand and led him, cut-ting through the clearing where they had met the second time, aiming straight for the silent gray structure looming above the surrounding countryside.

"No!" Phillip cried when he realized where they were going.

But just a few feet from the first outlying thorny vines, the noise behind them stopped.

Phillip and Aurora Rose slowed down clumsily, with heavy thuds of their feet, winded and exhausted.

Slowly, they turned around.

Between them and the forest was now an epic ravine.

The two staggered backward as they tried to see the whole thing from a single viewpoint. It was at least several furlongs across to the other side of the path.

"*I* wouldn't put this in a dream," the princess said shakily.

It was like the gorge was too large to be believable— like her mind couldn't encompass just how large it was. Her eyes kept darting to different points along its cliffs: where the dirt changed color, where there was a particularly large rock jutting out, where what looked very much like giant, ancient bones pressed up against the newly revealed earth. Anything to focus on and distract her from trying to comprehend the whole thing.

All was silent now, except for the occasional distant tumble of rock or *sssht* of a scree avalanche working itself free from somewhere in the depths.

Cautiously, without saying a word, Aurora Rose and Phillip shuffled to the edge and peered over.

The ravine wasn't *endlessly* deep, as each had probably feared, but it was *fairly* deep. And it was filling with water as rivers and lakes along it were being drained into its bottom.

Phillip and Aurora Rose looked at each other.

"If we go down to cross," the prince said hesitantly, "she could seal it back up over us immediately. Right?"

The idea of instant black death did not appeal to the princess at all. But neither did the idea of being stuck in the half-state of a dreamworld forever.

"But if she *wanted* to kill us outright, couldn't she have just opened the earth immediately below us? She's trying to lead us back—force us back into the castle. She needs us—or me—alive and close by. For now."

"Hmmm. Good point."

"Besides . . . do we have a choice?"

The prince sighed and shook his head.

"No."

He started his way down, testing the firmness of footholds before holding out his hand to her.

She took it, idly observing how in moments of need, at least, his touch was certainly becoming less strange. Her other hand she trailed along the cool dirt beside her, letting it tangle in roots. How much of this was the real world, and how much was secret layers of her own self?

"Well, it *wasn't* the stream I drank from," Phillip said with a lopsided smile. "That was the trap, I mean."

"No, it wasn't."

Suddenly, she didn't feel like smiling—didn't feel the urge to mirror his face. She felt weak and sick. The strength and determination she had felt just a moment before withered under scrutiny.

"It *was* a trap, wasn't it? She knows where we are. Somehow she knows I've figured everything out. She's trying to stop me. To *hurt* me, if she needs to . . ."

"Yes, and that's great!" Phillip said with a blindingly toothy grin.

Aurora Rose blinked at him. She found herself wondering if the two of them were, right at that moment, caught in different realities, like her and her real sleeping body. Because he wasn't making sense.

"I'm sorry?" she said, manners kicking in before what she really wanted to say managed to make its way to her lips.

"It means we're on the right path—don't you see? Every time Maleficent does something like this, every time we narrowly evade a trap or attack or whatever she sends after us, it means we're getting closer to our goal. The fairies. The way out!"

"Oh." She turned this over in her head. It made sense. It was also a way of thinking that was so utterly bizarre to her that she had trouble wrapping her head around it. "Bad things can mean good things. That's . . . unique."

"Nah, basic games strategy. Like when Sir Palomer starts sending all his one-point scouts after your first cavalry, you *just know* you've almost found where he's hidden the crown."

She studied him for a moment and decided to give manners a rest.

"I have *no* idea what you're talking about."

"Catch-the-King? Really? You've never played? Oh, it's a *great* game. Even my sisters . . ."

She just looked at him, raising her eyebrows a little.

"Well, anyway, the point is this." Phillip kept talking as he balanced on a giant piece of root, digging his nails into the dirt wall to balance. "It's a good metaphor, if I do say so myself. Imagine you're playing a very dangerous game with Maleficent. If you win, then you wake up, she dies— I assume—and everyone in the kingdom wakes up, I wake up, we all live happily ever after. If *she* wins, well, I assume she kills you, takes over the kingdom, and rains bloody hell on everyone and everything."

Now she really *did* feel sick.

Her stomach turned. When was the last time she ate? Was there anything left to throw up? Her legs felt rubbery. The view down to the bottom of the ravine suddenly seemed a lot farther. And the way back up impossibly steep. All she knew was rabbits and birds and banquets and balls. Nothing about life and death and saving kingdoms.

Phillip had stopped when she stopped, turning around to see what was wrong. When he saw her face, he gave her a sad smile. "You said you didn't know what it means to be a real princess. Well, now you do.

"Being a member of royalty means the lives of those you rule are more important than your own. You lead your armies into battle to protect your country from invasion. You marry people you don't want to, to keep the peace." He chuckled at the irony.

"And there is an *entire kingdom* of people asleep, at
Maleficent's mercy, depending on *you* to rescue them. This
is your quest. This is *your* adventure."

He reached out and gave her white-knuckled hand a
squeeze, then a comradely pat.

And then he turned around and started making his way
down again.

He was right. This was simply what she needed to do.
She had never been *more* needed to do anything in her
whole life.

Taking a deep breath, she followed.

"I cannot *believe* you've never played Catch-the-King!"
he went on, even as he nearly tripped over a narrow ledge
that shifted under his feet. His hands flew up for balance,
out of hers. "It's, like, the best game *ever*! I'm not great at
it—not even as good as Brigitte, between you and me—but
my uncle Charles, now *he's* the expert. What you do is set
up all the markers, without your opponent seeing. . . ."

As he prattled on, she found herself *not* listening to the
boy she'd thought was the most handsome in the world just
a little while ago.

Then, as he continued endlessly about the rules and
setup for the game, she wondered if this was another strategic move on the part of the prince: an attempt to distract her
from the weight of the burden she now realized she carried.

And after a while, the going became easier. The wide, gently sloping path a gigantic tumbling boulder had made on its descent allowed them to walk side by side for a little.

"Can I hold your hand?" Phillip suddenly asked, a little plaintively.

The princess looked up, surprised. "Sure. Yes. I suppose."

He grinned like a kid who had just been given a pony, taking her hand and squeezing it once. He swung it as they walked. All trace of near disaster was gone from his world. He was the handsome hero prince, for whom it was all in a day's work. The latest evil was overcome and now it was time to move on. No dwelling . . . despite the fact that they were several stories below the surface of the earth and deep in the ground's shadow. With no real plan of how to cross the water at the bottom.

"Thank you," she said after a minute or two. "For carrying me back there."

"Of course," he said, breaking off a root with his free hand as they walked. He looked at her mischievously. "But if I'm going to have to rescue you any more, you know, pick you up and throw you over my shoulder, it would be better if you wore softer shoes. Next time."

"There won't *be* a next time. I won't be needing that service again, thank you," she said haughtily. "I was just . . . caught unprepared."

"What is it with you girls and pointy shoes, anyway? Get yourself a nice flat-heeled pair of boots, that's all you need. . . ."

"I didn't wear shoes at all in the forest. I was barefoot all the time, and my skin was as thick as hides. I had *so many* shoes in the castle . . . all different colors."

She stopped, thinking about it.

Then she reached down with her free hand and slipped off her golden shoes.

With a gentle toss, Aurora Rose threw them into the ravine.

You're So Vain

"How long have we been walking?"

They were still a little soggy from tramping through the mud and water at the bottom of the ravine. Luckily, the stream wasn't as deep as it had looked from above, but it had still been cold and generally unpleasant. Phillip's boots sloshed a little as he stepped. Climbing back out of it took more time than going down, but she couldn't have said how much.

"A while . . . I don't know. A couple of hours?" Phillip said. "It's hard to see under the trees—I can't make a sundial here. It seems a little darker. Maybe the sun has set or is close to setting."

So this is real twilight, she thought. Not the graying-of-everything that evening at the Thorn Castle brought.

Shadows were blending with solid shapes, and everything seemed to be more blue or dark purple. She held her hand out in front of her; somehow it seemed more real, more detailed than it did in sunlight. But as she looked off to the sides of the path, directly into the heart of the forest, it was already as dark as night. Impenetrably black.

Except . . .

She blinked her eyes, thinking she was hallucinating.

No, it *wasn't* her imagination. *There were* tiny blue and orange wisps of light dancing just beyond the edge of where she could make things out clearly.

Fireflies? Will-o'-the-wisps? Sorcery?

And then one of the wisps bounced its way toward her.

She watched with wide eyes as it whisked this way and that and finally wound up bobbling in front of her face. Phillip continued on unheeding, muttering about finding food and whether or not dreamers needed to eat.

Inside the ball of light was, as she expected, a tiny, perfectly formed girl. Not like the previous ones; younger, with an almost childlike body. Her eyes were wide in surprise as she peered at Aurora Rose.

"You're a fairy," the princess stated, more for herself than anything else.

"You're a princess!" the tiny fairy squealed in amazement. "A beautiful, fairy-tale *princess*! In the flesh!"

The ball shrank down to the size of a pinhead, then

suddenly expanded and, with a pop, disappeared. The princess blinked. The fairy was now hovering in front of her, just off her toes, mostly human sized. She had what seemed like endless waves of chestnut brown hair, a rather shockingly short tunic, and a pointy little nose.

"Oh, how *pretty* you are!" the fairy said, dipping around the girl half on her toes, half in the air. The princess spun, trying to follow.

"You—are you from the real world?" Aurora Rose asked desperately. "Did the others send you? Are you from the cottage?"

The fairy didn't answer, too busy picking at the girl's clothes and hair and any other bits that stuck out.

"Hey," Phillip said politely. "Who's your friend, Rose?"

She shrugged helplessly. But she couldn't help smiling at the pretty, delightful, gold-sparkle-trailing creature.

"Please," she said, trying not to laugh at the thing's antics. "Were you sent by Flora? Or Fauna? Or Merryweather?"

"Oh, no." The fairy was now playing with the ends of the princess's golden hair, touching it with awe. "Those are important, serious godmothers. Tangled up in human importance. We are wood nymphs. Fairies of the forest. *Fialla! Livuua! Malailialaila!*" she called. The nonsense names quickly degenerated into bird trills and frog calls.

More wisps came quickly bobbing through the trees.

The prince and princess watched, astounded, as more and more fairies changed into life-sized forms and landed around them. They were all tiny, skinny, large-eyed, and wore very little. Not that there was much to cover.

"Oh! Look at your *hair*! It's like spun gold!" one of the fairies said. "But so dirty!"

"Oh, your hands! So delicate!" another said. The fairy's fingers were delicate, too—but *too* delicate, tapering to pointy nothings at all.

"Your skin is *flawless*," a third said, hovering in the air and examining her cheeks—a little too closely.

"Are you a prince?" a fourth asked, turning to Phillip and looking up into his face with reverence.

"Why—yes. Yes, I am."

"How did you know I was a princess?" Aurora Rose asked. So many fairies flew around her that she was practically cocooned in golden trails. The little sparkles were warm when they landed on her, like harmless crackles from a fire. She felt both crowded and swept up by the little army of magical girls around her.

"You *look* like one, silly!" one of the fairies laughed.

"You're so handsome," a fairy mooned at Phillip, her hands clasped.

"Well, I . . ." he said, blushing.

"Look at your gown!" a fairy wailed. "Your beautiful

golden gown, tarnished! Those rags are no fitting raiment for a royal princess!"

"And your *shoes*! *Where are your shoes?*"

"Come with us!" the first one said. "We will brush your hair! And magic you new clothes! And fix your nails," she added, with a distasteful look at the ragged, dirty, torn ones on the princess. Aurora Rose had a sudden urge to hide them behind her back.

"Nope. Not leaving the path. Not again," the prince said firmly.

"We can do it *here* then."

"We don't really have the time."

"It will stay your travels but a *moment*," the fairy pleaded. "Then you will be on your way. Refreshed and renewed—and properly dressed for the adventures ahead."

"You look like you could use your shoulders rubbed," another fairy said innocently, turning her big eyes to Phillip.

"Well, now that you mention it," he said.

"A *prince* and a *princess*! Handsome and beautiful!" the first fairy squealed, clapping her hands. "We are so lucky!"

Soon there were dozens of fairies flying around, lighting the area with their golden dust and creating a strangely room-like space under the trees. One made pine needles fly up together and dance into a low couch. Another conjured a mirror out of dewdrops. A third pulled tree branches together and coaxed them into forming a screen.

"No, no, no!" one fairy teasingly chastised Phillip, pulling him away from the princess to the other side of the screen.

Aurora Rose found herself surrounded by hovering, flitting bodies that changed size and dipped and flew up and down so much that she couldn't watch anymore. Their hands were gentle and carefully tugged at the ratty gown, flying it off over her head without any issue. The princess wasn't cold, as she had expected to be; the golden sparkles were keeping her warm.

"Here . . ."

She was led to the pine needle couch, where a fairy with a basket waited.

"Tip your head back," the fairy ordered.

She did as she was commanded. A warm cascade of water trickled over her head, getting to all the scratchy places. It felt like heaven. Her hands were being lightly scrubbed with what felt like pinecones.

"Your prince has no idea how lucky he is," the fairy buffing her nails said, leaning in close to whisper.

"He's not my prince," she protested halfheartedly. It was nice being so taken care of. Almost like being back home in the castle, but better. A perfect way to start the adventure.

Someone was very carefully combing the pitch and tangles out of her hair.

"It really *is* like spun gold," the fairy said with awe.

Wait . . . that sounded familiar. . . .

But before the princess could place it, another one was prattling on.

"We shall give you a dress as green as the pines that shelter you and *shoes* to match!"

Several fairies were working magic on a sapling, causing cloth and fabric to appear and drape around the tree like it was a mannequin.

Aurora Rose watched this and felt another pang of uneasy déjà vu.

"Why do you care about clothes? Why do *woods* fairies care about *human* clothes?"

"Silly, *we* don't. But humans wear clothes. And you're so *beautiful*. You need to wear beautiful clothes, too."

"But we're in the woods. In a dream. I *could* be naked. Like those dreams in which you realize you're naked?"

"Shhh," a fairy said, smoothing the princess's hair back from her face. "Your beauty comes with a trace of fairy magic . . . a fairy gift, if I'm not mistaken. You will probably be the most beautiful girl in the world. Lucky girl!"

"Um," the princess said, thinking about this.

Luck didn't seem to be a major contributing factor in her life. In either world.

As for beauty . . .

Well, she had indeed loved the way people had looked at her at balls in the Thorn Castle.

At the Forest Cottage, she had *played* at dressing up in the costumes her aunts had made for her. Only once was there a time in the real world when she had been dressed up properly and beautiful in front of a mirror. That was right before . . .

Right before . . .

She gasped in pain as the memory hit her.

The day she was going to tell her aunts about the boy she had met.

She had come home, having forgotten it was her birthday. Time was both important and irrelevant in the woods; stars marked seasonal changes, the moon waxed and waned, the solstices were strictly observed . . . but normal days and weeks and months weren't.

She burst into the cottage and there, waiting for her, was the most beautiful dress she could ever have imagined. No ragged seams, no patches, no spiderwebs or leaves holding bits together. It was fitted and radiant and like something out of a dream.

It was also hard to tell if it was blue or pink, which was sort of strange, because she wasn't color-blind.

She wondered where it had come from. None of the few villagers or woodsmen they interacted with had anything *like* the dress or even the materials with which to make it.

But that thought was quickly overwhelmed by joy: joy

at the pretty dress for her birthday, joy at the idea of spending the rest of her life with the boy in the woods, joy at the cake that was also somehow magically there and perfect, like something else out of a dream.

And then overwhelming sadness when she found out what her sixteenth birthday actually meant and what the presents were for.

The dress was there because she was a princess, about to get married—to a prince she had never met.

The three "aunts" who had seemed to love her so thoroughly her whole life vanished from the scene entirely when she was locked in the castle bedroom. For her *safety*, she was left alone—with nothing but loss and bitterness and hopelessness.

Aurora Rose gulped and took deep breaths, trying not to pass out from the memory, from the great wash of sadness.

Seeing *these* fairies conjure a dress out of thin air, she now realized where her sixteenth birthday gown had come from. *And* the cake.

Something like panic began to form in the pit of her stomach.

"Shhh, shhh," a fairy said, stroking her wrist. "What's the matter? Everything is fine."

Phillip's laughter rang out beyond the screen, boyish and loud.

"There!" a fairy said.

The magicked dress danced over to the princess. Despite her misgivings, she stood up to receive it—it would have been rude not to. The dress easily smoothed itself over her. Dark green velvet skirts, full and soft, twirled around down to her ankles. Golden buttons fastened themselves up the placket on the bodice and over the elegant, tight sleeves. From her elbows, wisps of dark green mist flowed to the ground for tippets. A collar around her neck drifted out into a cape of the same material.

"Truly, you are the most beautiful princess in the world," a fairy breathed.

Aurora Rose looked at herself in the mirror of dewdrops. She was indeed the most beautiful thing she had ever seen. Long neck, golden hair, wide violet eyes, narrow waist, lips perfectly pink and rosy.

She turned, just a little bit, to see how her figure looked from a different angle. The green velvet flowed softly and majestically, making delicious little noises when its folds rippled. As talented as the castle seamstresses were, the princess had never worn anything as elegant or perfect as this.

And yet . . . she thought about herself as a child in the dreamworld, hiding in neglected spaces of the castle, making friends with rats. She wore no dresses then. Nothing fancy or pretty at all until Maleficent came along and saved her.

She thought about herself as the child in the woods, playful and dirty.

Nothing fancy or pretty that wasn't pretend until her sixteenth birthday.

"Oh, that's nothing! Try this one!" another fairy squealed.

The princess found herself being gently prodded and pushed and combed and magicked, and her hair felt weird. When she was spun around to face the mirror again, she was in a yellow dress, waves of sunshine spilling down from her bodice to her toes. Her shoulders were bare, which was a little strange, but they were pale and perfect and delicate. *Swanlike*, she could hear the minstrel saying. Her hair was loosely braided over one shoulder, a yellow ribbon tying it off.

The fairies gasped.

"You are *sooooo* beautiful!"

"Even *more* beautiful!"

"Can it be possible?"

"Look at *this*," a fairy commanded. With a serious look and a wave of her wand, she transformed the princess again. This time her hair was piled high on her head in an elegant chignon, a simple ribbon holding it back. A light blue dress puffed out around her softly, like a cloud. The finest gloves she had ever worn covered her bare arms up to her shoulders. Funny little tinkling shoes felt chilly on her feet.

She put her hands on the skirt and twisted this way and that; what a dress to dance in! She would look like a fairy herself.

Or a bride.

"So pretty," a fairy said, touching her hair again.

"My turn!" another fairy said.

Little hands grabbed at her. It was disconcerting and a little frantic—but gentle. Far gentler than Lianna, who had also encouraged the princess to dress up. Who always said how pretty she was. How beautiful. How like a royal princess. Who made her stand in front of a looking glass and admire herself in her gowns.

For the balls. Which had been a distraction to keep her—and everyone else—from paying attention to the situation they were in, from figuring out what was going on.

"That's it. We're going."

Aurora Rose turned away from the magicked mirror. Tiny fairies were flung in all directions as she spun around.

She pushed the screen aside and grabbed Phillip's hand, pulling him after her.

He gaped and gawped at her outfit.

"Rose! You're . . . you're . . ."

"Beautiful. Yes. I know. Come on," she pushed her way past the fairies, who were gently trying to block her. "Thanks for the dress and the hair-washing and everything.

But we're on a quest, and I think we've already wasted too much time here."

"Stay! We just want to look at you!" one fairy wailed.

"So pretty!" another said, lacing its hands into her long locks. Its fingers were sharp and pulled.

"Thank you, sorry," the princess said, yanking her head back and wincing.

Little hands were pawing at her dress and her arms.

"Stay! You could be *our* princess!"

"So pretty, pretty!"

"Stay!"

Phillip was looking a little worried now.

"Should I pull out my sword?" he whispered as they began to shove through the growing press of winged creatures.

"No . . . not yet . . ."

The fairies began to cry.

"Stay! We'll treat you like the princess you *are*! We'll worship you!"

"You can be our beautiful doll!"

"We'll dress you up and feed you ambrosia!"

Aurora Rose closed her eyes as she marched forward. The grabby little hands grew claws. She felt her hair and dress begin to rip.

"Ow! Hey! Cut it out!" Phillip said. He was less gentle

than the princess, batting the fairies away with the back of his hand.

She didn't want to look down to see what was happening; she wanted to continue walking down the path calmly and have it all disappear once she could no longer see them.

"We won't let you leave us."

She turned.

The fairies were changing. They were elongating, their thin, wispy bodies growing strangely fluid. They were also changing color: slimy gray and oily green and sickly orange. Their eyes slid back over their skulls, yellowing in the process.

"Sssstay!"

They had claws and barbed tails now. Sharp, curved fangs and ugly horns. They lost their legs or grew extra sets or sprouted pointy, torn wings. They flew and gibbered and flowed around the trees and the prince and princess, swiping and grabbing.

"Sword. Now?" Aurora Rose suggested.

"Already out," Phillip retorted, trying not to sound nervous.

He swung his bright-bladed sword through the crowd of demons. Sometimes it caught an actual piece of flesh, causing one to shriek and peel away from the others. But mostly it just went straight through them, like they were made of smoke.

"I thought your sword was enchanted!" The princess covered her face and her head, trying to move faster in her ridiculous skirts.

"In the real world it was!" Phillip shouted. He winced as a six-clawed, three-eyed thing successfully got to his face. Six traces of blood flowed down his once perfect cheek.

Aurora Rose cried out as something snakelike launched itself at her waist and wrapped around her body, squeezing tight.

The demons converged on her, hissing and ripping and tearing.

She kicked and screamed. In neither world had there been much violence in her life—at least, not directed at her. She had never had to defend herself. She had no idea what to do when she couldn't run away. Her feet in their stupid new shoes were roped together by something living and cold. Something else horrible, rough and tiny, was easing its way under her hands toward her eyes.

Suddenly, Phillip was there. He had sheathed his useless sword and was now just grabbing the demons, throwing them off her.

One landed on the back of his head and clung there, sinking its teeth deep into his skull.

Phillip gasped with pain but ignored it, concentrating on getting Aurora Rose free.

When the demons were mostly off her, he roughly pulled her up.

"RUN!" he yelled, turning to fight the rest off.

"Not without you!" she said without thinking.

"Oh, I'm running, too," Phillip said. *NOW!*

And the two ran into the woods, all the creatures of hell fast on their footsteps.

Sing to Me, O Muse

In the world of the Thorn Castle, she had scurried. In the real world of the Forest Cottage, she had run races with rabbits.

Neither could compare to how fast she had run *twice on the same day now*, throwing out her legs and leaning forward, desperately gulping air.

Phillip was close on her heels, still wrestling with the thing on his head.

"To the left!" he panted. "The path splits and there's a smallholding up ahead! At least, in the real world . . ."

She made the mistake of turning to look behind her. The things were slithering after them just above the ground, spilling down the path like something boiling and spoiled that had been overturned.

The forest grew thinner. Though it was now well into twilight, with fewer trees blocking the last rays of sunset the land was still bright golden. The path widened into something like a dirt road, and its unruly banks changed over into orchards and rows of vegetables.

The creatures behind them thinned out, too; it was like the smaller ones couldn't leave the shadows.

Those that remained were looking more tentative now, curling around the bushes and scrub like smoke, skittering to the occasional protective lee of a rock, from which they would dart out and try to nip the fleeing prince and princess's heels.

But the larger demons, the stronger ones, still tore after their quarry, hissing and snorting and untroubled by the dying sunlight.

The closest one was the size of a horse and had horns above its evil yellow eyes. And it was gaining on them.

"THE GATE!" Phillip cried, pointing at a rough stile that marked the entrance to the smallholding. It was certainly not strong enough to keep the demons out and looked rather pathetic. On the fence next to it were tacked strange things Aurora Rose couldn't understand: garlic, a rope of wolfsbane, a tattered cloth painted with runes.

But the prince seemed to think the gate offered some form of safety, so she let him pick her up and hurl her over the side. He dove after her, landing in a roll.

The giant demon chasing them stopped short of the gate.

It looked ridiculous: this large, black, yellow-eyed, smoky, horned evil thing, swaying hesitantly in front of the comparatively small rustic fence with the bits and tatters on it.

It slowly lowered its head and began to fade.

In moments, it was gone.

Phillip let out a string of curses: the demon clinging to his head was still there, undispelled. He reached up and pulled it off, hurling it to the ground.

It howled, its face splitting almost in half. The teeth that it had sunken into the prince's flesh weren't long—but there were *lots* of them.

The prince yanked his sword out of its sheath and drove it into the thing's head through its wide mouth.

Perhaps many more times than strictly necessary.

It shrieked and hissed and squirmed and bled white bloodlike pus, finally disappearing in a curl of oily smoke.

Aurora Rose watched it all silently, trying to regain her breath. She wasn't sure why she wasn't crying.

"Dear God," Phillip swore, running a hand through his hair and looking at the thick smears of blood that covered it. "I think I would have preferred a dragon. Those things were *horrible*."

He wiped his sword on the ground to clean it.

"Why did they . . . why did that tiny gate stop them?" she asked.

"The protective wards. Didn't you see them hanging there?" he said, pointing at the brightly colored bits and herbs. "It's a pretty common thing in the more . . . rural villages. Never believed they actually *worked*, though."

"Oh." She decided she would deal with the philosophical implications—dream talismans effectively keeping away dream demons—another time.

A lone woodsman, returning from the forest, ax over one shoulder, looked over at the couple. Maybe it was the blood all over Phillip or the princess's *extremely* out-of-place dress, but he started walking faster. Away from them.

"Let's go see if anyone has some warm water. And bandages. And maybe dinner," Phillip suggested.

She put a hand to her head.

"But . . . none of this is real. We're not *really* wounded or hungry. Right?"

"It's real enough while we're here," he said with a shrug. "I don't know what happens to us in the real world if we're killed here. And I don't think I want to find out. So let's play by the rules until we figure out the loopholes."

She nodded. That made sense.

They started toward the village.

"So . . . another trap. Much cleverer this time," Phillip said.

"Yes. This time with a fancy surprise ending." Aurora Rose sighed.

"But *you* figured it out and managed to pull us out of it."

"I suppose I did," she said, thinking about it. It *was* all her doing. Up to the part with the demons.

"'Suppose'? You *completely* did. It was *amazing*! Well done!"

He was truly excited for her; his praise was real and enthusiastic.

Little warm waves worked up her body from the tips of her toes to her cheeks. He—*her prince*—was genuinely impressed by something she did. It almost eliminated the remaining apprehensiveness in her.

But not quite.

"What—what's wrong? We won, Rose. Why are you still upset?"

She took a deep breath and tried to sort her feelings.

"When you told the story of what happened in the real world before, you mentioned the fairies giving me gifts of beauty and grace or whatever, and I just sort of dismissed it. I thought it was poetic license. So when the . . . *back there* fairies, the demons . . . one of them said my beauty was a *gift*—a fairy gift—it suddenly sank in. It must have been literal. My beauty isn't even my own. It was given to me by someone else."

"Oh, Rose, don't be silly, of course—"

"The story *said*. The fairy *said*. But that's not the point. The point is that I realized, standing in front of the mirror, that wherever they came from, my looks *were never actually that important to me* in the real world. Other things were.

"*That's* when I figured out how weird the situation with those fairies or demons or whatever was. I didn't even start out caring about my looks in *this* world—the world of the Thorn Castle—not until I was actively encouraged. The fairies were acting exactly how Li—my handmaiden acted around me. With the dressing up and praising my golden hair. And *she* wound up being a spy for Maleficent."

Phillip frowned. "How strange . . . It seems like twice now in your dream life she has tried to distract you and trap you with dresses and . . . I don't know, your beauty and vanity. Which you don't really have much of. *Vanity*, I mean. You're plenty beautiful. But it seems like Maleficent doesn't have a very large range of scenarios for you. She just goes back to the same old thing."

"I think she might . . . underestimate me. I think she has a picture in her head of who I am. Silly pretty princess. I don't think she actually *knows* who I am."

"I hope I do," Phillip said with a grin, taking her hand and squeezing it.

"Do you?" she asked with a wry smile. "I'm not even sure I know myself."

The breeze turned, bringing the clear, teasing trill of a fiddle to them along with the smell of smoke and the sound of laughter. There couldn't have been a more inviting combination of sensations in the world.

"That must be the village up ahead," Phillip said, pointing.

The two picked up their pace and hurried to the center of the tiny village.

It was really nothing more than a cozy collection of cottages, with thatched roofs and smoke drifting from their stone chimneys. There was no bank or church or any more formal building than a smithy and a storehouse. Aurora Rose realized with a start that it might even have been one of the places her aunts—the fairies—went to get supplies. She was never allowed to go on those trips.

A huge red-and-orange bonfire crackled merrily in the commons. Two fiddlers and a jug player enthusiastically belted out high-spirited music. Children ran around in bare feet, mouths smeared with red and purple from the berries they were gobbling down. Adults clapped and danced. Everyone was dressed—well, if not in their *best*, then at least in their *nicer* clothes: big-skirted dresses for twirling, broken straw hats freshened up with ribbon, even the occasional washed face.

Humans weren't the only ones enjoying the fun, either: dogs and cats chased each other through the crowd. A gray donkey lifted its neck and brayed along with the music. Toddlers worked to keep a small flock of overexcited geese out from underfoot.

A table with a snow-white cloth was laid out with all sorts of pies and tarts along with a pile of bread and pots of dark purple jam. A cauldron of something that smelled like hot wine sat on a smaller fire nearby; a solicitous crone ladled out steaming portions into anyone's mug.

Aurora Rose's eyes widened in delight at the scene.

"It's the Berry Moon festival," Phillip explained. "If things work the same way here. They're celebrating the end of summer. I'll bet that's hot raspberry mash over there."

"I know that festival! They have it every year, but my aunts never let me go," she said wistfully. "Wait—"

Phillip sighed and put his hands out to catch her as she began to sway, hit by another stream of memories.

This time it wasn't *too* bad or too long. A series of very similar scenes presented themselves one after another: late summer, and despite their seclusion in the woods, the excitement of the festival reaching even the three aunts and Rose. She *begged* to go. If the breeze turned right she could smell simmering raspberries on the wind.

"Never, it's not safe," said Flora.

"I'm sorry, dear," said Fauna. "Maybe when you're older."

"How fun can it be, anyway?" Merryweather asked. "All those hu—uh, clodhoppers dancing around to those silly songs and eating pies . . ."

"YOU NEVER LET ME DO ANYTHING!" Rose screamed, stomping out of the house. At age thirteen, fourteen, fifteen . . .

Aurora Rose came to still upright this time, head pounding but buoyed by one clear thought.

"I get to go *this* time!" she said, grinning and walking ahead eagerly.

"Rose, it's not *real*," Phillip said, chasing after. "It's probably another trap. It's probably danger—"

"Don't. Even." She spun around and put her finger to his lips. "It's *my* dream, and I'm finally going to enjoy it."

But if the prince was expecting another trap from Maleficent, his suspicions were immediately allayed by what happened next: the music wound down awkwardly, the dancing stopped, and the crowd turned unfriendly stares on the couple.

The princess put a hand to the back of her head in embarrassment. They *did* look pretty strange, an armed prince and a ragged princess, covered in blood and dirt.

"Er. Hi," she said with a timid wave. She tried to remember who she was, and where she was from, and how people usually looked at her when she walked into a room.

At least in the Thorn Castle.

"Excuse us for interrupting."

"Where've ye come from, just at *sunset* and all?" an old man asked, not bothering to mask the suspicion in his voice.

"Oh, come off it, ye crazy old coot," swore a woman not dramatically younger than he, rolling her eyes. "That impudent gypsy *Ozrey* came in just a little before them, and ye didn't give *him* the third degree."

"We know who Ozrey is," the old man sniffed. "Never seen the likes of *these* two before."

There were murmurs and nods of agreement from more than a few villagers.

"We escaped from the enchanted castle," Aurora Rose explained calmly. "We were prisoners there and managed to escape the evil queen and her servants."

"We were chased by her demons. All the way here," Phillip added. "I killed the last one, who did this to me." He turned and showed the back of his head, torn and bloody.

And at *that* the crowd began to relax.

"I *thought* ye looked royal," a woman said, nodding her head knowingly.

" 'Swhy we have the wards," piped up an ancient lady, who had few teeth and many warts and a long, pointed chin. "Keeps the witch and her hellfire servants out of the town."

"For which we are indebted to you. Utterly," Phillip said with a graceful bow.

"Are there lots of other people in there?" another woman asked, looking worried. "Trapped?"

"Yes. We—we plan to get help. To *rescue* them."

There was no point in telling the whole story to these dream people who may have been asleep in the real world— or not in the real world at all.

"You'll need an army," a middle-aged farmer with a quilted vest said. A long piece of grass stuck out of his mouth.

"Aye. A big army. With siege machines and th'like," said another thoughtfully.

"You'd better not have your army tromping through my rutabaga patch!" a third farmer cried, pointing down to the ground with his finger like a judge. "I'll not have your army marching through here and ruining my rutabagas."

"We're not—there's not . . . All right, we promise," Phillip said, giving up. "No armies on anyone's rutabaga patch."

The farmer settled down, relieved.

"Well, then, come and refresh yourselves, you young heroes!" the crone at the cauldron cackled. "You're interrupting our party—you may as well join it!"

"We would be delighted," the princess said with a sigh.

The music started up again. Everyone began to clap, dance, or gossip, not bothering to disguise the curious stares they gave the newcomers. Someone handed them each a heavy-bottomed mug of hot raspberry wine. One sip of the sweet and syrupy drink went immediately to Aurora Rose's toes. Her foot began to tap to the music. She watched the children form a circle and begin a surprisingly complicated routine.

"Come!" a little girl said, running up to her and grabbing her hand. She looked at the princess with hope and awe; it was unlikely anyone as pretty or dressed-up as she had been to their village. Ever.

The princess, in turn, looked at Phillip.

"It's another trap," he said. "Probably."

"Doesn't feel like it," she said with a grin, and she let herself be dragged away by the little girl.

"Neither did the last two!" Phillip called after her.

The crowd cheered, and the adults joined together to make a larger ring around the children, dancing the opposite direction.

It was the exact opposite of the balls that Maleficent threw: no fancy dresses, no preening, no dissembling, no posing. The children were dancing for the sake of the dance itself. Energy, happiness, and light flew around, and Aurora Rose found herself swept up by it until she was laughing along with the little ones whose hands she held.

Phillip, on the other hand, looked uneasy; he kept smiling and toasting villagers but obviously didn't like the way that he was now separated from her by the ring of adult dancers.

The music slowed down. The circles paused in their gyres. Phillip moved forward and began to clap, relieved it was all over.

And then the music started up again.

The rings of dancers began their revolutions again.

"Wait now," Phillip said, to no one in particular.

No one heard, and the fiddlers played on.

Like a coach gradually accelerating on a downhill stretch, their strings plucked and thumped slowly at first . . . and then began to build speed.

The dancers followed suit, no longer attempting intricate steps but just circling round and round.

"Rose!" Phillip called, but she was swept up in the dance, her hair a golden smear, her smile a flicker that was there and then gone. Soon he could barely see the inner circle at all.

The musicians played faster. Their bows snapped back and forth across their fiddles like they were trying to saw them in half.

The dancers spun in circles so swift they became two blurry bangles of cloth and braids and feet and dust.

The adults put their joined hands together in the air and rushed into the center toward the children and Rose.

Phillip put his hand on his sword.

The music reached a fever pitch, the fiddlers pulling like their fingers would fall off. The notes sounded insane.

Phillip started to step forward . . .

. . . and then the music stopped. Just like that.

Everyone on the sides clapped madly. Both rings of dancers swayed, separated, and collapsed, all exhausted. They stumbled back to rest or have a drink.

The fiddlers shook their hands out and started again, a slow folk melody, to give everyone—including themselves—a chance to recover.

Aurora Rose's cheeks were ruddy and her smile was wild. She laughed when she saw the slow changes on Phillip's face: suspicion, then confusion, then grudging delight.

"I told you it didn't feel like a trap!"

"Neither did the last two," Phillip repeated, rolling his eyes. He started to hand her drink back, but she took both it and his own mug and set them down on a barrel, then grabbed his hand and led him out to the dance floor.

A reel was just beginning; a row of men and a row of women were curtsying and bowing to their partners across the way. The prince and princess tacked themselves onto the ends. If she had any doubts about the son of a king being able to perform a country dance, her fears quickly evaporated. Phillip gave her a not-too-courtly bow and immediately began the correct steps in perfect synchronicity with the boys and men around him.

She picked up her skirts and danced up to him as all the ladies danced up to—but did not touch—their partners. All they could do was look into each other's eyes, daring the other one to look away. The prince and princess's faces were less than a blush apart as she switched her feet in a series of tiny moves. She felt the heat from the drink spread back up through her body and flush her lips and cheeks . . .

. . . and then she was spinning back into her own line again, dizzy and giddy.

The lines moved, and they switched partners and clapped above their heads. Soon Aurora Rose was face-to-face with a short, bearded woodsman who had a cloth cap and surprisingly graceful feet. He was gentlemanly and had a serious expression, devoted to the dance . . . but gave her a wink when it was time to move on.

The music broke for a moment when a small child ran straight down the middle, crying and looking for his mother.

The princess immediately took him by his little hand and walked him around until they found her. The mother— unconcerned; it was a small village, with no real place to get lost—gave her thanks, but the boy kept staring back at the princess, awed at his royal rescue.

Everyone laughed and the dance restarted, and Aurora Rose was back with Phillip.

When it was time for him to swing her around, he put his full hand on her waist, thumb curving around her back so he had her entirely. She could feel the heat from his palm through the rich cloth and found herself swaying so he was supporting more of her weight than he really needed to. As if she would fall if he let go.

When he put his other hand on her waist to lift her up for the ladies' jump, he whispered in her ear. She didn't understand what he said at first, too focused on his lips just touching her ear, his warm breath on her cheek.

"Your dress."

She looked down when her whirling brain finally translated it.

She no longer wore the meringue-like light blue ridiculous thing. It was instead a strange mix of her outfit when she had lived in the forest and what she had escaped the Thorn Castle in. An old brownish skirt and black corset top—but with a golden shirt that flowed under the corset and over her hips like a tunic. The skirts were all ripped and in tatters.

And her shoes were once again gone.

She shrugged.

"It's *my* dream, isn't it?" she said, whispering in his ear.

Phillip raised an eyebrow, thinking about this.

And then the moment was over and they were returning to their lines.

After that dance ended a circle dance began, which was a little disappointing; she wanted to be close to Phillip again. But a dance was a dance, and she was having fun, so she joined in that one anyway—and the one after that, and the one after that. Phillip bowed out after a couple, his constitution for such diversions not as hearty as hers. He toasted her from the sidelines and was polite but not encouraging to the local girls who flirted madly despite his reticence.

Finally, he was forced to retreat to a quieter area where the horses were tied up and carts and wagons were parked for the evening.

The princess eventually took a break, collapsing next to Phillip on a pile of hay, leaning her hot and exhausted body next to him.

"Rose . . ." Phillip began.

"I know, I know, we need to go," she sighed, slugging down the last of his wine.

"Well, I don't know. . . ." He cast a worried look at the

sky. It was now fully dark and the stars were out. The bonfire blazed bright orange and red against the sky, smoke hazing the heavens. "Maybe we should spend the night here. It seems *safe*. I worry about another direct attack from M—"

He stopped what he was saying when a funny-looking man approached them. He had been hidden inside the prettiest of the covered wagons: peeling paint decorated the sides in a landscape of mountains against a blue sky. Once-brightly-colored pennants still flapped bravely.

The man was certainly not a local; his dress was just a trifle too fine and too untouched by the dirt a farmer or woodsman's life involved. His face was different, too, with a pointier nose and light blue eyes. He wore a multicolored cap that he touched when he sat down across from them.

"A fine night for a village dance," said he.

"Aye," Phillip said. "It is indeed. You don't seem like you're *from* this village, though."

"You don't neither," the man retorted, but toasted with his mug—a slightly dented metal one. "People say you're from that castle over there. The one where the witch keeps everyone prisoner."

"Yes," the princess said. "We escaped. We're going to go get help."

"And where are *you* from?" Phillip pressed.

"All over, my lad! All over! I'm Ozrey the traveling merchant," the man said, getting up and giving a little bow.

"Peddler of delights and displayer of fantastic finds. People come from all over when they hear I'm in town, to take a gander at my wondrous wares."

"Really," Phillip said. He didn't *quite* say it in disbelief, but Aurora Rose gave him a small kick anyway.

"Oh, I can see you're a sophisticated gentleman," Ozrey said with smile. "You've a sword of steel and have probably all sorts of boy toys at home. But *I've* been to the east and beyond, lad. I've been to Alexandria and Shanghai and Persia. I've traded with those who have been to R'lyeh and Carcosa. Tell me, have you ever seen anything such as *this*?"

Like a magician, he pulled out of nowhere a delicate wire bird cage, tiny and bell-shaped. But on the golden perch inside wasn't a real bird at all—it was a metal one, shiny and faceted like a gem. It had bright emeralds for eyes and a beak carved out of onyx.

"Amazing," Phillip said in wonder, putting his head close for a better look.

"Oh, that's nothing. Get a listen to *this*." Ozrey pressed a stud on the side of the cage and, suddenly, the bird came alive. It cocked its head and flapped its wings. Then it opened its beak and let out a pretty little trill just like a real bird.

"It's wonderful!" the princess breathed.

"She can sing real songs, too," Ozrey said with a proud

smile. "Not like you and me know, not the songs from around this great country, but songs nonetheless. Quite the companion on the long dusty roads."

He sighed, setting it down on the hay bale in front of him so the prince and princess could continue to admire it.

"That was from one of my trips long ago, to the east. Don't do that so much anymore. Mainly I come through these parts a couple times a year on regular rounds. Sell the good folks things they can't get here. Knives. Pots. The usual housewares. Pretty cloth from the city. And I pick up the things they can't get in the cities—mushrooms, wild herbs, the usual. Thought I'd stay for the party, but I'll be on my way tomorrow."

"Really?" Aurora Rose asked excitedly, finally drawing her eyes away from the bird and looking meaningfully at Phillip. "Maybe we can travel with you, for safety. You can hide us in your wagon."

Ozrey looked away, down at his drink, then over their heads toward the woods.

"Er, not that you wouldn't make pleasant enough company . . . but I'm afraid I've no desire to get the attention of that evil fairy back in there."

Phillip frowned.

"You *know* she will find out who helped you," the man protested. "Her spies are everywhere. I'm a coward, yes, but

I survived through more kingdomly squabbles and troubled times than many in my profession."

"We're not asking you to take us all the way through the woods," the prince said. "Just . . . part of the way. To the crossroads after the granite escarpment. We can part there."

"We can pay you," the princess added. "Um . . . somehow."

Ozrey started getting twitchy.

"If I *was* to take you, I couldn't take payment, now could I," he said, thinking desperately. "Not for helping the two of you out on your . . . *noble quest*. It would have to just be a good deed. Unless it gets me killed. In which case it was a stupid, stupid deed."

"It's a *good* deed," the princess suggested.

The man finally shook his head and stood up. "Well, I'll leave it to the fates like I always do. That way I don't make the decision myself. I can give myself up to what the gods will."

"How's that?" Phillip demanded.

"Well . . . can you sing, pretty bird?" the man asked, cocking his head at the princess.

"Yes . . . but . . ."

"So we'll have a singing contest!" Ozrey declared. "You against my own pretty bird here. You win, I'll take you wherever you want, as far as you want. *I* win, I'll take your man's pretty sword and hilt there."

Phillip put his hand protectively on his belt.

"We'll have no way to defend ourselves!"

"If you think a sword will defend yourself from Maleficent, you've already lost," Ozrey observed wryly.

Phillip shuffled his legs in exasperation but didn't contradict him.

"I'll wind her up once. Whoever sings longer without repeating a song wins. Is it a deal?"

Phillip looked at Aurora Rose.

The princess tried very hard not to roll her eyes—a habit she had picked up from the otherwise expressionless Lianna. The contest was a cinch. *Singing* was her thing: folk songs, religious songs, foreign songs, whatever the fairies taught her, whatever her music tutor or the minstrel did. Even her own made-up songs to while away the hours in the woods or her concerts in the castle.

In fact, this was very much like one of her performances. Just with higher stakes.

"Absolutely," she said.

"I'll even have the little wonder go first," Ozrey said, inserting a silver key into the thing's neck and winding. "Sort of gives you a head start."

The bird tipped back and forth once or twice on its perch, almost like a real one. But its movements were jerky and sudden, and its eyes didn't move, nor did it cock its head suspiciously at its audience, the way a real one might have. The carved-gem beak opened, and it began to sing.

The music that emerged was beautiful and perfect and unworldly, like tiny bits of metal or glass tinkling on a stone floor in surprising order. The notes were a little strange to the princess's ears, but she absorbed the new sounds eagerly—to try them herself later. It was a happy little tune. Just the sort of thing you would imagine a pretty windup toy would play.

And all too soon, it was over.

"Your turn, young miss," Ozrey said with a little bow.

For now the princess wouldn't show off; she would just concentrate on winning.

Without thinking she sang, *"Douce—douce dame jolie. . . ."* The last words from the minstrel before Maleficent's guards had hauled him away. In memory of him, she sang the whole thing through, which he didn't have a chance to.

She felt rather than saw Phillip watching her, enchanted.

When she finished, even Ozrey touched his cap again.

"That was amazing, miss, if you don't mind me saying."

"Rose, I've heard you sing before, but . . ." Phillip was at a loss for words. "Your voice is so sweet! Like an angel, or something perfect and pure . . ."

She blushed.

"All right, birdie's turn," Ozrey said.

It sang again. Another happy, spritely tune.

The princess sang again. A comic—but not too bawdy—ballad to match its tone.

The bird sang again.

Its tunes grew more complicated; sometimes it sang two notes at once to make a little chorus with itself.

The princess wasn't concerned in the slightest. She had a repertoire of hundreds of ballads, canticles, and rounds to choose from.

Slowly its songs began to change . . . from the simple country airs to tunes that were sweeter and sadder. It held its notes and trilled in minor keys.

When it sang, the princess listened, enraptured.

At the same time, she was impatient for it to end so she could begin her own response. It was almost like she didn't even care about the contest anymore.

Finally, it sang a song so sad that even the windup bird's unnatural notes brought tears to all of the listeners' eyes. Aurora Rose gave it an equally sad, shaky rejoinder. The thing paused for a long moment, fluttering its wings nervously.

It had used up its library of music.

Somewhat regretful the show was over, Phillip turned to Ozrey. "Well, seems like—"

And then it began to improvise.

Tentatively, at first. It began to sing a sad little tune—as if it was truly distraught over almost losing the contest. But then little arias built on themselves, climbing higher and higher, in dizzying complexity. The music turned joyful again as the windup toy sang its clockwork heart out.

Without waiting for her turn, the princess joined in, eager to be a part of such a beautiful thing.

Their duet was like nothing she had ever experienced. She thought she was following the bird, but then maybe sometimes the bird was following her. Could a toy do that? Or was she imagining it? She sang notes she had never hit before, higher than she had ever dared. Song *was* her gift. And for the first time ever, she was fully enjoying it.

"Rose . . ."

Phillip's voice came from far away, a little worried sounding. She almost laughed, almost missed a note. She would win the contest. The bird would wind down.

But, she hoped, not yet.

Her throat began to hurt a little.

The bird trilled an arpeggio that soared up and up—she sang a descant that climbed beyond.

She closed her eyes and held a single tone for what seemed like forever; she opened them to look up at the night sky. Each of her notes, each of the bird's notes, rose and became a star. A little bit of her soul, her voice, caught and rose and would now glitter in the heavens forever. Why hadn't she seen this before? She could sing the sky.

She held one note for so long that little flecks of blood came out of her mouth.

It was perfect, not disturbing. Her blood became tiny red stars, joining the notes and other stars; she was part of it all, her body and spirit and the music and the universe.

Then a single irritatingly off and banal note ruined everything.

The princess came to, forced to refocus her eyes closer to the earth; a tree branch resolved itself in black detail against the sky. Perched on it like a lump was a nightjar, an ugly, large-mouthed brown-and-black bird. It *chucked* and whistled its ugly call out into the void.

Was it looking at her?

Its voice was scratchy but nuanced, unlike the toy bird. It *carried*. Over the fields and even above the blurry din of the village dance and band, instead of disappearing up into the sky or falling tinkling to the ground, the male bird was calling plaintively for a friend, for a mate.

The princess forgot her song.

Ozrey was looking at her intently. Otherwise neither he nor Phillip was moving. But the little mechanical bird kept singing and glittering and jerking back and forth in its cage.

Its notes sounded silly. Toylike.

Aurora Rose suddenly felt sick and pained, her throat burning. She blinked at the little windup bird.

"That's it, then," Ozrey said, suddenly unfrozen. He

spoke nervously. "You've stopped singing. You've lost the bet."

Aurora Rose looked back up at the nightjar. She raised up a graceful hand. There was no reason the carnivorous and mostly shy bird should leave its perch and alight on her finger.

But it did.

How did she know it was carnivorous?

It burbled happily and did everything but rub its strange, whiskered beak on her hand like a cat. She stroked the back of its head.

"I'll have your sword," Ozrey continued.

"There *was* no bet," Aurora croaked, her voice ruined. "Another trap. He . . . tricking me . . . singing forever."

Phillip looked confused at first. His gaze moved from Ozrey to his bird to the princess and her bird, and then back again.

Then his face went white with rage.

"I should kill you where you stand," he swore, starting to pull out his sword.

Aurora Rose opened her hand and the little brown-and-black bird flew away. Saved by a creature of the forest. They remembered her and found her, even in her dreams.

Whatever happened, if she wound up alive and back in the real world, she would never, *ever* forget them. No matter what path her life took.

Ozrey wasn't reacting to either the prince's threats or the turn the situation had taken. His eyes were now strangely opaque, like Lianna's.

"How did you get past the protective wards, demon?" Phillip demanded.

"Oh, everyone knows old *Ozrey*," the thing that obviously wasn't human said with a leer. "Everyone helps open the gate and lets him get his wagon through. You might say my current . . . *role* . . . fits like a second skin. No one sees through it."

The princess coughed, the wounds in her throat itching and scratching. A small gobbet of blood sprayed out onto the ground.

"You do have a lovely voice, *Princess*," Ozrey said with a nasty sneer.

Phillip made an inarticulate sound of rage. Before she could stop him, he drew his sword and drove the blade into Ozrey's heart.

The thing that looked like a person squealed like a pig. He shuddered and vibrated and shook in a way that no normal creature did when it died. Black oily smoke poured out of his eyes and nose and the wound in his chest. But unlike the others, his skin began to collapse. Great swags of it bagged and pooled in dry puddles on the ground.

The smoke dissipated with a hiss and a terrible smell. All that was left was the thin shell of the original Ozrey, the human-shaped husk a demon had hollowed out and moved into like a mummer into a costume.

The princess turned and closed her eyes. *It's not real,* she mouthed silently to herself. But *was* there a real Ozrey, in the real world? Was he dead now? Was there a real demon in the real world as well? Was *it* dead, too? Where did the dream end and reality begin?

"Well . . . at least he won't report this back to her now," Phillip said shakily, wiping his sword on the grass again.

The princess coughed—a little less blood this time. She really *would* have kept singing forever. Someday, when she was awake, this would be a hard-to-keep-hold-of dream memory. The only thing that would remain would be a *feeling* that she had sung with the angels, that she was one with the universe.

And she would never do it again.

She wished she could talk so she could tell Phillip how she felt, how Maleficent ruined everything and hurt her in ways she never expected. But it was too painful—in every sense of the word

"Let's . . . get out of here," Phillip suggested. "Hide until morning, in case there are more of her spies around. We'll go out to the far fields—keep warm in a haystack maybe."

She didn't argue, exhausted and dispirited and unable to speak.

Out in the meadows, the last insects of summer were chirping comfortingly and the ground smelled of dry grass and clean dirt. The princess drew out of herself some, marveling at all the sensations. But she was still caught in her memories of being stuck in the castle, where all was sterile and dead.

Phillip chose a large pile of hay and dug into it, making a little hollow for them. After she clambered in and settled down, he got in next to her . . . then pulled out his sword and placed it between them.

She gave it, and him, a curious look.

"They do it in fairy tales?" he said. "You know, to keep from . . . It means that I can't . . . It's sort of symbolic. Oh, never mind. If anyone ever asks you about tonight, you can say there was a double-bladed sword between us and your chastity was safe."

She raised her eyebrows at him wearily. It was a strange thing to be concerned about right then. Considering none of this was even real.

"Just forget about it. Go to sleep. Rest. Whatever one does in a dream when one is tired," Phillip said, taking off his cape and laying it over both of them. "I know *I'm* exhausted."

She curled up, her back to him. It would have been warmer if the sword wasn't there. She wanted to be held. By

Phillip or her fake aunts or a real mother or father—or even Maleficent, the way she imagined her to be.

Tears began to fall silently from her eyes and soaked the hay under her head, faster and faster, until she finally slept.

And that's when she finally woke up.

To Sleep, Perchance to Dream

Someone was shaking her.

Aurora rolled over and saw concerned-looking adults—serious people in somber clothing and gold medallions of office. They crowded over her.

"Wake up, Your Highness. It's over. You're queen now. Maleficent has been overthrown. Your parents were, unfortunately, lost. We need you back at the castle. We can get you there. It's all a terrible mess."

Aurora blinked and let herself be pulled up. They were very insistent. And a little rough. She turned once to look at the prince, who should still have been sleeping, but it was like she couldn't see him.

"Phillip," she croaked, her voice still hoarse from the contest.

"Later," the apparent leader said. "You've a lot to take care of, my lady. Excuse me, I mean Your Majesty. I am the castellan—I worked for your father, the king. And now you."

She was shuffled to a waiting carriage, golden and royal, pulled by four beautiful chestnut horses. Before she could give them a friendly pet, the door was opened, she was ushered in, and they immediately set off.

She was bounced around and sleepy and sick, and in no time at all, they were out of the forest and pulling up to the castle—which was neither covered in vines nor looked like it ever had been; this was how she knew she was finally awake.

The moat was back and filled with water, and they crossed over the drawbridge and through a bailey uninterrupted by survival gardens or rain catchers. It was crowded with normal life: peasants, tradesmen, merchants, farmers, and animals.

"You must speak to the people," the castellan was saying. He held her arm as she stumbled out of the carriage, unable to tear her eyes away from the scene. "Your parents would have wanted this."

"My parents?" She blinked in the bright late-morning light.

"Please, Your Majesty, there is time to explain all that later," he said. There were lines on the castellan's face and a single age spot near his serious, straight brows. He wasn't a pretty person or an ugly person, either. That was another reason she knew she was awake and this wasn't a dream.

They pushed her into the castle and up a flight of stairs; someone hastily threw a purple velvet cape around her shoulders to cover up her rags; someone else stuck a very golden—and very heavy—diadem on her head. Her neck bent under its weight. A scepter was placed in her right hand.

Then she was shoved in front of a large window—the same window where she had last seen Maleficent, ordering her capture.

Horns sounded. The chaotic crowds below suddenly turned, almost as one, to look up at her.

Aurora stood as tall and erect as she could, trying not to gape like a goldfish. She was still sleepy, and her mind was clouded and the crown was heavy and the cape was hot. There were strands of hair in her face that were very tickly.

What should she say? What *could* she say to all of those expectant faces below?

What had happened, really?

She had fallen asleep . . . and then . . . Phillip said the fairies put everyone in the kingdom to sleep . . . and then they were ruled in the nightmare world by the undead Maleficent . . . and now they were free by means she didn't understand. But their king and queen were dead—her mother and father, whom she had never known in either world.

Didn't she get a moment to mourn that?

"Good people," she tried to shout. It came out as an ugly, croaking whisper. "You are now free."

Everyone looked expectant; a few people clapped.

Obviously, those who actually heard what she said knew that already.

"I am now your queen," she strained to say as loudly as she could. "Your old king and queen, my parents . . . are . . . gone. I guess? I am your *new* queen. And I'll try to do that to the best of my abilities. Being queen, I mean. From now on."

There was scattered, confused applause.

The castellan pulled a hand over his face. Men around him in important floppy hats looked similarly disappointed.

"Come, there are other things to be done," he said, trying to sound optimistic. "Much has fallen behind because of recent events."

She was whisked away from the balcony and pulled back downstairs. No one took the scepter, crown, or cape away. She wished they would.

They spirited her into the private audience chamber, the one she had never entered when she lived with

Maleficent. It was where the queen consulted with her closest advisors, where only the most serious claims were brought before her.

Aurora was plopped down in the large throne-like chair at the end of the room. The wood was hard and uncomfortable under her; she wished she could bunch up the cape and use it as a cushion.

This was also how she knew she was finally awake.

Men and women of all stations loitered at one end of the room, looking impatient and angry.

Another important-looking fellow immediately approached her. From his black velvet ensemble and pretty buttons that looked like coins, Aurora decided he was the treasurer.

"Your Majesty," he said. "The emergency coffers are dangerously low. Should there be a blight this year, we have nothing left to rely on."

"A blight?"

"Of *wheat*," he said impatiently. "As there was a decade ago."

"A wheat blight," she said, still unsure what that meant.

"Your Majesty, what shall we do?" he pressed politely, if impatiently.

"What . . . protocol . . . does one normally follow in these cases?" she asked, wondering if she had a right to feel proud about how well she had phrased the question. Didn't it sound regal?

"I recommend we raise taxes immediately," he said with a shrug. "An emergency tax of an additional five percent multure, plus a geld of two and a half. That should cover it."

"All right," she said slowly. "Let's do that. . . ."

There were howls of fury and stomping. She jumped in her throne, shocked by the outburst. The treasurer rolled his eyes.

"What is wrong?"

"They don't want to pay taxes," the castellan explained from where he stood on the other side of the throne—with her in between him and the angry crowd. "They think running a kingdom is free."

"What's a tax?" Aurora whispered.

The castellan gaped at her. Then he shook his head and turned away.

She turned back to the treasurer.

"What's a tax?" she repeated.

"Your Majesty," he said through gritted teeth. "Now is not the time for a lesson in basic economics. Now is the time for swift, decisive leadership. We need a decision. Now."

"I can't without knowing what all this means!" she protested.

"What kind of queen is *she*?" a storm-faced, craggy old

man with religious vestments spat. "What *is* this we've been left with?"

Aurora looked desperately through the crowd, hoping for a friendly face. But *all* of their expressions ranged from hate to confusion to disappointment. She wanted to run. She just wanted to get out of the room as fast as possible and run as far as she could. Back to the village where they had found her. Back to the woods. Back to her old hiding places in the dreamworld castle. She gripped the armrests on the throne to keep herself from leaping up and fleeing.

"What do I do?" she asked.

The castellan just shook his head again in disgust.

"What do I do?" she asked again, louder.

"WHAT DO I DO? WHAT DO I DO?" she screamed.

No one would answer.

Awakening. Sort Of.

"What do I do, what do I do, what do I do, what do I do?"

Phillip was shaking her.

She screamed hoarsely and constantly until her eyes finally registered the hay around her, the night outside, Phillip's face lit by the stars.

"Rose? Are you okay? Rose? It was just a nightmare." Then he paused, realizing how ironic and weird that sounded.

She blinked for a moment, taking it all in.

Then she began to weep.

"What's the matter? Rose?"

He put his arms around her and pressed her face to his

shoulder. Now someone was finally holding her, but she was too overwrought to enjoy it properly.

"My *gifts*," she said, still coughing a little. "The fairies gave me *grace* and *beauty* and *song*. That's what Maleficent was trying to trap me with: beauty and song."

"Yes," Phillip said, a little confused. His deep brown eyes were even darker with concern. He picked a strand of hair out of her face and laid it back with the others. "But we beat her! She didn't win. She *won't* win."

"No," Aurora Rose said, trying to form the words clearly despite her shakiness and hoarseness. "You don't get it. They gave me *beauty* and *song*, and then I was left in the woods to grow up for sixteen years before being handed over to you. I don't know *anything* about ruling. I don't even really know what *taxes* are. I was in the *woods* in the real world. In the dreamworld, I hid like a mouse and then organized *balls* and *parties*."

"Oh," Phillip said.

"Oh," he said again. "Well, my sisters aren't exactly being taught how to lead an army into battle. . . ."

"But they're not an only child!" she cried, instantly regretting it. Her throat burned. "Even if Maleficent was right—even if my parents were hoping to have a male heir after me, they *didn't*. Shouldn't they have had some sort of plan B?"

"Well . . ."

"And I'll bet your sisters are taught *something*," she went on. "I'll bet they know how to sew or organize the kitchen staff or . . ."

"Of course," Phillip said without thinking. "Bianca is known quite widely for her skill in embroidery, actually. And Brigitte began to take over some hostess duties after my mother died. My dad said that she actually had some quite innovative ideas about how to peacefully handle the tolls on the northern trade route. . . ."

The princess let out an incoherent, strangled cry of rage.

"Sorry," he said quickly.

"*WHAT ARE BEAUTY AND SONG GOOD FOR?* To a princess *or* a queen? It's not like I could join a wandering band of troubadours. These 'gifts' have nothing to do with running a castle or a country. And everything to do with being a perfect pretty wife for the prince I was engaged to marry *when I was a baby*."

"Hey, now," Phillip said slowly. "We fell in love. . . ."

"I know, I know, that's not the point," she said, irritably scratching her hands through her hair like a crazy person. She sort of remembered loving him, but it was strangely secondhand, mixed in with all the other memories that didn't feel quite real. Now she had no idea what she felt for him.

She began to weep again. Exhausting, racking sobs from

a girl with two false childhoods and too many memories and no past; grace and beauty and song and nothing more. And of course, despite the muddy tracks of tears down her cheeks, dusty with wheat chaff, and her tangled hair, and her strange dress, she was beautiful.

Phillip hugged her and stroked her hair down.

"Shhh. Try to get some more sleep. Or rest at least. We can't go anywhere until the sun comes up, so we might as well conserve our strength. I promise: no more nightmares."

The princess didn't want to fall asleep again.

But she did, and it was dreamless.

The next morning, she was woken by something uncomfortably sharp cutting into her side. Irritably, she moved aside and saw that it was Phillip's sword. Despite her resentment, she couldn't help admiring the delicately traced motifs winding their way up the grip from the pommel, the golden vines and decorated initials, the carefully faceted and inset gems.

She cautiously picked up the blade. It was lighter than she had expected but heavier than she could easily manage. Even to her inexperienced hand, it felt extremely well balanced; though it would take force for her to swing it, she could manipulate the tip easily with just a turn of her wrist. She ran her left hand down its sharp edges, feeling metal that was kept clean and sharp and grew noticeably colder the longer she had it out in the air. There was a tiny recent nick on the left side.

She put it down carefully next to Phillip. She was stretched beyond her physical limits, murky-headed, exhausted, and weak. Apparently, you *did* need sleep in the dreamworld, even once you knew it was a dream.

Phillip slept harder than she, innocent of troubling thoughts and incoherent pasts. It was quite a while before his handsome features began to twitch and his spirit began to surface to the waking world.

Aurora Rose watched him, contemplating his boyish face, which had just begun to lean out in the way of a man. Although her mind kept getting stuck on the concept of love at first sight, she could understand being struck by those looks. And already she was slowly being won over by his optimism and general wholesomeness.

But to promise yourself forever to someone you had just met?

Life in the woods must have taken an even greater toll on her patience and mind than she had thought.

Still . . .

Some pleasant dream pulled his lips into the tiniest smile.

Aurora Rose leaned forward with some idea of trying a kiss—a small one, before he woke up—just to see . . .

But suddenly, he was moving, stretching, and running a hand through his hair.

The princess hastily sat backward. He didn't notice.

"Morning! Boy, I haven't spent a night in a haystack in *years*," he said amiably.

"You've done this *before*?" she asked in surprise.

The prince looked chagrined. "You sort of chafe under the whole 'crown prince' bit after a while. You sneak out for a good adventure with your best lads. Hunting, hitting the taverns . . . waking up in an orchard with your head pounding and *starving* for that grouse you swore you were going to get . . . Don't look at me like that; I'm not the *first* prince to do so."

She wasn't sure what look her face made. It was an amazing, rebellious idea. She had never considered *actually running away* from anyone, even her aunts, except for that one night in the forest.

"Was . . . was your father angry?"

"Oh, you have *no idea*," Phillip said with a rueful grin. "He took my sword and bow away and forbade the stables from releasing my horse, Samson, to me. And I had an extra chapter of Cicero every night *for two weeks*. CICERO! The man couldn't end a sentence if there was a dagger at his throat. I mean, I guess there was, eventually. But it was totally worth it, though. For me, I mean. Not Cicero."

They got up, brushed away the worst clumps of dried

grass and dirt, adjusted their clothes, and set off again. The village was starting to come fully alive in the morning dream sun. The woodsmen had left a long time ago, but the other men and women were tending their kitchen gardens, heading out to the fields, going to forage in the forest with baskets to fill with berries and mushrooms. The *tink tink tink* of a smithy cold-forging something small echoed across the flat ground. The animals grazed or wandered or dozed or chewed contentedly. A couple of old palfreys hung around a tree, heads together like a pair of gossips.

"We could steal a horse . . ." Aurora Rose said slowly. "That would be faster than walking."

"No," Phillip said immediately. "No, we couldn't."

"But it's just a dream—who cares?"

Even as she said it, she wasn't sure if she believed that statement herself.

"So we could just steal and kill and rape and plunder and it doesn't matter?" Phillip said as if it was something he had already deliberated in his own head. "I don't believe that. We're still the people we were when we were awake. It's not . . . it's not always the *result* of the decision that's important; it's how we make those decisions. It's the sort of people we are. Oh, I'm not making any sense."

"Yes, you are. I wouldn't know how else to put it. There's more to it for me, though. I've lived two lives, and each seems equally real—and equally imaginary. I was telling myself before we met—this time—that all I have is my own eyes and hands to tell me what's real. Who knows how long I'll be living in *this* version of my life? It *seems* real to me. So I'll act like it is. Whether it's fairies or castles or evil queens or thorns . . ."

She stopped, thinking about the thorns.

How they disappeared under her touch.

"Yes? What is it? Thorns?" Phillip put a hand on her back, trying to push her along.

How her dress had changed . . .

"I want porridge," she said, unmoving.

"*Porridge?* Look, I know you're hungry—I am, too, *famished*—but we can't linger in the village anymore. We can't trust *anyone*; you've seen that. We'll grab something along the way. Nuts, a grouse, maybe . . . just talking about one earlier made me hungry. . . ."

Aurora Rose shook her head and set her jaw. "In the last few months at the castle—or minutes, or whatever they are in the real world—I started to see things. Things I *wanted* to see. Pictures of the way the world was before—well, before the fake apocalypse was supposed to have happened. I saw a vision of a bunny."

"A *bunny?*"

"Yes, a bunny. I wanted more than anything to see and

touch a real rabbit. And one appeared. And then the fairies appeared. And then when I was escaping, I sort of wished that the thorns that held me would let me go. And . . . they did."

Phillip looked at her, still confused.

"They did?"

"Could you please stop just repeating the last thing I said and actually *listen* to me? It's *my dream. My* touching the spindle caused all this. I'm the first one who fell asleep under her spell. It's why Maleficent had to lie and make up a sort of reason for us all to be trapped together; *she doesn't have complete control of this world.* Or whatever it is. It's part of me. You said so yourself."

"All right, that makes sense," Phillip said in a Serious Voice, arms folded and face frowny. "But what does this have to do with porridge?"

"*I want porridge!*" she said, exasperated. "That's all. I wanted a bunny before and *it* appeared, and now I want porridge. The way my aunts used to make it on cold mornings. Warm and buttery, with rich toasted acorns in it."

"Acorns? Really? That sounds . . . um . . . I mean, it's an interesting gastronomic choice."

She rolled her eyes. "We lived in the middle of a *forest*, Royal Prince. It was what we had. And a real treat in the middle of winter."

Then she proceeded to ignore him.

She closed her eyes and cupped her hands. She prayed and wished and imagined and begged.

Phillip stayed politely silent—though he did look around, sigh a little, and do all sorts of other things to obviously fret over the passage of time.

She tried to call up the feel of the wooden bowl in her hands: it warmed almost like flesh where the wood was thin and the heat of her fingers and the hot porridge mingled. She summoned the smell, a mix of dairy and things of the earth and the tall green grass and the woods. Sometimes there was even a dollop of honey on top.

She thought so hard she felt like she had to go to the privy.

Her concentration faltered for a moment when she distractedly wondered if that ever happened to Maleficent when she was performing an incantation. But after a few seconds she was back in her dream of porridge.

Time passed. . . .

"GOOD LORD!"

The smell in her head was giving way to a real scent in her nose now, with even that faint, almost *un*tasty burnt smell the acorns sometimes gave off.

She smiled and opened her eyes.

In her hands was a cracked wooden bowl full of porridge, just like she remembered.

"Can you get me some eggs and a drumstick?" Phillip

asked eagerly. "Maybe a tankard of beer to go with it?"

"Eat the porridge, greedy bird," she said, smiling.

"Oh, all right," he said with a sigh. "It is certainly a *lot* better than nothing. Well done and all! Shall we use our hands?"

She tried to summon two spoons. But which ones? The big wooden paddle Merryweather stirred their soup with? Or tiny teaspoons for fancy afternoons? Or . . .

Each one flitted up in her mind and then disappeared.

She shrugged apologetically. "I can't concentrate. Too hungry."

"Well, this won't be the first time," Phillip said, wiping his hands carefully on his cape. "Let's dig in!"

They did, giggling. As she licked the first scoop and the warm, familiar cereal filled her mouth, so too was she— filled with a warmth and happiness that she hadn't known in a long time.

Interlude

"I never realized just how infinitely boring the prattle of human teenagers was," Maleficent drawled. But her voice was even thicker than irony required; she seemed slow . . . like a mechanical bird winding down. "I hope we don't have to put up with much more of their *fascinating* discussion of philosophy and the nature of reality. Or the culinary delights of porridge."

"I thought the part with the porridge was fairly interesting," Lianna spoke up, perhaps emboldened by her mistress's weakness. "Especially the part where she *summoned it out of the air.*"

Maleficent's yellow eyes flicked toward her.

"Yes . . . that *was* interesting. And troubling. Who knew the girl had it in her?"

"You didn't," Lianna pointed out tonelessly. "There is much more to her than you originally thought. Considering how she has evaded all your traps—even the *particularly* clever nightmare inside the nightmare. It will be harder to kill her now that she is beginning to unlock the power of her own dreamworld."

"I don't need to *kill* her," Maleficent said with a satisfied smile. "All I need to do is *delay* her. She has one hour and two minutes to figure out how to defeat me and wake up. If she is in my power when the clock strikes twelve and the next day begins . . . I win.

"But you're right," Maleficent said thoughtfully, swirling the green and red liquids in the orb of her staff. "It might be time to step up the direct assaults on her personage. I need the work of my cleverest, strongest servants! *Eregral, Slunder, Agrabrex*, to me!"

Large, slow-moving, grinning black forms congealed from the shadows in the corners of the room.

And Lianna's opaque eyes might have shown a hint of concern.

They Hadn't the Foggiest

Hours later, it was still early . . . and Aurora Rose was already exhausted. Despite the porridge, her feet were dragging; it was probably before noon, and they had already walked at least six miles. She tried not to complain or slow down. Neither seemed like a princessy thing to do.

Instead of burning off entirely, the morning mist had risen and thinned out and now covered the sky loosely, like thousands of baby spiders leaving trails of silk behind them. The sunlight, so bright and yellow before, was sickly gray. The air was damp and chilly.

She kept her eyes on the ground to prevent tripping. The shadows were imperceptibly fading along with the light. Some colors in the background stood out more, though, like bright little poisonous mushrooms and the quick tail of an orange salamander. But everything else became shades of black and white and gray.

Sounds grew strange. If her heel crunched dead leaves, sometimes it seemed silent; sometimes it echoed loudly off rocks and logs.

"When are we going to get there?" she asked, trying not to sound whiny. Her throat still hurt.

Phillip sighed. "Honestly, if today is *entirely event free*— no more demons or sudden ravines or that many of your, um, spells—which are completely not your fault!—then just another half a day or so, I would guess. A few hours."

"All right." She took a deep breath, trying to be brave and stalwart like a prince.

But it wasn't long before the fog began to settle in earnest. At any other time, she would have been simply fascinated. The girl who was trapped in a castle had never seen anything like it, really, and the girl who was raised in the woods wasn't afraid of anything from the natural world.

But now . . . there was something *creepy* about it.

They passed through thick patches of gray clouds whose colony droplets were so large she could almost make out each individual one. Water seeped out of everything like magic; she saw a bead of dew appear and pull itself together at the tip of a pine branch like a living thing. For a moment she had a glimpse of the black-and-white world reflected in it, in reverse, before it fell silently to the ground.

The fog found its way through her clothes, which became heavy and damp. And then hot and itchy and freezing and itchy as her legs and body moved beneath them.

A few times it was so hard to see that they almost stepped off the path. Phillip let out an unprincely oath as he twisted his ankle on an exposed root.

The land began to slope downhill and the fog poured down beside them, rolling like a slow-moving liquid. Tendrils shot out before the rest of the clouds, as if feeling out the way. It curled and rippled around obstacles like trees and stones.

The princess began to be genuinely frightened.

"Here," Phillip said, stopping. "You look miserable. Take my cape—it will keep the worst of the damp off."

She turned to argue with him. Wondered if he would think less of her if she reached for his hand.

But fog quickly filled the space between them. The prince's body already seemed to fade and dissolve into gray. As he took off his cape and swirled it, the fog flowed along, blanketing him completely.

". . . not cold at all the splurble burbly . . ."

His words sounded strange and distant.

"Phillip?" she called out uncertainly.

"Right here." He sounded odd, like the words died inches from his mouth, like the mist stopped them and they fell to the ground. "Hang on, the . . ."

Whatever he said next was muffled.

"Phillip?"

She walked several feet to where she thought he was.

There was nothing but a wall of swirling white.

"Phillip?!"

She spun around. The fog made little trails behind her skirts and hair.

Finally, there was a muffled response, a little exasperated sounding.

"Where are you?" she demanded.

Her heart began to pound. She could *hear* it. She could hear that and the breath in her own ears and nothing else. Not even the noise of the pebbles she knocked around as she spun desperately looking for the prince.

She knew she should stay where she was. Somehow she knew that, from either growing up in the woods or some long-buried instinct that every child is born with. She should stay still like a fawn and let Phillip find *her*. If both of them moved around, they would be lost.

Harrumphhh.

There was a strange noise, like a grinding or a whuffing. Woods Aurora—*Rose*—thought it sounded a little like an angry bear. But it wasn't quite. It wasn't an entirely *natural* noise.

"Phillip?" she whispered. She wasn't sure whether she should scream so he could find her, or stay silent and let whatever that noise was pass by without ever seeing her.

Silence all around.

Heavy silence.

The silence of hiding under the stairs in a castle when everyone was looking for her—her *parents* actually looking for her, for once. All she had ever longed for was her parents wanting her, searching her out . . . but when suddenly it happened, she felt uncertain and had to ask *why*. Why *now*? Fear of the unknown reasons. And so she had hid, and the castle was mostly silent except for angry yells far away and the stomps of footsteps close by.

But they never saw her.

That kind of silence.

Her mind filled the empty, swirling fog with images.

Eyeless, leering, toothy smiles. The piggish bodies of Maleficent's demon guards. The strangely black and fluid forms they took out here—which would fit in so well with the fog.

And still there was silence.

And then the *nearly* silent scrape of gravel on the path.

"Phillip?"

Nothing.

Then: *Harrrummmpppph.*

The princess ran.

She aimed for what she thought was deeper into the forest; it didn't matter—it was all around her. She would feel safer under the trees. Things didn't look for princesses, for people, under trees.

Right?

She looked behind her; white streaked with gray to mark where she had come from, like a sticky shadow.

She looked ahead. It, too, was blank white and—

Thunk.

She smashed her head into the thick and spiky branch of a dead pine. An offensive, white-hot pain exploded from her forehead. She reeled backward, hitting her back on another tree.

Her right eye was clouded; when she tentatively put up her hand to see what was wrong, it came away covered in hot, fresh blood.

Harroomph.

She bit her lip and wiped the rest of the blood out of her eye.

"Phillip!" she cried halfheartedly.

This was like nightmares she used to have when she was very little, of being pulled away from her aunts, separated from them forever.

She watched the clouds twirl and swirl in front of her. *Something* was making them move. Something was making them slide and bubble, like foam on top of a pot being boiled clean.

She saw the smile first.

The black, toothless smile, wide and wider and then impossibly wide. Two yellow eyes above it opening into existence. And long, unlikely, skinny black arms, rising up to reach around and drag her in.

She screamed. A long, piercing, terrible scream—

—that never made it past her lips. Her mouth was open, and she felt her throat working and her lungs lose their breath, but no noise came out. Utter silence, despite how hard she screamed. No one would ever hear. . . .

The thing smiled even wider.

Aurora stumbled backward, hands out to either side, feeling for trees. There was nothing she could do. She couldn't run blindly deeper into the woods. She didn't have Phillip or even her own voice. She had *nothing*.

And then the last tiny part of her that was still Aurora Rose, angry and rightfully terrified, remembered it was *her* dream. She could have anything she wanted. If she knew what she wanted.

A sword appeared in her right hand. Without looking, she knew it was an exact replica of Phillip's. There would probably be a nick on its left edge.

The demon swayed sickeningly from one side to another, like a snake trying to decide which way to pounce.

Aurora Rose screamed again to give herself strength. But again, nothing came out.

The thing suddenly rushed at her. Inhumanly fast, with no warning.

She raised her sword.

In complete silence:

— Aurora Rose slowly bringing her arm down, her blade into the monster

— the thing twisting in surprise, spiraling around and around, turning its long neck and body back to regard her full-on

— her trying to scream for Phillip again, unable to make her lips shape the words, rocks in her mouth. Gripping her sword more tightly

— the demon dipping easily around her attack and circling her calmly. Two, three, four times as long as she thought it was. While she was trying to fight its front half, its endless tail forming coils about her legs

— bringing her sword down again on the flesh closest to her, sinking it all the way through with a strange, unlikely sound—

And suddenly, there was light and speed and *noise* again. The demon screeched and howled and whipped its forked tail around. The princess swung her sword again, trying not to lose her advantage by staring at where she had sliced the thing in half: the flat, raw wound and white-and-black ichor that issued from it. Its tail kept wiggling on its own while its head and body squirmed and drifted through the mist.

Sunlight slashed through the fog and suddenly her scream turned on, hoarse and ragged and horrible, and everything was bright and painful.

When her sword connected this time it made a ringing metallic noise—as if it had crashed against something equally metal and dangerous.

"*ROSE!*" Phillip cried out as he saw her raise her sword again.

It was *his* sword she had struck; it was his body she was aiming for. The fog had thinned some, and she could see his confused, defensive stance.

"You almost struck me . . ." he started to say, then noticed the piece of demon on the ground that twisted and sprayed viscous black blood from where she had hacked it off.

"But where . . ." he started.

The other half of the demon flung itself out of the fog at

the prince's face. Phillip immediately deflected the attack, hitting it to the side.

Before she could even think about it, Aurora Rose raised her sword and hacked at the thing again. While her blow didn't cut cleanly through this time, it *did* injure it, causing it to scrabble and scream on the ground, grinding its head into the dirt. Phillip took careful aim and stabbed the demon in the throat.

The two watched, heaving, as the thing hissed and died.

Phillip shakily ran his hands through his hair. It was unclear if he was recovering from the brief fight, the surprise attack, or Aurora Rose's almost killing him by accident.

"Nice job," he finally said, pointing at the two halves of the creature on the ground.

She looked at him—he was a little pale, to be sure, but he spoke as if she had just recited a poem from memory or some other little mundane thing. She didn't understand fully how he could be so . . . blasé.

"Thanks for the help," she said, trying to match his tone. Maybe it was the princely thing to do. "We . . . make a great team."

"We do indeed—although it seemed like you were doing pretty well on your own. A princess *and* a monster slayer. They'll be singing epics about *you*!" he said with a grin.

She gave a courtly curtsy in response. "All in a day's work."

"Nice *sword*," he added. "Where did you get it?"

She looked at the sword in her hand, which was balanced so well she had honestly forgotten it was there. It was almost a part of her already.

"Oh, this old thing? I, um . . . summoned it?"

"Handy," Phillip said, nodding.

The last bit of blood from the demon bubbled up and hissed into the ground. Its body faded.

"I wonder if there was a real demon in the real, waking world that matched this one," the prince said. "I wonder if it's dead over there, too."

"Well, it's dead *here now*. But there may be more. And we won't see them coming," she said, shivering. The fog was cold and swirled around them again. Icy little tendrils caught her ankles.

"Hey," Phillip said with a grin. "You know what *wind* is like, right?"

"Of course I know what wind is like! I didn't live in a windowless cave in *either* life. I'm not a . . ."

"So summon one and blow this all away!"

She stopped her rant and thought about what he had just said.

Of . . . course. Of course she could.

She closed her eyes.

She imagined the little bit of breeze that had managed to come through when she cracked a window in the castle.

The hot and dry—but not ostensibly tainted—air of the Outside. She remembered the bailey of the castle, the tiny dust devils that would sometimes wend their way across it, among the scattered and guerilla garden plots.

She remembered being in a meadow at the edge of the forest in the fall, feeling chilly but unable to stop watching the birds play in the growing ferocity of the air. The strong fliers, the jays and the woodpeckers and the crows, cavorted like eagles.

She felt something tickling her cheek.

She opened her eyes.

There was a small dust devil in front of her: it was lifting up twigs and leaves and scattering them, playing at her feet almost like a cat.

She arched an eyebrow—unconsciously imitating Maleficent.

The wind grew, widening its invisible arms and sweeping more detritus into its center. Then it shot straight up into the air. It stretched into the sky, its long, powerful tail whipping behind it. Everything loose and small was dragged up into its vortex: leaves, pebbles, the ends of the princess's hair and the tips of Phillip's cape—and the fog.

Great swathes of heavy gray mist funneled into the sky, turning the whirlwind dark.

The princess shielded her eyes as the sunlight grew

clearer and brighter, all of the darkness pulled away into the whirlwind.

In the forest surrounding them there were distant strange cries of demons being caught in the cleansing light.

It wasn't horrible, the princess realized.

It was strangely satisfying.

The winds grew wider and wider and slower and slower until they seemed to fill the sky . . . and then they gradually slackened, leaving the sky as clear and blue and perfect as a summer's day after a sudden thunderstorm.

Phillip was grinning like a boy watching a really good magic trick—even laughing out loud when it was over. He grabbed her and impulsively kissed her on the cheek—quick and hard and a little sloppy and wonderful.

Then he saw the blood on her face, the gash in her head.

"You're hurt!" he said, embarrassed that he hadn't noticed it before.

She shrugged. It hurt a little when she wiggled her brow; she could feel the skin pulling and cracking. Otherwise, it was almost unnoticeable.

"I was killing a demon," she said. "It happens in battle sometimes."

Phillip grinned.

"Right you are. Well, shall we?" he asked, indicating the path. She nodded and began to move forward, wishing she had summoned a belt and a sheath for her cumbersome sword. But she didn't have a good picture of what those things looked like from *either* life—and frankly, she was a little spent from summoning the wind.

"You know," he began casually, "even though the fog is gone, I think it's still safer if we hold hands. You know. Just in case. Don't want to get separated again."

"Of course," the princess said with a smile.

Somehow their footsteps were lighter now—despite the fog, the demon, the fear, and the blood. Somehow everything seemed easier and better.

She might not be able to remember her past correctly, and she still had to defeat Maleficent and deal with her parents . . . but she could summon and move things with her mind and had just killed her first demon. She could *do* it.

That was pretty great.

Double the Fun

The woods were definitely changing: Aurora and Phillip could no longer see the sky at all because of the ancient tall trees that stretched far overhead. Pines and other shaggy-barked species shot a hundred feet straight up on massive trunks, some of which were as thick around as a small house. The canopies that spread out at their tops blocked out most of the sun; only a rare dappled shaft made it through. But it didn't feel claustrophobic. The absence of light kept the underbrush low: moss on ancient fallen logs, puddles of shade flowers, mushrooms and tiny lilies. It was airy and endless like the largest cathedral ever imagined.

The prince and princess walked with light hearts, tiny figures in this primeval world, seemingly the only ones in it.

"We are now getting close to the heart of the forest—where the cottage should be," Phillip said cheerfully. "It doesn't *exactly* look like it does in the real world, but it's close enough. We should get there by late tomorrow morning."

But the more deeply they progressed, the more her memories came back.

Like suddenly being whacked in the head by a small rock, a crystalline image would explode in the insides of her mind, and she would reel for a moment:

— a hand that looked like hers but smaller, reaching for a perfect late-spring flower. A surprisingly large and yellow pollen-covered spider suddenly dropping out of its hiding place in the blossom's center

— her aunts not understanding the innate fear she had of a loud, violent thunderstorm, impatient and almost looking like they might rather be out there themselves but rocking her nonetheless, cuddling her close, uncomprehending but loving

— a sudden glimpse on one of her forest walkabouts at the edges of things: the end of the forest, the turrets of a castle . . .

Not only did the images come faster and longer, but each one raised a host of immediate questions and realizations that Aurora couldn't stop.

Why was I never brave enough to travel all the way to the castle?

Holy crow, that was my *castle!*

Wait, the real one. Without the thorns . . .

And then the headaches would begin in earnest.

Sometimes it wasn't a single image but a string of memories connected by a feeling or a thought. These hit her less like a rock and more like an angry bull, slamming her head and grinding her innards with its sharp hooves.

Like her studies, one of her aunts' whims. Several months of practicing beautiful runes that became gold no matter what she drew them with: ink and quill, chalk on rock, stick in mud. No problems at all remembering and copying them. Some flurry of realization from her aunts and then a replacement: twenty-five ugly letters that stayed the same color as the ink. These were just as easy to remember as the golden ones, though, and it was all a game. . . .

Not like learning in the world of the Thorn Castle. Not at all. The few things the fairies bothered to teach her came as easily as singing.

As the new/real memories revealed themselves, Aurora Rose found she had a growing collection of two different versions of the same scene, the same day, the same year— both of which fought for space and dominance in her mind.

She remembered being a young teenager, bored for days on end in the middle of the woods, impatient for something to happen, trying to hunt with the foxes, climbing trees as high as she could, lying in despair at their bases, no longer loving the happy, mindless burble of her aunts as they worked together to make dinner or wash the clothes.

Its sister memory in the Thorn Castle was of young Aurora confronting her neglectful parents, who, worse than being enraged by her sight, worse than ordering her out of their presence, just didn't care. Like she wasn't worth getting upset about. She found empty rooms in the keep and collapsed on couches for days, wondering what would happen if she died. Would anyone notice? She became hungry and would sometimes rally to find a bit of food, and she grew very, very dirty.

She didn't have time to succumb to these memories, to pass out. To be weak. To throw up and recover and stumble a few steps and then collapse again. Phillip had said that if she didn't have many more spells, they would be there in a couple of hours. And he was very patient.

But she *wanted* to go on.

Sometimes concentrating on one lovely thing about each memory helped her remain upright. Like the foxes . . . she had *hunted* with *foxes*! Beautiful red-coated beasts who sometimes tangled under her feet like cats and let her scratch their throats. That had really happened. Focusing on their beauty kept her walking—shakily—and kept her stomach from reeling.

Sometimes concentrating on one *enraging* thing kept her going.

How could the women who had loved her and rocked her and raised her *lie to her for sixteen years*? How could anyone do that and still claim to love you?

They could have told her the truth—that she was a princess in hiding—and at *worst* it would have been a lovely game for her to play when she dressed up. At best it would have been a distracting, interesting thing to ponder on her most monotonous days.

The jolt of fury about her false childhood in the woods and her aunts' betrayal of her trust was far stronger than her body's weak inclination to black out or lose breakfast. It even quickened her pace some.

But after several hours even that was getting hard to keep feeling worked up about and she found herself beginning to stumble.

"I think we'd better call it a day," Phillip suggested. "It feels like it's getting late—maybe an hour before sundown. Let's make camp and get an early start tomorrow."

She nodded, too tired to disagree or to say anything to make him feel better or to apologize. She sat there like a limp rag doll while he bustled around, pushing piles of unbelievably long, unbelievably soft pine needles into springy mattresses and clearing them entirely out of one area for a small fire. When he had the tinder and a nice little pyramid structure of twigs set up he coughed politely and pointed at it.

She nodded and flicked her finger.

In a moment, a cozy bright-orange fire was flickering, the only tiny light in the whole twilit forest.

Summoning a whole cottage might have been nicer—but it would have taken a lot more time and too much out of her.

Probably. She still wasn't sure how this all worked.

She didn't even have to snap her fingers or blink to make two bowls of porridge appear. Phillip tried not to sigh but took his as gratefully as he could manage.

"I think I understand a little how Maleficent's magic works," she said after a moment, thinking about magic. "The . . . events are different. But the feelings are the same," she continued slowly, trying to put it into words that made sense. "She's working with—she *worked* with—what was already in my head and just . . . gave it new pictures. Sort of. My 'confinement' in the castle was based on the feeling of being trapped. With no place to go, figuratively or literally. Nothing to do but pace my cage until I died. She built an entire world around that premise to keep me asleep and under her control. But in a weird way, she was the most interesting thing that happened to me in *either* life."

The direction her thoughts were taking was obviously making Phillip uncomfortable. He finished his porridge—still hungry, but not necessarily eager for more. He stretched back; despite his desire to press on, he was exhausted as well.

"Hey," he said, suddenly sitting up, eager. "Can I see your sword? The one you summoned?"

Glad to have *something* she could reward his patience with, she handed it over with a smile.

The prince pulled out his own to compare.

"It's truly amazing," he said, running his fingers over each. "A *perfect* copy."

"Funny, I never paid attention to swords before. Not even yours."

"Well, I didn't wear it openly when I traveled. I kept it under wraps, as it were. This is the sword of a royal prince— the son of a king. My father had it made for me when I turned sixteen. It would be dangerous to display openly."

"*Dangerous* to wear a *sword* where you can get to it quickly?"

"I am an *extremely skilled* swordsman," Phillip said gently. "But no match for a band of highwaymen. A feisty noble lad on a horse they might be willing to let pass. The son of a king is good for quite a bit of ransom."

"Ahhh," Aurora said, nodding. "So that's why I didn't see you with it when . . ."

She frowned, trying to bring up the memory.

"When . . ."

Phillip watched her uneasily.

"I never saw you with the sword," she said flatly. "Because you kept it hidden."

Phillip had a very unprincely, funny look on his face. Only she didn't find it funny at all.

"You never told me you were a prince."

"I was *going* to tell you," he protested. "I was going to tell you *that night*, in fact. . . ."

"That night?" she demanded. Despite her physical exhaustion she stood up, rage flushing her body straight. Her fists clenched of their own accord. "Why not, like, *immediately*? Just when was the *right* moment?"

"Rose, listen." He stood up and took her hands. She whipped them out of his fingers. "I was traveling that day to your father's castle. I was going to be formally introduced as a son-in-law to your parents and the rest of the court; to say hello to a bride I had never met and good-bye to a life I had barely begun to enjoy."

"So?" she demanded. "You decided you would have one last fling with some village girl or woodsman's daughter before being forced into a life of marriage?"

"No! *Listen*: I'm a prince. Outside of highborn ladies and princesses and what have you, you *can't* tell anyone you're a prince. Nobody likes you for just who you are. Girls . . . they want . . . they assume . . . everyone thinks they can *get* something if they have a prince."

His cheeks grew pinker and he began to stutter as he tried to explain. It did not change the severe look she gave him.

"As soon as you tell a girl you're a prince, they're all over you," he said desperately. "In the wrong way. They just hear *prince* and think riches or whatever. Especially if they get—I mean, if there's a—look, can we leave it at that?"

"No. No, we can't," the princess said. "You are . . . you *were* the one person I thought I could trust. The one person from my past. My real past. The love I forgot." Her lips began to twist, and she felt her nose seize up with incipient tears. "And it turns out *you*—also you, even you—*lied to me*! Like *everyone else in my entire life.* No one—*no one*—has *ever told me the truth about anything. Not even you.*"

"Well, *I* didn't know who *you* were . . . really . . . that you were a princess. . . ."

"Not my fault!" she snapped. "I didn't know that, either! Don't you *dare* think of blaming me or comparing us!"

Phillip took a deep breath. He looked up and around, as if trying to gather help from the sky or the air or the trees around them.

"I'm sorry. I really am. I realize there's no way to prove this to you now, but the day of our . . . of Princess Aurora and Prince Phillip's wedding, I told my dad I wasn't marrying the princess. I was marrying the peasant girl I met in the forest. Because everything else in your life might have been a lie, but my loving you wasn't. *Isn't.*"

She didn't say anything. She still glared at him, trembling with rage.

"I'm going to sleep now," she said through clenched teeth. "I'm putting *both* swords between us. I hope you cut your elbow."

They lay down on their pallets, Phillip sadly and wearily, she jerkily and angrily. She covered herself with pine needles. When he started to offer her his cape, she growled: *"Don't. You. Dare."*

He sighed and wrapped himself up.

"Good night," he whispered.

She turned herself on her side away from him. It was a long time before she finally fell asleep.

The next morning felt like just the sort of new beginning she needed.

Nothing was weird or indicative of anything magical or evil. She breathed in the clean air and listened to the breathtakingly still silence of the ancient forest. She looked up at the trees, feeling tiny and incredibly lucky and special. Small birds, hidden somewhere in the lightening not-gloom, made little echoey chirps.

She was overcome with the desire to *stay.*

This was nice. Here it was beautiful, and she had

incredible powers. Who knew what the real world held for her when all of this was done?

"Forgive me yet?"

And then all the exhaustion and emotional stress from the day before came crashing back down on her shoulders.

Phillip was on his side, chin resting on his hand, looking at her and trying to be fetching.

Aurora Rose grunted unprincessly and wished she had covers so she could roll over and pull them aggressively over her head.

"Please?" he asked, smiling winningly. He didn't *quite* bat his eyelashes.

"Let's just get this done with," she said, meaning *find the fairies, figure out how to defeat Maleficent, defeat Maleficent, and wake up.* And then deal with whatever aftermath there was. Were the two of them still engaged as prince and princess? What was she going to say to her parents? Everything made her irritable. Why couldn't he just have stayed asleep longer and let her enjoy the peace of the forest by herself for a few minutes? The rare peace of her own deep, innermost mind.

"Aw," he said with a pout. "What about a kiss? An 'I'll eventually forgive you' kiss?"

She stared at him, one eyebrow raised like Maleficent. The rest of her face was a very *un*Maleficent-like mask of shock and horror.

Then she let castle Aurora, ball-arranging princess Aurora, take over, and a smooth look of cool hauteur come over her face.

"I shan't even dignify that with a response."

She rose as primly as she could, resisting the urge to push the pine needles back into place as if she were making her bed, Briar Rose–style.

Phillip sighed dramatically and didn't get up, contenting himself with watching her. She kept her back to him.

Then Phillip came striding into the clearing, a string of fish over his shoulder.

"I was trying to think of some way of apologizing, but there don't seem to be any flowers here. In fact, there's not a lot of *anything* here, and I figured you'd be sick of porridge, too, and . . ."

He stopped, staring at the angry couple.

Aurora Rose stared at him.

Phillip-on-the-ground stared at him.

Phillip-with-the-fish dropped the fish and immediately drew his sword.

"Rose, get back," Phillip-on-the-ground said, leaping up. "It's another one of Maleficent's demons."

"*He's* the demon!" Phillip-with-the-fish said, cheeks flushed with anger.

"Right," Ground Phillip said, casually drawing his own

sword. "Who was sleeping here next to Rose *all night* while *you* just *happened* to come walking in."

"I got up two hours ago!" Fish Phillip said. "I couldn't sleep because of our fight."

"Really? Because I slept just fine," Ground Phillip said with a knowing smile. "And somehow *she* did. Right through your 'getting up' and . . . What is it you were doing? *Fishing?* Really?"

Aurora Rose looked back and forth between them uncertainly. The fish thing *was* strange, despite his obvious tiring of porridge. Did princes even know how to fish?

"I like fishing," Fish Phillip protested. "Even Roman emperors fished. To relax."

"Ha, now you *know* he's the demon," Ground Phillip said, laughing. "I'm *terrible* at Latin. You know that."

That was true.

But . . . was Ground Phillip acting . . . not like *Phillip* Phillip?

But then, who *was* Phillip? Besides a liar?

"Wait, hush," she said, thinking hard.

They both waited with the same patient, expectant expression.

"What's the name of your horse?" she said slowly.

"Samson," they answered at the same time.

Ground Phillip shrugged. Fish Phillip glared.

"All right. What . . ." She dug deep, into memories that had only recently been uncovered. "What kind of flower did you pick and give me the day we met?"

"Jonquil," said Ground Phillip.

"I don't know," Fish Phillip said, exasperated. "I don't know the names of flowers! It was tiny and yellow and smelled pretty. Like you."

"Nice," Ground Phillip said, rolling his eyes. "Real poetic."

She frowned. That *seemed* like a mean thing for the otherwise good-natured Phillip to say.

She tried to think logically—something she now knew was difficult in a dream. Maleficent was inside her head and able to summon an entire world out of her thoughts and memories. The evil fairy knew everything about Aurora Rose—and so, probably, did her servants.

But she didn't know everything about *Phillip*.

Not the things that had happened *before* he met the princess.

"Tell me . . . tell me your most important childhood memory," she said finally.

Fish Phillip spoke first.

"My father gave me my first sword, a wooden one, on my third birthday. I named it Cat. Because what I really wanted was a cat."

And Ground Phillip threw his hands up.

"You could make up *anything*," he said with exasperation. "*I* could make up anything. Rose wouldn't know the truth. Sure, I had a sword when I was three and named it Cat. I also kissed a dairymaid when I was thirteen, next to the fire in the kitchen. I absolutely did it. But . . . it's also the sort of thing any prince, any boy, could be reasonably expected to do. Is it true? Can you prove it?"

Fish Phillip frowned. Real hate began to burn in his eyes.

"I *did* kiss a dairymaid when I was thirteen. But it was outside, *near the cows*."

"See?" Ground Phillip said.

She bit her lip. He was right. Was there *any* connection to Phillip in the real world she could draw on? Something they both knew somehow, she in her forest and he in his castle?

Or . . . in the Thorn Castle . . .

"Your father," she said. "King Hubert. Tell me about him."

Both Phillips looked surprised.

Ground Phillip shrugged again. "Pompous. Loud. Bossy."

"Show some respect," Fish Phillip growled. "He's still your—my—*father*."

"What did he look like? *Really* look like? His face," she pressed.

"Old," Ground Phillip quipped.

Fish Phillip raised his sword. *"Enough,* I said!"

"Please, *use* this as an excuse to attack me," Ground Phillip spat. "Because you can't describe him at all, you *fake!*" He readied his own sword.

Fish Phillip sprang forward, beating the other Phillip's weapon aside with a clang that rang out disturbingly among the ancient trees. Clouds of tiny birds, high up, exploded from the leaves and flew away.

Both Phillips were fast—*very* fast. They were extremely skilled swordsmen, clearly trained by a master. They were perfectly matched—obviously. Neither could gain the upper hand, and each trick and tactic one came up with, the other had already thought about. Parry, spin, lunge, leap, surprise attack at the *legs* . . . It was actually quite beautiful. If it hadn't been such a dangerous situation, she would have enjoyed watching them.

But she found herself drawing her own sword. She would not be unprepared, no matter who won.

After a few minutes the twins separated, breathing heavily. Neither had drawn blood.

"You're well trained, demon," said one Phillip.

"As are you, demon," said the other, giving the first a little salute.

She didn't even know which one was Fish Phillip and which one was Ground Phillip anymore.

They clashed again, more furiously this time. One drew

blood on the other's side; the other delivered a painful-seeming blow with the flat of his sword to the other's head.

Aurora Rose winced with each one.

Finally, panting, they separated again.

"Here's the thing," said Phillip on the left, facing her. "There's no way you can trust *either* of us. Maleficent's magic is too strong and perfect."

"And here's the *other* thing," the second Phillip said with an arch look at his twin. "Why *would* you trust either one of us? You've already seen that the real Phillip, whoever it is—*me*, by the way—"

"It's *me*, you lying hell spawn!"

"Whatever. You've already seen that the *real* Phillip can't be trusted anyway. I lied to you. Just like you said. *Despite* falling in love with you. I could just as easily lie to you again. For good reasons," he added quickly, seeing the look on her face. "It could be for your own safety, or because it's too dangerous for us to be together . . . or whatever. How well do you really know me? Would you *ever* be able to trust me again? Now that you know I lied to you?"

She put a hand to her head. The other Phillip looked sick, seeing the logic behind his twin's words and where it would go. But he didn't protest.

"For your own safety, for the safety of this quest—for the good of all the people who are depending on you—it would really be best if you went on. Alone."

Aurora Rose felt a pain as great as the wound of a sword at these words—an invisible sword, in her heart. It was the truth.

And hadn't she always known that? She was always alone. She would always *be* alone. She was the only one she could trust. In *both* her memories. Whether she was hiding in the giant maze of the Thorn Castle or looking for something to do among the wild animals of the forest or lying on her princess bed, hoping Lianna would stay away, everything had always come down to just her.

The other Phillip also looked pained at the words.

"But . . . I love you . . ." he said desperately. "I want to be with you and protect you and help you."

"No, *I* do," the first Phillip said bleakly. "All those things. This is the hardest thing I've ever done. But it's what's best."

She knew she couldn't delay. If she did, she would be stuck there forever, trying to decide—another Maleficent trap. She turned to go, hoping she wouldn't hear the two boys begin their inevitable fighting again, clanging away in the forest of her mind forever.

Or until she woke up.

"*I stole my mother's pearl earring,*" a Phillip suddenly called out.

She closed her eyes and kept going.

"I *stole* it because it was *pretty*. That's all. Later when she was *dead* and they *found* it everyone asked if I stole it because I wanted a memory of her and I said *yes* even though I just wanted it because it was pretty and it was when she was still alive. But this way everyone was nice to me and I was forgiven and everyone felt bad for me!"

She couldn't stop herself from turning around.

What a weird thing for Phillip to say.

The other Phillip thought so, too; he looked at the first one with disgust.

"Why would you tell her *that* about us?"

But the first Phillip wasn't done yet.

"When I was ten, when I was waaaaay too old not to know better, I told my sister Marya that she was prettier than Brigitte. *In front of Brigitte.*"

The Phillip who spoke looked sick and racked with guilt.

The princess gripped her sword tighter but moved closer.

"Once I caught a mouse and put it in a room with my cat and watched the cat play with it until it was dead. It was horrible and I wept for days after and I went to confession about it, *but I did it.* I did it. Because I wanted to see what would happen."

"Sure, all right," the other Phillip said nervously. "Are we saying all this stuff now? Because I can do it, too. I don't know *why* you'd want to tell her all this. . . ."

"I wet my bed until I was thirteen!"

Aurora Rose and the other Phillip both looked at him in shock.

"I wet my bed until I was thirteen," Phillip continued, a little hysterically. "Not *all* the time. But on many nights. My father was angry and the chambermaid was sworn to secrecy and they *whipped* me and told me I was terrible, bringing shame to our name and lineage. Royal princes don't act that way. Royal princes do *not* wet their beds. But I *did*.

"Nobody else knows any of this. No one. I'm telling you because I love you and I trust you with all of my secrets— good and bad. I want you to know that you can trust me, too. I know I lied to you but I swear I will tell you *everything* about me from now on. All the bad stuff and all the good stuff, too."

He paused, looking bleak and weary. "Leave now, for the good of your kingdom and for your own safety. Just know that—if you succeed, if we ever meet again—I will never, ever lie to you about anything. Ever again. And I will spend the rest of my life doing whatever I can to make you forgive me."

The other Phillip opened his mouth to say something.

Which was the opportunity she took to drive her sword through his stomach.

The look on his face was human and terrible: surprise, hurt, horror. His hands came around the shaft as blood began to flow down it, as if he could pull it out and make everything better. Strange noises came out of his mouth.

She staggered back, horrified by the mistake she had made.

And then the blood turned black. And the noises turned to hissing. His body shivered and became something dark and not really there, snakelike and transparent. He vibrated and trembled and shivered.

Finally, he fell to the ground like all the others.

The remaining Phillip watched silently, his cheeks white.

It must be a horrible thing to watch yourself die, Aurora Rose thought.

But he recovered himself and strode forward, giving the thing a coup de grace, a quick death the demon certainly didn't deserve.

Then he dropped his sword, turned to the princess, wrapped her in his arms, and hugged her so tightly it almost hurt.

She didn't say anything. There were too many things to talk about: how she had figured out it was really him, how she still didn't forgive him for lying before, how he wasn't always the perfect prince he seemed to be.

How she would in private, for the rest of their lives, no matter what happened, remind him of the things he had said that day. Just because.

How she somehow just assumed she would know him for the rest of their lives. Forever.

But she had also just killed something that looked a whole lot like a real person when she stabbed him through the innards. That image replayed itself again and again in her mind.

What if she had been wrong?

So she stayed silent and let herself be held.

Interlude

A pile of bodies was growing next to Maleficent's throne. It was a little shocking—maybe even distasteful. Never in her life had the fairy been messy or allowed herself to be surrounded by filth.

The horde around her mostly didn't care, however; they looked at the corpses with hunger. Lianna rolled her eyes.

"You're going through them too quickly. There's not going to be anyone left for you to rule."

With a hiss and a movement that was far more redolent of a snaky dragon than a human queen, Maleficent cleared the space between her and the pig-footed handmaiden in the wink of an eye. She loomed over her, all arches and blackness.

Lianna didn't flinch.

"*I have less than an hour.* Excuse me, let me rephrase: *we* have less than an hour. If I don't get the princess back here by then, I could consume *everyone* in the castle and it wouldn't matter.

"And what help have *you* been, my dear?" she added with a venomous drawl. "I have attacked her through all her weaknesses . . . and sent my best servants after her. *All of which have failed.* What aren't you telling me? What dark secret of Aurora's heart can lead me to her defeat?"

"I have told you everything about the princess," Lianna said steadily. "*Excuse me, let me rephrase:* you already know everything I know."

The evil fairy and the strange handmaiden stared into each other's eyes for a long moment. Neither looked away.

The rest of Maleficent's creations grew nervous. They shifted from hoof to hoof or claw to claw and made uneasy whistling and *whoomph*ing sounds.

Maleficent pulled her lips back in a sneer and spun around, concentrating on the image of the battered princess and prince. Her cape flew and settled behind her. Still Lianna didn't move. If anything, she seemed a little bored.

Suddenly Maleficent looked thoughtful.

"But I don't *have* to know the darkest secrets of her heart," she said slowly. "All I have to do is . . . *encourage* them. . . ."

She raised her staff and looked into the depths of the orb, her yellow eyes further illuminated by whatever it was she saw there.

And she began to chant.

Void

The prince and princess traveled down the path in silence. Phillip put his arm out for her to hold and Aurora Rose tried to ignore it but finally accepted it, giving in to her present state and tendency to stagger.

She kept replaying the last few seconds, in which she had killed the demon.

It was harder to drive the sword into the thing's body than she had imagined it would be. But was it still, perhaps, easier than it would have been with a real human? Would there have been more resistance? Would she have been more hesitant? Would the fact that it was an actual person have stayed her hand some?

Or had the past few days changed her more than all her years in *either* reality?

Phillip was complicated now. She didn't want to think about him. His feelings for her were unbearably strong. His treatment of her in the Forest Cottage had been abominable.

Or had it?

Wasn't it just the way he would inevitably wind up, considering his life experiences up to that point? Did he have any reason to trust a random girl in the forest with the truth?

But didn't he *love* her?

She didn't want to think about that. It seemed like wherever she was, whoever she was, Aurora/Briar Rose was some sort of maelstrom of deceit, causing all who came near her to lie.

For the first time, she wished she was *out* of the dreamworld. Immediately. She wanted to wake up and see the actual world and face people and make them face her. She was exhausted. She wanted to slough off all the layers of falsehoods like the tired gray skin of a snake.

"How close are we?" she mumbled, finally breaking the silence.

"It's a little confusing around here. There are rocks, large ones, not that far ahead, I believe," Phillip answered, carefully trying to keep his voice neutral, not wanting to seem overly eager or grateful for the attention she was showing him, not wanting to scare her away. "As soon as we see them, it should be a straight shot to the house, alongside the little stream."

"I remember those."

Immediately another flood of memories pummeled her. She gasped but forced herself to keep walking. Now it was like a valve was turned on and couldn't close all the way. Even when the initial burst was over, the images continued to trickle in, never ending.

She could *feel* the rocks. She had climbed on them. She had rubbed her hands on them. She had found darker rocks in the stream that she could draw on them with. She had balanced on the rocks. She had pretended she was an eagle nesting on them.

"Get down! Ladies don't act like that!" Flora had yelled, catching her once.

The other aunts had looked at their leader with skeptical faces.

"Well . . . I mean . . . they don't. She won't be able to when . . . you know," she had continued in a way that hadn't made sense until now.

"Maybe if more princesses climbed rocks, the world wouldn't be in the state it's in," Merryweather remarked with her usual crankiness. At the time Rose thought she meant *princess* in a generally snarky way.

"Well, we *should* try to remain consistent," Fauna said reasonably. "Are we raising her to be a *lady* or a girl in the woods? We never discussed that, really."

"Oh, I don't know, that's a fair point," Flora said, putting a hand to her head. "She has so much natural grace and nobility. Let's discuss it further but let her be for now."

The young Briar Rose had latched on to the *let her be* part and had forgotten everything else.

The older Aurora Rose grudgingly saw their dilemma: they had been raising a princess who didn't know she was one. Their little lessons and flights of fancy were starting to make sense. Eating with the right utensil (when they had it), the steps to a few court dances . . . the few things that the aunts thought made a *princess*—that the fairies thought made a *human* princess. Fairies who really, until they re-remembered their task, let her run around naked and do what she wanted, because that was normal. For fairies.

What if she had been raised in the castle? She wouldn't, as Phillip said, have had what little freedom she had enjoyed in the woods. She wouldn't have hunted with foxes.

Of course, she would have had two loving human parents. Maybe.

Who might at least have been *all right*, like Phillip's— but nothing special. A prim kiss once a day before bed and after studies.

Who might have just been passing time until a son came along.

It was too much—being hit with the memories, suddenly

understanding them in a new context, almost sympathizing with those who had lied to her her whole life.

"Do you want me to carry you?" Phillip asked, putting a hand on her shoulder.

Aurora Rose cursed under her breath.

It was taking all her effort to stay upright, and there was something coming out of her nose that she was pretty sure was blood.

More than anything she wanted to be carried, the way her aunts had carried her when she was tired as a little girl, when she had played too hard or cried too much or just couldn't make it back to the cottage. She was exhausted and miserable and aching and in pain, and Phillip, good old Phillip, could easily take her the rest of the way and even enjoy it as penance for his previous sins.

"No." She set her jaw and kept walking.

Phillip didn't say anything. He just quietly kept pace with her.

The path dipped unsteadily at what was either the site of an ancient creek bed or a spot where rain naturally collected when it ran down the hill. Topsoil gave way to pebbles and rocks and little sharp divots that were deceiving to the eye. She stumbled twice before they had gone more than fifty feet.

With a burst of annoyance she spread her fingers. If

it was really her dream, her head, there would be wide, smooth roads, cobbled and drained, to where they needed to go. Or at least well-packed dirt.

The little rocks danced and sand shifted.

Phillip stopped, foot hanging in the air. At first he was unable to see the cause of the movements. His hand went tentatively to his sword.

Aurora Rose frowned, concentrating. Why couldn't the ground see where it was *supposed* to go? Fill *itself* in?

The rocks and sand and dirt acted like lodestones that didn't like each other, or raindrops on top of dry dust: they skittered around nervously, not wanting to go where she wanted them. The uneven places and holes remained.

She shrieked with frustration.

Phillip risked putting a hand on her arm.

"We're entering the deepest part of your mind, remember?" he said gently. "I don't think it's *supposed* to be easy to get to. It's a difficult path to who you really are."

"Spare me more philosophy. I'm *angry* right now."

"Well, how about this? You're not Maleficent—who had hundreds of years to perfect her magic."

The sound she made in response could have been either animal annoyance at or human acceptance *of* the logic in what he said.

So they traveled more slowly.

The path eventually opened up to an ancient clearing. The trees thinned out and a stream, which had been hiding shyly deeper in the forest, came close to them, rocky and gurgling. Gray stones emerged from the forest floor with moss and needles and even trees on top of them. They looked like they had just popped up their heads for a few moments to look around and would disappear back down below any moment.

"This is starting to look . . . to *feel* familiar," the princess said cautiously. She shivered—but in a good way. Finally something was starting to make sense, to feel right.

Phillip wasn't paying attention to her—which was strange, because he was *always* paying attention to her. Even when she was being mean. Or distant. Or both.

"Do you remember this? This is near where we met, isn't it?" she pushed.

But he made a motion with his chin in the direction he was looking, which was not at her.

Standing farther up the path, as if she had always been there, was a little girl.

She looked like a waif: maybe six years old, dressed in a grayish-pink shift that didn't cover her arms and fell thinly to her knees. An ugly, lopsided crown that looked like a child's drawing sat tilted on her head. Her feet were bare. She was as pale as a wisp of cloud, and dark half-moons rode beneath her startling violet eyes. She stood perfectly still. Not even a stray breeze ruffled her perfect blond hair.

Aurora felt cold horror creep its ugly fingers up her back.

The girl seemed perfectly calm. Complete stillness surrounded her like a heavy cloak. Although there were no clear shadows in the eternal twilight of the ancient forest, everything seemed dimmer and grayer around her, as if bathed in gloom.

She waited patiently for them to speak first.

"Who are—" the princess began.

"Kill it!" Phillip cried out, suddenly finding his voice. *"It's a demon!"*

Without a moment's hesitation he rushed at the girl, sword out.

Aurora Rose grabbed the prince—although she wasn't sure exactly why. It wasn't just because it was an unarmed, pretty little girl with long eyelashes that he was about to attack and run through with his blade.

Phillip was probably absolutely right that the girl was another one of Maleficent's demons. But there was something terribly familiar about her. About the air around her. The lack of color.

The girl smiled faintly, watching them.

"It's all right. He couldn't have touched me anyway."

When she spoke, it was like there was no distance between them at all; her voice sounded close to the princess's ear. Like the girl knew she would always be heard by the right person.

Phillip clearly did *not* like her tone. Frankly, neither did Aurora Rose. She didn't stop the prince when he launched himself at the girl a second time.

He was beautiful to watch, all grace and consummate skill, warmed up by the battle with his twin. The princess flinched, waiting for the thrust to the belly that would take the child down.

But the girl *flickered.*

Like a candle about to go out.

She was there and not there and there and not there, and when Phillip's sword would have connected with her flesh, she was suddenly a few feet away, in the same pose, with the same look on her face, as if she hadn't had to do anything—not even *think*—to get there.

To his credit, Phillip hesitated only a moment before spinning and lunging again.

The girl flickered, appearing a few feet away.

Phillip spun around and slashed, even faster than he had before.

It didn't matter.

They kept going at it: Phillip attacking and the girl

smiling and disappearing and reappearing and nothing else.

Aurora Rose felt sick. None of the magic, nothing they had seen in the dreamworld before, had looked anything like this.

Finally, Phillip fell back, exhausted.

"I told you," the girl said—not with a mocking tone but with one of infinite patience, which was somehow worse. "You cannot touch me, Prince Phillip."

"I do *not* intend to 'touch' you, demon," he growled. "I mean to run you through and keep your evil hands away from Rose."

"Ah. Well. Not everything in here is a *demon*, Prince Phillip. Or rather, not all of the . . . things . . . in here are *Maleficent's* creations," the girl said, strangely adult sentences coming in her high, young voice.

The prince and princess had matching expressions of confusion, which the girl obviously found amusing.

"Some . . . *things* . . . are from Aurora's own mind."

The princess sucked in her breath. There was something resonant in that statement. The girl did *not* look exactly like her. But the crown . . .

"Or wait . . . is it Rose now? What is it? Rose or Aurora? What are you going by these days?" the girl asked, brow furrowing in put-on seriousness.

"If you're from my mind, you should know," Aurora

Rose managed to say, trying to channel Phillip's usual insouciance.

"Ah, but *you* don't know, do you?" the girl said.

"From your mind? What is she talking about?" Phillip demanded. "Rose, what is she? What is this?"

All of her life had been inaction. All of her life had been waiting for other people to *do*. Ever since she had escaped the Thorn Castle, she had known she wouldn't last much longer if she continued this way.

Before she could talk herself out of it, she drew her sword and attacked.

She didn't question whether she could strike what looked very much like a young girl. She just screamed and threw herself into it.

Unblinkingly, the girl watched the princess come at her. At the last moment she put her hand up. A small wooden sword appeared in it, a clunky plaything.

When Aurora Rose brought her own sword down, the girl moved to deflect it.

The princess's sword bounced off the wooden sword with an unreal booming sound. It echoed sickeningly off the trees.

Her arms and upper body were shaken by the force of the rebound. She had been completely unprepared for how *solid* the girl and her sword were.

But Aurora Rose gritted her teeth and swung again.

The girl spun her sword and did a clumsy, childish parry and riposte. The tip of her toy didn't reach anywhere near the princess's body.

Aurora Rose raised her sword above her head, prepared to do the girl in. To cleave her head in half if she had to.

The girl made a concerned, *tch*ing sound.

"Are you *sure* you're up to this?"

The princess shook with the effort of holding the sword. It wasn't so big a thing, really, but it was solid metal and above her head. She could feel the blood draining down her arm into her shoulder and it ached terribly.

And what was the point?

They couldn't kill the thing. Whatever it was.

Her sword fell to her side.

"Rose, *kill* it!" Phillip shouted. "It's *not* a little girl!"

"I know," she said dully.

"Don't feel bad," the girl said. "You've only killed one other person, really. I'm not counting the mist sprite because your boyfriend here helped you finish it off."

Aurora Rose felt herself wilting. *Person?*

"That demon who looked like me was no person," Phillip said quickly. "It was *another* evil creature, like yourself, whatever you may *think* you are."

"Honestly, you seem a little tired," the girl observed, looking at Aurora Rose and ignoring the prince.

The princess collapsed to the ground. It was kind of a

relief. She didn't really want to kill the girl, anyway. And the ground was safe and comfortable.

The girl smiled sadly at her like a mother at an exhausted baby.

Phillip watched in confusion—but only for a moment. He took the opportunity to try a sneak attack, running up behind the girl with the pommel of his sword raised to knock her on the head.

The girl didn't even bother to look. She was suddenly a mirror image of herself, still turned to observe the princess, but now at the opposite angle.

Phillip fell over, with no plan in his mind for *stopping* once he had engaged the girl.

The girl stood there, looking mildly disappointed, both teenagers on the ground around her.

Aurora Rose struggled up from the inviting ground. She had to do this. She *had* to. She was just so weak, and battered-feeling, and exhausted. . . .

"No, no, stay there. Really. You look like you could just . . . use . . . a little . . . lie . . . down . . ." the girl said sweetly.

The princess lay down with her head in the dirt, feeling waves of not caring wash over her. It was just like when she was a little girl. . . .

"Rose!" Phillip cried. He leapt up. "*Rose!* What are you doing? Get up!"

"Leave her alone, can't you see she's done in?" the girl said with mock impatience.

Aurora Rose felt sluggishness pour over her like molten lead from her feet to her shoulders. It was a dark wintry day in either life, Thorn Castle or forest, when the sky was an ugly noncolor and it was cold, but not the kind that made you want to bundle up and be comforted with a cup of hot tea. It was the kind of day when you just lay, unblinking, and wished to die.

"Rose! Stop it! Get up! Why are you *listening* to her?" Phillip demanded.

"She's listening because I'm not telling her anything she doesn't already feel," the girl explained with a mysterious smile. "*I'm* not telling her to do anything she doesn't already want to do."

"That's not true," Phillip said—but he was hesitant. "Rose?"

She picked up her weary head to look at him. She couldn't do much more than that. This really was what she wanted: to be left quietly, at rest, alone.

Maybe it would be better if everyone just stopped talking.

"Behold your true love," the girl said through perfect tiny white teeth. It was almost a hiss. "A directionless, indecisive, despondent, *sad* little girl."

The princess wrapped her arms around her legs, each word dripping acid into her ears. It felt strangely good.

"That's not true!" Phillip said, going to her and kneeling down. He put his hand on her chin and turned her face so she was forced to look at him. His eyes were large and bright and passionate. "I fell in love with Rose because she was happy and lighthearted. I fell in love with her because she was beautiful and as cheerful as the sunshine. I fell in love with her because I heard her singing with her beautiful voice . . . as carefree as a songbird. I fell in love with a girl who danced and twirled across the meadows like an angel of happiness."

Aurora Rose listened to him. The words sounded sweet and he obviously meant each one.

But her chin felt awkward in his grasp and she began to think about what he had said.

"*That's* why you fell in love with me?" she asked, feeling a little bit of energy come back as she spoke, a little bit of anger rising through the sloth.

"Yes," Phillip said uncertainly.

"Because I *twirled*?"

"You were so beautiful when I came upon you . . . your hair sparkling in the sunlight. . . ."

"You *fell in love with*, as in *wanted to spend the rest of your life with*, a silly girl you found spinning by herself in the *middle of the woods*?"

"But," Phillip said, "it wasn't just that. . . ."

"No," she snorted. "It was the *singing* and the . . . cheerfulness?"

"You were the most delightful girl I had ever met," he protested.

"You were going to drop everything in your life for a pretty girl you thought was *delightful*?"

"It was either you or a princess I *hadn't even met yet*," Phillip pointed out. "You seemed like someone I could spend the rest of my life with."

"Because I was given the gifts of song and beauty and grace," she spat.

"It doesn't matter how you got them, it's who you are."

"I think we're going to run into some more trust issues here," the little girl interrupted. "Especially if you think you know Aurora. Rose. Whatever."

"It's *not* who I am," the princess said, ignoring the girl. "I am *not* cheerful and lighthearted. You caught me on a good morning, when I was going mad with loneliness from living in a forest with three crazy aunts and the overwhelming desire for a boy. *Any* boy. I was remembering a really great dream I used to have about meeting the perfect boy, which was as close as I had ever come to meeting a real boy except for the young woodsmen and villagers my aunts so carefully kept me away from. And then suddenly there you were, like out of my dreams."

"I know," Phillip said. "It really was perfect."

"Listen to me," she said, trying to fight the weakness that was overtaking her again—as well as Phillip's good-natured but not always insightful personality. "I spent—spend— many days in both worlds just . . . lying around. More time than I spent twirling. The joy I felt when you came was more than I had ever experienced at the cottage in the woods."

"But . . . it seemed so idyllic," the prince said helplessly.

"It was boring. Nothing ever happened. *Ever.* I wanted to . . . I don't know . . . *do* things. See things. I don't even know what I wanted."

"But isn't that normal? I know *I* felt that way."

"You say you *felt* that way. Past tense. What changed that?"

"Well, I went to university and made lots of new friends and . . ." Phillip trailed off.

The princess shook her head and looked at the ground.

The creepy girl gave a quiet laugh. "Oh yes, given *your* opportunities, perhaps she would have been all right. If she could have gone to a place where her other talents could have been trained. Where she would have been forced to work and learn and make friends and go out into the world.

"Honestly, even if she were raised *normally*, maybe she would be better in time and her sadness would become a passing stage. In a farm family, where there was work to do, things to learn and keep her occupied. Or a village family, where she looked forward to meeting boys at the dance every season. Or even as a royal princess, who had charity work to organize and . . . I don't know . . . tapestries to sew. But she didn't just *feel* trapped; she was. And she didn't even know it. She just felt it."

"You're speaking nonsense," Phillip said. The phrase was so odd for him Aurora Rose wondered if he had heard it often from someone else. "Everyone is sad once in a while. Rose is *fine*. She's not a sad person, or whatever you're trying to imply. You're filling her head with lies, demon."

And with that he rose and looked away—then dealt a blow to the girl in the face with the pommel of his sword.

It was horrible to watch.

The rounded metal end sank into the girl's nose noiselessly; there was no expected crack of cartilage or snap of bone. The girl's features simply crumpled around the metal like a pillow being crushed.

And then her face slowly popped back into place.

"Don't bother, Phillip," the princess said wearily. "It won't work. And besides, she's right."

"No, she's not!" the prince cried. "You're a happy, cheerful, beautiful girl, and she's trying to turn you into something you're not . . . to kill you with these ideas. . . ."

"I pricked my own finger!"

Phillip stared at her.

Even the girl looked surprised.

"How does the story go?" Aurora Rose asked tiredly. "The fairies took me to the castle, where, sad about losing the love of my life, I sat alone weeping and . . ."

"And Maleficent cast a spell over you," Phillip whispered. "She hypnotized you, worked her evil magic on you until she controlled your thoughts, and led you to the secret room with the spindle, where she guided your hand . . ."

"She *did* open a secret passageway to a room with a spinning wheel. At least, that's what I assume it was, never having seen one before," the princess admitted. "And yes, I think she *did* try to control my thoughts. But for goodness' sake—she appeared like an evil green ball of fire and told me to follow her. Who would listen to an evil green ball of fire? A total idiot?"

"But . . ."

"I had a pretty good idea of what was going to happen. The curse sort of gathered itself around me as midnight approached. I knew I was going to die or sleep forever or something *and I was completely fine with that.*"

The prince's face was a study of shock and surprise.

"Phillip," she said, searching for words. "I had been by myself in the woods for *sixteen years*. At least five years too long. And I had finally met you. You really were like someone coming out of my dreams and into my life.

"And then, as soon as that happened, it was over. It was like it was all on purpose. My aunts whisked me away on the night you were supposed to meet them and threw me into a whole new situation with parents I had never known and a wedding to someone I'd never met—set for the very next day! It was too much. I wanted out. Death was better than living through that much disappointment. And sleep was more than welcome."

Phillip looked away from her to the ground, eyes bright with tears.

"Well, *that* was a deeply buried secret," the little girl said. "Even *I* didn't know about it."

"Why didn't you just . . . run away?" Phillip cried. "If you were so scared and miserable."

"I don't know," the princess said, frustrated with herself. "It didn't even occur to me. I didn't *think* to. The spindle seemed like the only reasonable option."

"No, there are always options other than *killing yourself*," the prince said, shaking his head. "You could have . . . I don't know . . ."

"And that's the nature of her, let's say, *sickness*. Her, well, *me*." The girl spoke politely, like a professor whose clever students had finally figured out the answer themselves. "The mind traps itself. She couldn't see any way out. Everything seems too hard. Too difficult. Too tiring. Too unlikely. Too prone to failure. Too inescapable."

With each pronouncement Aurora Rose wilted: each thing the girl said was absolutely true, had always been true. It was as if it was finally recognized by her mind and body as she said it. The familiar black lethargy came over her.

The little girl smiled, far too widely for her tiny features.

"Go to sleep, little princess. This world—*any* world—is too much for you."

Aurora Rose felt her eyes become heavy. The ground seemed to grow up through her, both supporting her and pulling her down into its embrace.

Between blinking images she saw Phillip struggling to reach her. It didn't seem he was trying very hard, though. He wasn't coming anywhere close to her. Maybe he was giving up, too.

Or possibly it was the black thorny vines that were snaking up out of the ground and wrapping around his limbs. Holding him back.

It didn't matter.

Her eyes closed, filled with a permanent sap, and her limbs relaxed.

She heard Phillip rustling but finally growing still.

All was silence and peaceful blackness.

And then:

A single sound.

A quiet groan from the stalwart Phillip, who never complained about anything.

She cracked open her eyes.

The prince was now lashed tightly to a tree by the vines, and they were still tightening. Thorns pressed into his flesh. His face was white as he struggled to breathe but was obviously losing that fight.

There would be no rescue by him. Or *for* him.

Or for the hundreds of people lying asleep in a castle somewhere in the real world.

And it's your fault, Aurora Rose.

Usually being yelled at—even by her own mind—only made her want to run away more. To escape into herself. She winced and shifted uncomfortably.

There is an entire kingdom of people asleep, at Maleficent's mercy, depending on you to rescue them. This is your *quest. This is your adventure.*

This *was* her quest. This was her *duty.*

The little girl must have noticed something shifting in the princess's countenance; she barely moved and another heavy black wave of lethargy crawled over Aurora Rose and pressed against her like a physical weight.

What *could* one princess do against a powerful fairy? A fake world? An army of inhuman guards? What was the point in trying? She was only going to fail.

And then a single image came forward and burned itself into the back of her eyes.

Lady Astrid.

Lady Astrid bleeding out on the floor, a once energetic and funny little woman reduced to piles of lifeless flesh.

Somewhere out in the real world her husband wouldn't even know that she was dead yet.

Aurora Rose began to struggle to her feet. Her legs felt like stone. Her arms ached like she was sick. She ground her teeth together, stepped forward, and swung her sword.

The girl deflected the attack but stepped backward as she did so.

"You should give up," the girl whispered.

Defeat loomed, ugly and unavoidable, around the princess. She staggered under the fear of failure.

With a moan she stabbed poorly at the girl again, trying to move, trying to continue the fight. Trying to stay awake.

The girl knocked her sword aside easily.

And then she lunged.

It didn't seem like a blunted wooden toy sword could do any damage. Its painted tip just grazed the princess's left thigh, but it sliced through her flesh like cloth. Aurora Rose fell back, gulping in pain. It looked like a clean cut, with the precision of the line and the immediate flow of blood; it *felt* like a jagged, ugly ripping of her skin and the pain of a thousand swords dragging across her.

Like it had been made by the rippled knife Maleficent had used on Lady Astrid.

The noise that came from her was an animal scream of pain.

"You cannot destroy me," the little girl hissed. "I am *you*, Princess. I am your *sadness*. I am your *melancholy*. I am your *despair*!"

She moved to lunge again.

The princess just barely brought up her own weapon in time to block her.

"You. Can't. *Sword*. Fight," Phillip struggled to say with a few gulps of breath.

"*I KNOW THAT!*" she shrieked, almost throwing her blade away. What *could* she do? Nothing. She had no useful skills, no strength, no . . .

And then she stopped.

Phillip was looking at her desperately. *Meaningfully.*

She couldn't *sword* fight. He was right. He was trying to tell her something.

So what *could* she do?

The little girl waited patiently at the ready, knees bent, anticipating her next move.

She probably didn't expect an attack from something *other than* the princess.

So . . .

The girl suddenly stumbled backward as a rock grew out of the ground, right under her feet, like it was heaved up by frost—but quickly, making wonderful little grinding and crunchy gravel sounds as it rose.

The girl steadied herself.

"Clever," she said. "You—"

Aurora Rose imagined another rock.

The girl pitched forward.

Another, and another and another rock.

She concentrated on raising *all* of them, in a circle around the girl's feet. Her opponent fell forward and backward like a rag doll shaken by an angry child.

As soon as she found her footing, the girl shot the princess a look and hissed a single word: *"Disappointing."*

Immediately, Aurora Rose sank under the weight of the meaning. The ground rushed up to embrace her again as she remembered all the people who found her utterly *disappointing*:

— her aunts, who asked her to do so little, returning home and seeing nothing was done, not even her own nook swept. She was still in bed, contemplating the clouds

— Maleficent, humoring the princess but obviously disgusted with her studies. The queen's patience with—but disinterest in—the balls, and dismissal of Aurora's desire to help

— Aurora Rose, at her own inability to find an escape
from a marriage she didn't want in a family she
didn't love, resorting to death because it was easy

She closed her eyes, frowning as hard as she could, trying to force pain into her head, trying to will some little bit
of spirit and anger. She tried thinking of Lady Astrid again
but this time felt only sadness.

"Rose . . ." Phillip croaked. "You were going to end it
all . . . thought you had lost me forever. But . . . *I'm here.*
Always be here. For you. Telling you . . . *not* to go to sleep.
To . . . get up."

The princess tiredly regarded the scene: the prince tied
up in the background; the girl with her tiny sword; the tall,
ancient trees, growing up into forever, surrounding them.
The trees, which might have had something to do with her
subconscious thoughts. Her memories made solid. Twice as
many as a normal person had. Twice as *useless.*

The girl raised her wooden sword.

"Rose!" Phillip sobbed.

There was a creaking sound. A very, very loud creaking
sound.

The girl looked around, confused.

Time became strange: it seemed to take forever for the
infinitely tall, infinitely old tree to fall. The little girl looked

back and forth anxiously, trying to find the source of the sound. Then there was a skip in the connected moments, like when the girl flickered out of existence, disappearing from one place and reappearing in another.

The enormous tree was halfway down . . . and then mostly . . . and then . . .

It smashed solidly on top of the little girl, just brushing the princess's feet.

Phillip cried out in anguish: *"Rose!"*

The depression and somnolence drained out of her as the demon hissed and bubbled and died.

"I'm all right," she called back shakily.

The exhaustion, pain, and weakness remained, however.

"Was that . . . you?"

"Yes," she answered with a faint smile. She forced herself up, using some of the branches for balance. There was no sizzle of buried thoughts. The tree was dead. She apologized to it, to the memory it represented.

When she got close she saw that unlike the other trees in the rest of the forest, it was riddled with bird holes and had large barkless patches of black, slimy wood. Not a healthy tree to begin with.

What did it all mean?

The trunk was too immense to go around so she clambered on top. She paused there, balancing for a moment among the prickly dead pine branches, and surveyed the scene below her. It was a new perspective, seeing Phillip from above.

She filed that thought for later and carefully went down the other side.

The upper part of the little girl's body was exposed— the tree had crushed the rest of it. Her limbs and head were turned at impossible, sickening angles, and a trickle of *red* blood leaked from the side of her mouth. Her eyelashes were long and golden, and it was hard to focus on the fact that she had just been trying to kill the prince and princess. In death, at least, she seemed almost like a normal little girl.

"Sorry?" the princess said, unsure if she meant it.

The girl's eyes shot open. Violet irises focused on hers.

"You haven't won, Princess," she said with a voice that creaked. "Hear this, and let's see how you deal with it: *your parents are dead.*

"Maleficent has just killed them."

Interlude

Many people were dying.

As midnight approached, first one and then another and then another court noble suddenly began to start bleeding. They thrashed and gasped and choked like fish thrown out on dry land.

Fauna and Merryweather flew around, frantically trying to tend to them, staunching the wounds with clean bandages here, trying a healing spell there. Nothing worked, and sometimes all it seemed to do was prolong their agony.

Flora stayed as calm as she could in the midst of it, hovering in the air, *willing* the universe to help her as she tried to reach Rose again. She had broken off a piece of her soul and sent it into the sleeping nether realm Maleficent ruled.

It was a terrible place, this inside of her adopted niece's head, with the evil fairy running rampant in it.

The sleeper tossed and turned and moaned because of whatever had happened in there, and her pricked finger had started bleeding again.

Flora bounced through dream forests and nightmare castles, fogs of worry and large blank places of stark depression and madness. The golden sparks that represented her loosely held together consciousness barely glittered in the gloom that blanketed the world.

Only later, when she had time, would she think about her poor Briar Rose and how it was possible that none of them had seen this darkness within their adopted daughter.

Now, however, was the time to *act*.

She felt the tether tying her to the real world grow taut and thin; she couldn't go much farther. She urgently flung out her consciousness, looking for something, *anything*, that could help. But all she could see was murky, worthless gloom and confused shadow people whose spirits were entirely enslaved to Maleficent's spell.

There! Up ahead.

Another consciousness. Not as bewitched by the false world around it. Not entirely coherent, either, but it would have to do. It was aware of itself and seemed more than harmless—it seemed like a friend.

YOU! Help her!

The soul spun around in a tizzy, looking for the source of the communication.

FIND HER! Flora ordered frantically. *She is . . . that way.*

Golden sparkles aligned themselves in the direction of the blackest part of the world, the deepest part of Rose's mind—the place Flora couldn't go.

Your release . . . everyone's freedom depends on it. HELP HER ESCAPE. Help her find us. . . .

And then, like a wet stocking pulled too tightly on a clothesline, the strongest of the three fairies was pulled back, painfully and quickly, to the waking world.

"Flora!"

She opened her eyes, torn between fury and worry. Her cohorts were unlikely to have summoned her for anything that wasn't important.

Merryweather had her by the arm and was already dragging her. Her eyes were bright; fairy tears, sparkling and sharp, coursed down her cheeks.

"It's *them* this time!" she cried. "Oh, Flora, she got *them!*"

Not wanting to believe what she suspected, Flora let herself be led into the throne room.

There, Fauna was hysterically flitting from king to queen, who just scant minutes earlier had been peaceful and sleeping in their giant seats. Now they shivered and convulsed like rag dolls as blood poured out of their hearts.

"But *why*?" Flora cried. "She doesn't *need* them!"

In life King Stefan was both a good king and a faintly humorous man, with his droopy mustache and calm demeanor. Now he rocked and heaved inhumanly, his long face pale, his skin ashen and waxy. The heavy state robes he wore in anticipation of the royal wedding day were thrashed into rags as he tried to escape his own death, still asleep.

And Queen Leah . . . her mouth twitched and pulled from side to side like a hideous puppet's, her sad, peaceful features melting and expanding with desperation.

It had been terrible to watch the others be killed this way, but the fairies had known the king and queen since long before they had taken the throne. These humans and their daughter, whom the fairies had watched over, were the closest things to *children* they had ever had.

So they might be forgiven for missing a few tiny sounds, easily lost in the calamity of the sleeping castle but surely audible to the ears of a fairy.

The sound of stone cracking. The sound of shards falling away, tinkling like glass.

The sound of triumphant black wings stretching out of their stony prison. The cackling caw of an evil fairy's raven, taking flight to discover what had become of his mistress.

Her power was growing and the raven was flying home.

O Fool, I Shall Go Mad!

The thorns holding the prince back were already turning black and crumbling away. Aurora Rose helped them along, pulling and ripping, but she didn't really need to do much; they decayed into nothing under her touch.

"Rose!"

As soon as his arms were free, Phillip wrapped her in a tight hug. She bore it because it felt nice and she was too tired to do much else.

Then she collapsed on the ground like a young child or an old doll.

"Oh, Rose," Phillip said, kneeling down next to her.

"I'll never know," she said, voice empty. "I'll never know why they thought it was safer to send me away. I'll never know if they missed me. I'll never know if they really wanted a son instead. I'll never hear them say 'I'm sorry.' Or 'I love you.' Or 'It was the worst mistake we ever made.' Or even 'Someday, when you're a queen, you'll understand.'"

"Rose . . ." He stroked her cheek.

"I will never know what they really *looked like!"* she shrieked. She was finding it hard to breathe. Her lungs moved and her chest heaved in great, sudden gasps, but it didn't feel like any air was getting in. "How . . . they . . . *walked* . . . or *hugged* . . . or *laughed* . . ."

"Shhh." Phillip took her in his arms again and held her tightly. "Shhh. Quiet. Breathe now. I know. It's a terrible thing to lose your parents. Even ones you didn't know."

"Even ones?" she hiccupped angrily.

Phillip bit his lip and took a deep, patient breath. "Rose, my mother died. Remember? I had issues with her, but she was still my mother. She's gone. She won't see me married or made king, or enjoy any grandchildren I would have given her."

"Oh."

Suddenly, she felt stupid and even *more* miserable. What a selfish, horrible beast she was on top of everything else. It was like the only things that mattered were things that happened to *her.* Here was this—albeit somewhat *duplicitous*—prince with an entire past that was very real for him. And she didn't even think about it.

"I'm an idiot. I'm sorry."

"You're not. And my tragedy doesn't diminish yours. You just found out your parents are dead. Grieve for them—it's right."

"I can't do this, Phillip," she finally said, covering her eyes with her hands, trying to squish the rest of the tears out. She felt completely drained, beaten up, bloody, weak, and *done*. "I can't. . . ."

"You have to," he said firmly. "Take another moment, and then get up. Now that your parents are gone, your people really have no one to lead them. You are the only one. You have to save them and then lead them out of the chaos when we all awake."

"I DON'T EVEN KNOW WHERE WE'RE GOING!" she shouted in despair. She pointed around the tall cathedral of trees, then at the path, which petered out. "I don't know if our cottage even *exists* here! It was all a long shot, wasn't it? Find the cottage, maybe find the fairies, maybe find a way out? We don't know if any of this will really work!"

And that was when they heard the singing.

> *"A mighty woodsman swings his ax,*
> *Alone among the trees-o,*
> *Lonely with no girl or wife,*
> *Until a maid he sees-o. . . ."*

"I can't take much more of this," she said in a low voice.

"No, wait," Phillip said, cocking his head. There was a strange look on his face. "I know that song. . . ."

"*It's going to be a demon!* Or a sociopathic villager or a rabid fox or some sort of horrible little boy who looks like you with a giant spiky mace. . . ."

"FEAR NOT!" the voice called, coming closer. "I HEARD SHOUTS. I AM SENT ON A QUEST TO GIVE SUCCOR AND AID. I SING, YOU KNOW, TO KEEP THE BEARS AWAY. IF THEY HEAR YOU COMING, THEY SORT OF JUST AMBLE ALONG AWAY FROM YOU.

"FEAR NOT! A KING APPROACHES. A KING OF THE WILDS! IF YOU BE TRUE, YOU HAVE NOTH-ING TO FEAR. . . ."

"Let's go," the princess said, finding the strength to leap up. "Come on. Let's avoid this."

But Phillip held her and pointed in the direction the voice was coming from, like a hunter waiting for a stag to appear.

"BUT IF YOU'RE ONE OF THOSE DEMONS SENT BY THAT HAG MALEFICENT, I WOULD STAY AWAY. FOR I WIELD A MIGHTY STAFF AND CUDGEL. . . ."

Out from behind a tree stepped someone who was very probably not a demon.

He wore a ragged black-and-red cloak with torn orange sleeves and undershirt. His boots had probably once been fine but now were bound up and relaced with vines and awkward pieces of badly cured leather and sinew. What was likely white hair sprouting in all directions from his head and brow and neck and chin was gray and brown, well dusted with dirt and twigs and leaves.

One of his eyes was missing, the skin hanging loose over the socket in sad bags.

He did indeed have a mighty staff—or, more precisely, a giant branch used as a crude walking stick. His cudgel was just a large skull-shaped rock he carried in his other hand.

"Father . . . ?" Phillip whispered.

"Phillip . . . ? No . . . it cannot be." The old man's voice fell and he looked around distractedly. "I am seeing things again. Like I used to. Before I lost the bad eye that made me see things that weren't there. Before it was put out, to keep it from lying to me."

"Father, it *is* me," Phillip said, choking.

He ran forward and threw his arms around the crazy, dirty old man.

The princess watched in silence, trying to put it all together. It was too shocking to make sense.

The king began to weep and clasped his bearlike arms tightly around Phillip.

"Phillip . . . Phillip . . . I wish you were *not* here, glad as I am to see you. I only remained sane at all by assuming you were safe, away from all of this, slipped out to be with your little peasant girl. . . . You were right about getting away from the castle. . . . It *is* the *fourteenth* century, after all. . . . Isn't it?"

"Oh, Father. You *have* been out here all this time . . . by yourself . . ." Phillip said, his own eyes wet.

"The Exile . . ." Aurora Rose murmured. "I am so sorry. . . ."

"*YOU!*" King Hubert rounded on her. "Maleficent's little ward!"

"No, no," Phillip said. "It turns out *she* was the peasant I thought I was going to marry . . . but she's actually Princess Aurora. She was in the woods because she was sent away to be raised by the fairies."

"Wait, I remember that, I think," King Hubert said, raising his eyebrows. It stretched the skin over his socket oddly. He scratched it thoughtfully. "Wait. What?"

"Maybe we should start from the beginning," Phillip said. "But quickly. Time is short."

"Time?" King Hubert asked bleakly. "I've been wandering in these woods for years, lad. All I *have* is time."

She let Phillip do the talking. It was strange, once her adventures outside the castle had begun, to suddenly be sitting aside and letting someone tell the story. It was both restful and unsettling.

"But I don't understand . . . tell me again. *Why* was he exiled? What did he do?" Phillip finally asked when he finished the story. He turned to her, as if sensing she felt left out.

She shrugged. "I think . . . it wasn't much, really? He wanted some say in the ruling of the castle. But it probably had more to do with his presence in the castle." She frowned, thinking. "There was no easy explanation for his being there. He was there in the real world because of our wedding. I'll bet Maleficent was afraid of some sort of . . . irregularity in her dreamworld. Of him or me remembering something."

King Hubert nodded. "When that witch threw me out, she said something like 'And now we'll have no problems from *you*, King Hubert.' But it was in a nasty tone. Nasty woman."

"And then . . . what happened to you?" Phillip asked, reaching up as if to stroke his father's brow. Then he stopped, seeming to think better of touching the king in so casual a manner.

"ONCE EXILED, DID I GIVE IN TO FATE?" the king demanded. "I did not! The damn fools in *there* thought the world was dead out *here*! Didn't even take a look. Just took

her word for it. It was beautiful! Green and glorious! Got to go on walkabout. Haven't done that since I was a lad. Ate off the *land*, children! Nuts and mushrooms and rabbits and fruit of the trees! HEALTHY, I tell you!

"Sometimes I would run into some of Maleficent's minions," he added philosophically. The skin over his missing eye twitched. "Had to arm myself. Didn't have my father's sword anymore . . . made myself *new* weapons. King of the Wilds! Hubert may be exiled, but he is still KING!"

Aurora Rose found herself putting her arm around the old man as he got worked up again. At her soft touch, he jumped and looked around. Then he smiled and settled down.

"I couldn't find my kingdom," he continued quietly. "It shouldn't have been hard. Stefan and I could see each other's towers on a clear day. We joked about putting up a rope between them . . . making quick work of a visit. But it wasn't there. . . . It should have been there . . . but it wasn't."

"This is the world inside Aurora's mind, Father," Phillip explained gently. "She's asleep. We're in her dream. She has never been to our kingdom."

"Quite right, quite right. Lost in some girl's sorcerous dream," Hubert said faintly. "Nothing *is* ever quite what it seems. The further I got from that blasted castle, the more things got confused. But also clearer. Memories of another world came back . . . the real world, I suppose. Stefan and Leah—as *good* people. Good friends. It was all mixed up. Rather like the mind of a young lady, I suppose."

Instead of taking umbrage at that, the princess asked the question that had been bothering her. "Isn't it odd that you found us just when we were talking about my parents? When I was about to give up on the quest?"

Hubert drew himself up and looked smug. "Nothing is odd in these woods, dear lady. I was *called*. By a higher power. Some being, an angel, a protective spirit, guided me to you. Told me you were lost. Told me that I should seek you out and guide you home."

"The fairies," Aurora Rose whispered. "It must have been them."

"Fairies?" the king asked, intrigued. "I suppose it could have been. All golden and twinkly, now that I think about it."

"Brilliant! It's all coming together!" Phillip said with a sigh.

"But *can* you help us with what we're looking for?" she asked, pressing him. "We need to find a cottage in the woods. Looks like the one where I grew up, in the real world, with my aunts. Small, with a thatched roof . . . I think. . . ."

"I know *all* these woods, dear lady," the king said, getting up and giving her a deep bow. "Even when they change. Which they do. I *knew* duty would call. And here I am, answering! Needed, at last! Follow me, children!"

He marched forward, a serious look on his face, holding his staff high and his rock firmly.

"He wasn't like this in real life," Phillip whispered as they set off after him.

Aurora Rose gave him a look.

"All right . . . maybe a little. But a lot of it was for show. Underneath he was a stern, solid ruler. Big drinker, big eater, and a very good friend to those who were good friends to him. But if it came to executing criminals of the realm, he had no problem taking a sword and doing it himself."

She shuddered, though she wasn't sure if it was for the Hubert of the past or the Hubert of the present. Phillip was speaking about him like he was already gone.

They followed him on what seemed at first to be a random meander through the trees, completely at odds with where they had been walking before. Hubert strode like a proper king, as if his robes were still long and thick and trailing behind him. But he also kept a watchful eye on everything around him: shadows, the world above, the distant movements. He wasn't *nervous*, precisely. Just aware.

It also looked like he occasionally waved to certain trees and rocks.

The princess decided not to call him out on it. From the way he almost saluted one large boulder, it was obvious that whether or not he actually had discourse with the landscape, he definitely recognized it. And Aurora Rose, broken and beaten up, grieving and wounded, was just relieved to let someone else take the lead for a while. It took all of her concentration just to keep up with the father and son, swinging her stiff and injured left leg into place with every stride. Her side hurt when she breathed; it was a strange pain that felt *wrong*, like bones were doing something they shouldn't.

She wondered what they would have done if Hubert hadn't come along—if the fairies hadn't figured out how to send him.

For the first time on the journey, Phillip walked ahead of her, keeping pace with his father. They didn't talk about anything serious; they just exchanged the occasional strange, manly platitudes that seemed out of keeping with the present situation. Phillip would remark on the weather, and his father would guffaw and tell a story about a terrible downpour during which he had hidden in a small cave— along with two foxes and a badger.

Aurora Rose wondered if she had made that rain. She wondered if it reflected something else that had gone on in her head.

Eventually Phillip seemed to remember the princess and dropped back to be with her.

"You doing all right?" he asked.

"Not great. But all right," she admitted.

"We're almost there," he assured her.

They wandered down the path, not quite touching, not quite bumping shoulders.

The sun must have climbed high beyond the trees; time passed and the light shifted, filtered though it was.

"My lady," King Hubert said. He swept his hand forward dramatically and bowed.

There, starting in the middle of nowhere, was a path of neat little mossy flagstones that led into the darkness of the forest.

Her heart began thumping.

The path didn't look *familiar*, exactly, but she was overwhelmed with nostalgia. Which was strange when she thought about it. In the real world she was less than a day away from her home in the forest, and less than a day had passed since she had left it. And in this world she had never been there at all. But she felt oddly tall, huge really, as if she was coming back to some place she hadn't seen since she was a small child.

She started to run down the path, but Phillip grabbed her hand and held her back.

"Doesn't this look familiar to you?" she whispered.

"It looks very much like the area where we met," Phillip said guardedly. "But not exactly. The trees and the plants are the same, and the . . ."

"Rocks!" she cried in delight, seeing a giant gray boulder with sides so tall and straight it was like a small mountain with sheer cliffs. This time she *did* try to run and was rewarded by stumbling over her bad leg and experiencing a painful tear in her belly.

She bent over, hand to her waist.

Phillip and Hubert looked at her with worry.

"Are you all right?"

No, she realized. Her body wasn't up to much more adventuring.

But she shook her head, put up her hand; she was fine.

"Let's just continue on," she suggested.

Then there was a crackle in the underbrush behind them, where they had come from. It wasn't loud and it wasn't heavy.

It was, however, extremely ominous.

"I thought none of Maleficent's demons could make it here," Phillip said warily. "Here, in the deepest part of Rose's mind."

"That wasn't a bear," Hubert pointed out. "I know from bears."

"The little girl back there wasn't a demon," the princess

said wearily. "And she could be just, you know, *waiting* for us. To come back out. We can't hide in the deepest part of my mind forever."

There was another—very tiny—shuffle of leaves. And the sound of air sucking in from someplace else. A very unnatural *hoooomph*.

"CALLED UPON AGAIN!" Hubert said enthusiastically in response, straightening his robes. "I'LL DEAL WITH THE DEMON. You two go on. Finish your adventure."

"What?" Phillip cried. "No, we should all stick together. Father . . ."

"No, lad," the old man said with a sad smile. "This is my part of the story. Yours lies ahead."

"He's right, Phillip," Aurora Rose said gently. "It's the best plan. Maybe he can delay whatever's out there until we get done whatever we need to."

"Listen to her, my boy. She's a smart one."

Phillip looked back and forth between them desperately for a moment. Then he set his jaw and nodded.

"All right. Thank you, Father. We would never have found it without you," he said, embracing the old man warmly.

"We will see you on the other side," the princess said gratefully. "When we all wake up."

Hubert gave her a funny look.

"The peasant is the princess, eh? I don't think you're either, young lady. I don't know *what* you are. Maybe you don't, either. But . . . I don't think you'll see me on the other side. Exactly the same way, I mean."

"What—what do you mean?" Phillip asked, trying to keep his voice calm.

"What I'm trying to say is, well . . ." The king flustered and fought for words. "Son, I've been lost in these woods for years now. I've had some absolutely top-notch—*top-notch*—adventures and made quite a few furry friends. Put some dreadful demons out of my misery. But I don't think all of me has been entirely found. Do you understand?"

"No," Phillip said with a worried look.

"Ah, well." Hubert clapped him on the shoulder. "Don't worry about it now. You have bigger issues to deal with. Kingdoms to save. Princesses to—well, I don't know. We'll talk later. I wish . . . I wish we could have talked *before*. *Really* talked."

His remaining eye grew glassy.

Then he raised his branch in a kingly salute.

"I shall DEFEAT anything that would ATTACK YOU AND HINDER YOU IN YOUR GLORIOUS QUEST! And WHEN I HAVE PERSEVERED, I shall make my own way back to that infernal vine-covered castle. You may have further need of my aid later on when dealing with that witch. And honestly, I should like to be there when she gets her what's what!'"

He gave one last smile. Then he turned with great, slow dignity and headed back into the shadows of the forest. He had disappeared, like a wild animal, in thirty paces.

Phillip watched him go. Emotions struggled for dominance on his face.

"What . . . just happened?" he asked in a strangled voice. "What just . . . Something just happened. I feel like we just said good-bye somehow."

Aurora Rose put a hand on his arm—her first urge to touch him since their fight. But she wasn't thinking of an *us* or a *we* or a *him*; she saw only Phillip, the boy who had been upbeat and brave and inspiring on this journey, brought to the edge of tears.

He looked down at her hand; the movement dislodged a single drop, which flew to the ground, dampening a salty spot on the leaves.

Then he shook himself and patted her hand.

"Let's go," he whispered.

She nodded.

She could almost ignore the little pains all over her body, lost in the satisfaction she felt from her surroundings. Familiar oak leaves crunched on the ground, tracing their strange shapes in pale dirt, looking like harmless baby monsters.

The smells they made as she crushed them were so heady she wanted to swim in the air. It was fall here, she suddenly realized, while it had been other seasons elsewhere in the dreamworld. Fall was her favorite after spring. Small burnished brown acorns, with their cute tan caps, littered the ground. She used to collect them and . . .

It was difficult to stay present; her consciousness had to be constantly and reluctantly pulled back to the world around her. Every part of her wanted to sink into the memories, the warm ocean of completeness she knew was there now, easily dipped into.

"Come on," the prince said, giving her his arm to lean on. This time she took it right away.

She spotted the cottage first.

"It's . . . *sort* of like that place I was kidnapped from," Phillip said.

It was a pleasant little shack, wood and thatched roof, funny little rooms added on higgledy-piggledy, and one tall chimney reaching up, crooked, above it all. Little puffs of smoke came out.

But it wasn't quite right. She was pretty sure the stones had been normal stone colors, not bright, shiny browns and whites and blacks, like a picture painted by a child.

And there hadn't been a flower garden on the roof, sweet peas dangling over the sides in front of a window.

But it was close enough, she decided.

There was a woman waiting in front of the door, which somehow neither of them noticed at first. A simple dark green dress and a lighter green apron fell in clean, crisp folds over her body. A pair of thick graying braids hung from the sides of her head, behind her ears. Her face was smooth but for a few deep wrinkles. She seemed inclined toward peace and kindness.

"Come in, come in, children," she urged them. "Quickly now."

"It's another trap," Phillip said uncertainly, but even he could feel this was different somehow.

"I . . . know her?" the princess said, confused but intrigued. "No, this is all right, Phillip."

"This cottage is the safest place in your mind, Aurora Rose."

The girl jumped at her full name—what she had begun to think of as her *proper* name.

"Please hurry," the woman urged them.

The princess looked Phillip in the eye, and for once she was reassuring *him*. He accepted her near-motionless nod and the two stepped forward.

Childhood Haunts

Aurora Rose blinked.

· Instead of the expected dark-but-homey cottage with the usual paraphernalia—tidy hearth, pots, a broom—the interior was much, much larger than it should have been. And also brilliant, blinding gold.

When Aurora Rose's eyes finally adjusted, she saw where they really were: in an ornate, almost *over*decorated room in the castle. *Her* castle. A room she had never seen before. The walls were draped in tapestries of golden animals: rabbits, deer, birds, a unicorn. An orange fire blazed merrily within a positively giant fireplace whose mantel was white marble inlaid with gold. Huge windows with leaded glass panes let in shafts of happy white sunlight. Thick rugs of white and gold thread covered the floor. Brightly colored swags and garlands of flowers hung from every exposed surface.

In the middle of the room was a golden cradle. Above it stood two tall, motionless adults.

Aurora Rose felt something in her throat, a sob or a cry of joy, as she realized who they were, and whom they were gazing at.

She crept forward, almost like a forest creature, hands clasping each other.

She peeked in the cradle.

There, kicking and pink-faced, was baby Aurora.

Grown-up Aurora knew herself immediately.

The eyes were the same, the pale wisps of golden hair the same.

But while *most* people would have been endlessly fascinated by the chance to observe themselves at such an early age, grown-up Aurora Rose more wanted to see something— some*one*—else.

She turned to look at the two adults who loomed over the cradle.

Queen Leah.

Almost like an older version of Aurora, but with slightly browner hair. Slightly browner, thicker, *friendlier* eyebrows. The princess saw where her cheeks would eventually wind up, shed of all their remaining baby fat: sailing above the high cheekbones she also inherited.

But her mother's looks didn't matter; it was the look she gave her *baby* that mattered. The queen was completely and utterly enraptured by her daughter in the cradle. Her eyes were wide and unblinking; a very slight smile was on her parted lips. Nothing could distract her from her watch.

King Stefan.

Skinny. A little tired-looking. Kind brown eyes above a not particularly royal mustache and beard. His robes gave his body some depth; the fire gave his cheeks a little ruddiness.

"Mother," Aurora Rose breathed. "Father."

The parents she had never known. The parents she was supposed to have been reunited with—only to part from—on her sixteenth birthday. On her wedding day. The ones who had given her life and then given her away.

And this was the only way she would ever get to see them again—in her memories. Her mother's beautiful, loving face. Her father's, well, kingly one. She couldn't talk to them, ask them questions, hug them. She would never be able to find out why they had done what they had. She would never be able to curse them or forgive them.

Phillip coughed quietly, clearing his throat. Reluctantly, she looked up.

Standing by the fireplace was the woman who had let them in, along with two other women.

One was in all different slightly faded shades of blue. She wore robes and belts and scarves and scraps of cloth and even had quick blue eyes that matched—although *they* weren't faded. Her hair was as brown as a polished chestnut and tied up in crazy buns on the back of her head with sticks pointing out all over to hold them in place.

The third woman was huge: tall and muscled, strapping and strong. She wore a red tunic over rust-red leggings and boots. Her dark blond hair hung to her waist and was pushed back from her face with a simple leather headband. Her skin was tan and a little windburned, and her light brown eyes were dancing.

"The fairies!" Aurora Rose cried.

"Sort of," she added.

Her memories still weren't perfect, but there was something off about them. Weren't they a little younger than her aunts? Or maybe they were older. They certainly dressed differently. And their eyes were . . . different.

"They don't look exactly like the twinkling ladies who rescued me," Phillip whispered. "But they *feel* like them?"

"Nothing is exactly the same in the dreamworld," the one in blue said. "Just as in a dream your own house seems different, with more rooms, or things within it placed strangely. Everything here is a result of your perception and edited by the quality of your memory. Reality is entirely subjective."

"She means don't worry," the one in green said. "Things aren't what they seem—but that's not always a bad thing."

"You tried to rescue me in the castle," the princess said. "You appeared to me and told me to wake up."

"Not precisely, not us," the blue one said. "That was a manifestation of the real, waking-world fairies. As was the one who sent Hubert to guide you."

"Trust me, if *we* could have come to your rescue," the one in red said, "I would have come with my sword drawn and a thirst for Maleficent's blood."

Phillip looked at her with something like affection.

"Here in this room, you are in the only part of your memory completely free from Maleficent's reach," the woman in green said. She spread her hands and smiled. "These are your deepest, oldest, most untouched memories. You guard them very carefully—as do we all."

"But that horrible girl thing attacked us not too far from here," Phillip said accusingly. "Just a little ways that way."

"Ah," the woman in green said sadly. "The manifestation spoke truly: mostly, she was a piece of Aurora Rose herself. A monster from her own mind. Maleficent may have given her a nudge, or awoken her fully, but she has always been close to the princess's heart."

"I don't get it, myself," the woman in red said frankly. "If it were up to me, I would have slain that nasty thing years ago. In the real world."

"Focus, please," the one in blue said to the red one. "Aurora, this all comes back to the fact that *you are the dreamer*. You, in the end, are responsible for this world. Inadvertently the beginning and deliberately—hopefully— the end. Only you can end the curse and wake everyone.

"What we are experiencing now are the final effects of a magical promise made sixteen years ago, sort of a balancing out of a magical equation. To wit, Maleficent publicly cursed you to die on your sixteenth birthday. Then Merryweather fixed it a bit with the amendment about you falling asleep. But unbeknownst to all of us, Maleficent tied her soul up in the curse. Had you actually died, your life force—and that of everyone else in the kingdom, to a lesser effect—would have been transferred to her. Instead, when Phillip killed her, Maleficent's soul was still bound to you and followed you into your sleep. And, of course, we can all see what the result of *that* was."

"Her controlling me and the world of my dreams," Aurora Rose murmured.

"And, unfortunately, the lives of everyone else asleep with you," the one in green added sadly. "An unintended consequence of a little bit of good the fairies thought they were doing by tying the fate of the kingdom to yours so that even if it took a hundred or a thousand years for the curse to be broken by true love, you wouldn't wake up in a world you didn't know, surrounded by the great-great-grandchildren of people you knew."

"All of which is neither here nor there," the blue one continued. "What is important is that a curse of this magnitude and complication can only be broken by spilling royal blood."

"*Queen* Maleficent," Aurora Rose murmured.

The one in red smiled at her appreciatively. "You must return to the castle and defeat her," she said, hand on her sword. "You must kill her once and for all. The moment she is finally dead and royal blood is shed, all will from their slumber rise and return to their waking lives.

"We will aid you, of course," she added with a bow.

The princess let out an audible sigh of relief; she hadn't even realized she was holding her breath. Just the thought of the one in red battling by her side was encouraging. And having the other two around . . . well, they might at least be good for moral support.

"But as the dreamer, you already have incredible powers at your disposal," the one in green said, "as you have discovered yourself. In the end, this is *your* world. You control it."

"All right," Phillip said, tapping his own sword. "We

have our own sorcerous Rose, two good hand-to-hand fighters, two, uh, whatever you green and blue ladies can do . . . against dream Maleficent. That *sounds* good. But what can *Maleficent* do, really? I defeated her with help before."

The green one looked uneasily at the princess. "She has been growing stronger of late. I believe you can feel it—because *we* can."

The red one lowered her eyes and kneeled for just a moment before rising again. "I'm sorry, Your Majesty, but the death of your parents has only made her more powerful. She has now fed upon royal blood and is much stronger."

Your Majesty.

Aurora Rose shivered.

It was like the nightmare she had had in the haystack . . . what they had called her . . . because her parents were dead. And they were now. She was queen. *Queen.*

She looked at Phillip, who gave her a sad smile and the straight-backed bow royalty gave those of higher rank.

She swallowed hard.

Forget the word, she told herself. She had to *act* like a queen.

"Maleficent *killed* them and is more powerful. Like she did Lady Astrid. Does she . . . She then takes something from them. Their blood. In her staff? I saw but didn't quite understand. . . ."

The blue one nodded.

"She took my parents' *blood* . . . and used it . . ." the princess repeated, feeling the first stirrings of anger.

"You shall have your vengeance," the red one said grimly.

The green one shook her head sadly. "Vengeance will not bring them back. Aurora Rose was on the cusp of meeting her mother and father, from whom she was separated for sixteen years. It is a miracle that even *this* memory of them still exists. She will never be able to talk to them, blame them, learn from them, hate them, or love them for themselves now. She can only deal with the results of their actions."

The red one shrugged. "Vengeance might make her feel better."

"Also, it would wake everyone up," the blue one pointed out brightly. "A win all around."

"Show a little compassion!" the green one hissed.

Now the blue one shrugged. "Not my thing. That's all you. I'm here to strategize."

Aurora Rose looked back and forth among the three women, gladly distracted from the sad events by the puzzle before her. The fairies in real life had their own personalities, of course, despite their superficial similarities as ageless, chatty, loving aunt figures. Flora tended to try to lead and made decisions for them. Merryweather seemed to understand the basic workings of the world better, although she rarely acted on this knowledge and instead chose to comment snarkily on it. Sometimes she got sneaky and went behind Flora's back. Fauna was the one who hugged the princess the most and often acted as an intermediary between the other two.

The green one, "Fauna," seemed more concerned with how Aurora Rose was feeling—how *everyone* was feeling. She was the one who had been waiting outside the cottage for the prince and princess. Like she was the one who *cared*.

And the blue one "Merryweather" seemed *incredibly* quick-minded and brilliant. And even snarkier.

"Flora" was brave and powerful and ready to plunge into any physical combat. And not for nothing, she was built like a gladiator.

They were *all* acting like extreme versions of their real selves.

What did it mean?

She found herself drifting to the window. As she suspected, it did not look out on the lands beyond the outer wall. It was the view from her room in the cottage in the forest: apple trees where birds nested and squirrels scampered, birch trees whose golden leaves lit up the meadow in fall, a corner of the tiny kitchen garden the aunts tended. A peaceful scene that combined wild and tamed nature in a way that was so familiar it hurt.

"I'm . . . never coming back here in real life, am I?"

The three women looked at her sadly.

"Probably not, child," the green one said. "Or not for a long time."

"With your parents dead and no male heir, there will be a terrible mess when you all wake up, assuming we defeat Maleficent," the blue one said. "You will either take over the throne and defend it from the spurious claims of distant cousins, or marry Phillip and combine your kingdoms, or some variation of those situations, none of which will leave you much time to visit childhood haunts."

Aurora Rose sucked in a deep and sudden painful breath.

It was the word *childhood* that stung. Before the dreamworld, she would have rejected the term: she was sixteen and a woman, for heaven's sake! She had chosen the love of her life and had planned to run away with him.

But now the looming permanent closing of a door on her past life seemed a little too inevitable and sad.

"I wake up and I'm grown-up," she said dryly. "*That's* some subtlety there."

Phillip, who had been silent through the whole exchange, looked at her with concern.

"Rose . . . you didn't used to be so . . . cynical . . ." he said, scraping for words. "Sarcastic? I know the death of your parents has been a grievous blow, but you're becoming—no, changing into—something . . . I don't know. . . ."

She just looked at him.

"Not that I don't like it!" Phillip added quickly. "You're just different. That's all."

"Oh, he's a regular genius, that one," the blue one said.

The green one whacked her on the arm.

Aurora Rose smiled faintly. "Maybe I'm becoming *myself.*"

She took Phillip's hand and pointed out the window.

"Come here, let me show you something. I used to climb that tree there—the biggest apple tree. I always thought the best apples were the highest up. I pretended the lower branches were a horse. You can just see the pea trellises there. I loved making them with Aunt Fauna, out of dried vines and twigs. It was like weaving with plants. And I loved the little curlicue ends of the peas. . . ."

"I would love you to show me around where you grew up," Phillip said gently, squeezing her hand. "Whatever you feel for me now . . . I would enjoy it. Someday."

She gave the prince a quick, sad smile, then took his other hand and clasped them both for a moment.

"I know. I know. But . . . we have other things to do."

The three women looked at her approvingly. They moved to the other side of the room and stood by a door

Aurora Rose was sure hadn't been there before. She squared her shoulders and walked forward, head held high, imagining she had on robes of state, swirling behind her. Phillip followed.

"First thing is to properly suit you two up," the blue fairy said matter-of-factly.

They entered a long, broad hall lined with suits of armor and closets and chests of clothing stuffed to overflowing. Dresses, doublets, capes, and underskirts were all crammed so tightly that it looked like the furniture was choking to death on ripples of bright colors. Helmets, snoods, caps, gloves, tippets, girdles, and other accessories were piled haphazardly on shelves.

At one time Aurora Rose would have been *thrilled* to try on all the new and different gowns. But now she strode forward, looking for a nice pair of gauntlets that would fit instead.

Phillip was like a child in front of a table strewn with candy and sweets. He picked up helmets, held them out and regarded them with a serious eye, then put them down . . . only to skip over to the greaves and cuirasses, practically bubbling with delight.

"Can't Rose just magic us up protection? Like an invisible shield or something?" he asked, trying on a breastplate for size.

The green one gave him an indulgent smile. "The less

she has to *think* about, to concentrate on, when the battle is joined, the better. Having these already on may buy you a few extra moments."

At first the princess went for the ugliest, most clumsy-looking pieces, in defiance of . . . of . . .

Of, well, being a princess.

But when she went to the tarnished silver oval that served as a mirror and observed her slit-mouthed metal mask, the grotesque gray gauntlets, and the huge-shouldered, spiked breastplate, all she saw was a monster.

She cocked her head and so did the monster. What was it thinking?

Slowly, she turned away from the mirror and went back to the racks and cupboards.

"You want something to inspire your subjects," the green fairy said gently, helping her take the mask off, "not frighten them."

"I know," Aurora Rose said glumly.

The green fairy squeezed her hands through the gauntlets.

"It's not fair that you don't have time. To try on all the different possibilities."

The princess gave her a wry look. "My *subconscious* isn't all that *subtle*, either, is it?"

"In our defense, your world experience and reading habits haven't led you to being the most sophisticated person on the planet," the blue fairy said, blowing the dust off what looked very much like a child's shield, complete with big shiny gems set in it. She raised a knowing eyebrow.

"I didn't know I had it in me to be so *snarky*, either," the princess said, putting her hands on her hips.

The blue fairy shrugged.

"Just calling it like I see it."

The red fairy disentangled herself from Phillip, with whom she was having a broad laugh about the comparative weight and density of different kinds of steel.

"Try these," she suggested. She held out a pair of simple long gauntlets that were almost as fine as gloves, chain underneath and plate on top. Aurora Rose carefully took off the ones she wore and slipped the others on.

They fit perfectly.

"This is a bit more your style," the blue one said, approaching her with a breastplate that was almost as big as she was. It was curved femininely to fit Aurora Rose's body, but not ridiculously so. A staid design of roses and thorns was inlaid along the sides.

It was sturdy, and *heavy*.

The princess had to readjust the way she stood to support it while everyone helped buckle it on the back.

"And for the top . . ." the red one said, looking around.

"Let *her* choose," the green one suggested gently.

Aurora Rose walked down the aisle slowly, getting used to the weight of the armor. She passed each of the women and then Phillip—dashing in his shining cuirass and silver-white greaves, like a soldier from ancient Rome. Her eyes swept over everything, everywhere, pausing nowhere. Golden helms, intricate onyx headpieces, spiked and dangerous-looking crowns, plated metal turbans.

Finally, she saw what she wanted.

She strode forward and lifted a helmet—one she *knew* would fit—off the top shelf. A point came down the middle of the forehead to protect her nose and was also vaguely reminiscent of Maleficent's headpiece. But instead of horns, silver wings swept back over the ears.

With slow, sure movements she put it on.

It *did* fit.

Perfectly.

She turned around to show the others.

Phillip sucked in his breath.

"You look *magnificent*, Rose. Like—like an ancient goddess of war."

"Like victory," the green one said softly.

The edges of everything around them changed—quietly and unobtrusively. The five found themselves in a large, silent room that was a strange mixture of what a child might imagine a throne room looked like and the cottage in which Aurora Rose had grown up. The stones that made up the walls were all far too big and simple-looking, the throne giant and garish and gold. There were several fireplaces around the sides instead of the one grand one the Thorn Castle had, and they all looked cozier, each with a little pot and broom by it. The floor was packed dirt with no rugs, and the tables were ridiculously fancy, with huge carved feet and yellow-and-blue runners down the middle—but set with crude wood and clay bowls and tureens of porridge.

"Damn acorns again," Phillip swore humorously, lifting a steaming lid.

"We're not quite as skilled as Maleficent at manipulating your dreamworld," the blue one apologized. "This is what your mind came up with when we asked it for a practice room."

"Let's get to work," the green one said politely but firmly. "We haven't much time."

"We need to work on *summoning* first," the blue one said. "But do not turn to it immediately in battle. There are rules, even in this world. The creation of something from nothing will exhaust you unduly—as you may have already noticed. Better to make do with the things already around you. Keep this as a last resort."

"You made a sword before," the red one said, tilting her chin at the empty space on Aurora Rose's girdle where it had hung previously. "Can you make a dagger?"

Aurora Rose twitched her nose. Had she ever seen a dagger? In the Thorn Castle, some men and boys affected them. She had never seen the blades used for anything more than cleaning fingernails (the uncouth) or stabbing food (the slightly more couth). She was pretty sure she had never held one.

"What about a *knife*, then? Just . . . a knife? A *sharp* knife?" the red one asked impatiently.

Aurora Rose could manage that. Her aunts had never seemed to care when she handled the one very sharp little bronze paring knife. They had let her hold it even as a toddler.

She closed her eyes and held out her hands. She remembered the bone handle. She remembered the dull golden gleam. She remembered the sharp, slightly curved tip, perfect for starting to peel the thick rind of a fruit or vegetable.

She felt its weight in her hand even before she opened her eyes.

"Well done!" cheered the green one.

"Good, good," the red fairy said impatiently. "Now summon two more. Quickly."

Aurora Rose bit her lip.

The additional daggers appeared in her palm, which was now sweaty.

"Great job!" Phillip said excitedly.

"Now throw them at the throne," the red one urged.

Aurora Rose blinked, then did what she was told. She was good at that.

She was not so good at throwing three daggers one-handed. They flew not very far and went every which way, clattering on tables and dirt floor.

Everyone stared at her.

The princess reddened.

"With your *mind*, you ninny!" the blue one snapped.

The green one did not hit the blue one, though it looked like she was sorely tempted.

"You won't win against Maleficent in a fair hand-to-hand combat," the red one said politely. "In this protected part of your mind, she can't see in; she won't know how strong your control over your own demesne has become. So. Um. Try again. With *magic*."

Aurora Rose chewed her lip, feeling embarrassed and hot. She closed her eyes—

"Not a good idea in a fight," Phillip said gently. "Keep your peepers open."

Aurora Rose took a deep breath and forced her eyes to stay open, not blinking. She held out her hand. Three daggers appeared in it.

She looked at the throne.

The three daggers launched themselves through the air and whistled as they flew. Where they hit the back of the giant chair, the tips buried themselves in the wood.

She let out her breath.

Everyone cheered.

That was a strange thing, she realized as she panted and felt her cheeks cool down. Almost like people believed she could do this. Like she *could* do this.

"Great!" the red one said. "Now grow a hill out of the middle of the floor."

The Really Long Journey Back to the Castle

It was hard to tell how much time she spent practicing, but it *felt* like an infinite number of afternoons of summoning the rocks from the walls to come to her and rebuild themselves into a barrier. Unending hours of bringing anything weak and breakable down from the ceiling onto the head of her imagined enemy. Days of causing the very earth itself to ripple like the ocean under the feet of her assailant—without a break for snacks.

And yet it still wasn't as much time as they needed.

"We must go soon," the blue one told Phillip in a low voice while the princess made chairs fly up and around the room. "Time passes slowest in this, her most buried memory, but it passes nonetheless. Maleficent has abandoned all pretense of being good and may just keep consuming people until every one of them is gone."

"But once we leave here she'll know where we are, won't she?" Phillip asked.

"Unavoidable," the red one said, polishing the end of her sword. He watched her deft movements with frank admiration. "We must progress back to the outer edge of her dreams, where the queen holds sway. She will not come to meet us."

"A bird helped trip one of Maleficent's traps on our way here," the prince said eagerly. "Maybe along the way we could gather some more? Have them help us?"

"Birds?" The blue one looked at him blankly. "Oh, sure. Yeah. Birds. Why not? Any help, right?"

The green one patted his knee encouragingly.

Phillip twisted his lip in a suspicious pout.

The chairs dipped in the air and almost fell as the princess tried not to laugh.

"All right," the red one said, giving her sword a final swipe with the leather strop she had been using. "Let's go."

The little procession made its way back through the room with the cradle, where the princess said a silent good-bye to her parents and her baby self, who seemed so happy in the moments before she was whisked away to the woods for sixteen years.

They filed through the front door, into the twilight gloom—which seemed utterly appropriate for the beginning of their secret journey.

The three women were suddenly wearing travel robes, though no one had said a thing or lifted a finger. Phillip raised an eyebrow.

"Shouldn't we magic up some provisions or supplies for the return trip?"

"Don't be silly, you don't *really* need to eat," the blue one said. "You're not really here."

"It's like being dead," the green one said helpfully. "You realize you only *think* you need the stuff the living do."

Phillip's look turned to one of comic dismay as the implications of what she said began to sink in.

Meanwhile, Aurora Rose was thinking furiously in the pause before the storm. She had never done anything violent in her life before these adventures. She wasn't sure she could *plan* to now. *Kill* someone? Someone she knew? Would any of her remembered affection for Maleficent slow her hand when they faced off?

It certainly wouldn't cause a moment's hesitation from Maleficent.

She discreetly juggled two or three rocks at her side with her mind. It helped distract her.

"I'm going to miss this," she said aloud with a sigh. "All this work and when I wake up I won't even have these powers anymore."

"You didn't have them to begin with," the red fairy said pragmatically.

"But she has experienced it *now*," the green one said. "It's hard to go back to not having something so wonderful. Plus now she also knows she was living with fairies the whole time! And *that's* gone, too. She's going back to being a regular human girl in a world where princesses are used as pawns and never have any sort of real power of their own."

"Thanks," the princess said. "I was trying not to think about that."

"Hey," Phillip whispered in her ear as he caught up with her. "I think I've figured it out! The blue one is the smart one? And the red one is the brave one? And the green one is . . . nice? Or compassionate or something?"

He really was just trying to help.

"Oh . . . *yes*—I'll bet that's probably right," she said slowly, trying to make it sound like she meant it. "I was sort of coming to a similar conclusion myself."

Phillip smiled, pleased with her praise.

"Wish I had my horse. Samson could take at least two of us. Or maybe three. He's really strong, you know—just a bit temperamental. Did I ever tell you he was part Nisaean?

You wouldn't guess it from his color. Definitely has war horse tendencies, I can tell you that."

She understood that he was excited by the return journey to the castle, probably a little nervous about the final showdown, and perhaps showing off a bit to the one in red.

"I *do* wish there was a faster way to the castle," she said instead of *shut up*. "I'm worried about the time we're wasting and Maleficent's being able to see what we're—"

Interlude

Time became disjointed.

Her head grew muddled and thick. For the very first time in the world of the Thorn Castle, she *knew* she was asleep: groggy and aware things weren't making sense, as if in the middle of a very deep dream.

Her Return

"Be careful what you wish for, my dear."

Aurora Rose was not altogether surprised to see that they were back in the throne room of the Thorn Castle.

She blinked her eyes muzzily and was transfixed, for just a moment, by how out of place her little party looked. She, in armor and golden rags. The three strange ladies, dressed in red, blue, and green. The prince, who looked somehow more alive and glowing than any of the murky people around the edges of the room.

A blinding green light shone from the orb at the top of Maleficent's staff; it bathed the room in a sickly cast and confused the shadows. Her visage, never that healthy-looking to begin with, was also a throbbing green. But the queen's purple-and-black robes lay thickly and luxuriously around her as always, and she sat with less of the tense elegance she always had; now she seemed more relaxed, almost *sated.*

A raven perched next to her wrist on the throne and seemed to smile evilly. The princess was confused; Maleficent had never kept a pet. The shallow, visual similarities between the two were not subtle: both familiar and mistress were black, yellow, angular, and vicious-looking.

The princess turned away from the pulsing green light and blinked again to take a better look at the rest of the room. The people pressed against its walls were those she had spent the last subjective decades with—the people whose real bodies were elsewhere, sleeping. They seemed strangely unfamiliar now, like someone was forcing her to name people in a portrait who were hard to distinguish and resembled others she might have known.

Maleficent's unnatural servants stood guard in front of them. There were more of the nasty goblin-like creatures with yellow eyes than Aurora Rose remembered. They stood insolently with their spear tips crossed to make an improvised fence to hold their prisoners back. Obviously, the queen had given up all pretense; the poor nobles and servants and peasants now all knew what she was saving them for.

"Sorry, what?" Prince Phillip asked, clearly a little disoriented.

Maleficent looked annoyed.

"*What* what?"

"What did you just say? I missed it."

"I *said*, 'Be careful what you wish for,'" the evil fairy hissed through her teeth. "You were just wishing to arrive here faster. I arranged that for you."

"Yes, yes, we get it. Very clever," Aurora Rose said, a little impatiently. That was *one* nice thing about all this: she realized that the guilt she felt for her irritation with Maleficent's more annoying habits was irrelevant now. She could be honestly irked by the woman's penchant for the dramatic.

She looked deep into the woman's face, trying to recall everything she had felt for her, and why. How she had wanted nothing more than respect, friendship, and love from her. But there was not a lot that was human in that face, she now realized. Or even "normal" fairy. She saw the queen through two different sets of eyes, and her new vision was rapidly overtaking the old.

This was an unapologetically evil, power-mad, and furious creature in front of her.

What would a real queen do in Aurora's place?

"Please step down from my throne," Queen Aurora Rose said coldly. "And release me from this curse."

Maleficent was genuinely taken aback for a moment, her yellow eyes flaring in surprise.

Then she threw back her head and laughed. The raven cackled in unison with her. Her other evil servants gibbered and hooted as soon as they felt it was all right to do so.

"And *what*, oh beneficent princess Aurora? You'll deign to spare my life?"

"No, but I shall grant you a dignified and quick death."

She felt rather than saw the change in stance of those around her; she would bet that the prince was smiling grimly.

Maleficent cocked her head and gave a knowing look. She stroked the raven for effect.

"Well, my, my, a few short days in the world outside the castle and suddenly you've become a cold-blooded killer."

"I haven't become anything of the sort. In my authority as queen of the realm, I am executing a known criminal, assassin, and enemy to the state."

"Why not throw me in a prison and have me rot there forever?" Maleficent asked philosophically.

The younger woman raised an eyebrow at the fairy.

"Apparently, killing you *once* isn't enough to get rid of you," she said dryly. "I hardly think prison bars—*dream* prison bars—would hold you."

"Oh, you flatter me," Maleficent said, looking down and touching her chest coyly. But her grin was all evil and hell-fire. She hissed: "Of course, you also flatter *yourself* if you think you can get within a foot of this throne without my obliterating you on the spot."

She ducked her head like the dragon she had briefly been—prepared to strike. Prince Phillip flinched.

When the evil fairy hunched over, Lianna was revealed standing behind the throne, her black eyes unreadable, her face impassive.

"Greetings, Lady Lianna," Aurora Rose said coldly, nodding toward the girl. "I'm delighted to see things worked out so well for you."

"Oh," Maleficent said, putting on a moue of surprise and concern. "Did you—did you think she was *replacing* you? As my 'ward'?" Her face twisted into a sneer. "She's nothing, don't you know that? Just a little bit of my essence and a lot of clever magic. With some help from the powers below."

At this, Lianna's eyes hardened. She didn't move.

Aurora Rose had a comeback ready, but it died on her tongue. All her queenliness shifted for a moment, slipped aside as a twice-orphaned girl broke through.

"But did you feel nothing at all for *me*?" she whispered.

Maleficent looked shocked at the question.

The room was silent. Everyone else also seemed surprised by this turn of the conversation.

"All of those 'years,'" Aurora Rose said, pressing her, advancing slowly on the throne, "all those talks we had, all those meals we shared, all the things we did together . . . did you really feel *nothing* for me?"

Maleficent gripped the top of her staff tightly; her fingers over the orb caused the hideous light in the room to dim. Every human shuddered in relief.

"You were my means to an end," she finally said.

"You're not answering my question," Aurora Rose made herself say. It was hard but felt good. Never, in either life, had she ever questioned someone in authority before.

"Whatever *feelings* I may initially have had in the rearing of a human child, in the end, were irrelevant," Maleficent said. "Through your death I would live again. After being murdered so callously by your *prince*."

"Murdered? *YOU WERE TRYING TO KILL HIM.* Because he was trying to save *me*. Are you that deluded, Maleficent? All of this—*all of this*—came about because of the curse you put on me as a *baby*!" she yelled. "A *baby*. Because you weren't invited to a *party*!"

"Your parents had no respect for me and the powers that I wield."

"You. Cursed. A. Baby. Because. You. Were. Slighted."

Prince Phillip moved quietly up to be next to her, hand on his sword.

Maleficent shrugged one elegant shoulder.

"And? Do not slight those of great power. I believe that's the lesson to be learned there."

Aurora Rose suddenly felt the urge to draw a weary and exasperated hand over her face. She was losing this verbal battle. She was losing her own train of thought. There was nothing to reach in Maleficent. The princess had been raised in a dreamworld by a madwoman. She had been looking for a mother in a monster.

The three fairies and Prince Phillip moved in close around her, sensing a change. They faced Maleficent together.

"What made you so horrible, Maleficent?" the blue one demanded. "What made you into this monster of a fairy?"

"Was it something in your childhood?" the green one asked. "Is that why not being invited to a party irked you so much?"

"Who cares?" the red one said, brandishing her sword. "She's evil now. Let's get her."

"What if I had some little power?" Aurora Rose interrupted. "What if I had some ability in me, like yours? Would you have *kept me close and taught me well, schooled me in the arts of magic*?"

Maleficent was speechless for a moment upon the realization that Aurora had overheard that conversation with her parents.

"But you have no powers," she finally said. "It is irrelevant."

The two women looked each other in the eye.

Then a dagger flew through the air and buried itself in the throne next to Maleficent's head.

The evil fairy's eyes widened in shock.

"But what if I did?" Aurora Rose whispered fiercely.

"Doesn't count," Maleficent said slowly. "This world isn't real."

The princess almost threw her hands up in frustration.

"What about all of those special tutors you assigned to me? What about all of those things you did that seemed a whole lot like caring?"

"It was just a game," Maleficent said lightly. "To keep me amused in this dreadfully boring place."

But she couldn't look the princess in the eye. She faltered under Aurora Rose's stare and turned to pet her raven to get away from it.

She would never, ever reveal the truth. Even if there *was* some last, lingering thread of humanity about her.

"You have no idea," Aurora Rose said with a mix of relief and disappointment, "how close I actually was to being able to forgive you. Killing you is going to be so much easier now."

Maleficent recovered herself quickly. "*Easier?* Killing *me?* I think you speak too soon, mighty queen."

"I am *less than a foot from you*," Aurora Rose whispered into the fairy's face, "and I'm not obliterated."

There was utter silence in the castle as all watched the evil fairy with the horns and the princess with the silver helm glare at each other, their noses no more than an inch apart.

Maleficent's jaw worked twice before fury overcame her. She thrashed her staff arm impatiently.

Vines—thick, rubbery, and strong but sickly-looking—twined up the princess's legs and torso. Suddenly, she was being pulled backward, sliding across the throne room floor.

"Rose!" Phillip cried, trying to grab her.

When she was about twenty feet away, the vines hardened into woody trunks that glued her to the floor and pinned her arms to her sides.

Maleficent rose, her cape and robes billowing behind her, caught up in the eddies of magic she was beginning to summon.

At once the green fairy was flying between the two of them.

It was a little shocking; the three women hadn't shown any fairylike abilities up to that point. And seeing a full-grown middle-aged lady go buzzing overhead—albeit one who seemed to get slightly smaller as she went—was slightly unnerving.

"Be reasonable, Maleficent," the green fairy said, sounding like a disappointed mother making a last effort with an unruly child before punishing her. "This is *Aurora's world*. You can't hope to win. You're in *her mind*."

"Oh, I have no fear in that," Maleficent said calmly. Her raven cackled once. "The little girl barely can figure out her own feelings, much less what she wants or how the world works. *Now out of my way, you useless firefly!*"

She pointed her staff and a flash of purple lightning crackled out. The green fairy dipped and just barely avoided it; the bolt hit a stone in the ceiling above her, which exploded, leaving a sooty black mark where it had been. The green fairy gave Maleficent a chastising look.

"People change. People *grow*, Maleficent. *Normal* people."

The queen ignored her and kept letting the lightning bolts fly.

Despite the green fairy's size and billowing dress, she managed to deftly avoid most of them. The throne room lit up with purple flashes, and she buzzed around them as they illuminated her features—in fact, very *much* like a firefly.

One bolt veered off and shot over one of the prisoners; he ducked, but it still managed to set his hat on ugly purple fire. The poor man threw it to the ground and stomped on it despite the warning growls from the guards.

"Can we do this someplace else?" the green fairy demanded worriedly. "There are a lot of innocent bystanders who will die in the real world if they're hit in this one."

Aurora Rose wondered if the green fairy knew how incredibly stupid she was being.

Maleficent did what anyone who knew Maleficent at all

would expect: she grinned a toothy, lips-pulled-back, skull-like grin and pointed with her staff.

A purple crack of lighting exploded from it and roared its way across the room, then ended its path in the heart of a man. Aurora's old painting tutor.

He groaned once and then crumpled. The smell of burning human flesh filled the air.

Aurora Rose swore in rage and struggled against the vines. At least they didn't cut into her skin, protected as she was by her breastplate and gauntlets.

Then she remembered she didn't need to *be* anywhere to do what she needed to do. She tried not to close her eyes and calmed her inner self.

"Not yet," the blue fairy whispered to Aurora Rose. "Let us do the initial battle. Wear her down. Keep your attack as a surprise at the end."

"But more people will die!"

"*Everybody* will die if Maleficent wins!" the blue one shot back. "Try to think *tactically!*"

"*MURDERER!*" the green fairy howled, and dove for the queen.

Maleficent aimed around her, picking out another person in the crowd.

The green fairy banked to the side to intercept the bolt. She held out her hand; suddenly, there was a wand in it. A crackle of golden energy flashed out and knocked the purple magic aside. Gold and purple sparks rained on the room as they canceled each other out.

As if she was choosing flowers, Maleficent calmly aimed her staff at different people in the room and then fired.

The green fairy dove and twisted, shot high and rolled, parrying each bolt with a bolt of her own.

Maleficent twirled her staff and bit her lip but didn't seem that concerned; it was more like she was playing a difficult game than trying to kill people.

Her attacks came faster.

The dream prisoners cowered and ducked. Gold and purple light made terrible shadows behind them, multiplied the prisoners by a thousand shadow prisoners. Maleficent's evil servants laughed and only occasionally tried to avoid the bolts.

One got hit.

He exploded on the spot, fangs and tusks and yellow eyes and trotters all disintegrating immediately and becoming black soot. There was nothing wet, nothing animal, nothing real or alive about the death.

His compatriots standing on either side hooted and laughed at his fate, at their luck.

And then Maleficent suddenly turned and aimed her staff directly at the green fairy.

With a toothy snarl she sent a giant bolt arcing across the room.

The green fairy dove, but she was too slow, too late, too concerned with saving other people's lives to worry about her own.

Her legs and arms flailed outward as the energy hit her directly in the heart; purple rays erupted from her eyes.

There was a huge, brilliant explosion.

Aurora Rose turned away, unable to look.

When the light faded, a small, dim green ball hung uselessly in the air where the fairy had been. It dipped and bobbed a little, unintelligent and barely animate.

"Begone, little firefly." Maleficent laughed.

The red fairy let out a strangled cry of rage.

She ran forward, sword drawn, making straight for Maleficent's heart.

Maleficent dipped her staff experimentally at the woman.

The red fairy deflected the purple bolt easily, parrying it away as if it were nothing more than a fly.

Maleficent fired again.

The red fairy deflected the lightning again.

Maleficent frowned and sent out a spray of bolts—dozens of them, one after the other.

All that resulted in was the red fairy's slowing her advance to defend herself from the attacks. She didn't *stop*.

Her arms moved quickly, her muscles flexed beautifully as she contorted herself into different positions to avoid being hit. Her brow furrowed with the effort, but her eyes remained clear, full of concentration and anger and not a hint of fear.

She managed to inch her way forward a little at a time.

Prince Phillip, still beside the mostly frozen Aurora Rose, tensed his own muscles and reached, unthinking, for his sword.

"*Not yet,*" the blue fairy whispered. "Your lives are short and precious. Save the wasting of them to the end, if we have failed."

Phillip nodded but didn't take his eyes from the fight.

Lianna also watched the fight unblinkingly. The sparks from the magic and flashes from the red fairy's enchanted sword glittered in her eyes.

With everyone watching the incredible battle in front of the throne, it was unsurprising that no one noticed two of Maleficent's servants creeping up on either side of the red fairy until it was almost too late.

"*LOOK OUT!*" Aurora Rose shouted.

"*ON YOUR LEFT!*" Phillip cried.

The red fairy didn't turn around but instead thrust her sword *back*, up under her armpit, surprising the creature behind her. Her blade sank deep into its chest. But she didn't waste a moment watching him gurgle and bubble and sputter and die. She spun and dove, slicing the second creature's feet out from underneath him.

"Doesn't have a leg to stand on," the blue fairy quipped, unable to help herself.

Maleficent swung her staff and a purple bolt grazed the red fairy's left calf.

She staggered and fell to her knees. No cry escaped her lips; she sucked in her breath and shook with pain. But she still forced herself to rise.

Maleficent muttered something unintelligible and aimed again. This time, instead of large purple bolts, little sickly-green fireballs shot from her staff. These flickered strangely and were connected to each other by syrupy strands of magic.

The red fairy looked confused for a moment. But she beat each away easily: one, another, a dozen . . .

But once they hit something, the balls didn't dissipate the way the purple bolts had. They drifted to the floor, the sickly green strands that flowed behind them taking much longer to fall, slowly arcing to the ground like cold honey.

The more she hit the balls away from herself, the more the strands built up around her. They stuck to her clothing, her feet, her arms and legs—everything except her sword.

Before long the red fairy was completely entangled.

Big gobs of the glowing green stuff dripped from her arms, dragging them down. They pulled her sword arm closer to the floor even as she still tried to parry the attacks.

Soon she couldn't move at all.

Maleficent smiled widely with satisfaction. Then—as gently as if she were a dewdrop fairy anointing a flower—she tipped her staff lightly at her opponent.

A giant purple flash erupted, engulfing the red fairy and her bonds and everything else within a few feet.

Aurora Rose screamed and turned her head. Phillip put his arm around her but didn't look away.

A weak red ember glowed amid the scorched, foul-smelling residue of the evil magic that burned the floor.

Maleficent tossed her head back and laughed. Likewise, her raven cackled. She put her free hand out to scratch its throat.

"Well?" she asked. "You're all going to die eventually. Who wants to be next?"

"And when we're all gone—then what?" Aurora Rose growled. "You prance self-importantly around an empty castle?"

"You think ruling a bunch of pathetic humans is my ultimate goal?" Maleficent asked with put-on surprise. "I really don't care a whit about you festering house apes or your ridiculous kingdoms."

"No, you only care about the parties they throw, and whom they invite," the princess said archly.

Prince Phillip grinned.

"*Nice* one," the blue fairy said, drifting forward. She turned once in the air, giving Aurora Rose a mock military salute. The fairy had little doubt about the outcome of her assault.

But she didn't approach Maleficent directly. Instead, she drifted toward the edge of the room, to a far corner, and hovered just over some prisoners and their guards.

"All right, Maleficent," she said. "*Do* at least try to remain consistent. If you don't care about humans at all, you shouldn't care about killing them. So leave them alone."

Maleficent, still stung from Aurora Rose's jab, set her chin and leaned back, putting her concentration into a bolt of immense size.

The blue fairy delicately bounced out of the way.

The bolt struck the floor between two of the guards, enveloping them both in purple fire until they burnt away to nothing.

"I repeat my question from earlier, Maleficent," the blue fairy said almost casually. She floated to the other side of the room like she didn't have a plan beyond keeping as much distance between her and the queen as possible. "What *happened* to you? You weren't *always* this insane. A bit touchy, perhaps, and malicious, but not hell-bent on evil."

"It is not *evil* to want to live, to continue my life that was cut off so prematurely," Maleficent snarled, hurling another bolt at her.

The blue fairy ducked, revealing the guard she stood in front of. *He* received the full of the blast and exploded in surprise.

Aurora Rose began to smile, seeing what she was doing.

"She's trying to even the odds for us," Phillip whispered excitedly.

"I know! Shut up!"

"And I can tell you, from personal experience," the blue fairy continued, slowly drifting down the line of prisoners and guards as if she were inspecting them, "that royal parties are really not as much fun as you would imagine. I like humans more than you, don't get me wrong, but they're shockingly smug. Especially their kings and queens."

With inarticulate rage Maleficent hurled bolt after bolt at her. The blue fairy dipped her head and bowed and twisted out of the way, moving as little as possible to avoid all the attacks aimed at her.

Almost every missed bolt hit another guard, sending it back to hell or wherever they came from.

"And golden dish domes. Really. Who needs them? I've got at least half a dozen from various birthdays and christenings over the centuries. They just sort of clutter up the place. Trust me, you didn't miss much at that party."

Four more bolts. Four more guards.

The fifth bolt singed the back of the blue fairy's dress, but she didn't even wince; she just continued her maddening little flight.

"*I DESERVE MORE RESPECT THAN THAT!*" Maleficent hissed.

"Yes, you keep saying that. Have you ever thought that maybe they were afraid you'd make a rather *unpleasant* party guest? I mean, I can't imagine *why* they would think that, but . . ."

This time she couldn't help letting out a yelp as an extra-large, furious purple bolt shot from Maleficent's staff. She dove out of the way, holding her head.

But the blue fairy was not as agile or quick as the red one; the magic caught her full in the side. Purple flame crawled over the left half of her body, singeing her flesh as she struggled to keep going.

"*So touchy,*" she croaked through scorched black lips. She limped, half flying, half walking, toward Maleficent.

"*DIE ALREADY, YOU ANNOYING GNAT!*" Maleficent swore.

The blue fairy suddenly lunged, diving at Maleficent instead of moving away from her. When the killing bolt got her, it was too close to the evil fairy for her to entirely escape its burning aftermath.

Maleficent shrieked as flames licked up her face, leaving charred tracks on her cheeks.

The blue fairy gave a wink to Aurora Rose and Phillip with a swollen eye, then vanished into the fire. Only another weak little will-o'-the-wisp remained, blue, hovering over her ashes.

The evil queen wiped her face with the back of her hand and looked surprised by the blood she saw there. If she appeared merely unhealthy before, now she was positively frightening, bloody and burned and still pulsing a ghastly green.

She managed to cackle hoarsely.

"No matter. I will be whole in a matter of minutes now. Guards, bring me a victim."

There was a pause.

"Guards," she ordered again.

There were only a couple of the inhuman things left, and they looked unsure of themselves now, shaken and unmoving. With most of their cohorts wiped out, they were no longer gibbering and hooting at death.

"Don't you dare," Aurora Rose said. "You've killed your last innocent."

"Oh no I *haven't*," Maleficent hissed, striding forward with her staff. "It's *your* turn now, sweetest.

"And there's no one left to save you."

Another Denouement

The prisoners looked on with horror. The prince put himself in front of Aurora Rose, between her and the fairy.

But the princess was no longer paying attention.

The will-o'-the-wisps, the little green, blue, and red embers, had begun to bob in the air, making their way over to her. They passed practically under Maleficent's nose—and the evil fairy looked more shocked and confused than angry.

Bouncing slowly in the air as if they had all the time in the world, they crossed the open space while everyone watched silently.

When they finally got to Aurora Rose, they suddenly

gained speed—slamming into her flesh with hot sparks.

"Rose!" Phillip cried.

Aurora Rose began to . . . *laugh.*

Maleficent didn't blink; like a snake, she showed her surprise by freezing in place.

And the princess kept laughing.

Not a giggle, not hysteria, not the sounds of someone who realizes she is about to die and is therefore going mad, but a genuine, full-throated laugh.

"Rose," the prince said slowly.

All her memories fell silent. The dream of the Thorn Castle and her childhood in the Forest Cottage both faded before the realizations of the here and now. She felt *alive*, as if for the first time. Fully awake and present. Her blood sang with the desire to protect her kingdom, the will to fight for the lives of her subjects and for Phillip—and the knowledge of how to do it.

"I will not show clemency despite your apparent insanity," Maleficent said carefully, obviously confused by what had just happened and trying to pretend she wasn't. "You will still die."

"No," Aurora Rose said. "This changes *everything.* And I'm *not* going to die."

She stretched like she had just risen from a long sleep; it was a big, luxurious stretch. The magic vines and branches

fell away from her like they had never been. She glowed—
not like Maleficent, but with a healthy heat behind her eyes
and under her skin.

"My true gifts," she said. "Returned to me."

"Truly *useless* gifts," Maleficent said. "What good are
grace and song and beauty—especially to a dead girl?"

"Not those gifts. Those were bestowed upon me by
others. These are my true, *natural* gifts: *Intelligence*. Bravery. Compassion.

"Those three you 'killed' weren't actual fairies at all—
they were parts of *me*. My *true* self. Hidden from me by
you. Dampened. Darkened. Just like everything else in this
wretched realm. Just as I myself was hidden away from the
world, first in the woods, and then in a dream."

"Bravery? Intelligence? *Please.* You're nothing but a
silly little princess," Maleficent spat.

Aurora Rose couldn't have controlled her anger if she
had wanted to.

Maleficent suddenly flew backward, buffeted by a mad
wind that came out of nowhere, a devil of dust and air that
exploded and then disappeared.

The evil queen managed to keep from hitting the floor
only by clawing at the throne. Her raven cawed and flapped
its wings to stay upright.

"I am not. A silly. Little. Princess," Aurora hissed. "I am

Aurora Rose, rightful queen of this kingdom and your judge and executioner, you *silly little fairy*."

Maleficent forced herself to stand upright, the pain of it obvious as she straightened her back. Her eyes flared.

"How *dare* you . . ."

"That's all you are. A silly little fairy grown too big for her britches. Thinks she's the big, bad powerful sorceress because she's queen of a *dreamworld*."

The stones in the floor grew. They pushed up in columns and pillars all around Maleficent and the throne, groaning and shrieking as they scratched against each other. The wall they made around the fairy looked like the teeth of a very old woman. Like they would swallow her whole.

It would have been a nice ending, but Aurora Rose wasn't at all surprised when, after barely a moment's silence, the granite palisade blew apart. Shards of glass-sharp rock rained on everyone in the room. Maleficent's prisoners cowered and screamed and covered their heads. One of the remaining guards took a chest full of shrapnel, crumpling to the floor.

None of the shards hit Aurora Rose, though; they just avoided her.

When the dust settled, Maleficent was revealed standing in a very un-Maleficent pose, fists curled in anger and legs bent, ready for another attack. Her teeth, the only thing about her that remained white, were bared and animallike.

Lianna, behind the throne still, was picking herself up and calmly brushing herself off.

"Insolent whelp!" Maleficent hissed.

"It's the truth, Maleficent," Aurora Rose said evenly. "It's not even your world. It's mine."

"I still have your *blood*, dreamer! You may think you are in control of the world, but *I* control *you!*"

Maleficent shook her staff. The green liquid, the blood transformed, swirled around in it strangely.

Aurora Rose suddenly felt sick.

Her mind and stomach wobbled. All the strength and energy she had felt just a moment earlier drained out of her through her feet, like when she was getting a cold or it was the first day of her moon blood or . . .

Everything seemed pointless and gray.

"Rose!" Phillip cried out. He put his hands on her shoulders and shook her. "Rose! She's doing it to you! It's not real!"

Maleficent was grinning. She raised her staff.

> *"For my help, in these last few hours,*
> *I summon thee with my dark powers:*
> *Golem and demon and efrit and imp,*
> *Heed my call and . . ."*

"No incantations," Aurora Rose said weakly.

A powerful wind rose and spun around Maleficent, ripping her capes and sucking her breath and words away.

It might not have been *quite* in time.

A thing appeared. It was black and half-formed, with sunken red eyes that glowed like the last embers in a dying fire.

It looked around once and then charged.

But instead of heading for Aurora Rose, it made for closer prey: the residents of the castle.

The poor prisoners had just begun to realize that without Maleficent's servants guarding them, they were free to escape—but were faced with gargantuan piles of rubble and stone blocking the exits, a floor that didn't exist in places, and now a giant demon-thing that hungered for their blood. Servants, children, once-dignified ladies and noblemen all began to run from one end of the room to the other, looking for a way out. There was a lot of chaotic spinning around and screaming.

Aurora Rose started to gather her concentration again.

"I'll deal with that," Phillip said, interrupting. He drew his sword. "You take Maleficent!"

The evil queen was already taking another deep breath and gesticulating with her staff again.

Aurora Rose tried not to close her eyes.

She pictured the roots she had often sat on or napped between when she lived with the fairies. Big, strong tree roots, friendly and ancient . . .

Almost like a retort to the sickly black vines that had held her, healthy brown oak roots grew quickly through the stones of the floor and the doors and windows of the room. They even came down the chimney. Little green leaves sprouted here and there, as if they wanted very badly to become a tree.

Maleficent lifted one foot and then the other, swiftly, trying to avoid being tripped up as they slipped around her.

But physicality was not Maleficent's strong suit.

In a matter of moments, stout brown ropes twined up her middle and began to squeeze, hardening. Little twigs crept across her face but couldn't quite make it over her mouth.

A loud huff from Phillip broke Aurora Rose's concentration; she turned to look.

The half-formed demon had clapped him on the side with a ridiculously large and stumpy hand, knocking his breath out. Possibly cracking a rib. Phillip staggered, then turned that into a stunning riposte in which he drove his sword up into what passed for the creature's belly.

While Aurora Rose watched, distracted, Maleficent managed to finish another conjuration.

It would have been almost funny if it hadn't been something out of Aurora Rose's worst nightmares.

Standing before her was a three-legged, seven-foot-tall attenuated and unnatural monster with two heads. It looked like a child's poor drawing, a *joke* of a demon.

Except that one of the heads was her mother's, the other her father's. They wore crowns.

They gibbered meaninglessly at her, their long arms swiping the air.

But she could understand their words in her head.

Is this how a princess behaves?

You are no queen!

"I am," Aurora Rose said, swallowing, forcing herself to look into their insane, brightly colored eyes. "You're dead. You're not real."

It takes more than death to make a queen.

We can help you. . . .

Take our wisdom and love.

Aurora Rose made wood and stone rain from the ceiling between her and the parent monster. Then *on* the parent monster. Each time the thing was struck, it howled and their strangely familiar, distorted, and pale faces contorted and pouted.

We love you.

Come here.

It was a mistake.

They put out their long, sinuous arms.

Maleficent rolled her staff, spoke to the blood.

And Aurora Rose had the faintest moment of doubt.

Would it be so bad, really, to die, believing she was finally in the arms of her real parents? Believing that they truly loved her? It would be the only chance she ever had. Everyone died eventually. Did it matter when? Did it matter *how*? She would probably die in this battle anyway. At least she would be blissful for that last moment.

The hand on her mother's side brushed her arm.

Aurora Rose reacted without thinking, a sword suddenly in her own hand and the creature's arm suddenly on the floor.

Her doubt was over; the spell was broken. The evil fairy had been controlling her, causing her not to care. Pulling on her overwhelming desire to be loved.

But Aurora *had* parents already. The three fairies were the ones who had raised her.

And Stefan and Leah were gone.

Now she *was* queen. She had to survive and save everyone else.

The parent monster hooted and howled.

Ungrateful child!

Hide behind your prince!

DIE, LITTLE GIRL!

With terrible, gargling cries, it bore down on her, flailing oversized hands at her head.

Sick with anger, Aurora Rose willed the rest of the ceiling to pour down.

It funneled onto the parent monster like a giant whirlpool, sucking at it. The whole floor above was eaten away in their destruction.

"You're *sick*, Maleficent," Aurora Rose spat.

Through her rage she felt the world around her again, the world that was a part of her. All of it was a weapon.

Eyes closed and chanting, Maleficent ignored her.

More *things* were appearing as she summoned them: scaly, many-footed creatures with long beaks full of teeth. They ran off, snapping and rending and ready to kill, the moment they appeared.

The castle dwellers crowded into the remaining corner of the throne room as Phillip tried to protect them.

Aurora Rose desperately imagined all the stones in the castle, reminded them who they owed their allegiance to.

Boulders and cornerstones ripped themselves from the walls and the towers.

The evil fairy flung out her staff.

The stones stopped in midair and flew to the side, blocked by an ugly green wall of flames that curved around Maleficent, protecting her.

She grinned in nasty triumph as the bones of the castle were engulfed by her fiery wall.

But the light on the staff's orb was growing dimmer.

The shrieks of men and women and children rose as Phillip attempted to drive off the beasts that were attacking them. Aurora Rose tried not to let her concentration falter, tried to focus on what she needed to do. Killing Maleficent was the only way to save them.

One of the demon-beasts rose in front of Aurora Rose. It snapped its jagged black beak in her face. The stench of decay and rot enveloped her. Its claws raked across her chest. Sparks jumped from its talons.

If she hadn't been wearing armor, it would have torn her open from rib to belly.

Then she remembered: she also had a sword.

She brought it up between them. The demon leapt on her anyway and knocked her to the ground.

The thing tried to take out her eyes with its beak, slavering and whistling insanely as it thrashed. Its body was hot and slimy and all over her, its weight crushing.

Aurora Rose tried to protect her face with the hilt of her sword. The monster's beak snapped over the blade with a terrible clang, shattering orange cartilage everywhere.

Far from stopping it, the pain only drove it madder.

She panicked, flailing violently. All she wanted was for it to be off her. She didn't think of magic. She didn't care what happened to Maleficent.

She screamed.

"GET *OFF* OF HER!"

And then the weight was gone. Phillip was above her. He had the creature in his bare hands, was throttling its writhing neck, sword forgotten. His face was a mask of fury, his eyes flashing red.

"DIE, beast of hell!"

He knelt and smashed it on the floor. Again and again and again, he crushed its head against the stone.

It fought its death in unnatural silence but for the scrape of its claws against the floor.

Finally, it went still.

"You all right?" Phillip asked gruffly.

Aurora Rose nodded.

"I love you," he said—and then he was away, after another demon.

Aurora Rose staggered to her feet, hand on her face where blood flowed and her skin burned from the demonic creature's spittle.

Maleficent was laughing.

"Aww, look at the little princess who needs a *prince* around to save her. Can't even fight her own fights."

"Needing someone once in a while doesn't make me *weak*, you pathetic harridan. It makes me *human*. Who is on *your* side, Maleficent?"

And in a fit of pettiness the princess hadn't even realized she had, a cage of roots grew out of the throne and around the fairy's raven before it could even squawk.

Aurora Rose imagined the blue fairy muttering, *"Birds of a feather . . ."* and then she smiled, knowing it was something *she* would say.

At first glance, Lianna seemed to be watching this with mild interest, either waiting for a similar punishment or merely intrigued by the concept. But she was also gripping the back of the throne, her white knuckles revealing that the fight had finally stirred some sort of survival instinct in her inhuman psyche.

The castle was in ruins now, most of it obliterated in the battle with Maleficent. A strange sky glowed overhead, scraps of blue and white and rips of midnight black, complete with stars. The people in the castle howled in despair as the world literally crumbled around them.

Phillip wrestled with the last of the monsters; Aurora Rose hurried it along with a wisp of a thought. One of the remaining castle walls collapsed on top of it, neatly avoiding the prince.

Maleficent was chanting again.

"I said no incantations," Aurora Rose repeated wearily. The ground buckled beneath them, rolling and churning like the surface of the ocean in a storm. She wondered

vaguely if she had ever seen an ocean in either world. She couldn't remember. Well, it was like a giant mole pushing up the dirt. That worked.

The castle floor broke, a puzzle ripping apart along its edges. A single finger of stone heaved up suddenly, right under the queen.

Maleficent was tossed into the air unceremoniously. She landed with a surprisingly violent snap on the ground in a heap.

Better make sure.

Aurora Rose closed her eyes then.

The walls of the outer keep, now visible through the ruins of the castle, flew apart like apple blossoms caught in a wind, and paused for a moment, swirling over Maleficent.

Then they crashed onto her body with a satisfying and delicious crack.

Consider the Dragon. Again.

For the first time since the battle had begun, there was a hush: the demons were all dead. The people in the castle looked around at each other, guardedly hopeful. Aurora Rose let out a deep breath. The excitement of the fight, the adrenaline high of survival, was leaving her. She slumped, feeling exhausted.

Her dreamworld was destroyed. The Thorn Castle was no more, torn down to its very elements in the battle against Maleficent. Distances were messed up; things that were far away were too clear and large, as if they had been drawn in wrong. Clothes and beds and golden bric-a-brac littered the ground like an oversized dollhouse had been smashed by a giant child.

The remaining denizens of the castle looked pitiful and few now exposed to the mad sky. They pressed against the crumbling remains of the giant thorns that were the only things left to mark the borders of the castle walls. The vines no longer prevented anyone from leaving—but neither did they offer any protection.

The raven began to caw; it might have sounded piteous to some, but to Aurora Rose it sounded like fingernails on slate, and it took all her willpower not to crush the bird in its woody cage.

"I don't think she's done yet," Lianna said unexpectedly.

The evil handmaiden had spoken neither excitedly nor disappointedly; she was just making an objective observation. She looked interestedly at where the body of Maleficent lay buried underneath the giant pile of debris.

"*Obviously*, Lianna," Aurora Rose said disgustedly. "We're all still here. *Not* awake. She's not dead."

Lianna looked shocked, maybe even a little hurt, by the princess's tone of voice.

"You're right, of course. I hadn't thought. I thought logic didn't work in dreams," she said a little philosophically.

"Yes, and you also thought I was a lot *dumber* than I really am, and . . ."

Then, across the silence of the strange world was the tiniest noise of pebbles shifting.

Of dust sifting down through an unseen blackness.

A clink of small rocks being shoved aside, one at a time.

A laborious shifting of weight, one rock grinding painfully against another.

A single piece of rubble fell off the top of the pile, ominously bouncing and sliding its way down to the ruined and uneven castle floor.

Then everything was silent.

Aurora Rose turned to say something to Phillip . . .

. . . and a hand shot up out of the pile, stabbing its way to the light.

A big, *clawed*, black hand.

"No . . ." Phillip whispered.

As if it was gaining strength from the sheer possibility of release from its stony prison, the creature underneath the rocks began to shift and move. Waves and waterfalls of boulders and rubble tumbled heavily to the floor.

Aurora Rose quickly used up what was left of the castle trying to crush the horrific thing that was slowly emerging. Giant beams, bedrock, furniture, statues, the walls and windows and turrets, the very tower she had jumped from. It all converged on the spot, forced itself into impossibly small spaces as she imagined crushing the life out of Maleficent. Stones screamed and exploded. Burning, liquid scree filled in gaps in the stones, sealing it.

There was nothing left.

A hot, dusty breeze scoured the desolate plain that had once been a castle. The only things that remained unbroken and upright were the throne and the strange hovering oval that showed the real, sleeping Aurora. Her face was twisted, contorted, her dreams of battle and violence causing her to react in her sleep. But the dreamer made no noise.

Everything was silent.

And then the dragon burst forth.

It rose from its cracked, stony prison like a lizard from its egg. The thing rose higher and higher into the sky, enormous, nearly as tall as the castle had been, black and purple and yellow. Not like a proper storybook dragon at all: too skinny here, too lumpy there, wings that were little more than useless flaps on ugly, blackened stumps of shoulders. Long, narrow beak-like mouth full of teeth, like those of the demons Maleficent had summoned. It screamed, the terrible noise ripping across the empty land.

Horrific. Like something from the end of the world.

It shrieked and shook rocks off its seemingly endless scaly back and continued to grow into its new skin.

"Get out," Aurora Rose said to Phillip without moving her eyes from the dragon. "Get everyone out of here."

"I'm staying with you. Princes kill dragons. That's what we're all about."

"You didn't kill her *enough* last time. Help me after you get everyone away."

Phillip opened his mouth to argue but was interrupted by a shout from behind.

"GOOD SUBJECTS OF HOUSE STEFAN!"

King Hubert stood on the path that led to the forest, as tall and unmovable as a mountain despite the ragged clothing flapping around his ankles. On his legs and arms were fresh wounds: deep, ugly gouges still weeping blood.

But his good eye, clouded before, was clear and icy. He clasped his stone as if it were a royal orb, and his stick a mighty staff.

"Father," Phillip whispered in wonder. "You're alive. . . ."

"COME TO THE SHELTER OF THE FOREST!" Hubert ordered. "FOLLOW ME, AND AWAIT THIS BATTLE'S END OUT OF HARM'S WAY! *NOW!*"

As if just waiting to be told what to do, the straggling crowd immediately ran to him. He stood aside and gestured them past with his stick like a stern shepherd. And so Aurora Rose's subjects fled into what must have looked like a different kind of death to the dreamland sleepers: the forest they had been told was dangerous and deadly.

The princess felt a surge of warmth and gratitude, something she had rarely felt for an adult other than her aunts. People could be surprising. Not *everyone* in the world was untrustworthy and disappointing. Not everyone lied to you or failed you.

Quietly pleased, Phillip watched his father with a smile.

As the last little child ran past him, the king turned— and gave a big old-Hubert-style wink. He shook his stone and stick and whispered: "I'll defend them with my very blood."

And then he was off behind them, shouting exhortations and marching very precisely.

Aurora Rose put a hand to her head. Maleficent's transformation had taken an absurd amount of power, and the blood magic resonated soundly in the princess's body. It was *her* power the evil fairy stole. She was weak and not ready for what would come next.

The dragon reared up. It belched a wide stream of ugly green fire from its beak.

Phillip grabbed Aurora Rose and swung her to the other side of him, then stood in front of her.

Lianna still stood, strangely uncowed by the fire that seemed like it could have just as easily consumed her.

As the flames neared them, Aurora Rose whipped up a wind that swept the fire aside and into the sky in a vortex of smoke and ash. The dragon shrieked in frustration.

But how could she *defeat* it? What would disable it? What would, at the very least, trip it up?

Gorges. She remembered them from her time in the

woods. Steep and narrow. At the bottom were shallow, pebbly streams. . . .

The world fell out from below the dragon.

The ground caved into itself and tumbled into the bottomless pit that opened up. The giant lizard shrieked and fell backward, clawing desperately to try to stay upright.

Aurora Rose felt a tugging inside her head.

Give up. You cannot defeat me so easily.

The dragon was slithering its way out of the pit, tail and legs moving so quickly and strangely it was like it was climbing the air itself to get out.

Prince Phillip ran toward it, sword out. Just at the edge of the pit, he stopped and sliced at the thing's neck, which was now level with the ground.

It didn't even scratch a scale.

Maleficent threw her head back and laughed, yellow eyes narrowing.

That was the only thing, perhaps, that saved Phillip from an eye-level blast of hellfire.

He ran away, past the dragon, zigzagging over the ruined castle floors, through what had once been the kitchens, the chapel, the treasury. He stopped on the other side of the pit and taunted Maleficent—trying to draw her attention away from Aurora Rose. He clanged his sword against his cuirass and hooted.

"Too slow, Maleficent!"

The dragon was now entirely out of the pit. It snaked after him, moving and twitching and shuddering like it hurt to stay still.

Aurora Rose pushed her hands apart. She imagined opening up the earth like a giant book.

The dragon ran headfirst straight into a hill that suddenly rose before it. It staggered, stunned for a moment.

But then it rose, shaking its neck and head—and wobbling a bit—and immediately scrabbled over the ground after Phillip again.

Aurora Rose looked around in desperation. What else could she do?

The trees.

With a sad twinge, Aurora Rose remembered seeing them for the first time when she escaped the Thorn Castle, how amazed she was that they still existed.

Now they pulled themselves out of the ground with creaking, groaning screams. Branches flew off as an invisible hand stripped their trunks to deadly points.

She sent them after Maleficent.

The first one slammed the dragon squarely in the back. It swung its head around in annoyance, brushing it off like a twig and fluttering its useless wings angrily.

Aurora Rose threw a dozen more after that, one after

another screaming through the air like large, deadly arrows.

Maleficent roared, then scampered toward her on ugly, flailing legs, doing little to avoid the trees.

The wooden tips blunted, the trunks cracked in half, the missiles bounced off the armor of her skin. When they hit, she merely flinched.

Twigs and leaves cannot hurt me, you silly girl!

Phillip was chasing after the dragon again, slashing at its tail to get its attention.

Maleficent's head whipped around faster than seemed possible and she belched a river of green fire at him.

Aurora Rose screamed.

Ugly, hissing black smoke rose where Phillip had been.

It drifted, ghostlike, over the piles of rocks and boulders.

The dragon threw back its head and roared out laughter like bile.

Then it turned with a certain regal slowness, as if savoring the next bit.

Aurora Rose swallowed a sob. She had to *not* think about Phillip. She had to think about the hundreds of people who depended on her, everyone who needed her to live, and win, and wake up. So *they* could live.

What kills dragons?

"Think, Aurora," she said aloud, panicking. "What kills dragons? Phillip—"

Phillip had his magic sword. . . .

Aurora Rose imagined a dozen of them.

They rained on Maleficent from the crazy sky like metal drops, plinking against her skin.

The dragon's flesh shuddered, crawling and puckering, where each one hit. A few scales, the size of war shields, fell. But no blood was drawn.

No weapons of man can destroy me! I am a mere fairy no more. I am the greatest thing in this world!

The dragon's tongue, forked and giant, came out and raked over its lips in expectation. The beast slithered slowly up on Aurora Rose and raised its deadly claw, each nail twice as long as the swords she had summoned and as black as death.

And then, suddenly, Maleficent's neck snapped back. She screeched in pain—a horrible sound that carried across the world.

Standing under her, looking grim, was Lianna. She had her little bodice knife sunk deep in the flesh of Maleficent's ankle and was twisting it.

"But weapons from hell can take back what they are owed."

There was a very faint but definite smile on her lips. She pulled her dagger out and sank it again, this time in the flat of the dragon's foot.

Maleficent roared with rage and spasmed, shaking her leg to free herself. But the dagger stayed stuck.

She turned to bite Lianna in half.

Suddenly, *Phillip* was there, popping up from behind a boulder. His hair and clothes were singed and there were burns across his face, but otherwise he seemed unharmed.

He cleared the distance between him and Lianna in seconds. He grabbed her around the waist like she was no more than a ball in a game, and kept running.

Maleficent whipped her tail like a club. The tip just touched his side, but it was enough to knock him down. He landed with a sickeningly heavy thud and Lianna fell out of his grasp.

As fast as a cat with a mouse desperate to escape, the dragon leapt over Phillip to pounce on the handmaiden.

"No!" Aurora Rose cried, trying to summon the earth to move, to make a canyon between the two.

It was too late.

With a look of pure hatred, the dragon ripped its front claws over Lianna's face and body. Their needle-sharp tips shredded her flesh and opened her innards to the light of day.

And then, as if it had merely been an annoying task to be dealt with, the dragon was done. Maleficent spun around and faced Phillip and Aurora Rose, not even bothering to gloat over her kill.

"Lianna!" Aurora Rose cried.

"Sorry . . ." her old handmaiden wheezed.

Then her black eyes froze in place.

It was too much. From friend to betrayer to friend and savior. To *gone.* Aurora Rose couldn't process all of it.

Stop, she told herself. *Mourn her later. THINK NOW!*

From somewhere unseen, a clock began to strike the hour.

Phillip and Aurora Rose and even Maleficent paused in confusion.

There was nothing left to the castle. Except for the forest, the whole world looked destroyed and grim, flat and featureless in all directions. Yet the distinct bong of a clock could be heard, eerily and perfectly, everywhere at once.

Cold dread washed over Aurora Rose.

Maleficent reared up on her hind feet, the left one splayed from the dagger. She laughed.

Midnight on the day after your sixteenth birthday, Aurora! Now you die—and I live again!

Aurora Rose thought desperately. What could she do? All this was because of the curse. All this was because she pricked—

Suddenly, she knew. She *knew* what she had to do.

Although she had only ever seen one once in the real world, she could bring up a perfect image of it in her memory.

The spinning wheel.

Bits and pieces of the ruined castle—chairs and tables and beams and other chunks of broken wood—began to fly through the air. They spun and interconnected and wiggled until each piece fit, sucking together like lodestones. Aurora Rose frowned, concentrating hard to get the trickier bits in place.

They made an ugly, enormous spinning wheel.

Maleficent laughed and belched green fire.

The spinning wheel caught flame immediately and started to burn away—all but the spindle, the bright black nail with the sharp tip.

The dragon looked confused for a moment.

Aurora Rose drove the spindle into its heart.

The dragon screamed.

It spewed fire that changed different, hideous colors: bloody red, sickly black, hellfire yellow.

Purple and scarlet and black ichor throbbed from the wound in a giant-sized echo of what had happened to Lady Astrid. Aurora Rose watched with a grim, horrible satisfaction.

The dragon clawed at its wound, trying to pull the spindle out, perhaps—but all it succeeded in doing was ripping out patches of scales and flesh.

It toppled, falling so hard that the ground shook. The princess was almost thrown off her feet.

The dragon writhed and scrambled on the ground as if trying to claw its way back to life. It shuddered and hissed and convulsed.

Its wings and legs and scales and tail billowed and fluttered and seemed to shrink, to become raggedy flaps of cloth. These finally shredded and collapsed around what would have been its giant body—except that there was no body anymore, either.

Just a black and purple and yellow stain on the ground, with little pieces of silk flapping in it like a dying butterfly.

The End.

And this was when, Aurora Rose was pretty sure, everyone was supposed to wake up.

The End?

"I'm still here," the prince said—rather unnecessarily, Aurora Rose thought. He ran a hand through his thick, dirty mane; chunks of broken and burnt hair came out. "At least I *hope* I'm still asleep."

Aurora Rose regarded the pile of filth where Maleficent had died. In the middle of it, like it was the only real thing left, lay the giant spindle, still gleaming and sharp.

Lianna lay nearby, broken and torn apart. Her black eyes were open to the apocalyptic sky above.

A cold wind blew over the degrading landscape. Aurora Rose took comfort that someplace beyond the trees, her people were safe.

"They said royal blood would break the spell," Phillip continued. "You killed the evil queen . . . what's going on?"

"She wasn't a real queen."

Her voice was strangely flat because of the desolate world, the lack of anything for sound to bounce off.

She took a deep breath and winced when it hurt her ribs and chest.

"Hey, look," Phillip said, pointing to the only other distinctive thing among the piles of trash and rubbish. It was the image of the real Aurora, asleep on her bed. He approached it and tried to walk through, like a door. But he just pushed through it like it was air and wound up looking at it from behind.

For just a moment sleeping Aurora stirred, and dream Aurora felt hope rise in her chest.

But all sleeping Aurora did was drop an arm over the side of the bed. Her fingers uncurled as she relaxed back into deep sleep.

A single crimson drop fell from the tip of her wounded index finger.

"Royal blood," Aurora Rose murmured.

Royal blood.

She knew what to do.

Aurora Rose squared her shoulders and straightened her helmet.

Then she turned back toward the spindle.

"Don't you dare," Phillip said uneasily. "Rose—what are you doing . . . ?"

She ignored him.

"Rose, *stop*!"

He leapt up just as she reached the sharp, ugly black thing.

But all she did was touch her finger to it.

Phillip sighed in relief.

Aurora Rose stiffened.

The pain that ripped through her body wasn't that of a single pinprick. It was as if fire climbed up through her veins and then out through her ears, through her mouth, through her nose, into the world.

She gritted her teeth and tried to ignore it. That was what a queen would do.

Cradling her bleeding finger, she walked slowly and carefully to the image of the sleeping princess.

She looked at herself. The hollow cheeks, the beautiful hair, the slender neck, the spotless gown.

"What a mess," she murmured.

The little girl the young woman—who could figure out an escape from her fake life and arranged marriage only through death. Who had never known enough to question anything.

She took one last look around the bleak, terrible world where she controlled everything. It could be a paradise if she just imagined it.

She took another deep breath, reached through the

image, and held her own hand, touching blood to blood. The last time she had pricked her finger, it was to sleep. Forever.

This time it was to wake up and *live*.

Happily Ever After

Princess Aurora Rose woke, suffocating in heavy corseted gowns. She had sworn she would go right to work but was surprised by her own skin.

"I was older in the dream," she said aloud, surprised by her own voice. Several years had passed with Maleficent. Here she was still sixteen.

She swung her uninjured, younger legs around to the side of the bed, where Phillip was stretching and yawning.

"Wake up, Prince," she said, clapping his shoulder. "We have a lot to do."

Their moment of peace and transition ended quickly. Screams, inevitable but still shocking, began to ring out from different areas of the castle. Some people were *not* waking up. Some people were as dead as they had been in the dream.

Three tiny creatures, red, blue, and green, buzzed into the room and rapidly became familiar, very welcome little ladies.

"Aunts!" Aurora Rose cried, surprised by how glad she was to see them—the rush of feeling that overcame her—despite their betrayal mere hours before in *this* world. She leapt up and gathered them in her arms, squeezing tightly.

"Rose!" Fauna cried happily. They all had tears in their eyes, even Merryweather.

But still.

"We," Aurora Rose whispered in Flora's ear, "will talk. *Later.*"

"Well, yes, of course, my dear, but—"

"MY LADY!"

One of the faster, smarter guards—Aurora Rose made a mental note to review him later, with a possible eye to promotion—appeared at the door, face haggard and aghast.

"The king and queen—your parents—are dead! Murdered! As well as countless other nobles and servants . . . *here* . . ." he added, a little unsure of himself. None of the others who had slept had the advantage of knowing the full story of Maleficent's true intentions and the point of the dream. Doubtless they would be confused and terrified.

"Thank you," she said politely. "Sadly, I am already aware of the situation. This is all the result of the evil that Maleficent wrought."

Phillip was finally upright, still stretching and grim with the loose ends of the adventure.

The guard's eyes kept flicking to the prince's.

"I need you to take as many guards as you can and scour the castle for any remaining of Maleficent's servants," Aurora Rose said. "Kill them all. Afterwards we need to send a unit to go to her lair and destroy it utterly. Set fire to it and all its contents. I don't want a repeat of . . . recent events. We must make sure that every aspect of her is dead and gone."

"Absolutely, my lady," the guard said. He looked relieved that someone was taking charge of the situation—but hesitant about carrying out those orders. "Perhaps Prince Phillip or your cousin the prince of Fendalle—"

"*Can both help out with the search*," Aurora Rose said, putting some spit into her words. She changed her mind about his promotion. "If they are up to it. All able-bodied men with swords are welcome to do so. Nay, encouraged."

She moved purposefully out of the room, still with the infinite grace she had been born with. But there was iron immobility to her shoulders.

Fauna sighed. "Already a queen, that one."

The three fairies, and Phillip, hurried after her.

In the real world she had been in the castle as an adult for only a few hours. But it was, with some superficial differences, nearly exactly the same as the Thorn Castle. She had no trouble finding the throne room. If nothing else, the sounds of chaos would have led her there.

For just a moment Aurora Rose caught herself, viewing the room she had destroyed just moments earlier in her mind. The real one was different in ways that made her queasy: lengths and heights of things were changed; colors and decorations were off. It was set as if for a party. . . .

My wedding, Aurora Rose realized belatedly. She stood halfway down the grand staircase she was supposed to have descended with Phillip, her arm in his, to greet their parents. Gold and blue tapestries hung everywhere; shiny horns with pennants hanging from their bells flashed in the light.

But this was not the scene the musicians had prepared themselves for. Beautifully dressed ladies dragged their priceless gowns through pools of blood and wept. Men tried to comfort them or each other, or they themselves wept. Bodies sprawled on chairs and the floor in terrible poses.

"PEOPLE," Aurora Rose shouted, trying to channel King Hubert's lusty call from the dreamworld. Only a few looked at her. One, however, was a horn player. Aurora Rose impatiently gestured at him.

He complied immediately. Like the guard before, he was only too happy to have someone giving orders.

He played a loud royal flourish—and could perhaps be forgiven if it wasn't perfect.

At *that* the crowd turned around. Strange noises, murmurs of recognition and astonishment, rose from them. They remembered her from their dreams. They remembered the battle, her facing off against the dragon.

"Noble ladies and honored gentlemen," Aurora Rose said as demurely as shouting would allow. "It is a sad day for our kingdom. My heart goes out to all we have lost and those who loved them. I know that no words of mine can stem your grief.

"Even so, there is much work to do. Those who aren't in need of immediate assistance, please return to the rooms in which you are staying. Our servants will care for your every need, and we will send for you all as soon as things are . . . tidied."

There were a few mumbles of protest, but otherwise everyone who could leave seemed glad to do so. No one went alone—all were in little groups, whispering and discussing and sharing what they remembered, the strange experience they had all endured while asleep.

A man in severe black robes and a soft hat strode over to Aurora Rose. Other men in similar robes followed behind him. They all wore thick golden chains with heavy gemmed pendants on them. Ministers or secretaries or some such, Aurora Rose decided. Like the ones who had yelled at her in her dream within the dream.

It seemed that, sometimes, sleep did indeed mirror life.

"Your Highness, it is very good of you to take this under your own personal direction," the first man began. "But as you are new to the kingdom and have had no experience with such matters . . ."

"And are a woman, moreover," another man put in.

"And a woman," the first man continued. "Your delicate constitution may not even survive the *viewing* of your parents, much less what else needs to be done. What I'm saying is perhaps you should leave the sorting-out of things to us, your father's advisors . . . and maybe your uncle Prince Jaundry. . . ."

Aurora Rose regarded him mildly, trying to conjure memories of the beautiful girl full of grace everyone was supposed to fall in love with so easily.

"Did I not face down a dragon, unarmed, while the rest of you fled to the protection of the woods?"

The man blanched.

"I haven't a . . ."

"Oh, yes, you remember it well, please do not pretend it wasn't *real*," Aurora Rose said firmly, trying not to hiss the way Maleficent would have. "After such an ordeal, believe me, I am quite capable of taking over civic matters. If you have some disagreement with my manner of doing things, you may of course bring it up later in conference with me. *Privately*. Also, from here on out you will address me *correctly*: as *Your Majesty*."

"Yes, Your Majesty," the man said, nervously glancing at the men around him. None would meet his eyes.

"Excellent," Aurora Rose said. "Thank you. I look forward to meeting with all of you later to discuss how to proceed."

She strode forward out of the knot of men, Phillip and the fairies trailing smartly like an entourage. The prince was trying very hard not to smile.

It took her a long time to make the short journey to the thrones. Noblemen and -women, who had looked so alike and unreal in their perfect dresses and matching raiment in the other world, became human through tragedy in this one.

It took her a moment to recognize Duke Walter of the Five Trees, the short, sensible middle-aged husband of Lady Astrid. The princess had never had much to do with him in the Thorn Castle; only his wife.

His cheeks were wet and red and he held Lady Astrid's head in his lap, refusing to let anyone take her away.

Aurora Rose knelt and clasped his hand.

"I am so sorry," she whispered.

He nodded, not really paying attention. Even a brave princess who fought dragons and saved everyone—including him—couldn't distract his attention from loss and grief.

She steeled herself and moved on.

The young, powerful, and now dead Marquis and Marchess of Longbow had left behind three children, the oldest of whom was twelve. He tried to look brave, but hysteria leaked from the edges of his eyes with tears.

"Maleficent hasn't paid enough for her crimes," Aurora Rose murmured after she kissed and hugged each of the children, unable to do anything else for them in the moment.

Finally, she came to her own tragedy: the bloody and lifeless bodies of King Stefan and Queen Leah, still propped up on their thrones. No one had dared touch them. No one knew what the protocol was.

Aurora Rose leaned over and looked into their faces, but the dead told no secrets.

"I forgive you," she whispered, because . . . because there was nothing else she could do. She kissed each one on the forehead, then summoned a servant to cover them and take them away.

King Hubert had apparently fallen asleep near the royal couple, having been in discussion with them as they waited for Aurora's arrival. His face was sopping wet with tears, but now he was talking to a guard, to a servant, to a dazed-looking noble, to anyone at all who would listen.

"*Years* I lived in the wilderness, after that blasted fairy exiled me. *Years.* Once I ate some mushrooms out of extreme hunger . . . didn't know what they were . . . but they didn't kill King Hubert! No, I tell you! Takes more than that to take *me* out! Hey, Phillip, my boy!"

His eyes lit up when he noticed the couple.

"I was just telling this lad here . . . one of the many Israelites I was leading through the wilderness. Like *Moses*, I was. Eh, boy?"

"Absolutely, Father."

"Say, I don't suppose your mother came back with the rest of us, did she?" he asked eagerly, looking around the room. "She was lost somewhere, too, but maybe . . . maybe she came back?"

The prince looked searchingly into his dad's face. Something was broken in the old man. Roaming the forests of the dreamworld by himself for years had indeed altered him—just as he had suggested.

Phillip wrapped his father in a tight embrace. Aurora Rose saw, for just a moment, tears quicken in Phillip's eyes before he screwed them shut and willed them away. He sobbed a huge, shuddering sob of loss for all the things he had endured but didn't name.

The dreamworld had changed everyone. Even the boy-ish, unflappable Phillip.

"But what's wrong, lad?" King Hubert asked in wonder. "We're all all right now."

"Father . . ."

But whatever he was about to say next was interrupted by someone calling desperately from across the room.

"My lady!"

The guard Aurora Rose had sent off to organize the search for Maleficent's servants came running back to her, looking a little pale despite his exertion.

"We found something that might be . . . the remains of Maleficent or the dragon," he said unsteadily.

Aurora Rose set her shoulders, feeling grim. "Show me," she ordered.

She and Phillip and the three fairies hurried after him, picking up a half dozen of the more quick-witted guards as an escort. Back through the chaotic throne room, past the tables in the great hall, out to the courtyard and then through the gate, over the drawbridge—like it was no big deal. The princess tried to keep from gawking. She was just *walking* out of a castle she had seemed to be trapped in for so many years. . . . And the thorns on this one, receding now, were small and pretty and covered in flowers.

On the other side of the outer wall, bushes and fields still smoldered from Phillip's battle with the dragon. A blackened, steaming crater outlined where the dragon had fallen. Phillip's sword was still there, pinning the tattered remains of Maleficent's capes and robes to the earth.

But instead of Maleficent lying among them, it was Lianna.

In this realm, she was more pig monster than human. Though she still had her beautiful black hair and wore the vestments of a lady, tusks protruded from her mouth at awkward angles and her delicate hands ended in strange claws.

She looked over at Aurora Rose without moving her head and smiled faintly.

"You're still alive," Aurora Rose said, kneeling beside her.

Lianna gave a painful snort. "I . . . was never *alive*. In this world or the other. I'm . . . just a piece of Maleficent and some dark magic. *Semantics*. I'm dying now, or a reasonable version thereof. And the last of Maleficent dies with me."

Aurora Rose took Lianna's hand-claws in her own hands and squeezed them.

"Why . . . why did you save me?"

"You were my friend," the creature said simply.

Aurora Rose felt the tears welling up, more than the day could hold.

Lianna's eyes turned toward the sky as if she didn't want to see.

"I *learned* that. I *learned* that you can care for someone, and be cared for by someone. Even . . . if you're not . . . *created* with that as part of you, you can learn that. Maleficent could have learned that, too . . . but she never did. Things could have been so different."

Her breathing was ragged now and growing shallow, the sound made worse by the tusks. She shifted uncomfortably.

Biting back a sob, Aurora Rose gestured to Phillip. Without needing to ask, he ripped off his cloak and handed it to her. The princess folded up the cloth and placed it as best she could under the girl's head, tucking it around her neck.

A look of relief spread over the creature's face.

"Thank you. For this and . . . everything."

And then, just like that, her eyes grew filmy and still.

Aurora Rose let out one desperate cry, a shriek of helplessness, anger, and loss. Phillip put his arms around her and held her tightly.

"Look," he murmured.

Lianna's face began to shift and melt—her whole body did.

But instead of dissolving into the black, hissing soot and filth the demons usually became, her features transformed.

Lying dead on the floor before them wasn't a pig thing. It was a young woman with beautiful long black hair and high cheekbones—and black horns sprouting from her skull. A tiny, pleasant smile sat on her lips. She looked at peace.

"It's Maleficent," Aurora Rose whispered. "As she was, originally. As she could have been."

Phillip shook his head and swore, kicking the dirt in frustration.

"*This*," he muttered. "*This* is our happy ending?"

Epilogue: All Good Things

Aurora Rose sat at the head of the ponderous, heavy table, arms resting gracefully, regally on the edges of the throne. She regarded the men putting forth different thoughts on the economic ramifications of consolidating the kingdom's power under a single princess—no, *queen* . . . no, wait, *girl*—with a gaze that was just a shade warmer than cool, amused detachment.

It wasn't an unconscious decision to adopt some of Maleficent's trademark moves; why not learn from her, even if she had been an enemy?

Behind her throne, to the left, stood Flora, Fauna, and Merryweather. Their presence added just the touch of mystical power that kept people in line whenever they started to think about using the term *princess*.

On her right sat Phillip, honored guest of the kingdom. But he sat away from the table and didn't speak. If anyone tried to address him, he replied with his usual affable demeanor and directed them to their queen.

A tapestry was pulled aside from the door, and a trusted butler entered.

"Your Majesty, it's time for the speech. All able subjects have been gathered in the outer bailey."

"Thank you, Christer," Aurora Rose said, trying to sound more *polite* than *incredibly relieved*. "And thank *you*, gentlemen. We shall continue these discussions later, after the coronation."

She said this warmly and with a smile that made each man in the room feel like he, personally, was being thanked. Only a few looked unhappy as they filed out.

As soon as they were gone, she sank down in her throne, hand to her head.

Not that long ago, she could have conjured a mug of cider or caused the scrolls on the table to fly around the room amusingly like a flock of sparrows.

But then, of course, she had woken up.

"Oh, that was marvelous, simply marvelous," Fauna said, putting a delicate, weightless hand on Aurora Rose's shoulder. "You certainly have a knack for this whole leadership thing."

"Yes, it was very well done," said Flora. "You have them eating out of your hands."

"I think you should turn the one in the corner into a toad," Merryweather said, bunching her fat little face into a scowl.

Aurora Rose nodded with a faint smile, taking their praise as graciously as she could. They *did* love her. She had just sort of outgrown their ministrations.

"I still haven't forgiven you for lying to me about my parents all those years," she warned them. "Don't think you can flatter your way into my good graces."

"No, of course not, dear," Flora said with a sigh. "Please see it from our perspective, however. While we are here, we are bound by the laws of your kingdom. And it was what your *parents* wanted, Rose."

"What my parents wanted? Did they *show* any great insight or ability in *parenting*?" she demanded. "Whose idea was it to lock me in a bedroom by myself on the eve of my sixteenth birthday and not even *introduce* me properly to my own parents?"

"It made some sort of sense at the time," Fauna said thoughtfully, a finger on her lips.

Aurora Rose stared at them blankly for a moment.

"I pricked my finger on the spindle because I thought I would never see Phillip again and my life was over!"

"Yes, well," Flora said, looking chagrined. "We didn't expect that to happen. Honestly, we never realized how sad you were. You were our first baby."

Phillip muttered something unprincely and *very* rude.

"Well, *you* try being bound by human kings and human law," Merryweather snapped. "Which of you brilliant house-apes came up with the idea of people just *inheriting* the rule of a land? Instead of choosing the best person for the job? We had to do what the king said. Your own rules, people."

"We *loved* Rose. We still do. Even if we didn't make the best choices as parents," Flora said wistfully, touching Aurora Rose's hair.

"We'll do better with our next baby," Fauna promised.

Aurora Rose felt her heart stop.

She loved her aunts. She forgave her aunts. She was growing less bitter and angry with every second she spent with them. She *did* have, in her own way, a freer childhood out in the woods than many a princess did.

But she would never *ever* give up any child of hers to them.

If I ever have a daughter, you can be sure I will keep her close, and teach her well, and school her in the arts of reading and math and kindness, and make her strong and power-ful enough to protect herself, and I would never let anything come between us.

She smiled as she thought the words.

"Come on. Let's go," Aurora Rose said, rising from the throne and heading to the door. Phillip's face still brightened at seeing her moving so gracefully, her golden hair now pulled back in a more businesslike braid down her spine.

In the antechamber to the speaking balcony, King Hubert was seated comfortably on a padded stool. Several polite-looking young men, nobles and servants alike, clustered around and listened.

"The thing is, lads, the thing is, once upon a time. Once upon a time I was in an endless dark forest. No—*actually endless*, I tell you! In another world! I wandered for ages all by myself in the woods. My wife died years ago, you see. I don't know where my oldest boy was. My little girls and lads were safe at home, I think.

"Once upon a time we were all together, in a castle, you know, but things change. Wives die and eldest sons grow up and chase after princesses and peasant girls, riding away from you forever. . . ."

"Good afternoon, King Hubert," Aurora Rose said, kissing him on the cheek.

"Young lady!" Hubert said with delight, taking her hands in his. "I was just telling them. Are you the princess . . . no . . ." He looked at her and paused, searching her face. "No, my mistake. Are you the *queen* my son is going to marry today?"

"Not today, King Hubert," Aurora Rose said with a smile. She brushed a stray lock of snow-white hair out of his eyes.

"Oh, well, soon then, I hope. Grandchildren will fix everything, I think," he said pensively. "Grandchildren *love* stories."

"We'll see you in a moment, Father," Phillip said with a quick, formal bow. Then he patted him on the shoulder, unsure what else to do.

They looked toward the balcony, where horn blowers stood at the ready, gold and blue pennants streaming from their polished instruments. A maid appeared in front of Aurora Rose with a crown resting on a pillow. It wasn't the small princess one the fairies had gifted her with, nor was it the giant golden crown of state she would be given later at the official coronation. She had gone through the treasury very carefully and chosen an ancient gold circlet, simple and thick, that would be unmistakable as anything *but* a crown to the crowds below.

Aurora Rose took it and thanked the maid, sending her on her way.

"I wish Lianna were here," she said, trying to sound a little flippant. Sadness came through anyway, weighing on her as much as the diadem she pressed onto her hair. "She would do something fancy with this. Loops or buns or something . . ."

"You look *gorgeous*," Phillip said, taking her hands and squeezing them. "Don't worry about winning over the people. If they're like me, they'll fall in love with you on first sight."

"You really did," she said, shaking her head. And perhaps she had once, too.

She thought about their adventures together. How he had never given up on her. How he had forced her on. How he had constantly, annoyingly remained cheerful and upbeat in any situation. How he had killed demons and always talked about his stupid horse and ate porridge that he hated.

No, she hadn't fallen in love with him on sight the second time around.

It had taken a few days.

"Hey," she said with a grin. "Ask me a math question."

"What? Oh—to prove we're awake." He grinned back. "What's four plus four?"

"Eight! Too easy. Give me another."

"What's . . . twenty-eight minus fifteen?"

"Thirteen! Again!"

"All right, Princess Smarty-Pants, what's two hundred twenty-five divided by fifteen?"

"Fifteen, silly! It's the square of it."

They both paused, equally surprised by her answer.

"Well, what do you know?" she said slowly. "I *really am* a smarty-pants princess."

Phillip took her hands and clasped them in his own.

"No, you're a smarty-pants *queen*."

Aurora Rose looked down at their hands and took a deep breath.

"Are you going back home after today?"

"Yes. I think . . . I think I have my own . . . ah . . . transition of power to deal with," Phillip said, looking at his dad with a sigh. "I think I might finally have to grow up and do all those things I was trained for."

"Hey, at least you were trained for it," she said with a wan smile.

"I think you'll do just fine."

"You think?"

"Absolutely. Also, I think there's going to be a lot of talk about our two kingdoms . . . with young leaders. . . . Young, unmarried leaders . . ."

"Can we please drop this for just, like, *two minutes*?"

"I'm just saying . . ."

"I know, I know. You're right. There are a lot of . . . advantages to combining things."

They were silent for an awkward moment. The noise of the people could be heard below, shouts for the queen and exhortations from the guards telling people to calm down. Also just a lot of general yells.

"Hey, Queen Aurora," Phillip suddenly said, an impish look on his face, "before this all starts . . . and things get *too* complicated . . . and we have to figure out what we're both going to do . . ."

"Yes?"

"How about a kiss?"

Aurora Rose's face broke into a surprised, pleased smile.

"Absolutely. But just a small one."

And Prince Phillip took Queen Aurora Rose in his arms and kissed her, deeply and passionately, and she held him tightly, and they drew strength and love and support from each other.

And they *did* live happily ever after . . .

. . . if not, exactly, the way they had originally expected.

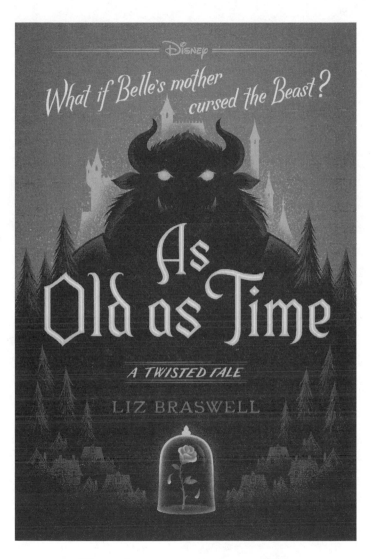

Turn the page to start reading
Liz Braswell's twist on *Beauty and the Beast*.

Once Upon a Time

Once upon a time in a faraway land, a young prince lived in a shining castle. Although he had everything his heart desired, the Prince was spoiled, selfish, and unkind.

But then, one winter's night, an old beggar woman came to the castle and offered him a single blood-red rose in return for shelter from the bitter cold. Repulsed by her haggard appearance, the Prince sneered at the gift and turned the old woman away—although she warned him not to be deceived by appearances, for true beauty is found within. And when he dismissed her again, the old woman's ugliness melted away to reveal a beautiful enchantress.

The Prince tried to apologize but it was too late, for she had seen that there was no love in his heart. As punishment she transformed him into a hideous beast and placed a powerful spell on the castle and all who lived there.

"You have until the eve of your twenty-first birthday to become as beautiful on the *inside* as you were on the outside. If you do not learn to love another—and be loved in return—by the time the last petal of this rose falls, you, your castle, and all within, will be cursed and forgotten *forever*."

Ashamed of his monstrous form, the Beast concealed himself inside his castle, with a magic mirror as his only window to the outside world.

As the years passed, he fell into despair and lost all hope—for who could ever learn to love a beast?

It was a very good story.

It often entertained the woman who lay in her black hole of a room, manacled to a hard, cold bed.

She had enjoyed its repetition in her mind for years. Sometimes she remembered bits differently: sometimes the rose was as pink as a sunrise by the sea. But that never resonated as well as *red as blood*.

And the part at the *very* end, where the Enchantress is waylaid upon exiting the castle, thrown into a black carriage, and spirited into the night—well, it didn't sound as epic and grand. She never included it.

Almost anyone else would have run out of thoughts by

this point. Almost anyone else would have given in to the finality of the oubliette until she forgot herself entirely.

A few of her thoughts *were* crazy, spinning around and around the dried teakettle that was now the inside of her head. If she wasn't careful, they would become too speedy, break free, and seek escape through the cracks of her mind. But that way lay madness, and she wasn't quite there yet.

Ten years and she had *almost* forgotten herself. But not quite.

Footsteps down the hall.

She shut her eyes as tight as possible against the madness from without that tried to intrude upon her black personal madness.

Chattering voices. Another set of footsteps. The swish swish of a rank mop against the endlessly slimy floors. The clink of keys.

"No need to do that one. It's empty."

"But it's locked. Why would it be locked if it's empty?"

She had to scream, she had to shake, she had to explode—*anything* rather than let the dialogue repeat itself yet again as it had for the last four thousand days, in only slightly different iterations:

"Ooh, this one's locked. But do you hear something inside?"

"This door's closed. You think it's locked?"

"The one down here is locked—but I don't remember any-one being put down here."

It was as if God were trying out all the different possible lines in the mummer's farce that was her life and still hadn't gotten it quite right.

The next two minutes were as predictable as the words from a parent to a child who knows she has misbehaved and chafes under the inevitability of the sentences hurled at her.

Turn of the key in the lock.

Door creaking open.

A hideous face, hideous only in its familiarity, the same look of surprise as always and every day since forever began. The face's owner carried a tray with her in the hand that didn't have the keys. Behind her, in the hall, stood the woman with the mop. And behind *her* stood a large and silent man who was ready to subdue any of the prisoners not tied down.

The prisoner found herself opening her eyes, curiosity getting the better of her survival instinct. Today's tray had *four* bowls of broth. Sometimes it was five, sometimes it was three. Sometimes there was only one.

"Lucky for you I got an extra," the one with the tray said, settling herself down in a filthy tuffet of skirts and aprons.

This line never changed. Ever.

The prisoner screamed, unable to contain herself, unable to keep herself from looking forward to that one thing each day—the thin gruel that passed for nourishment.

The woman with the mop muttered indignantly.

"I didn't hear nuffink about a new one, I can tell you that. Thought they done a right good job clearing these sorts out of the world."

"Well, there's one now. There you go, finish up now."

The woman said it with the same false tenderness she expressed every time. The bowl tipped faster, broth trickled down the sides of the prisoner's neck and, despite herself, she got desperate, straining against the chains and sticking her tongue out to get every last drop before the bowl was removed.

"This one is old enough to be a mother," the gruel woman said without a trace of emotion or sentiment. "Think of that, them having children and raising them and all."

"Like animals, all of them. Animals raise their children, too. I don't know why they keep them around. Kill 'em and be done with it."

"Oh, soon enough, soon enough, no doubt," the broth hag said philosophically, getting up. "They don't last long around here."

Except, of course, it had been ten years now.

This time the hag didn't bother to toss some platitude

over her shoulder as she left; the prisoner's existence was forgotten the moment she touched the door and was on her way out.

It would be all new again for her and her horrible companion tomorrow . . . and the next day . . . and the day after that. . . .

The prisoner screamed one last time, finally and uncontrollably, as the darkness closed in.

She had to start the story again. If she just started the story and played it through, everything would be all right.

Once upon a time in a faraway land, a young prince lived in a shining castle . . .

Before the Beginning

Once upon a time, slightly longer ago than before, there was a kingdom whose name and very existence have long since been forgotten. While the rest of the world was fighting for control of new lands across the seas, inventing ever more deadly weapons, and generously gifting their own religion to foreign people who didn't want it, this kingdom just splendidly *was*.

It had fertile croplands, dense hunting forests, a neat little hamlet, and the prettiest postcard castle anyone had ever seen.

In happier years, because of its removed location in an out-of-the way valley, it was a lodestone for the artistic, the different, the clever: *les charmantes*. They fled there as the modern world closed in on the rest of Europe. The little kingdom passed the Dark Ages and the Renaissance peacefully and uneventfully. Only now were the diseases of civilized man finally catching up.

Even so, here there were still fortune-tellers who could actually tell your fortune, farmers who could pull water from stone during a dry season, and performers who could really turn boys into doves. And sometimes back.

The kingdom also drew those who didn't have *powers*, precisely, but their own unusual natural talents and quirks— those who felt comfortable among the other folk. Misfits and dreamers. Poets and musicians. Nice oddballs, finding refuge there in a world that didn't want them.

One was a young man named Maurice. The son of a tinker, he had both the will to wander and the skill to fix and invent. Unlike his father, however, he felt a change in the ancient air of Europe. Wonderful, mechanical change: a future filled with weaving mills powered by steam, balloons that could carry people to far-off lands, and stoves that could cook meals all by themselves.

Determined to be part of all this, Maurice looked to both the past—the steam engines of Hero—and the present, desperately chatting up anyone who had a firsthand account of the marvels he had read about. His longing took him all over, chasing down gears and pistons and demonstrations of science.

But he realized that a life of wandering would get him

nowhere; he needed someplace he could sit and think for a while and tinker with really big things—machines that required huge fires and mighty smelters. Someplace he could store all his junk.

In short, he needed a *home*.

Following his heart and rumors, he wound up in a corner of Europe that was just a bit out of sync with the rest of the world.

First he stopped at a tiny village on a river that was perfect for powering waterwheels. But after observing the provincial little lives of the people there and enduring their horrified looks at his handcart filled with goggles and equipment and books, he realized that it was not the right place for him.

He crossed the river and went on through the woods, winding up in the strange kingdom where it wasn't unusual for someone to be seen whispering to a black cat—and the cat whispering back—or having a drink at the local pub, still covered in silver soot from the day's work and wearing dark mica goggles. Where he would fit in.

Maurice immediately struck up a friendship with some local lads and ended up renting a place with one of them. Alaric, more into animals than machines, managed to get them a cheap room at the back of one of the stables where he hired himself out as a groomsman.

While the lodging itself was tiny and reeked of horses, it

did include access to a large common yard. Maurice immediately set about constructing a forge, kiln, and tinkering
table.

He happily betook any hard labor that would bring him
closer to getting the right bits for his latest project. While he
picked rocks out of fields or hauled sheaves of grain on his
shoulders, his mind was far away, thinking about the tensile
strength of different metals, the possibilities of alloys, and
how to achieve the perfectly cylindrical, smooth shape he
needed for the next step.

"Old Maurice Head-in-the-Clouds," his fellow strong
lads would say, clapping him on the shoulders. But it was
always said with a smile and respect, the same way they
called Josepha the tavern maid "the Black Witch." Her
punch was strong—and the shocks she could deliver with a
snap of her fingers to irksome customers even stronger.

At the end of summer, all of the able-bodied young
men were working in the fields—even Alaric, who preferred
horses to the oats they ate. Sunburned and with aching
backs, they staggered into town every evening, throats
parched but still singing. And, of course, they made their
way directly to Josepha's.

One night, while his friends piled into the tavern,
Maurice hung back to dust himself off as best he could—
and to get a better look at a bit of a commotion occurring
just outside.

A giant and solid-looking man stood with his legs spread aggressively and a dangerous look in his eye. This was interesting, but not as intriguing as what *else* was going on.

Sticking her face into the man's was one of the most beautiful women Maurice had ever seen. She had the poise of a dancer and the body of a goddess. Her hair glowed golden in the sunset. But bright red spots of rage flushed her beautiful cheeks, and her eyes flashed green with indignation.

She waved a slim alder wand in the air for emphasis:

"Nothing is unnatural about us!" Her words were perfectly formed and accented; it was emotion that caused her to nearly spit. "Anything God makes is natural—by definition. And we, all of us, are the children of God!"

"You are the children of the devil," the man said calmly, lazily. Like someone who knew he was going to win. "Put here as a test. You shall be wiped from the earth like the unnatural dragons of old, you mouthy hag. Unless you purify yourself."

"Purify?" The girl *actually* spat this time. "I was baptized by the monsignor himself—so that is at least one more bath than *you've* ever had, you son of a pig!"

The man made a movement, a very slight one, reaching to his waist. As good-natured as Maurice was, he had traveled enough to know what that signaled: a knife, a pistol, a backhand across the face. *Something* violent. He acted immediately, moving to run over and help her.

But it was all over before he took a single step: there was a flash brighter than lightning, completely silent. Everything went stark white.

After a few moments, Maurice could see again. The girl was storming off angrily but the man still stood there. There was indeed a pistol in his hand that he had meant to use. It fell to his side, now forgotten. More pressing business occupied the man's attention. Where his nose had been, there was a now a bright pink snout.

"Son of a pig . . ." Maurice repeated slowly, beginning to smile. *"Pig!"*

He chuckled to himself and finally went into the tavern.

He found Alaric with the usual gang, along with someone new: a thin, drawn-looking young man who folded his body over and brought his shoulders together like an insect, a very unhappy one. His clothes were dark and the expression on his face nervous and dour—in every way the exact opposite of the fair-haired and sunny groomsman.

Maurice moved toward them slowly, still thinking about the incident outside. Not the flash or the fight or the pig's nose, but the way the setting sun had gleamed on the girl's tresses.

Alaric impatiently pulled him down into a seat between himself and the brooding fellow.

"Here, sit already! Have you met the doc yet? I don't think you have. Frédéric, Maurice. Maurice, Frédéric."

Maurice nodded absently. He hoped he wasn't being rude. Without being asked, Josepha placed a tankard of *cidre* down in front of him.

"Pleased to meet you," Frédéric said crisply, if gloomily. "But I am not a doctor, I keep telling you that. I was *meant* to be one, once . . ."

"What happened?" Maurice asked, trying to remember his manners. Frédéric, he noted, had a tiny glass of something expensive. He must have come from some learned, professional background.

"My parents sent me away before I could complete my studies. They sent me to this . . . *lovely* little place. They paid me off to come here."

"Frédéric here has a talent," Alaric said meaningfully, tugging on the end of his cap. "He can see the future."

"Oh, aye?" Maurice asked, impressed.

"Not really, not always, only a little," Frédéric protested, shaking his head. "Just enough for my family to exile me here . . . to be with 'people like myself' who would 'understand it.' Or, possibly, remove it with more magic. I was in university. I was going to apprentice to a great surgeon. I was *going* to be a doctor."

Alaric caught Maurice's eye above Frédéric's head and made a face.

"I've been trying to get him to move in with us," the groomsman declared, taking a swig of beer and then wiping the foam off in one easy, well-practiced motion.

"I don't need to," Frédéric said, but not meanly. "I have money and I don't wish to live with animals, thank you very much. Also, I already have a bit of an additional income. The king and queen summoned me to attend to their royal infant. A *cold*," he added quickly. "Nothing else wrong with him, and nothing I—or a real doctor—could fix. *Ignoramuses!* Anyway, they have hired me as their occasional consulting physician, and I do not require your charity, thank you."

"C'mon, don't you want to bunk with a couple of lads your age who can show you around? Rather than rent a room all by yourself at the top of some widow's drafty attic?"

"Thank you for your concern," Frédéric said, again, not unkindly. It was more like he didn't know any way to be other than per-fect-ly polite. But it left a strange hole in the conversation.

"Alaric, that girl . . ." Maurice began. "Outside the tavern before . . . there was a beautiful girl with golden hair . . . she turned a man's nose into a pig's snout . . ."

"Oh, you must mean Rosalind! That one's a card!" Alaric said, laughing.

"It's a bit excessive," Frédéric said, making a sour face. "That's the problem with witches."

"He was being very insulting," Maurice said, finding himself rising to the defense of a girl whose name he hadn't known a moment before. "He was accusing her of being unnatural, and saying that magic was impure."

Alaric clicked his tongue. "Ah, there's a lot of that these days, I'm afraid. Before you came, there was a terrible row. Two boys, a *charmante* and a normal one—like us—fought over a girl. It came to blows and the *charmante* won and the other boy died. By magic. The palace guards were sent to break up everything and there was a bit of a riot, accusations being flung back and forth. Some of the guards got caught in the crossfire . . . with rather more permanent afflictions than pigs' snouts . . . which, knowing Rosalind, she will remove the next time she sees him."

"You can hardly blame the *normal* ones, 'like you,'" Frédéric said with bitterness. "Here these people are who have powers and can do things that you can't. There's no control over their behavior and nothing anyone—palace guards or people with muskets—can do about them. They . . . *we,* I suppose . . . need to be controlled. Or made less dangerous."

"It was two boys fighting over a girl," Alaric pointed out patiently. "It happens all the time. Boys die over that sort of thing in normal duels. This one just happened to involve magic. You can't get all worked up about it."

"At the very least, if there must be . . . unnatural

things . . . people should hide it rather than flaunt it. Besides, magic always comes back on itself. Everyone knows that. *She* should know that. Rosalind, I mean."

"*Rosalind,*" Maurice said, trying the name out on his tongue.

"Oh, no," Alaric said with wide eyes. "Maurice! Say it isn't so! Not so soon in our relationship!"

"Her hair," Maurice said thoughtfully, "is the exact color of the inside of my kiln, when it is hot enough to melt iron."

"Oh, good, we're all safe then," Alaric said with a sigh, shouldering Frédéric companionably. "With lines like that, we don't need to worry about coming home to find a ribbon on the door and being forced to find another place to stay the night."

"I have said I am not rooming with you," Frédéric repeated patiently.

But Maurice was no longer listening.